MODERN SOCIETY;

OR,

THE MARCH OF INTELLECT

THE

CONCLUSION OF MODERN ACCOMPLISHMENTS.

BY

MISS CATHARINE SINCLAIR,

AUTHOR OF "MODERN ACCOMPLISHMENTS," "CHARLIE SEYMOUR," ETC., ETC.

"Thus happiness depends, as Nature shows,
Less on exterior things than most suppose."

NEW YORK:
ROBERT CARTER & BROTHERS,
No. 285 BROADWAY

1854.

THOMAS B. SMITH, STEREOTYPER,
216 WILLIAM STREET, N. Y.

ROBERT CRAIGHEAD, PRINTER.

PREFACE.

An attempt is made in this volume to contrast the happiness offered to us by our Maker with the happiness which we invent for ourselves,—to exemplify a wide difference between the "living fountain and the broken cistern." In our own experience, we find that the one resembles the purity and clearness of the early dawn, which grows brighter and brighter till the perfect day, while the other may be compared to an evening twilight, beginning in still gaudier hues, but growing gradually darker, till it settles into the gloom of night.

While thus representing two opposite states of enjoyment, which might justly be called a parallel, since they are lines which can never be made to meet, no hesitation has been felt in representing worldly as well as spiritual enjoyments in the brightest colors, because the superiority of the latter are more conspicuous in proportion to the accuracy with which both can be depicted. Those, indeed, who have experienced the blessedness of Christian peace, require no demonstration of its unrivalled excellence; but the case is otherwise with those who are ignorant of the Gospel, and have never felt that joy "which no man knoweth, saving he that receiveth it." Many, also, who would close at once the page of formal instruction or grave rebuke, may be induced to bestow attention on a familiar narrative, exhibiting the development of taste and feeling in the genuine Christian character, and to acknowledge that the highest achievement of fashionable education is to make us *appear* amiable, and *appear* happy, while it is the peculiar province of Christian principle to turn these appearances into reality. Works of imagination have this additional advantage, that they may take cognizance of faults in temper or conduct too trivial for the notice of treatises or essays, yet so frequent in their recurrence as to form the chief moral peculiarities of the individual. Life, as Dr. Johnson observes, is not a series of great events and illustrious actions; it is from minute particulars and casual indications of feeling that we form our estimate of those around us. Mere moralists too readily coincide in opinion with the mistaken poet, that, "his creed can't be wrong whose life is in the right;" while we have equal reason to deprecate a new reading, which would seem to say, "His *life* can't be wrong whose *creed* is in the right." It is not the handles of a clock which constitute its actual value; but still, if they do not point aright, during every moment of the day, and every day of the year, we know that something is amiss within; and though it may continue gravely and solemnly ticking the hours, no one will take heed to its admonitions. The superstructure of Christian conduct cannot be justly appreciated without exhibiting the inward machinery of the mind by which external actions are directed or controlled, and therefore the authoress has, with reverence, attempted to portray those thoughts and principles which render the pleasures, the hopes, and the emotions of Christians entirely different from others whose apparent circumstances are exactly similar, and with whom they may be unavoidably thrown into habits of continual association.

That fictitious narrative is a proper mode of instruction, is demonstrated to every Christian by the highest of all examples. Some excellent persons, however, who admit the usefulness of little tracts and histories representing, in proper colors, vice, infidelity, and superstition among the lower orders, inconsistently object to similar delineations as respects the higher; yet the success of such writings in the one department seems to encourage the hope of usefulness by corresponding exertions in the other. Mrs. Hannah More remarks, in her novel of Cœlebs, "how little justice has been done to the clerical character in those popular works of imagination which are intended to exhibit a picture of living manners. So many fair opportunities have thus been lost of advancing the interests of religion, by personifying her amiable graces in the character of her ministers." The authoress feels encouraged to attempt this interesting task, from a grateful consciousness that she has enjoyed more than ordinary occasions for appreciating the enlightened devotion, the active benevolence, the disinterested labors, the learning, the consistency, and the zeal of those who are in heart, as well as by profession, the servants of God. At the same time, on no one occasion, in any of her past or present pages, has she drawn the portrait of an individual, and no circumstances can ever induce her to do so. Every reader of a fiction would *cast* the characters differently; and it is to be hoped that all have known some whom Lady Olivia Neville's imaginary virtues might fairly represent. Three originals for this sketch have been confidently named, any of whom do honor to the success with which female excellence has been represented, though the fancied resemblance in every case is only such as all Christians must exhibit to each other. There are many lively girls like Eleanor, without her faults, and many gentlemen as prosing as Sir Colin, to whom, while the authoress has never seen them, some resemblance may easily be imagined "to give the airy nothings place and name." It is requested that every young lady will believe she was intended for Matilda,—that every gentleman will discover that he is portrayed in Sir Alfred, or Mr. Grant, and that each will feel assured, in whatever quarter of the United Kingdom he resides, that Dr. Murray is certainly intended for the clergyman of his own parish,—

> "This is a likeness, may all men declare,
> And I have seen him, but I know not where."

With respect to the white poodle, Blanco, he is not meant for any poodle in particular, but is a fair representation of drawing-room dogs in general, with all their faults and good qualities, seeing that they occupy a place of distinction in society now which entitles them to prominent notice in any work professing to take cognizance of the more important actors in fashionable life.

Having formerly delineated the progress of education, it is now proposed to trace its results on the character, temper, and morals; but each volume may be read, either in connection, or as a separate story. The original intention was, not to carry the same narrative on, but many readers objected to the want of a regular *dénouement* in the previous work, where, according to established etiquette, virtue ought to be rewarded, and vice brought to condign punishment. This is very appropriately termed "*poetical* justice," because we observe no such results in actual life. It may be well, however, to exhibit the triumph of virtue in scenes of fancy, where the characters cease to exist with the closing page; but it should be remembered, that while the universal desire for final equity seems to be implanted in the human breast by Him who now promises, and will one day execute it,—this world is not the place of retribution. Temporal happiness is granted irrespectively of merit, and frequently those who seem most deserving of success receive the smallest share of worldly prosperity from the hands of that Great Benefactor who knows its real worthlessness. The favored children of our Merciful Father are not the most pampered and indulged now; but that in which they differ from others is the inward feeling with which the inevitable afflictions of life are borne.—As we frequently see the more precious exotics in a garden first planted and cherished in darkness, that they may attain a higher and a nobler growth, so the Christian is often reared in the gloom of adversity, and watered with tears, while we likewise see that winter's stormy blast is necessary to the stability of the oak.

MODERN SOCIETY

CHAPTER I.

Sorrows like show'rs descend, and as the heart
For them prepares, they good or ill impart.
Some on the mind, as on the ocean, rain,
Fall and disturb, but soon are lost again:
Some, as to fertile lands, a boon bestow,
And seeds that else had perish'd live and grow.
Some fall on barren soil, and thence proceed
The idle blossom and the noxious weed.

CRABBE.

IT has been mentioned as an ancient Jewish tradition, though not recorded in Scripture, that, among other tests to which the Queen of Sheba put the wisdom of Solomon during her visit at Jerusalem, she held up, at some distance, two large groups of flowers, the one real and the other artificial, desiring him to discriminate between them. Unable at once to do so, and resolved, nevertheless, not to be baffled, the monarch instantly commanded a window to be opened, at which a multitude of bees flew in, and settled on the natural flowers, after which there could no longer be any difficulty in pronouncing a correct judgment. It cannot be doubted that the loveliest blossoms of spring may be so imitated by art that in form and color they shall seem equalled, or perhaps excelled, and the eye, transiently glancing at both, may be most attracted by greater brilliancy in the one, though the freshness and fragrance of nature must, on nearer acquaintance, prove their own superiority, and add a charm to the creations of an Almighty hand which all the ingenuity of man could never confer. Equally similar in external appearance were the two heroines of our story, Eleanor Fitz-Patrick and Matilda Howard. In all that could give grace and beauty to their earliest girlhood they were alike; but, while Eleanor was embellished with every outward attraction which art or ingenuity can add to the gifts of nature, she wanted that inward spirit which can be only supplied by Almighty power, and which gives life and permanence to all that is precious in the heart. Both the cousins were fitted to bloom amidst the sunshine of life's gay morning, enlivening every scene on which they entered; but the brightness and beauty of merely human excellence like Eleanor's, must fade amidst the storms of earthly sorrow and temptation, while the grace and the sweetness derived, like Matilda's, from an eternal source, may indeed be bowed down and blighted for a time, but cannot long remain obscured, and are never entirely lost, being of that "nature" which "dies and lives again," and which, whether in sunshine or shadow, is under a wise, unerring cultivation for an endless and glorious existence.

On the death of Lady Olivia Neville, to whom they were both alike indebted for that tender affection which had constituted the happiness of their childhood, and for that judicious kindness which had watched over them in subsequent years, the two cousins mourned over the object of their earliest attachment, who had shown them all the endearing and devoted interest of a mother, and each in her separate home wept bitter tears for the days that were past, when every thought of their hearts had been dear to her who could now hear them no more. Few had ever occasion to weep for a friend more deservedly beloved; and so essential had her friendship become to both her nieces, that it seemed to their young minds scarcely possible that death had indeed caused a final separation. That voice, now silent in the grave, had been the first to impress on their thoughts the fleeting nature of every earthly tie, and taught them to reflect, that, as soon might we anticipate day without night, or an ocean of perpetual calm, as that this changing scene shall continue to smile on us as brightly as it beams on the early dawn of existence; but no reverse had yet brought them so acutely to feel that mournful truth, until the last solemn event which set its seal to all that they had been taught.

When the melancholy news reached Barnard Castle, Eleanor was overpowered with amazement and grief. She delivered herself up to a tempest of uncontrollable emotion, which soon exhausted itself, and she conjured up the remembrance of everything that could add bitterness to her sorrow. Her feelings were on most occasions like the ripple of a summer breeze on the surface of a stream, or like breath on a mirror, which flits rapidly away, leaving it as cold and as bright as before. But Eleanor now mourned for a time, with almost frantic grief—she admired in herself every excess of sensibility; and amidst tears and hysterics, she spoke as if the very sunshine of her life was set forever, and the only remaining comfort that could cheer her would be to live all her remaining days as if Lady Olivia Neville were the witness of every thought and action.

Sir Richard Fitz-Patrick proposed that they should hasten immediately to Edinburgh, as he wished to show the last mark of respect and attachment to the memory of one whom he, along with every one who had known her, felt desirous to consecrate in their most sacred and respectful remembrance; and to this suggestion the young heiress readily acceded, glad to find any refuge from her own depressing thoughts, and from the mournful inactivity of grief.

To a casual observer, the earliest burst of heart-breaking sorrow on the part of Eleanor Fitz-Patrick would have appeared to call for greater sympathy and more anxious solicitude than the deep, unobtrusive grief of Matilda Howard, who wept silently and profoundly, though she fortified her mind against the inroads of immoderate affliction by incessant and fervent prayer, and struggled against the excess of that grief which she felt conscious could only end with her life. Some minds have a wider grasp of sorrow than others, and hers was one which felt intensely and suffered long. There are depths in our thoughts and in our feelings, which we ourselves can only fathom when trying events lay open the inner recesses of our own hearts; and in this hour of anguish and distress, Matilda seemed as if she had never known before what it was to think or to suffer: but still she could now place all her happiness implicitly in the hands of that Gracious Being whom she supremely loved, in humble trust that hereafter His unerring designs would be revealed; and thus she felt that to a Christian, in the utmost sorrows of life, *one comfort* inalienably belongs.

Amidst the intensity and anguish of her feelings, Matilda shrunk from the notice of every one except her parents, to whom she revealed without reserve all the passing emotions of her heart, and in return she received such consolation and sympathy as they could suggest for the time; though long before her grief was alleviated, they each thought that it might have been almost entirely subdued; and Lady Howard, whose heart had become, by constant intercourse with the world, as hard as a well-beaten highway, having one day surprised her in tears, thought it necessary to remonstrate.

"My dear girl," said she, "we have all suffered a great misfortune, which it would be most unnatural not to deplore; but if the sorrows of life are felt so very acutely, your spirits will be depressed beyond all remedy, at the very commencement of existence. The bodily health may be restored after severe injury, but the spirits once thoroughly broken, can never be revived; therefore you must really save up some cheerfulness to stand the wear and tear of future years, and for my sake and your father's, let me entreat that you will exert some fortitude."

"There can be no use in cherishing grief," observed Sir Francis. "I would have willingly cut off my right hand to preserve Lady Olivia's life, and no one can lament her more sincerely; but still it is vain to think of it, and we must learn to turn our minds away from inevitable misfortunes. My receipt for banishing melancholy thoughts is, to take a good hard gallop on horseback, or to smoke a double portion of cigars—but anything is better than to sit down and make sorrow a welcome companion."

Matilda ventured to reply, that she found it a better restorative to encourage reflection than to stifle it, but she promised that nothing should be wanting on her own part to attain peaceful and Christian resignation, while she looked forward with ardent hope to the arrival of Eleanor Fitz-Patrick, when she might have the additional comfort of finding sympathy from one who mourned like herself. Her frank and affectionate heart was incapable of reserve with those she loved, and in her present hour of sorrow she would rather have spoken to a statue than smothered her grief within her own breast,—what, then, could exceed the longing desire with which she anticipated that moment when, with the companion and friend of her childhood, they should mingle their tears together, and wear out their sorrow by talking of it.

Before the stunning effect of surprise and grief had been sufficiently alleviated on Matilda's mind to admit of her shedding any tears, those of Eleanor had been entirely dried up. The long journey from Inverness-shire—the daily change of air and scene—the exhilarating effect of rapid motion—and the thousand future plans and prospects which flitted gaily through the magic-lantern of her fertile imagination, prevented the young heiress from dwelling very intently on the past, and when she reached her destination, she felt but transiently affected by the solemn event which had brought her there.

Matilda flew into the arms of her cousin when they met, and burst into a flood of tears. Confident that she was at last with one who could enter into the utmost excess of her feelings, and who would look back with her on every endearing remembrance of the past, she now wept unrestrainedly in all the intensity of natural emotion. Heedless of all but the sacredness of her own sorrow, and forgetful of everything relating to Eleanor, except the unbounded confidence of their once-happy childhood, she felt soothed by the undoubted certainty of their mutual sympathy and affection, while she struggled to regain her composure, and to say all that the first impulse of her feelings directed. A tear glistened in the eye of Miss Fitz-Patrick, at the sight of her cousin's speechless distress, and she returned her embrace with considerable warmth. Their first interview might have almost satisfied the feelings of Matilda, for it was short and affectionate; but, when longer and more frequent intercourse occurred, she became sensible that a degree of restraint and embarrassment was but too obvious in the manner of Eleanor, and she could not remain blind to the coldness of her expressions, and to her absence of mind, which recalled to unavoidable remembrance, that she was the brilliantly-endowed heiress of Barnard Castle.

"I have become excessively nervous of late, and might have been sure that our meeting would be too much for me," said Eleanor one day, assuming a melancholy tone, in answer to some of Matilda's reminiscences. "I wonder that you are able to speak of our affliction at all, as, for my own part, the most distant allusion to it overpowers me, and I must entreat that, till we have somewhat recovered this dreadful event, you will never say anything at all about it to agitate me."

"But, Eleanor, we have such consolations, that it seems ungrateful not to reflect on the goodness of Providence in sending them, for truly in the midst of judgment He remembered mercy; and our beloved aunt's death, in peace of mind and body, seemed almost like a translation into glory. Surely you would like to here the message she left for you, dear Eleanor, and all she said that day; for it was so like herself, kind and consoling."

"Not now!—I have told you already that it must be at some future time, when I can bear agitation better," replied the young heiress, hastily. "Miss Marabout very truly remarked, that I am prodigiously altered within the last ten days since we have been here, and she earnestly entreats me to avoid all emotion; for she observes, what every one must see, that I have only too much sensibility. We should endeavor, Matilda, not to water the road of life with our tears more than can be helped, for there is both sunshine and shadow to be found there, and my object shall be to linger always in the first, and to avoid the other entirely when I can; but you will probably do exactly the reverse."

"No! indeed I shall not," replied Matilda; "it is my desire to receive every event of life precisely as it is intended. We have instructions, both how to be merry and how to be sad; so the time may come when I shall be cheerful again, but not *now*, Eleanor, not *yet*."

"We are very differently circumstanced," observed the heiress, in a tone of importance. "Many affairs must necessarily occupy my thoughts during the short time we remain in town, which take me off from dwelling incessantly on the subject of our regret. You have no conception what a multitude of things have to be settled before we leave Edinburgh. I must bespeak a new pony carriage, as my present one is an ugly color, and hung too low;—then every nursery-garden in the neighborhood has to be ransacked for new plants to decorate my American garden, which was in a blaze of glory this summer. After that, I must select a wagon-load of new books to replenish the library, for at present it is all so ancient, that one might suppose it to be the ghost of the one at Alexandria. You have no idea what ruin is brought upon me by all my friends having become authors now; and I find it quite an effort of memory to send for their books, and to lay them on the table conspicuously, whenever the 'accomplished writer' comes to Barnard Castle. I pointed out yesterday to papa, as a great natural curiosity, a gentleman who is supposed never to have published! and he would scarcely believe it possible. My most difficult task, however, has been to find an Italian confectioner, as our French cook, newly imported from Paris, is quite a *cordon bleu*, and expects to have an *artiste* under him."

Matilda felt amazed at the grave look of dignity with which all this was uttered; and she could not but remember a time, not long past, when her lively cousin would have been the first to ridicule, and even to burlesque, such an outbreak of ostentation from any one else. Her immediate impulse was, forgetful of every restraint, to speak with the frank, good-humored gayety of former days, and to rally Eleanor on her sudden assumption of magnificence; but an indefinable barrier was arising between herself and the companion of her childhood, which she could scarcely comprehend. That mere wealth should cause such a disparity as to forbid the unrestrained exercise of all their former confidence, was what her young and ardent mind had never anticipated. Matilda felt herself free and unfettered by obligation—she had no object to gain from her cousin, nor would she have hesitated to show such deference as was due to Miss Fitz-Patrick's superiority of station; but to find herself, as she now did on many occasions, unaccountably treated like a humble friend —a sort of *souffre-douleur*, who must study her cousin's humors, and implicitly follow her lead in conversation—filled her with surprise, and with a degree of indignation, which was foreign to the natural gentleness of her disposition. Matilda Howard's spirit was not proud, but it was independent; and the longer she associated with Eleanor, the more difficult she felt it to preserve herself from subservience, and at the same time to maintain that Christian meekness which was her duty in the sight of God. If Eleanor asked her to drive out, or to visit a shop, her tone was that of a superior dictating to a protegée; and every day she seemed more hurried for time, and more anxious to escape all confidential intercourse, which Matilda could scarcely regret, as not only was Eleanor's extraordinary vivacity unsuitable to her own feelings, but she was hurt on account of Lady Olivia, to see how soon and how entirely the sacred remembrance of her virtues and affection was extinguished from the memory of one who owed so much to both; and her good taste, as well as her partial affection for Eleanor, were irresistibly hurt by the vulgar-minded ostentation and glaring selfishness of her whole conversation and conduct.

"Matilda, why do you never wear rings?" asked Eleanor one day, looking at her beautifully-formed hands, while she plied the needle with busy activity. "I should require some additional fingers to wear all mine upon; and this turquoise hoop cost me as much yesterday as would be the whole annual income of *some* young ladies. It appears quite undressed to be without any; and really, Matilda, with that industrious, painstaking look, you might pass for a sempstress who does plain work at eighteenpence a-day.

"It would be necessary for me to turn an honest penny, in some way or other, before I become curious in rings and bijouterie," replied Matilda, smiling. "You know perfectly, Eleanor, that I can scarcely keep myself in shoe-strings and hair-pins, so if ever I put on a ring, it must be taken down from the bed-curtains."

"Very true. Now, I do think that old quiz, Lady Barnard, treated you shockingly!" replied Eleanor; "it is, in my opinion, a complete case of swindling, when rich old people receive *very excessive* attentions from *any* one, and slip out of the world leaving them nothing. I protest it ought to be actionable!"

"But my dear Eleanor, you quite mistake me"——

"Yes! yes! I know all that you expect me to believe—disinterested kindness, pure charity, and so forth; but, Matilda, I know the world. What pleasure could there be to you in reading several hours a-day to that peevish old woman, and giving up every sort of engagement to sit with her in the evenings? People may act as they please; but I must think and speak as I please, for the motive to exertion is always as plain to me as if it were inscribed in legible characters on the face of it, and nothing diverts me more than to see how people can deceive themselves and others."

"You might as easily suspect right intentions as wrong ones, Eleanor, and it would be much the more agreeable occupation. I often think of a man mentioned in the Spectator, who had a deformed and a handsome leg, so he always judged whether people were inclined to take the favorable view of others or not, by watching which their eye most readily fixed upon; and we should endeavor to be among those who contemplate the presentable leg."

"*A propos*, Lady Susan Danvers dined with us yesterday; and her large red arms were so covered with glittering bracelets, that they reminded me of the raw flesh which Sinbad the Sailor threw into the Valley of Diamonds."

"You will allow, then, that it is better to be deficient in ornaments than to be overloaded with them. Some of our *nouveaux riches* exhibit so much jewellery now, that they look like Queens of the Sandwich Islands, or Roman Catholic images from abroad."

"'*Do you mean anything personal!*' as one gentleman

said to another, who was kicking him down stairs," exclaimed Eleanor, laughing. "That hard hit was evidently levelled at my splendid gold ear-rings."

"No, indeed! you know me better than to suppose it possible; but I had entirely overlooked them, and you used to coincide in my antipathy to much carving and gilding in our dress and decoration, Eleanor, in which, perhaps, we still agree; but, however that may be, I shall not feel entitled to animadvert very severely on you, unless your hair is curled with bank-notes, or I see you hung in chains of gold all day, like the city magistrates."

"Matilda! I never observe you dressed for dinner without a smile, for you still wear the same perpetual necklace that we had in the school-room. Do you live and sleep with it on?"

"I like everything that reminds me of old times, and of the friend who gave it," replied Matilda, fixing her large, deep, speaking eyes on Eleanor. "She never leaves my thoughts, and everything connected with her is dear to my heart. The very ground she trod on, has an additional charm for me; and I walked all over the garden at Ashgrove yesterday, Eleanor, tracing impressions of the stick with which she supported herself last time we walked there together. I sat in her favorite seat. I recalled how she looked, and what she said, and I tried to realize the idea of that blessed country where she now is eternally happy. Oh, how sweet and how sad our lovely garden looked. It seemed as if the rose-trees should not have bloomed so gayly, and as if the bright carnations were ungrateful, to be sending up their fragrance, when the hand that had reared them was no more; and the laughing, joyous sunshine which sparkled and glittered on all around, showed no sympathy with my own mournful feelings. I remembered that the last words of comfort and affection have been spoken from those lips which are now closed forever, and I seemed yet to watch the last glance of tender interest which gleamed upon me from her dying eyes. The truest friend we have ever known, Eleanor, employed her latest hour in praying for *us*."

Matilda paused a moment in profound emotion. Her voice was harmony itself, and it deepened into a tone of intense sensibility while she spoke. The rich full notes of a flute could not have died away more softly on the ear. She faltered, and became silent; but after pausing a moment, and watching in vain for a look of answering sympathy in the bright cold eye of her cousin, she gently endeavored to vary the subject, though she could not at once dismiss it.

"Aunt Barbara is at Ashgrove still, but so altered, you scarcely could have recognized her. I burst into tears when we met, more affected by the change on her than even by the sorrow that afflicts myself. May her consolation be from above, for no earthly friend can afford her any, and she says, that in the whole range of future events, there is not a single circumstance which could give her one gleam of pleasure. That must certainly be wrong, because a true Christian cannot know such a word as despair; but I could not leave her for several hours, nor get the remembrance of her miserable countenance a moment out of my head since."

"Pshaw, Matilda!" said Eleanor, contemptuously; "Barbara's very sorrows formerly were always absurd and frivolous. I remember, as a child, seeing her often in tears; and, being then young and tender-hearted, I used to watch her with commiseration, summing up, in my own mind, all the causes of grief that she probably endured—her solitary existence; her brother's sudden death; the evident indifference of every one towards herself; the approach of old age, and infirmity; the scanty pittance she had to subsist upon, and the awful consideration of a future state. These were all grand, legitimate subjects of agitation; but whenever I wasted any good sympathy upon her, and investigated beyond my own imagination into the origin of her distress, it turned out to be some petty affront which she had fancied. Mamma had given another person the precedence of her to dinner, or I had occupied the chair she usually sat in, or had picked up the book she was reading, or papa did not take wine with her. In short it never was a real, impressive distress that touched her feelings."

"But we must spare her now, Eleanor, for she is sadly humbled. Did you hear that Aunt Barbara has insisted on accepting in earnest the offer which papa lately made her in jest, of permission to occupy Ptarmigan Cottage, in Argyleshire, where she means, with the income recently bequeathed, to devote herself to doing good in that neighborhood? Mamma and papa did their utmost to detain her with ourselves, but her melancholy reply was, with tears in her eyes, 'Ah! now that Olivia is no more, who could bear with *me!*'"

"Who indeed!" exclaimed Eleanor, superciliously. "But now, do let us call another subject, for I hate people to be, like Paganini, always harping on one string, especially if it be a melancholy one. Do you know, Matilda, I am going to have all the Barnard diamonds newly arranged in the form of an enormous butterfly, and the ear-rings are to be set transparent. I must be off now, to order some additional plate and furniture for the country, so adieu! *au revoir!* I shall try to call again before we go to Barnard Castle next week; but you can have no idea what it is to be torn in pieces with engagements as I am. You may think yourself a very lucky person, Matilda, to enjoy the privilege of moping all day over a fire, without any one asking or caring where you are; but if I disappear for half an hour, there are shoals of visitors crowding into the drawing-room, or else the butler, and housekeeper, and all my people waiting, as if they had no business on earth but to torment me. I shall probably find a whole host of company at home—notes waiting to be answered—and shopkeepers with things upon sight: so you should be properly grateful for my bestowing so much precious time upon you already. Come and see me sometimes. I am always glad to have you with me Matilda, *when I have nothing else to do!*"

"Eleanor! I sometimes scarcely know whether to laugh or to cry, you are so ridiculous!" said her cousin, coloring, and endeavoring to smile. "Let me now exercise, probably for the last time, my old privilege of being allowed to speak out my whole mind. There is a change in you, Eleanor, which cannot but be obvious to us both; and if a short time has already produced so great an alteration in the tone you assume towards me, I cannot but anticipate the hour when there may be that in your manner which I should feel scarcely entitled to overlook. Our affection was such as I believed neither time nor circumstances could alter; and I thought you had known the worth of that which no wealth can ever purchase; but we have gradually became estranged from each other's confidence, I scarcely know how or why! I almost feel as if it would be less painful not to see you at all, than to see you so changed. I may be hasty,—wrong,—imprudent to say this; but if we do not come to a right understanding at first, I shall never know when to speak. The evil increases every time we meet, while my courage to notice it will diminish; for our former equality in affection is already almost obsolete and forgotten. Dear Eleanor! my spirits are already weighed down by the sense of our irreparable misfortune; do not add to it the grief and mortification of mourning for your loss as well as hers, and in a way so very comfortless and unexpected. You know how often we were taught to pray that our hearts might be preserved from inordinate anxiety about earthly happiness; but if anything could infallibly subdue and chasten my worldly affections, it would be the deep disappointment that your alienation would occasion to me. Let us continue, then, as we once were, dearest Eleanor; let us remember the time when we were friends before either of us knew what worldly honors meant; and oh! let us remain so until all earthly distinctions are at an end."

"Certainly!" replied Eleanor, hastily tying on her bonnet, and gathering her splendid cashmere into graceful folds round her sylph-like figure. "You know very well, Matilda, that I prefer you to any one else, and it would be very wrong and ungrateful to do otherwise; but pray make due allowances, considering that I have no leisure either to look back upon former times, or forward to the future, there is such a *perfect scramble* for my immediate attention among country neighbors, victims, would-be lovers, and Scotch cousins to the remotest generation."

"Yes, Eleanor! you really are the 'hare with many friends,' and I must not be captious about trifles. Excuse me, then, if I have been hasty and unreasonable. Your regard is necessarily scattered among the many claimants who court it, while mine may be reserved for the few who will seek and value it. I shall try, therefore, to think you unchanged; and, happen what will, it shall be noticed no more; for, perhaps, in the solitude of my heart where an aching void must long remain, I may have looked with too keen an eye on the only friend to whom my whole feelings could have been unreservedly opened. The fewer friends we cultivate, the more precious they must become; and in our case, Eleanor, I might apply that beautiful Persian proverb, 'The moon looks on many flowers, the flowers see but one moon.'"

CHAPTER II.

I fondly thought
In thee I 'd found the friend my heart had sought;
I fondly thought, ere Time's last days were gone,
Thy heart and mine had mingled into one!
KIRKE WHITE.

ABOUT ten days after the preceding conversation, Sir Francis Howard had concluded a long philippic against luncheons, in the way in which gentlemen usually end them, by sociably drawing his chair towards the table, and becoming the greatest beef-eater of the party himself, when Sir Richard Fitz-Patrick entered, accompanied by Eleanor and Miss Marabout, who were now inseparable companions, for the young heiress would have felt as great a privation without her *ci-devant* governess as the unfortunate man did who in a rash moment parted with his shadow.

"Howard! when are you coming to beat up our quarters in the North?" asked Sir Richard, while scientifically employed in selecting the trouffles from a *paté Perigord.* "You shall be up to the chin in turtle and venison every day at our chateau."

"Captain Ross has promised me a passage next time he goes your way, and Captain Back is to pick me up, if he ever returns."

"But seriously, my good friend, we have admirable sport, if that will be any inducement—you may shoot partridges at the door, and catch salmon out of the window, besides having a shot at the red deer, which abound in our forests. I saw a prodigious herd the day before we left Barnard Castle, and my neighbor Alderby persevered in stalking one for fifteen miles. The sport is so unrivalled in its way, that when once a man is thoroughly initiated in deer-stalking he never enjoys anything else."

"Then never attempt to 'initiate' me, for depend upon it, that all my happiness in life would be ended if ever I became disgusted with hunting. Let me be put in my coffin as soon as the huntsman's bugle loses its attraction."

"Bring two or three of your hunters, then, next month, for we are going to try the experiment of starting a pack in my neighborhood. De Mainbury is to hunt our country for the first time this year, and we expect capital sport."

"Rather a hilly country to ride across," cried Sir Francis. "I shall certainly have a steeple chase over Ben Nevis."

"We are plentifully peopled with foxes," continued Sir Richard eagerly; "the only danger is, that three at least will be starting in different directions, and we have only one pack of hounds; but a most numerous field is likely to turn out. Colonel Pendarvis, Major Foley, Alderby, Fletcher, unumbered Mackenzies, and countless Grants. *A propos*, Tom Grant has returned from picture-gazing abroad, and writes me that his present intention is to aid and abet Sir Alfred Douglas in canvassing our neighboring boroughs, with which laudable intention they are to set out some weeks hence for that strange, old, ivy-covered castle of the young candidate's, which looks almost as grand and frowning as himself—but my reply to their announcement of to-day was, that unless they both make Barnard Castle their headquarters I shall vote on the other side. They must positively use a little bribery and undue influence with me, and my stipulations were peremptory."

At this moment, Eleanor inadvertently upset a basin of sugar, and Matilda started forward to assist her; while Sir Francis laughingly observed, that it was the first time he had ever seen her commit an actual *gaucherie;* but he hoped that, as it was considered unlucky to throw down salt, it must be the very reverse to overturn sugar. "But, my poor Matilda! what a fright you must have got, for I have not seen such a brilliant carnation exhibited on your cheek for months. It is lucky that none of my hunters are so easily startled, for you shy at everything of late; and really, Maria, we ought to do something for that poor girl, she is becoming thinner every day, and quite out of condition now; we must have change of scene, for she is positively vanishing into thin air altogether, and I would lame my best hunter to set her on her legs again. Perhaps a trip to Leamington might be of some use, as no one can be in health now without consulting the magician there; and it would suit me quite as well to hunt for a season with the Warwickshire hounds."

"Pshaw! nonsense!—Let Matilda go with us to Barnard Castle," exclaimed Sir Richard, earnestly. "Eleanor is flapping her wings to take flight thither next Monday, and will be enchanted to have her of the party."

There was no suitable look of enchantment at these words, however, in the heiress's countenance, who seemed intent upon her occupation of paring an apple, which, to judge from her expression, might have been the apple of discord.

"What do you say, Matilda?" continued the hospitable baronet, who never read looks, and always supposed his daughter's mind to be a duodecimo edition of his own. "We have a spare corner in the britschska, for I shall ride all the way, so Eleanor and Miss Marabout only want you to complete their agreeable trio. You might sing catches and glees along the road, eh? Matilda—'All's well'—or, 'When shall we three meet again,' eh?"

There was both thunder and lightning in Eleanor's glance at this unexpected proposition of her father's; but she hummed broken snatches of the last new opera, and tried to seem unconscious of what was passing, until an opportunity occurred, when, having caught his eye, she attempted to stop the current of his eloquence with one of those family frowns which are like freemasons' signals, perceptible only to the initiated.

"I know your drift, Eleanor," continued Sir Richard, who was never very easily dismounted from his hobby; "but I am not reckoning without my hostess. The seat in our carriage is really vacant, for Charlotte Clifford has accepted the Chiltern Hundreds, and cannot leave home till nearer Christmas, when she is to follow, instead of accompanying us. I thought you had known this already. But now, Matilda, can you have all the necessaries of life ready by Monday morning, or must we linger till Tuesday? You are well worth waiting for, and if *I* think so, what must Eleanor feel?"

"I thank you a thousand times," replied Matilda, coloring deeply; "you are very kind, but"——

"I never like a sentence ending with a '*but*,' and beginning with a multitude of thanks—it always betokens evil," interrupted Sir Richard, hastily; "but you shall not get off very easily, for I mean to be as pertinacious as the Scotchman who told Mr. Pitt that he considered every refusal a step; so tell me now, what little whimsical reason are you going to give for disappointing us? This is the only com pensation we can make to Eleanor for being jilted by Charlotte Clifford; and, indeed, now that I think of it, you ought certainly to have had the precedence of her; and I wonder it was not all arranged sooner, for there is nothing I enjoy so much as to have a circle of cheerful, merry young faces round me."

At the mention of cheerfulness, Eleanor stole one of her own peculiar glances at Miss Marabout, satirically directing her attention towards the downcast expression of Matilda's countenance, who was painfully embarrassed, because, little as she wished to accept the unexpected offer of this excursion, and nothing could be farther from her intention, yet she felt wounded and surprised at the marked coldness of Eleanor's manner, who had not said, nor looked, the most transient expression of common civility on the occasion. The preference given to Miss Clifford had also astonished and mortified her. Matilda never imagined that with the confident tone of superiority constantly assumed by Eleanor in their intercourse, there was mingled a rankling feeling of jealousy towards herself, and yet nothing had been more carefully instilled into the mind of her pupil by Miss Marabout than a spirit of angry and contemptuous competition against Miss Howard. It was, indeed, surprising how much Eleanor had succeeded in blinding herself to her cousin's beauty and good qualities. She had fully persuaded herself that neither could be discernible in her own presence —that Matilda's eyes, so "deeply, darkly, beautifully blue," were not comparable to the lustre of hazel,—and that the more subdued vivacity of Matilda's conversation could never be preferred to the sparkling brilliancy of her own. Nevertheless, she had on a few occasions found herself unaccountably eclipsed, and without being led by that circumstance into any diffidence of herself, it merely produced a determination to keep her cousin as much as possible in the background, as she would rather have seen any one on earth promoted to an equality with herself than the companion of her childhood; for it had been one chief pleasure of her own advancement, to see how far she had left Matilda behind.

Meantime, Sir Richard was far on in his negotiation, without any doubt of bringing it to an equitable adjustment, telling Lady Howard that he would keep Matilda as a hostage for Sir Francis coming at Christmas; and that Eleanor would show her cousin all the projected improvements at Barnard Castle, and introduce her to a numerous flock of beaux who were soon to emigrate northwards. Nothing could well exceed the surprise of the whole assembled party, only excepting the hospitable baronet himself, when Lady Howard at length remarked, that she saw only one objection to the invitation.

"You know, Sir Richard," she said, looking at Eleanor, "no motion can be carried until it is *seconded.*"

"Indeed, Aunt Howard," said Eleanor, seeing that she must speak, "papa leaves nothing to be said when once he begins making speeches for any one, and especially for me. I feel like the strolling player who forgot his part, and another advanced as his substitute saying, 'This gentleman's name is Norval! on the Grampian hills his father feeds his flocks,' &c., &c. I shall, of course, be, as papa says, '*enchanted*' to take Matilda north, and '*delighted*' to act as show-woman of the lions at Barnard Castle; but she will find it odiously dull, with only Miss Marabout and me for two months. I quite dread the thing myself, though, if my cousin will endeavor to endure it, we must do our best to render ourselves tolerable."

Matilda's refusals now became more earnest and decided than ever; but all her ostensible objections were good-humoredly combated by her uncle. The skirmish continued for some time with great spirit on both sides; but her defensive operations were suddenly and finally defeated by Lady Howard, who interposed again, with a peremptory acceptance of the "very considerate and kind invitation which Sir Richard AND ELEANOR had been good enough to *volunteer* so opportunely."

"Pray feel no scruple about leaving me," continued she, determined not to see her daughter's beseeching looks. "I know you are scrupulous about that, and it makes me only the more desirous to indulge you, my dear Matilda. It will be of the greatest benefit to your health, and we little thought you would so soon enjoy an opportunity of lionizing Barnard Castle."

"No more did I!" exclaimed Eleanor, pertly; "Matilda may say, when she arrives there, like the Pope at Paris, 'of all the wonders in this place the greatest is to see *me* here.' But papa, you do everything now in such a hurried extempore way, that one never knows what to anticipate."

"Ah!" said Lady Howard, delighted to teaze and draw out her neice, "that is so pleasant; for when a surprise is agreeable, the more unexpected the better."

"Yes," replied the heiress dryly, "when it *is* agreeable!"

"How very kind, Eleanor! I was sure you would be overjoyed to have Matilda; and she seems *quite as pleased* about the arrangement *as you are*," said Lady Howard, stealing a satirical look at the heightened color and distressed countenance of her daughter; "what you say about the want of company will be an additional inducement to your cousin, who is only too fond of being alone, and would prefer your quiet fireside to all the 'dignity dinners' and county balls you could offer her. She will explore the beauties of Inverness-shire with untiring delight, and copy all its 'birks and braes' into her sketch-book."

"Yes; if it had been summer!" cried Eleanor, eagerly. "I am sure Matilda would like the place best in June or July."

"What a good kind creature you are, Eleanor!—If you make such a point of her returning there in summer, we may perhaps consider of it then; but I could not think of allowing Matilda to remain much beyond Christmas now, though we are equally obliged by your importunity on the subject. Sir Richard, my niece has quite inherited your hospitality of disposition."

"But virtues in excess amount at last to vices," added the young heiress, peevishly. "Papa knows how I always teaze him about his pressing five gentlemen to stay all night with us, in Cumberland, knowing as he did, that we had only one spare bed in the house—and when Sir Colin Fletcher called last week, the butler said papa was not at home, but had left orders to inquire if he could dine with him that day. The poor baronet thought we had picked up in the Highlands a little second-sight, to know for certain that he would come; but it turned out that Martin had a general order to invite every gentleman who called to make up a party. But, papa, may I tell the story about your asking Lady Montague's ci-devant butler to dinner? My father knew his face perfectly, but forgot everything else, and supposing him some old friend whom he had known long ago, he asked him to fill up a spare corner at our dinner-party, and take his mutton with us at six. The poor man nearly died on the spot with astonishment, and said, according to the usual phrase, that he would be most happy to WAIT UPON US, which he certainly did, in one sense, for it was with a napkin in his hand, behind my chair. We shall soon be quite a revival of

'The worshipful old gentleman who had a great estate,
And kept a brave old house at a hospitable rate.' "

Matilda made one more vigorous attempt to evade her impending fate; but, though she ran some risk of irritating and mortifying Sir Richard by the pertinacity of her refusal and her eagerness to escape his invitation, it was all in vain, for she was allowed to have no more influence on her own destiny than a trout on a fishing-hook; and Lady Howard, having settled all the preliminaries to her own entire satisfaction, took a cordial leave of her visitors, and then throwing herself on the sofa, she indulged in a hearty fit of laughing.

"My dearest mother, let me hope you have been in jest all along, and that I am not really going to be banished from you;" said Matilda, anxiously. "Pray relieve me by saying so."

"On the contrary, I never was half so serious about anything in my life," replied Lady Howard, decidedly; "and let me request that not another word may be said on the subject. I have a particular reason for wishing that you should spend this Christmas at Barnard Castle, and it is from the very same cause, in all probability, that Eleanor would avoid it; but I can always manage good worthy Sir Richard, who is all liberality and kindness, without the *soupçon* of a manœuvre. How I enjoy teazing Eleanor now and then! But, Matilda, I do pity you certainly, for you feel all her absurdities too acutely; and why do you, who are ten times cleverer than Eleanor, not give her a hit now and then, to show what you can do?"

"Impossible in her own house. *If I am to go*," observed Matilda, dejectedly, "I shall even lose the comfort of independence there."

"Matilda!" said Lady Howard, with a certain slowness of speech and compression of the upper lip which was meant to be unanswerable; "when did you ever gain a point with me by importunity—*c'est une affaire finie!* You ought to be seen in the world now, and there cannot be a better opportunity than this to 'come out.'

'Where none admire, 'tis useless to excel,
Where none are beaux, 'tis vain to be a belle.'

You will see a number of *eligibles* at Barnard Castle; and considering, as I do, that marriage is a woman's profession, it is as much my duty to place you in the way of advancement in that line, as it is incumbent on me to send your brother Frank to India, or Tom to Sierre Leone, if that be likely to facilitate their promotion; therefore, I lay a positive command upon you to remain in the Highlands until it is my pleasure to come there myself."

Matilda was stunned and silenced by this unexpected address; but, finding that she had done all in her power to avert the long penance forced upon her, she felt that it was now her duty to bear with submission what could not be avoided; and in her well-exercised mind there was no room for a repining thought. Much that was painful to nature she anticipated during her intercourse with Eleanor, but nothing that she could not endure with cheerfulness, if it became really inevitable; for, however trying to a sensitive mind are the slights or the caprices of altered friends, and few things can be more painful, yet she knew that they might be necessary to check the excess of that affection and confidence with which she would have given her whole heart to her cousin, and expected an unbounded and unchangeable return. Matilda had often heard it remarked that our hopes of happiness rest successively on worldly objects, like a bird on the branches of a tree. If he be driven from perch to perch, he wings his way at last towards Heaven; and thus, while mourning the earliest changes which had afflicted her own heart, she felt that if the cords were cut which bound her most strongly on earth, her hopes and desires might perhaps thus be elevated to a better world.

CHAPTER III.

> "Où allons nous, Madame?
> Nous ennuyer à la campagne"

THERE is a luxury in being waited for, which seems universally understood by great people, though to the subordinate actors in life it is a pleasure quite incomprehensible and unknown. On the morning of their setting out for Inverness-shire Eleanor Fitz-Patrick detained her cousin in momentary expectation of her arrival fully as long as personages enjoying a certain degree of self-importance think it usually necessary for those who are considered their inferiors; but at length the open britschska with four horses swept up to the door about half-past one, to claim the very unwilling and unwelcome inside passenger who had been booked for the journey.

"These are good travelling hours, Eleanor!" observed Sir Francis, handing Matilda into the carriage, and bidding her an affectionate farewell.

"Yes!" replied the heiress; "papa is already a stage in advance, but I am no admirer of sunrise, when, as some poet *beautifully* observes—

> 'Like a lobster boil'd, the morn
> From black to red begins to turn.'

The only advantage of travelling in my own carriage is, to choose the hours that suit me best."

"True—it is only irrational animals that keep what are vulgarly called rational hours. A young lady of fashion must be distinguished from the common herd who travel in coaches and steamboats, which all start before the peep of day."

"Yes," replied Eleanor, glancing with visible alarm at Matilda's baggage, "and in another respect I differ from those public conveyances, in a total incapacity to accommodate many packages besides my own, for the carriage will certainly *burst*, if we add much more to the load it already carries."

"Shall I order a post-chaise to follow with Matilda's dressing-box?" asked Sir Francis dryly. "You fill up more room in the world now, Eleanor, than in the days when I took Matilda and you, three in a gig, to Argyle-shire; and your baggage might then have been tied up, like Mr. Dowlas's, in a pocket-handkerchief."

The young heiress made no reply. She always felt a mixture of fear and respect for Sir Francis Howard, whose rallying manner and ready humor had acquired a sort of influence over her which no one else could have possibly preserved. His quick sense of the ridiculous, and unrivalled turn for mimicry, often enabled him to show her up in a way that made Eleanor conscious how absurdly she had acted or spoken; and frequently, when she could have braved Lady Olivia's affectionate remonstrances, the keen shaft of Sir Francis' eye, and the cutting sharpness of his ready wit, kept her in awe; and yet she liked him as well as her blunted feelings could enable her to like any one, and enjoyed a frequent war of wit with him, in which species of mental gladiatorship it was difficult to say whose weapons were the brightest, or which came off victorious.

"Have you heard that Barbara set out this morning for Argyleshire?" inquired Sir Francis. "Poor soul! she is sadly altered. I declare it is melancholy to see how amiable she has become now! I have lent her Ptarmigan Cottage during pleasure, and we hope she will soon become *quite herself again!*"

"I hope not, for *anybody else would be better*," replied Eleanor, laughing; "you should change the name to Termagant Cottage, till she abdicates it."

"I shall postpone that alteration till you are settled there," answered Sir Francis gravely. "You are as pungent as a vinaigrette this morning, Eleanor!"

"There is nothing more dangerous than a bad example."

"Well, adieu! You are longing to be off, I suppose, and to reach the rural plains of Inverness-shire. 'Oh! for a lodge in some vast wilderness—some boundless contiguity of shade!' Eh, Eleanor? Long life to you, then! and take care of my precious Matilda. I grudge you every hour of her society that we lose, for she is the very light of my eyes now. But, my dear girl, write constantly; keep a pen behind your ear, and as long as you are absent I trust we shall hear that Time has had his wings '*parfumées de bonheur.*' "

When the carriage stopped in Maitland-street for Miss Marabout, Eleanor turned to her cousin, saying—" By the way, Matilda, have you any objection to sit backwards? it would be such a charity! for Miss Marabout is subject to headaches, and it kills me outright, the seat is so narrow, and the back so perpendicular. I have less scruple in venturing this proposal, because you are such a good creature; and we young ladies are seldom promoted to any other side."

" No more are governesses in general; but I shall willingly give up this place, in memory of old times, when neither you nor I, Eleanor, could dare hardly to sit down in her presence at all," replied Matilda, with her wonted vivacity of look and manner, for she could not help feeling diverted at Eleanor's extreme absurdity.

The heiress gave her cousin a good-humored, but a rather patronising nod when she vacated her seat; and for some time after the carriage had driven on, Matilda was occupied in realizing to her own mind that the proud, consequential-looking personage opposite, wrapped up in ermine fur and Chantilly lace, with a grave, dignified aspect, and a pompous, commanding voice, could actually be the lively, frolicsome companion of her own juvenile days, with whom she had once lived in the free interchange of every thought, and in the happy confidence of unbounded, and, as she then believed, unalterable affection. " Cease ye from man," thought Matilda; " alas! how early am I taught the frailty of human friendship! By the changeableness of one, and by the death of another, I have *equally* lost the two who were dearest to me on earth. Oh! may the sorrow of this hour only serve to confirm the more gratefully my dependence on that eternal Friend who will never either disappoint or forsake me!"

Meantime Eleanor and Miss Marabout had thrown themselves gracefully back into opposite corners of the britschska, almost buried alive in cloaks and cushions, while they became deeply engaged in an animated discussion of all that everybody had said or done for the last few months, during which nothing could exceed the skill and perseverance with which Miss Marabout flattered her *ci-devant* pupil, unless it were the readiness with which her *douceurs* were accepted; for frequent practice had taught her to suit the bait to those she wished to catch, and Eleanor was becoming every day less fastidious in respect to the quantity or the quality of adulation which she could believe to be sincere as it was well-merited.

"That was so like you!" Miss Marabout was in the act of saying, when Matilda first aroused her attention. "As soon as I hear of anything generous or amiable, it instantly reminds me of Miss Fitz-Patrick, for we so rarely see the heart expand in proportion to the fortune; but yours were formed to suit each other.

'Large was her bounty, and—and—and—'"

Miss Marabout was apt to run aground in her quotations, to which Eleanor had long been accustomed, so she did not supply the cue, but continued the train of her own thoughts and plans. "I always wished, as you know, to transplant the Muckleraith family from Ashgrove, but Lady Olivia entertained some odd notions on the subject. The old man is dead now, so I have taken that rustic beauty, Nanny, whom we have so long raved about, into my service, and she looks like a perfect fairy. The plain elder sister may blush unseen, and remain with her mother, who will be a picturesque-looking old woman for attending to my fancy dairy and poultry-yard."

"How very kind and judicious!" exclaimed Miss Marabout; "but I always foretold that you would be a model for the rich as well as a friend to the poor, and few people combine so much power and inclination to be both."

"That silly girl Nanny imagined herself attached or engaged to the under-gardener, William Grey, though I hope she will learn better taste in my service than to fancy such a clownish-looking youth; but, with my usual good-nature, I have engaged him to work for me in the Highlands—and my greatest achievement of all remains to be told. Poor old Millar is already at Barnard Castle. She can make herself of no earthly use; but in every large country-house there must inevitably be an old nurse, or superannuated housekeeper, who is a pet in the establishment, with nothing to do but drink oceans of tea and grumble at the other servants So I have taken Millar as a necessary grievance, and shall let her be *at grass* while she lives.

Matilda felt surprised at the contemptuous tone in which Lady Olivia's faithful, attached servant was noticed, and she was hurt that none of these interesting communications were addressed to herself; but anxious not to be "overcome of evil," she listened with animated attention, and tried to appear as if the oversight was entirely unnoticed, by joining in the conversation with a degree of cheerfulness suited to the tone of her companions, though they were so agreeably occupied with each other that neither seemed conscious of the remarks which Matilda occasionally intruded upon them.

"With respect to your old victim, Sir Alfred Douglas," continued Miss Marabout, complaisantly, "I have it from undoubted authority that he admired no young lady abroad."

"Of course not, for you know he had *seen me*," replied Eleanor.

"Ah, very true! He is said to have become handsomer and more repulsive than ever, if that be possible; for Lady Montague says that all Florence was in an uproar about him, and the most diverting anecdotes were in circulation of the hauteur and indifference with which he kept every body at a distance last winter; but the more he tried to repress people's attentions, the more they were obtruded upon him."

"Of course! that is the way always!—whenever you wish to get on in society, begin by cutting three or four perfectly respectable people."

"Lady Montague mentioned a curious circumstance about Sir Alfred," continued Miss Marabout, evidently wishing and expecting to be asked for the sequel; "but she told it me under seal of the strictest secrecy."

"Oh! delightful!" exclaimed Eleanor eagerly; "it gives such zest to a story when people have promised not to tell it. Now go on!"

"But——" said Miss Marabout, with a hesitating look at Miss Howard.

"Nonsense!" cried Eleanor, impatiently, "you know very well that if Matilda had been Blue Beard's wife, she might have been alive yet, for any danger of her prying into secrets or repeating them. So now for your story."

"It was very much whispered that, a few days before Lady Amelia's death, she sent for her son, and extracted a promise from him that he would neither marry nor engage himself, for a certain length of time which she specified; and it appears, from what Lady Montague can learn, that his mother had some very eligible match in view, but that he prefers another, whom she does not think desirable. I cannot understand the business, having always been certain that he was devoted to you, and Lady Amelia would have felt too thankful for the slightest prospect of making *that* out, which would have rendered her son the most envied man in existence."

"I hate 'dying requests,' because they are sure to be always something so disagreeable or inconvenient that no *living* person could expect them to be granted! We must have an act of Parliament to annul all such extorted promises!" exclaimed Eleanor, indignantly. "I can now explain the whole enigma of Sir Alfred's conduct, for there need surely be no doubt that he was an admirer, in his dry, distant, odd way; but some 'good-natured friend' has certainly shown Lady Amelia the caricature I drew of her, as a bear-leader, taking about the young Baronet with a rein round his neck. The sketch was thought so inimitable that it circulated more than was prudent, and very probably fell into Lady Amelia's hand, who would certainly be angry, because her own portrait was *dreadfully* like; so it becomes evident that she wishes to prevent his proposing to me in a spirit of very laudable vengeance. As long as there are old people in the world, the course of true love never will run smooth."

"But your conjecture can scarcely be correct," interposed Matilda, trying to speak with the same indifference as if she had been dissenting from Eleanor's verdict on the weather, or setting her right about the day of the month, though a rebellious blush rose on her cheek and dyed it with crimson. "You must have mistaken Lady Amelia's opinions, because I heard her admiring you in terms that would satisfy even Miss Marabout. You used to say that she puffed off her favorites as if they were quack medicines, and that Lady Amelia should be poet-laureate to the japan blacking: so on this occasion your opinion would have been quite confirmed, for she was all in superlatives."

"Then what took Sir Alfred abroad, unless she had doubts of his being accepted, which would be quite reasonable and proper, for I am not at all sure upon that score myself; but one would, at any rate, like to be asked, if it were only for the good it would do Sir Alfred to be surprised with a refusal. I shall set about it as soon as he comes to lionize Barnard Castle at Christmas, when he will of course renew his attentions."

"Attentions!" exclaimed Matilda in undisguised astonishment. "I thought, Eleanor, you complained that he never spoke to you! I have heard you call him Harpocrates, the walking gentleman, and twenty other names, to indicate his perpetual silence."

"Yes—but every man in the world has a different way of being in love, and Sir Alfred's is not loquacious. True love seldom is talkative; and gentlemen often speak least to those they think most about. For instance, Sir Alfred addressed more of his conversation to *you* than to me—but the manner is everything on these occasions, and I would have been quite mortified if he had seemed as much at ease with me as he was with you. Charlotte Clifford carried on a flirtation all last winter with a gentleman who never even ventured on being introduced to her. She remarked him frequently watching her when she danced—he always contrived to be opposite to her at dinner parties, and very constantly passed by her windows in the forenoon."

"You cannot be serious, Eleanor! for I never heard a case worse argued in my life! As long as the gentleman looked in health he was probably thriving on hope, and if he had died it would have been of despair."

"Poor Charlotte certainly has a slight hallucination of intellect upon that subject, for she is so continually expecting to be fallen in love with," replied Eleanor, laughing. "She is, as your mother used to say, 'a silly flirt, who is good for nothing but to be married.' I have always observed that it makes a girl intolerably conceited to be, as she is, the best looking of three plain sisters, for *parmi les aveugles un borgne est roi*, and if there is but one eye in a family there must be always a beauty among them. Do you believe, Miss Marabout that Charlotte has really refused Sir Colin Fletcher?"

"It is difficult to say; but no man could be worse spared in society than poor Sir Colin, for he has such a philandering way that every young lady of his acquaintance gives out annually she has refused him; and I make a principle of believing them all."

"Charlotte Clifford is never acquainted with any young lady for an hour without asking to be her *confidante*, and on these confidential occasions there must be something to tell; but she has scarcely her equal in the world for getting up a romantic story impromptu. She gave me a splendid edition of Sir Colin's disappointment, and then asked me to return a Roland for an Oliver by serving up poor Lord Alderby."

"Those who confess a petty theft to their friends expect to be told of a murder in return;" said Miss Marabout, complaisantly; "and you have already a multitude to answer for. I understand that we are to have a visit from 'that diverting vagabond, Mr. Grant,' as Lady Susan Danvers calls him."

"Yes," replied Eleanor, slightly coloring, "we could not be off asking him, because he acts as Sir Alfred's second in canvassing the neighboring county, and they are quite inseparable. Mr. Grant's little property '*marches*' with mine, though we do not *march* long together, as his whole estate is scarcely so extensive as one of my largest farms. Yet you would be astonished what influence he has acquired in the neighborhood, as well as on his uncle Sir Evan Grant's extensive property near mine. All my people talk of his old descent, and his high principles and extensive benevolence, as if he were really a man of consequence."

"Mr. Grant may say, like Sir Lucius O'Trigger, though the mansion-house and dirty acres have slipped away, our honor and the family pictures remain as fresh as ever," observed Miss Marabout, with a contemptuous laugh.

"I shall not be sorry to see him back, however," added Eleanor; "he amuses me beyond measure; and besides, when Sir Alfred Douglas and Mr. Grant started off with one accord to the continent, it really seemed as if all my hangers-on had *struck work* at once."

"You really do task them very hard, and hold out but little hope of future reward," replied Miss Marabout, in her usual fawning tone. "Positively Lord Alderby's attentions to your white poodle are quite beyond praise."

"Poor dear Blanco! it will be my greatest joy on returning home to meet him again," exclaimed Eleanor, affectedly. "He sent me a wag of his tail by the last letter I had from the housekeeper, and Lord Alderby has certainly been an admirable tutor. Blanco sits at the piano, and makes sounds not much more discordant than Lady Susan Danvers, when she sings her *only* song, 'Di Tanti Palpiti;' and I am told, when you ask the dear dog what he would do for papa, he barks like a fury; but if he is asked to show what he would do for me, he falls down dead. That was really no bad idea of gallantry for an elderly gentleman like Lord Alderby to teach him."

"If you could only grind his lordship young again, and get a carpenter's plane to diminish his enormous physiognomy," said Miss Marabout, "he might be, with the earl's coronet, a very endurable person. What a pity it is that such a man should ever grow old; but I remember our hearing, last time he dined at Barnard Castle, that the only tooth in his head was aching; and he is accused of being rheumatic, which shows him to be very much broke. In short, it seems like summer and winter when you and he are together."

"Did you ever hear the fable," asked Matilda, "that once upon a time, Cupid and Death having fallen asleep, Mercury very mischievously mingled their arrows, which accounts for young people sometimes dying, and for very old people falling in love?"

CHAPTER IV.

"The yew-tree lent its shadows dark,
And many an old oak, worn and bare,
With all its shiver'd boughs, was there."

During the progress of their journey, in that singularly bleak and desolate stage between Dalnacardoch and Dalwhinny, the evening had nearly closed in, when Matilda was surprised to observe a well-mounted equestrian, in a long horseman's cloak, and very much muffled up, who rode alongside of the britschska, and stared incessantly at the whole party, as if he were resolved to identify them; but the instant that Eleanor perceived the stranger, she let down her veil, put up her parasol, and looked at Miss Marabout, who immediately did the same, while they began to exchange a few whispering exclamations of surprise and annoyance. Matilda rapidly ran up quite a little romance in her own mind, as to who this mysterious incognito might possibly be, and she thought his appearance fitted him admirably to act the villain of the piece. He had a dark, Schedoni-looking countenance, and his large eyes were so extremely prominent, that, whenever he winked, it seemed an equal chance whether his eyeballs were shut *in* or *shut out;* he was apparently about fifty years of age, but still in the vigor of his strength, and rode extremely well. It is astonishing, when people are travelling, how intense is their curiosity to know the name of every individual who may happen to lodge at the same inn, or to pass on the road. Matilda had wearied herself with conjectures about the probable rank of their fellow-traveller, when, next morning, Sir Richard mentioned, in a tone of apprehension to Eleanor, as if he anticipated an explosion of indignant surprise, that he had "accidentally met Armstrong, who offered to breakfast with them at the next stage." This intelligence was received in angry silence, and Matilda then remembered to have heard very frequent complaints from her cousin, that an old friend of Sir Philip's had almost forced himself into Barnard Castle during the previous summer, and steadily kept his position there in defiance of every stratagem which Eleanor's ingenuity could suggest to dislodge him. Matilda had laughed often at the stories she heard of the heiress's contrivances to affront him out of the house, and of the dogged unconsciousness with which her hints and sarcasms were all received by the object of them; and she could scarcely help smiling, when at length Mr. Armstrong entered their sitting-room with a sort of awkward swagger which is usually assumed by those who are doubtful of their welcome and determined to brave the worst. Eleanor gave him a look of tall contempt, and scarcely bent her head in return for a bow of almost exaggerated respect with which the intruder saluted her. Not a word passed between them; yet Matilda could not but observe an expression of fierce malignity which glittered for a moment in the large prominent eye of Mr. Armstrong while he bent it on Eleanor's haughty countenance and then turned to Sir Richard, who received his guest with that air of easy, good-natured hospitality which nothing could alter.

Few words passed between them, however, as both gentlemen had good travelling appetites; and now began "the war of waiters, the wreck of butter, and the crash of egg-shells," while Mr. Armstrong "troubled" Eleanor for as many cups of tea as if he had been Dr. Johnson. Towards the close of breakfast, when Miss Marabout accidentally addressed Miss Howard by name, Mr. Armstrong suddenly started round, with an expression of surprise, and held his tea-cup suspended in his hand, while his large eyes became fixed upon Matilda, and he repeated the surname again, as if to assure himself of her identity, while she looked at him in return with astonishment to perceive the sensation which had been so unaccountably occasioned; and Eleanor whispered to Miss Marabout, in a tone of satirical wonder—"Quite a dramatic start! It was really equal to Kean in Macbeth!"

Mr. Armstrong instantly made an effort to recover himself on hearing this remark; but Matilda observed, with perplexity, that frequently during the progress of breakfast he stole an examining glance towards the place where she sat, and still the "wonder grew" why her name should be an object of such peculiar interest to a person whom she was never conscious of having met before.

When the travellers were about to resume their journey, Matilda was unexpectedly accosted by Mr. Armstrong, who remarked, in an under-tone which seemed intended to be confidential, and with a very peculiar look, to which she vainly endeavored to assign a meaning, that "he was delighted to see HER on the road to Barnard Castle, as no one on earth had a better right to enter that house."

"We both derive our right from the same origin, Mr. Armstrong," replied she, smiling. "Sir Richard's kind invitation is our best passport."

"Perhaps I could show you a still surer one," muttered he in a mysterious tone. "It would be worth a trifle to me were mine half as good; but if Sir Philip's old friends are not better treated, your satirical cousin may yet have cause to remember a certain fable about the cow who stuck herself with her own horn. What would *you give me*, Miss Howard, to solve *that* riddle for you? Perhaps I may, if you promise to make it worth my while."

"It is worth every man's while, Mr. Armstrong, to do what is right, and nothing can ever make it worth your while to do wrong, therefore I can only leave you to judge for yourself, whatever the case may be," said Matilda, turning away with unconquerable dislike from the sinister expression of his countenance. "All I venture to recommend is, that you should neither act nor speak upon an angry impulse."

"You are the last person on earth who should have given me that advice, replied Mr. Armstrong with a loud laugh which grated harshly on the gentle ear of Matilda, and she hastily sprung into the carriage, where Eleanor wasted a number of witticisms on her cousin about the impression she had so suddenly made; but the career of her humor was changed into a burst of indignation when she heard Mr. Armstrong call out, in an apologetic tone, to Sir Richard, who looked little less astonished than his daughter, that "he should scarcely be able to reach Barnard Castle *before Christmas*, as he was torn to pieces with engagements, but would certainly reserve a week or two for their hospitalities at that time."

Before any one could frame an answer, and before the angry flash of Eleanor's eye could be followed by the sharp word that was ready, the incorrigible offender had finished a civil speech with which he expressed his consciousness of being "always so kindly welcomed;" and waving his hat with a look which showed how fully he understood the real state of the case, Mr. Armstrong spurred his horse and gal loped down the hill.

Matilda Howard's youthful spirits rose with the buoyancy of health and natural cheerfulness, her cheek was restored to its wonted bloom, and the light of joy and good-humor shone in her bright blue eyes, for she encouraged in herself that continual expectation of pleasure which is in itself a pleasure—yet she had many difficulties and discouragements to encounter from Eleanor, which, if she had allowed herself to dwell upon them, might well have checked and repelled a mind so sensitive as hers. If she was silent, her cousin sneered at "people" who thought nobody *good* enough to converse with—when she remarked on the weather, Eleanor seemed to think her common-place—if she spoke of books, it was pedantic—if she broke forth into admiration of the landscape, she was ridiculed as being sentimental; and the most cautious approach to religion was received by both her companions with marked disapprobation. As long as the talk was of Eleanor's lovers, her estates, her jewels, or her horses, conversation flowed smoothly on with unabating animation: even the outrageous mistakes of her footman, or the follies of her French maid, were subjects of legitimate attention, and her very lapdog was promoted into an object of excessive interest; for it may be observed, that when people are exceedingly self-important, a part of their system is to raise the dignity of every creature belonging to them. At the inns where they stopped to dine, Eleanor instantly sent the waiter to order "a chop for Fancy, done without pepper, and to be served up immediately, as she did not agree with irregular hours;" and it was the young heiress's whim to make her dog of more consequence than any one except herself.

As Eleanor persevered in an aristocratic time of setting out late in the forenoon, Matilda gained many hours every morning, during which she enjoyed a solitary ramble amidst those glens and mountains which are scattered along the Highland road. By the peep of day, while the heiress and Miss Marabout were buried in deep repose, her early steps were brushing the spangled dew from the grass, while the clear, cool breeze played among her hair, and brightened the bloom on her transparent cheek. Matilda's sylph-like figure had lost nothing of its juvenile grace, and she looked like a blossom of spring, while she glided along the shady paths, or stood beside the stream, listening with rapture to the morning song of the skylark soaring rapidly aloft, or to the brilliant chorus of blackbirds and thrushes, which seemed in gay emulation to drown each other's notes. Matilda's voice was sometimes raised in the deep solitude of nature, and tuned to a hymn of praise, while her thoughts arose in ardent gratitude to Him who formed those glorious scenes, and had placed her there to appreciate and enjoy them. "Can any artificial pleasure of life be compared," thought she, "to that which the God of nature provides in such a world of beauty as this!

'Surrounded by his power we stand,
On every side we feel his hand,
Oh! skill for human reach too high,
Too dazzling bright for mortal eye!'"

Nature may well be said to reward all her lovers without disappointing any; and never had she a more ardent admirer than in the pure mind of Matilda Howard, who gazed in unwearied delight on the last bright smiles of autumn, already clothed in her fancy dress of many colors. She watched the rising sun struggling through the morning clouds, and observed, with almost poetical interest, the various and singular effects of mist upon the distant hills and moorland solitudes. At times, the fog seemed like a boundless ocean, waving beneath her feet, while here and there a mountain-top appeared, like a distant island on the sea, and frequently the hills were only screened from her sight by a thin coquettish veil of mist, which hung in graceful draperies on the height, or stretched in wreaths along the mountain-top, till at length, floating off in transparent clouds, it displayed their massy outlines and Alpine forms, broken into a rich variety of light and shadow.

Matilda wandered for hours enjoying the unrivalled loveliness of Kinrara, where nature has been extravagant in her gifts of splendor and beauty. There the broad sweep of the majestic Spey flows on between its rugged banks, glittering with gay and dazzling brightness, or else cast into shadows of inky blackness, by the majestic forests of natural wood which wave over its deep and silent waters,—while the drooping tresses of the birch-tree floated over the gigantic rocks and Ossianic heights, around which were festooned wreaths of ivy and periwinkle. In the distance arose the lofty peak of Craigellachie, where tradition tells that the last wild boar was slain, though Eleanor remarked that *bores enough* were still remaining as long as Sir Colin Fletcher survived.

Much as Matilda enjoyed those lonely rambles, she yet felt the want of one who would say to her that "solitude is sweet," and with whom she could live in the interchange of thought and feeling. Her disposition was peculiarly social, and she had long felt conscious that, even in religion, it is almost essential to have some one with whom we can exchange the communication of those joys and sorrows which can only be imparted in the most perfect confidence, and in which she had once enjoyed a degree of entire sympathy which could never be looked for again. The thoughts of her departed friend brought a tear of tender and mournful remembrance to her eye as she glided on with no sound to accompany reflection but that of her own light elastic step upon the path.

There was one forbidden hope that forcibly obtruded itself on her mind, and which seemed to recur the oftener the more carefully it was banished. Who does not know that *Vouloir oublier quelque chose c'est y penser?* and our heroine could not entirely forget the more cultivated scenes of Douglas Priory, where conversations which had lasted but a few moments had fixed themselves on her memory forever. Sir Alfred Douglas was the only person Matilda had ever met with who seemed thoroughly to understand her sentiments, and to whom she scarcely found a necessity for expressing them, so entirely did his thoughts sympathize with her own. He had shown so much pleasure in consulting her taste upon all his projected improvements at the Priory, and she was conscious of his having adopted so many of her suggestions, of his intense delight in her music and conversation, and of his frequent manœuvres to be near her, that nothing but his unexpected departure for the continent had occurred to check her increasing belief in his attachment to herself, which his conduct in several respects had partly served to confirm. On one occasion, when he had requested her to gather a bouquet of wild-flowers, and she presented him with a group of heart's-ease and forget-me-not, Matilda could not cease to remember the look of sensibility with which he had remarked that it was impossible for him to *keep both*, upon which he threw away the heart's-ease, and insisted on dividing the forget-me-not with herself. Time, which had obliterated many subsequent scenes and events from her memory, had left that hour as vividly present to her mind as ever;

but, always anxious to place a proper control on her natural susceptibility of disposition, and conscious that, in every circumstance of life, there is a duty to be done, Matilda felt that she ought certainly to consign into oblivion any idle imagination which interfered with the serenity and peace that are the best accompaniments of true devotion, and which were never in so much danger of being disturbed as when some of those words or actions occurred to her memory which had once led her young mind to believe that she was an object of secret preference to Sir Alfred.

To Eleanor, her cousin's unaffected delight in the wonders and the beauties of creation was a subject of ridicule and incredulity. "Why, Matilda, you are quite in a fine frenzy," exclaimed she, sipping her coffee, and looking sleepily at her cousin's glowing, animated countenance. "You remind me of the tourists' guide-books, which not only describe what we are to see, but how we ought to feel. 'Here the spectator will be enraptured.' But I never follow any one's lead, and would not have spared a single exclamation, nor a line of poetry, for your cascade. It is the sort of thing I always detested, lionizing waterfalls; and indeed upon that score I am sadly like Madame du Deffand, who complained that she tired to death of '*innocent pleasures.*' How often I have been obliged from complaisance to set out on what is cruelly nicknamed a party of pleasure, to scramble up a steep, slippery, ill-kept path, with occasional chasms of several feet to leap over. A canopy of dripping trees overhead, and a deep abyss of green leaves below, through which you occasionally catch a peep of some stones and gravel, said to be the channel of a river. Then comes the cascade, not much fuller than my shower-bath, streaming and trickling down like a squirt. I am certain we might drink up all the water you have seen to-day; and that if a register were kept of wet feet and torn petticoats, it would be carried *nem. con.*, that '*le jeu ne vaut pas la chandelle.*'"

"No, no, Eleanor, you must have admired it. The birds were all crazy this fine morning, they sung so beautifully, and the deep bass of the waterfall made a splendid accompaniment of natural music."

"I always think, in such a scene, of the comparison that a cascade is like a scolding woman, beautiful to look at, but in a perpetual brawl."

"Yes, it is indeed perpetual, and makes me feel like one of the summer flies that skim along the surface of the stream, when I hear the voice of its waters, and see the tumult that has been raging there, with so much life and animation, ever since the world began, and which will continue in all its vivacity for ages after we are swept away and forgotten."

"Matilda, one would imagine you have visited the Falls of Niagara *at least*, to-day; but I have no turn for rhapsodizing about frowning mountains, and murmuring streams, and *fleecy-hosiery* clouds. Perhaps one may do so occasionally in society for effect; but to come blazing in, as you have done this morning, in a real fit of genuine ecstasy about nothing, is quite out of my line. With a wide domain of one's own to admire, where, like Robinson Crusoe, 'I am monarch of all I survey,' the country is endurable; but otherwise give me any town on earth, Berwick, or Mutton-hole, in preference."

"I always feel like Cowper, that God made the country, and man made the town; and mine is like the sensation of a bird escaping from its cage, when first we emerge into green fields and gay shrubberies again. I could have embraced the first tree on our road, for it seemed like a long-absent friend restored to me again."

"'*Chacun à son goût*;'—but if you want mountains, Arthur's Seat is quite sublime enough to satisfy me. For varied scenery, take a circuit of the Calton Hill; for umbrageous shades, give me a parasol; and for a romantic, loverizing promenade, scramble up the steep sides of the Castle rocks. Then for moonlight you may indulge in a stretch along Prince's Street, watching the splendid shops, glittering like Aladdin's palace, with gas lamps shining picturesquely though a long perspective of gauzes, feathers, and artificial flowers; the apothecaries' shops sending forth a stream of green and rose-colored light; the pedestrians lounging about with cigars in their mouths; and the New Club, which blazes for an instant, like lightning, as you pass, showing a momentary glimpse of its members, picturesquely grouped on the sofas and chairs. How I wish the whole building, with its contents, could be transported to my gate, for Barnard Castle will be as dull as a hen-coop during the next two months. There is no resource in the house except Blanco, and not a single victim to be captivated but Lord Alderby, whom I shall be almost tempted to accept, for something to do."

"Many girls marry for no better reason," said Matilda.

"True enough!—I verily believe that if *trousseaux*, favors, white satin, feathers, blonde, and marriage-jaunts were abolished, and that no paragraph in the newspaper was allowed to commemorate the event, and no happy couple permitted to set off in a more splendid cavalcade than they are daily ascustomed to, half the young ladies who fancy themselves desperately in love would remain very rationally at home. That newly-invented word *excitement*, is the pleasure which we are all in pursuit of; and, whether it be dancing or matrimony, therevolution of kingdoms or the death of acquaintances, all contribute their quota to that degree of *excitement* which is become an actual necessary of life."

"So much stimulus to the mind is like drinking brandy; it may produce temporary exhilaration, but leads to a painful reaction afterwards. How different it is, Eleanor, from that mental composure and peace which the Scriptures point out as our natural state of enjoyment, and which alone can be permanent and wholesome. This life has been truly called a changeable scene—a procession of trifles—the chief interest of which is not derived from the incidents themselves but from the use we make of them in correcting our own dispositions and habits of thinking."

"Matilda, you shall be fined for preaching without a license! I am always afraid to articulate three syllables now, because a sermon is so sure to explode in my face. Pray talk occasionally without attempting my reformation, or considering yourself a home missionary appointed to convert me; for really, my *good* friend, if Mrs. Stevens at Knaresborough ever wants an assistant and successor, I shall make a point of recommending you."

"I have perhaps been unguarded, Eleanor; but the time was *once* when I might have thought aloud without the danger of being misconstrued; and you know perfectly that I never *talk at* any one, but often make these common-place reflections, more to school my own mind than others, for even the frequency with which they have already been made proves their importance; and I am anxious to forget nothing that may strengthen the clue with which we shall be safely guided through the labyrinth of life."

Advancing towards Inverness, the features of the country became more majestic, and Matilda's heart expanded with astonishment and delight when their carriage swept round the projecting elbow of a hill, and her eyes first dwelt upon the unrivalled splendor of Cromarty bay. Its broad expanse shone like a sapphire, amidst an amphitheatre of rugged mountains, clothed to their summits with patches of natural wood, tinged in all the richest hues of autumn, while here and there a brilliant sunshine glittered through the branches, and painted every leaf upon the ground beneath. No painter could have ventured to mix such bright and varied tints on his pallet, as were glowing in gaudy splendor beneath a setting sun, on the sparkling waters, the glittering sails, and the waving forests of Cromarty. A light "*skiff*" of rain, which fell in the sunshine as they passed, looked like a shower of diamonds, and the glorious arch of a rainbow, which stretched across the sky, was reflected like a magic circle in the mirror beneath.

Tears of admiration sprung into Matilda's eyes when she looked upon this profusion of beauty; but she dared not give vent to a single thought that filled her heart at the moment when it overflowed with devout and holy joy. No answering look was elicited when she turned to Eleanor and Miss Marabout for sympathy, but giving a cold glance of indifference at the brilliant panorama, accompanied by an impatient conjecture whether Sir Richard had yet reached Dingwall to order dinner, they resumed an interesting discussion relating to the intolerable stupidity of Pauline, and her extreme dislike to her deputy, Nanny Muckleraith, many strong evidences of which were related by Eleanor with infinite zest and only slight disapprobation.

"I never see that poor girl now; for Pauline is outrageously jealous of her being so excessively admired, and I scarcely dare mention her name. You know one must keep on good terms with an Abigail, *coute qui coute*, and mademoiselle never does my hair tolerably unless she is in good humor."

"Then Pauline may be considered as a viceroy *over* you," observed Matilda; "and poor Nanny, when exposed to all the whim and caprice you describe, must often look back with regret on the garden at Ashgrove, and wish she had still to *sow* turnips instead of handkerchiefs."

"Pray send for her sometimes then, and be melancholy together," replied Eleanor, laughing. "She has almost broken her heart lately, I am told, about some foolish attachment to William Grey, the under-gardener, and it really provokes one to hear of such intolerable stupidity. I told her once that nature had made a mistake in giving her such a name and station, but that, if she pleased me I would rectify the blunder."

"Most generous, indeed," said Miss Marabout.

"She was very grateful at the time, but Nanny is never two hours of the same mind, and has become so flighty and odd of late, that I sometimes think she is scarcely in her right senses. You know her father was once in confinement for a year, and there is a glare in her brilliant eyes that sometimes almost alarms me, especially since this affair of William Grey, and all her *brouilleries* with Pauline. Luckily, they have not a language in common to quarrel in," added Eleanor, laughing, "as each is obliged, for indispensable reasons, to prefer her own; and it is fortunate in another respect, as Pauline is quite a Frenchwoman in her principles, if she can be imagined to have any principles at all: she flirts prodigiously, and is not supposed to be of very immaculate reputation; but I must turn a deaf ear to all gossip on that score, seeing that I could not exist, or at least dress, without her."

"Is there likely to be a change of ministry soon?" asked Matilda; "you seem to find great faults in the present administration."

"No, no! as Charles the Second observed, there may be oppression and injustice against my subjects, but I see nothing against myself," replied Eleanor, in a tone of great complacency; for it is a favorite piece of self-importance with vain people to set themselves above general rules, and to boast of doing what no other person could venture; so that when Eleanor talked of keeping a maid whose character appeared questionable, it was to show with what impunity she might brave Matilda's opinion, or that of any one else who was tied down to ordinary customs in their actions and thoughts.

CHAPTER V.

This castle hath a pleasant seat!
MACBETH.

MATILDA had not imagined it possible that any accession of dignity could take place in the demeanor which Eleanor assumed throughout their journey; but when her carriage at length reached the princely domain of Barnard Castle, she seemed to swell out with fresh importance, while, assuming a studied air of indifference, she pointed out all that might enhance the estimate of her extensive possessions, saying, in the careless, accidental tone usual among landed proprietors, "All the grounds on each side of the road now are mine. I am *Marquis of Carrabas*, whichever way you turn."

A fat, unwieldy, consequential-looking old woman swung open an enormous iron gate, surmounted by armorial shields bearing the Barnard arms, and flanked by two ivy-covered lodges which were so handsome as to give promise of future magnificence, and the approach was entered by a dense wilderness of trees, like an Indian jungle, through which the road cut its winding way, till it emerged upon the noble and extensive park, stretching, with its verdant glades and lofty woods, to the utmost verge of the horizon. Large groups of ancient trees bowed their majestic heads on every side; while Eleanor, in the exuberance of her spirits, bowed to them in return; and the graceful fallow deer might be seen pasturing in distant herds, or occasionally tossing their branching horns, and bounding across the velvet sward. A broad river, which flowed impetuously through the park, swept almost round the house, and was lost in a lake of such crystal clearness, that the variegated tints of every tree were reflected on its bosom; and the whole was closed in by a distant range of craggy mountains, crested by dark thickets of pine, which were seen in bold relief on the evening sky. Matilda stood up in the carriage, partly to indulge, but chiefly to conceal the emotion with which she was filled by such a scene, and her heart whispered, in a tone of devout admiration and praise,

> "'Twas great to speak this world from nought,
> 'Twas greater to redeem."

"Miss Marabout," said Eleanor, gazing with proud exultation at some wide-spreading oaks which skirted the terrace, "I should not like to be as old as the very youngest of those trees; but it would certainly be desirable to resemble them in one respect—becoming always more beautiful the older they grow. What changes I shall have to make here," added she, glancing a magnificent look around. "No alteration has been attempted for centuries, and if my great-grandfather Sir Hildebrand himself could come back for a day or two, he would scarcely discover any innovations; but I shall cut and carve in all directions, to show what the finger of taste can do."

"Those mountains, hills, and valleys will not be easily altered," thought Matilda. "It is in such scenes as these that men have doubted whether the natural beauty of the world was not allowed to continue unimpaired, while its moral beauty has been defaced. I often meet in society the most pleasing natural characters, and I look at such scenes of natural beauty as these, till I imagine them fragments and specimens, as it were, of what *has been once*, and of what *will be again.* We shall yet see a new heaven and a new earth of unimaginable beauty, inhabited by a people of inconceivable holiness, whose enjoyments will remain undisturbed by those longings after a 'better country,' and after a more heavenly frame of mind, which we now experience, and which it is the business of our present lives to encourage."

"I mean to prove myself a model of taste, as well as of all the other virtues and graces," continued Eleanor. "You know, Matilda the genius of most ladies is confined to planning improvements on a cap, or to meandering over mazes of muslin and tulle; but mine shall be immortalized on vistas, flower-beds, clumps, and plantations which will astonish your weak mind. And now let me introduce you to my chateau."

Miss Howard turned her eager eyes, and beheld, on the declivity of a neighboring hill, the noble, commanding site of Barnard Castle, which was a striking specimen of feudal magnificence, with its lofty circular towers, and venerable, time-worn battlements, shooting upwards amidst a veteran battalion of aged fir-trees, which seemed to protect the walls, and bid stern defiance to the gayer and more modern tenants of the park. A flight of noisy rooks expressed their terror and annoyance at any symptoms of human habitation, by cawing and croaking vociferously; while everything around testified to that neglect and indifference in which the place had remained during the period when Sir Philip wasted his years in an Italian villa, and allowed "spiders to hang their tapestry" on the walls of that splendid home which Providence had assigned him.

The interior of Barnard Castle corresponded with Matilda's expectations, though the floors were all so polished, and the roof so elaborately decorated, that she nearly lost her equilibrium in looking upwards, and would have entered the house with a series of prostrations, like the Hindoo devotees, had it not been for Sir Richard's hospitable alacrity, who met her at the door, and handed her in with a truly gratifying degree of *empressement* and kindness.

"It would require a twenty-horse power to move this chair," said he, placing her safely in one, which stood beside a blazing fire. "Probably some of your progenitresses wore out a pair of eyes in embroidering those beautiful designs."

"I hate *designs*, and designing people too; but there are some of my relations still left who are of that class," exclaimed Eleanor, in a peevish tone, which was loud enough to reach Matilda's wondering ears, while the heiress stood at a full length mirror, arranging her shining curls, and catching the reflection of her aërial figure in the numerous antique looking-glasses which hung around the walls, in massy frames of oak. "How frightful I look, after our long cold drive to-day!"

"So you do!" replied Sir Richard, archly. "Only think, Eleanor, what successive generations of beauties have admired themselves in that ancient mirror."

"But the last is *not the least*," interrupted Miss Marabout, with flattering emphasis.

"Dear Eleanor, what head could stand all this!" thought Matilda, listening with affectionate regret to the fawning adulation which followed, while she also contemplated, in silent admiration, the gorgeous splendor of her cousin's newly-acquired possessions. Once more, while she rose up and strolled, neglected and alone, into the quaint old library, Matilda revived her resolution to view Eleanor's conduct towards herself with partiality and complaisance; to bear all things, to believe all things, to hope all things, and, far from bringing on estrangement by that captiousness in anticipating affronts which is too common on the part of old friends towards those who are suddenly elevated, she resolved, in all the firmness of Christian principle, not even to "harbor a suspicious thought;" and she turned speedily back, to participate in the joyful meeting which took place between Eleanor and her professed idol, Blanco, on whom the heiress lavished every term of rapturous endearment, speaking all the time in that peculiar tone of nonsense which ladies reserve for the entertainment of lapdogs and babies. At length, this scene having been prolonged to the utmost possible duration, and Eleanor having afterwards given to Pauline a million of orders and counter-orders, she felt at leisure to take Matilda a tour of the sitting-rooms, which she displayed with all the gay delight of a child exhibiting its last new toy, turning frequently round to her cousin, and exclaiming, "Now! don't you envy me, Matilda?"

"Certainly," replied she, with that good-humored sympathy which was as ready for the joys as the sorrows of her friends. "What you have shown me to-day reminds one of Hafiz, in the Arabian Nights, who borrowed an ointment which enabled him to behold all the treasures of the world; but when he wished inordinately to possess them, you know, Eleanor, he tried a second application, and lost his eyesight entirely; so let me beware of deserving such a fate. My business is to learn how to be abased, while you must study how to abound, because both situations are appointed to us; and I feel such implicit confidence it the unerring wisdom which directs our different circumstances, that I could almost feel as Fénélon did, who once observed that he would not be at the trouble of lifting up a straw to make anything in life different from what he found it."

Sir Richard, who only lived from meal to meal, had dropt several emphatic hints on the propriety of being rigidly punctual at dinner, before Eleanor condescended to appear conscious of their import, till at length she started up, and proposed to show Matilda her room. "But, in the first place, like all ladies doing the honors of a country house, let me deliver a set speech, hoping you will be perfectly comfortable, make yourself quite at home, ring for tea nine times a-day, if you choose, and for every other necessary of life that may be requisite, &c. Pauline is such a fine lady that I dare not ask her to attend on all the stray misses who wander here without Abigails, therefore Nanny has orders to be in every corner of the house at once, to arrange all the dresses that require to be put on for breakfast and dinner. As for hair-dressing, those who cannot manage to do their own must wear bonnets, for Nanny is scarcely fit to comb Blanco's, and Pauline, who learnt from the first friseur at Paris, finds it quite troublesome enough to please me."

"If you are superstitious, Matilda, we can soon *faire dresser les cheveux à la tête*," said Sir Richard. "You are aware that an old castle in the Highlands would scarcely be considered respectable without its own particular ghost, and we have a 'murder room' here, in which some 'Mystery of Udolpho' was transacted long ago. It must be passed on the way to your apartment, so look well about you, though nothing very supernatural has occurred in my time, except that the window-sashes are supposed to open and shut of themselves occasionally, and a terrified kitchen-maid once protested she had seen the ghost of a leg walking past there in the evening."

"Probably a leg of mutton," observed Matilda, smiling.

"You forget, papa, that a noise of steps may be heard at midnight, running up and down stairs, often; and do you not remember, one evening, when Miss Marabout and I watched, she at the top landing-place, and myself at the bottom, with an arrangement that we were to fly to each other whenever the noise began? The agreement had not been made above ten minutes before we both heard foot-steps, and flew to meet; but though she came down, and I ran up, we saw no *living* creature 'on the way.'"

"You were probably both much excited, and mistook each other's steps for something supernatural," observed Sir Richard; "but I remember long ago a Ghost Club at Bath, for which you might both have been eligible candidates, as no one could be admitted without telling a perfectly new and well-authenticated story of an apparition. The 'murder-room' in this house is certainly very singular, as it had been shut up for ages and completely forgotten, till, in moving an old picture, the door was discovered by Sir Philip, who told me that nothing could be more strange than the first *coup d' œil.* Whoever had been the last inhabitant, every article remained precisely as he had left it a hundred years before. The bed was turned down, ready to be slept in,—towels were laying about the room"——

"His very boot-jack and slippers, I suppose," added Matilda, laughing. "It reminds one, in a small way, of Herculaneum, and I feel quite delighted to hear that we pass near it in going to my lodging, that I may drop in, for a moment,—only for *one* moment, Sir Richard, to lionize."

The baronet looked at his watch, and shook his head; but Eleanor beckoned to her cousin with an air of more easy familiarity than she had condescended to assume lately, and they both hurried up a narrow, perpendicular back-stair, near the summit of which were two opposite doors, one leading into Matilda's room, and the other, which Eleanor opened first, ushered them into an apartment more singular in its aspect than her guest had been at all prepared to see. It was a large, low-roofed, dark-looking gallery, filled with lumber, and the extent was so vast, that in a dingy twilight, which penetrated through one or two narrow-pointed casements, the distance was lost in obscurity, though enough was revealed at one glance to afford the ready eye of Matilda a field of unbounded diversion and curiosity. Close to the wall were ranged a double, and in some places a triple pile of foreign pictures, many in frames, and others only stretched upon wood. A few of the subjects were laughably grotesque, and others appeared to be splendid specimens of art, which Sir Philip had probably meant to suspend in the drawing-rooms when he returned home. Packing boxes on every side had been recently opened, and the floor was strewed with mutilated statues, Herculaneum vases, casts from the antique, models of Rome, Pére la Chaise, and the Alps; cabinets, gems, marble tables, grotesque jars, and Roman enamels. High above all, as if contemplating this scene of devastation and disorder, stood a full-length portrait of Sir Philip Barnard, in all the bloom of youth, and of that handsome exterior for which he had once been celebrated. Matilda paused a moment to contemplate it, and she felt as if a whole lifetime were comprised in that single glance. He seemed then just entering into manhood, full of buoyant animation, and rich in the gifts of nature and fortune. All had now passed away—and what had been the result? No domestic affection had brightened his enjoyments—no grateful tenantry had blessed his liberality—not a tear had been shed over his grave—not a human being had been benefited by his existence--but a multitude of statues and pictures were transplanted from Rome and Florence at his command.

which now surrounded him in apparent mockery of his wasted years and scattered income.

"It will divert me some wet morning to arrange the best of these portraits in the entrance-hall," said Eleanor. "My grim-looking ancestors have literally returned to the dust, they are so encrusted with it. Most of them were collateral relations, old maiden aunts, or admirals and generals who performed the parts of uncles in their time, but I am about to dignify them all with new names. The family pedigree has furnished me with a list of innumerable peers and ladies of quality, who connected themselves with us ages ago, and I shall have their style and titles engraved in gilt letters on these frames."

"But, my dear Eleanor! what a want of historical veracity!—you cannot seriously intend turning those worthy, respectable ladies and gentlemen into arrant impostors! Though this house has been so long shut up, visitors might come who could detect the alteration, and you may then perhaps feel, like the valet in the play, that it is easy to tell falsehoods, but it hurts one's conscience to be found out."

"I see no harm in the joke at all!—every body's ancestors look precisely the same. For instance, that lady with the large nosegay in one hand, and a hawk resting on the other; or this smiling sylph, with coral lips and an invisible waist, is extant in all the galleries I ever entered; and ditto the gentleman in pink cheeks, full-bottomed wig, and steel armor, with a cannon just going off at his back. Their duplicates may be found in every old house you visit, with different names, so why should not I indulge my whim, seeing that it is the only plan which will enable me with any advantage to display them? The collection is so large and miscellaneous, that I shall be obliged to decorate the outside wall of the house with pictures at last, and as for the statues, I wish many of them could be broken into stones for the road, they are such mere lumber."

"I cannot really stay to hear you quizzing these venerable antiquities to their faces, and making me too late for dinner," said Matilda, leading the way to her own room. "You know, Eleanor, that the only subject on earth in which the whole civilized world has agreed, is in admiring such ancient specimens of art as these, and I shall take many opportunities here of improving my acquaintance with them."

Miss Fitz-Patrick proceeded to stir up her cousin's fire, which was already like a furnace, and after indulging in a critical examination of her simple, unadorned dressing-box, she carelessly expressed a hope that Matilda would be comfortable, and lounged towards the door, humming an opera tune, as was her continual custom, for wherever she went Eleanor might be heard, like a linnet, all over the house. "I shall send up Nanny to unpack your *valuables*," said she, satirically; "but really, Matilda, that plain, uncut crystal in the dressing-case looks so like a gentleman's paraphernalia, that I consider it *quite improper*."

Matilda was disturbed from an interesting reverie into which she had fallen after Eleanor's departure, by a gentle tap at the door, and immediately afterwards a smart little figure entered, most fantastically dressed as a French soubrette, with her face shaded beneath a torrent of ringlets, and a light soufflet of a cap put on in the last extreme of affectation. Having looked at the intruder for some moments in silent perplexity, she suddenly exclaimed, with unfeigned astonishment,—"Nanny!—can it be possible!—you are so altered that I really did not recognise you!"

"Probably not, Miss Howard," replied she, dropping a very rustic curtsy, and looking exceedingly conceited; "Miss Fitz-Patrick said, when she sent me here, ma'am, that I was so improved you would scarcely know me."

"I did not say you were *improved*, Nanny, but altered, and not, I fear, as far as can yet be seen, for the better; you know well how much I am interested in your welfare, and that since the time when we both were children, my feelings have been the same, therefore it gives me real regret to see that you have become thin and pale. Ribbons and millinery cannot conceal the real fact from an old friend like me, Nanny, and I am perfectly convinced you are unhappy, though I will say no more on the subject now, unless you want advice, or wish to intrust me with the cause of your uneasiness."

The kindness of Matilda's manner, and the gentle, though sorrowful tone of her voice, recalled old feelings and associations to Nanny's mind—her newly-acquired affectation vanished at once, and she hung down her head in silence, while her color went and came with alarming rapidity. Matilda proceeded with her toilette in silence; but at length, before she left the room, Nanny had recovered her voice, and seemed anxious to tell the whole history of her distresses, from which Matilda plainly gathered how deeply she was attached to William Grey, her former lover, though Eleanor's advice, and the ridicule which had been thrown upon his rustic manners and appearance among her own new associates, had induced her hastily to break off an engagement which had long subsisted between them, and the struggle of love and ambition that became obvious when she spoke would have caused Matilda to smile had the subject been less serious in its consequences than appeared probable. Nanny spoke with a husky voice and a quivering lip, while she hastily plaited up her apron into every possible shape, and occasionally stole a glance at the mirror, which generally altered the current of her expressions from the sincerity of nature to an artificial tone of rather comical conceit.

"I often think, Miss Howard, of the time when William was such a good scholar at your Sunday-school—what a clever workman he is, too!—and then such beautiful flowers as he brought to church for me! Many an evening he twisted garlands of roses and honeysuckles in my bonnet while we sat by the river singing our hymns together—but that is over now. We can never be friends again as we were, and often I can neither rest nor sleep for sorrow to think how all is ended. Every one says it is for my good, and that I shall do much better, because William is too poor to marry," added Nanny, catching a glimpse of the looking-glass. "I should have had no comfort with him, but hard work continually and coarse food. Indeed, Miss Howard, it is impossible to do without my tea twice a-day, now that I am used to it; and we have everything so grand at the second table that I can never get accustomed to any discomfort again. How astonished William Grey would be! But he never comes to the house now, for he can only be admitted to the kitchen, and I could not help laughing the last time he went there at the way he was ridiculed and taken off by Sir Richard's gentleman, who can speak as like him as possible, and answered all he said in a vulgar voice, the same as his own, but rather worse."

"This is sad indeed, Nanny! I am sorry for what you tell me about William. He was an honest-hearted, well-principled young man, who would probably have made you happy, and the trifling reasons that have caused a change cannot long satisfy your own mind; but it is well when people alter before marriage rather than after their engagement is irrevocable."

"Yes, ma'am," said Nanny in a very doubtful tone and with tears in her eyes.

"I trust you will now find all for the best and never repent of your decision. But, Nanny, you are in new and trying circumstances here, which makes me feel most anxious on your account. Think for an instant of your kind benefactress who is now no more, and reflect what would have been her feelings if she could see you at this moment. The change is great already since you first learnt to repeat at school such texts as these—'Be ye clothed with humility—be not high minded—let not the prince of this world gain dominion over you.' Alas, Nanny! the friend who would have advised and warned you is now no more, and who shall supply her place to either of us? She dreaded your being placed in a situation of such difficulty and temptation as this; but once having entered it, you may find strength sufficient for every trial, if you seek it aright. Do not destroy the simplicity of mind and manners that you once had, for be assured nothing can be gained that will compensate for the loss, and you may become ridiculous even to those who appear most friendly. You move about the room now with as many contortions as an eel, and none of the faces you make in speaking are better than the face you have by nature. Let me hope, then, that when you attend on me I may see the Nanny of former days to remind me of Ashgrove, and be assured that I shall feel the warmest interest in your welfare as long as you continue to deserve it. I little thought at one time that such a doubt could be possible; but the true test of principle is *consistency* in small matters as well as in the greatest, and before long I hope to see your dress and appearance more in accordance with the sober and rational mind you once had, and with the self-denying doctrines which we have both been taught."

CHAPTER VI.

That weariness of all
We meet, or feel, or hear, or see.
COLERID .

It is difficult to realize in our own conceptions, that the noiseless foot of Time invariably advances at the same pace, neither accelerated during our seasons of joy, nor lingering in the days of our weariness. Months passed on at Barnard Castle in the tranquil uniformity so agreeable to those who have mental resources, but most tedious and intolerable to the many who, like Sir Richard Fitz-Patrick and his daughter, depend for happiness on external amusement. Eleanor, "stretched on the rack of a too easy chair," fretted and complained forever, protesting that Time had certainly put a drag on his chariot-wheels on purpose to tease her, and Miss Marabout laboriously tried to beguile the weight of present ennui by holding out the promise of future amusement when Christmas festivities and an approaching election might be anticipated as the certain harbingers of gayety—every night she remarked, in a tone of satisfaction, that one day was over, and on Sunday mornings her regular salutation to Eleanor was, that another week had passed, and that Christmas must be at hand.

"Yes," replied she in a tone of peevish resignation, "as the tenant said who wanted a lease of his farm for several centuries, 'a thousand years soon passes away,' and it must be almost as long since we came here—even the post-bag is empty to-day, which always happens on a rainy morning."

"It would be an excellent expedient," observed Sir Richard, "to hire a few gossiping correspondents, who shall write regularly, and be paid like a magazine, at so much a line, and double price if the letter comes on a bad day. I would deduct, however, all paragraphs of apology for not writing longer, or sooner, or oftener—all professions of friendship, and everything in the slightest degree sentimental."

"What havoc you would make at the post-office, if these were all expunged," said Matilda; "many of our letters would reach their destination as blank sheets of paper."

"I wonder that no quack advertisement ever proposes an infallible cure for ennui!" exclaimed Eleanor, languidly.

"Fling but a stone, the giant dies," replied Matilda; "nothing can rid us of it entirely but exertion."

Meantime Eleanor never seemed to think of planning any excursions to lionize her guest over the beautiful scenery around; but she cantered off on horseback alone, leaving Matilda to explore, in solitude, the romantic glens, and almost inaccessible hills in the neighborhood; while her sketch-book became filled with views of the wild, deep ravines, the ivy-covered bridges, the tangled thickets, the foaming torrent, and the green retreats, to which she wandered in silent, but exquisite enjoyment. Like all amiable minds, Matilda's never fully enjoyed any pleasure till it was communicated; and often did the words of Solomon recur to her meditations—"Wo to him that is alone!" she continually found the want of a friend whose feelings might be an echo to her own, as even in religious enjoyment the mind seeks communion with a kindred spirit, that "as face answereth to face, so may the heart of man to man." Frequently she stood on a lofty bank that overhung the village green, watching with animated sympathy the joyful groups which assembled there; and on all occasions, in witnessing the amusements of others, those pleasures that seemed most natural were those in which she felt most ready to participate. The group of laughing girls in a hay-field,—an old woman basking in the sunshine at her cottage door,—or a child carefully cultivating its flaring wall-flower in a broken tea-pot, all in succession caused her to stop and contemplate them with benevolent interest, while she seldom forgot in an evening to station herself at the library window, from whence might be observed the moment when old Janet Muckleraith retired, after her daily labor. She could discern a clear blue column of peat smoke, which curled upon the distant hill-top, showing that the cottage fire was lighted, and then Matilda knew that the mother and daughter were sitting down, with thankfulness and praise, to their evening meal.

Few recreations were so delightful to her as visiting the poor people around, for amongst them she discovered an infinite variety of character and circumstances, while the strongly-marked features which may be traced in unpolished minds, form a subject of interest even to those whose motives are unsanctified by religion. Many there were whose genuine worth rendered them objects of real esteem, others whose eccentricity was so broadly exhibited, that she could not be otherwise than amused; but, wherever she went, her first aim was to diffuse consolation amidst the sorrows of those who were depressed or afflicted. Her most frequent visits, however, were paid to the cottage of old Janet, whose busy wheel was laid aside for the short period of Miss Howard's visit, with a look of such honest, heartfelt gratitude for her attention in calling, that Matilda scarcely required her repeated thanks to prove how cordially she was welcome; and Martha's tidy appearance, and still tidier house, seldom needed the apology, which was nevertheless invariably made, for its supposed disorder.

Nothing could be more pleasing to Matilda's young and buoyant mind than to observe the devout and thankful spirit which both mother and daughter continually maintained. Their lives consisted not in the abundance of the things they possessed, but amidst hard labor and many privations, they spoke of countless blessings. Old Janet once remarked, that it was not sufficient for Christians to speak in general terms of the mercy they received, but that each individual should be able to recount some advantages peculiar to himself, for which he ought to be especially grateful, and hers was a catalogue of considerable length. Matilda observed with regret, that, latterly, when her children were named in the number of her comforts, the old woman paused in the recapitulation, while a tear struggled in her eye, and a look of anxious care clouded her usually cheerful countenance.

"These are changed times with Nanny," said she, giving a furtive, agitated glance at her visitor; "and oh! Miss Howard, I wish it may all be well, for when Satan wrestles with poor weak sinners like us, he often lifts us up, that we may be more easily cast down, and that the fall may be greater. She looks ill; and has a strange, wild way of talking sometimes, that frightens me. I am sure her quarrel with William preys on Nanny's mind, but she will not speak to me about it, and seldom comes here at all. There are plenty of good excuses; but where the will is, we soon find the way. I wish she would settle at home once more; but Nanny is sadly spoilt for that now."

Matilda had little reason to doubt the truth of this last

assertion, and would have seen still less could she have been present sometimes when the young beauty visited her mother at Gowanbank cottage, where her tone of conscious superiority, and fine-lady airs, formed a striking contrast to the blithe and happy looks of her elder sister. William Grey still occasionally met Nanny there, though not apparently with any intention of doing so; but all his leisure hours were spent at old Janet's, while he assisted her more active daughter in the garden, the dairy, and the poultry-yard. No employment came amiss to him when Martha required his aid. He nailed up clustering jessamines and honeysuckle on the rustic porch; he cut down the hay for her cows in the neighboring paddock, and planted out, with a group of lilacs, the view of some rather ruinous pig-styes, which Nanny complained of as tormenting her eyes, whenever she crossed the garden.

"William," said Martha, one day, in the exuberance of her gratitude, "I must once more get you and Nanny reconciled, though both very troublesome people; I have nothing to do now but keep peace between you."

"It passes the power of any one to do that now," replied he, gloomily; "she has set me an example which I am very glad to follow, and I no more think her a fit wife for me than she does herself."

"I am grieved to hear this, William; for Nanny loves you still; and, though she is a little spoilt now, it cannot last. I am sure when the novelty of her fine situation wears off, she will be the same as ever, and you may both be reconciled."

"No, Martha! I never should have thought of her, and I never shall again; it has been a mistake all along, a boyish fancy—but now I know my own mind, and I prefer some one else."

"You! oh, William, it is impossible!—Nanny would break her heart; but you are not in earnest? You are angry now; but remember old times, William, and do not quarrel with us for a trifle. Think of the days when we went to school together, and you helped us across the burn, and gathered daisies in the fields, and berries on the hedges; we had no quarrels then, William, and why should we have them now?"

"Not with *you*, Martha," said William, coloring, and speaking rapidly; "you must have seen long ago—you—you surely know that every day has shown me how miserable I should be with Nanny, and how happy I might be with —with *yourself*."

Martha started and turned pale at this unexpected declaration; but, after a momentary struggle, she answered, with perfect decision of voice and manner—

"No, William, I cannot listen to this; you mistake a little anger against Nanny for a preference of me; but it must not be thought of or ever mentioned again. She loves you, William—indeed she does. I know Nanny's whole heart, and her sister must not be the person to break it."

With all the eloquence of natural feeling and true affection, Martha entreated William's forbearance, and spoke in defence of her absent sister, while he listened in silence, and turned away to hide his emotion.

"I seem changeable, Martha, and do not deserve that you should trust me at once," said he, earnestly; "but time may bring all things round. If you are convinced of Nanny's indifference, and of my constancy to yourself, shall we then be happy? I used to think, Martha, before I ever spoke to Nanny on the subject, that you liked me; and I sometimes thought even then that I preferred her more on account of what other people said, than because I loved her myself."

Martha turned away, but could not reply—her cheek became pale, and her step uncertain; but she hurried to the house and closed the door.

Many days elapsed before William saw her again, and it became evident that she was resolutely bent on giving him no opportunity to renew the agitating discussion which had taken place between them; for it was only in her mother's presence that they had at last any intercourse. For some time Martha's countenance seemed paler than usual, and there was an unconquerable tremulousness in her voice when she spoke; but these emotions were speedily and resolutely subdued, so that no traces remained of her remembering what had passed.

Martha usually possessed, in an eminent degree, that "joy of countenance" which is produced by a "glad heart," and the beauty of holiness might be seen in all she said or did; for like the salt that seasoned her food, was the prevailing zest given to every action of her life by the unseen presence of religious principle, and her life might be considered as a continual prayer, from the consciousness under which she lived of an all-seeing eye being upon her. William Grey continued his attendance at Gowanbank, notwithstanding the conscientious discouragement with which she persevered in avoiding him; and could he have known how great was the effort which it cost her to do so, his estimation of her heart, as well as her principles, must have been greatly enhanced; for it was no common generosity which caused her to conceal every emotion, while she continued doing all in her power to bring on a reconciliation with her sister. Nothing could have served more strongly to exhibit the superiority of what is genuine over all that is false, than to see the two sisters together. Martha, in her printed cotton gown, checked apron, and mob-cap—active, neat, and cheerful, with a clean house, a bright fire, and a contented mind, seemed every way suited to be the wife of a hard-working laborer like William Grey, who felt completely at ease and at home when he was with her; while her more elegantly-attired and far more beautiful sister, assuming a listless air of conscious greatness, addressed him with the tone of a superior, and wore such a look of condescension in her manner, that his usually blithe and merry countenance became clouded with displeasure whenever she spoke. Far from being apprehensive of any change in his sentiments, Nanny attributed his silence and restraint to diffidence, and became only the more delighted with herself, and the more capricious and consequential in her manner to others; so that even the gentle Martha, whose whole pride and affection had once been centered in her sister, felt hurt at the oblivion to which she had apparently consigned all former times, and sometimes even thought it necessary to drop a good-humored hint on the subject.

"How strange it feels," observed Nanny one day, with a contemptuous toss of the head, "when one walks on this floor, to feel the sand gritting under one's feet like a gravel-walk."

"Yes," replied Martha, smiling, "we have been all our lives so accustomed to Turkey carpets, that it does seem odd; but Miss Howard never complains when she comes here."

"And those oat cakes you are baking will taste as if they were made of sand also," added Nanny, pertly; "I cannot manage to eat them at all, they are so like a mouthful of dust."

"Nanny," said old Janet, shocked at her daughter's supercilious looks, "always enter your mother's house with a proper feeling of respect, or do not enter it at all. I can bear any distress more easily than to see a child of my own look as you do now. It is a Christian duty to govern my own family with decorum, and to preserve the authority that God gives me in it; therefore let me desire you will be dutiful both in your thoughts and speech while I am present."

There was a look of maternal command in the old woman's expression and manner which was very impressive; but yet her lip quivered and her voice faltered. William Grey fixed his eyes upon Nanny for a moment with grave anxiety; but no external symptom of compunction appeared on that beautiful face, for her eyes were fixed on the ground, an angry frown had gathered on her forehead, and she seemed completely occupied in tying the ribbons of her bonnet. He looked indignantly away, and tried to direct the attention of Martha to what passed; but she was apparently too busy with household affairs to notice him, and he might have supposed her entirely unconscious, but for the flushed cheek and the tearful eye which were caused by her mother's agitation, and which she vainly tried to hide.

When William Grey got up soon after to go away, Nanny also took leave, apparently expecting that he would offer, as had been his custom formerly, to accompany her across the fields towards Barnard Castle; but not seeming conscious of her movements, he whistled a tune, and hurried off in another direction. The young beauty glanced after him with angry contempt, and then turned to bid her sister farewell; but Martha slipped her arm affectionately into Nanny's, and looking at her, with an expression of almost maternal affection, she suddenly burst into tears. "Nanny! dear Nanny!" said she, sobbing with grief, "why are you so changed? Why do you distress our poor mother, and quarrel with William? Who will ever love you as we do? Oh, come back before you are lost entirely! I see it all! you will learn to despise us, and be miserable yourself. What will fine people or fine clothes do for you without peace of mind? William will be lost forever, and——"

"No great loss either," interrupted Nanny, angrily. "There are some as good as he, and many better, to be met with any day. But I am sorry to have distressed you Martha. Never was a kinder sister in this world, and I must be very wrong indeed before you think me so. It was not right to speak as I did when our mother was by; and I cannot go home without telling her how sorry I am for all that passed."

Before Martha could reply, her sister had darted hastily back to the cottage, and entered it with flushed cheeks and in breathless agitation. The old woman's head was sorrowfully leaning on a table when her daughter returned unobserved. A deep sigh escaped from her breast, and she did not look up, supposing it to be Martha. Nanny gently took her hand, and tried to speak; but her voice was inarticulate for some moments, and she looked at her aged parent's solitary grief with feelings of severe self-reproach.

"Mother," said she, in a faltering tone, "you are to be pitied for having such a daughter. I have been foolish and ungrateful to-day, but I was always a poor silly creature, easily led away. You must take me home again, or I shall soon forget myself altogether. That grand house is not a place for me."

The old woman rose up and threw herself into Nanny's arms. "Come back! my child! It is a blessing to know that you are still willing. I never wished you to leave us, and thankful shall I be for the hour when you are once more safe with Martha and me. We can easily get you work about the garden and fields; for William Grey says——"

"I do not care what William says," interrupted Nanny, as her sister came into the room; "he is nothing to me now, and we are best asunder. The only objection I have to leave the Castle next term is, that it would seem done to please William, who is the very last person in the world that I care about. Sir Richard's gentleman says he mistook him one day for a cherry in the garden, his face is so round and so red."

The splendid monotony of Eleanor's life grew more wearisome the longer it continued. Every luxury of existence had become as essential to her comfort, and nearly as imperceptible to her senses, as the air she breathed, while the exaggerated view she took of petty annoyances caused her to be fully convinced that she actually endured that large share of trial and vexation which falls, sooner or later, to the lot of every created being. While she wished to be envied by all the world, and by her cousin in particular, Matilda, on the contrary, frequently thought with pity and regret how little an undisciplined mind can enjoy even the brightest portion of earthly felicity, and how singularly unprepared Eleanor was for the inevitable vicissitudes of life.

"What a bore!" exclaimed Miss Fitz-Patrick one day, about the beginning of December, throwing a note peevishly down on the breakfast-table after a hasty perusal. "I have never been to church but once since we came here, the distance is so great for a carriage, and the foot-path so impassable for any one except a bog-trotter like you, Matilda, and here is a formal intimation from your paragon, Dr. Murray, the parish clergyman, saying that he proposes coming here to-morrow, according to his usual custom of giving prayers and instruction once a-year in every house to the assembled family. He hopes, if that time is inconvenient, that I will name any other day which would suit me better."

"What an excellent and venerable custom that is!" observed Matilda, brightening with anticipated pleasure. "I like in all the great old English houses to see how universally they contain a little private chapel consecrated to family worship; but that admirable practice is so nearly obsolete now, that I am told almost the only infallible proof of a mansion being really ancient is when you find in it an altar to the living God."

"What shall we do, Miss Marabout?" said Eleanor, twisting the note into a variety of contortions, and finally throwing it into the fire. "You know I have an appointment to meet some of Mr. Burn's people at Grassfield about the new dairy, which must not be postponed, and, as Sir Lucius O'Trigger says, one cannot possibly be two gentlemen at once. It would be useless to name any other day for Dr. Murray to come, because I never in my life made an assignation that it was convenient to keep, and the whole ceremony will be so formidable that I am glad of a good pretext to evade it. Matilda you should personate me!—we have never met, and it would be a pleasure for you to be in my place a single hour. Pray receive Dr. Murray, and say everything proper as Dame du Chateau."

"Masquerades never take place in the morning, Eleanor, and you would not wish to pass a jest upon that good old man when his errand here is so solemn and important. But if you positively cannot, or at least will not, postpone this architectural excursion, I shall be very glad, with your leave, to meet Dr. Murray, though on account of the servants, as well as for your own sake, I still hope your decision may be revised."

"He is a man of extraordinary character, but quite out of my line," observed Sir Richard, carefully stirring his coffee. "A few such people in the neighborhood are very advantageous in keeping up a good understanding between rich and poor, besides that one likes to see a clergyman act as he preaches, and Dr. Murray's whole life is a perfect sermon. The only thing in the world that he seems to be proud of is his profession, for no one can be ten minutes in his society without becoming aware of it. There is a great deal of dignity in his manner too, and his eloquence and talents are so highly spoken of, that several vacant churches in Edinburgh have successively been offered to him lately; but he declares that it is his intention to finish his labors where he began them. His remark is true enough, that clergymen, like forest trees, should not be transplanted after they are old."

"Matilda," said Eleanor, with a transient look of seriousness, "it is no small compliment to say that you will suit such a visitor better than I shall, though the time was—— but no matter. He might perhaps bring back some of my old Ashgrove feelings, and I *do* sometimes remember those days with a kind of sorrow that *you* never can know."

Matilda took her cousin's hand in silence, and a pause of emotion, on both sides, succeeded. Before either of them could speak, however, Miss Marabout hastily interposed her word—"If you once see Dr. Murray, Miss Fitz-Patrick, there will probably be no end to his demands on your benevolence; for a person's purse is no more his own, in the hands of a philanthropist than of a highwayman. Dr. Murray and his sister are the most indefatigable pair I ever heard of, and establish all sorts of institutions; each of which you must subscribe to instantly. Sewing-schools, knitting and spinning clubs, cottage readings, Bible societies, dispensaries, blind asylums, hospitals for incurables, catechising visits, and Sunday classes for the old, and for the young, and for the middle-aged. I really wonder if it all does any good."

Miss Marabout knew that it was easier to get blood out of a stone than money from Eleanor Fitz-Patrick for any purpose unconnected with ostentation or personal enjoyment, and the effect of her exaggerated representation was, as she expected, instantaneous, though Matilda made a vain attempt to oppose its pernicious tendency.

"You have built more hospitals and asylums in a minute, Miss Marabout, than Dr. Murray has done in a lifetime," said she dryly. "There is nothing of the kind at Gaelfield. He seems, from all I hear, to be so intent on the good of others, that one would suppose neither he nor his sister had any affairs of their own to occupy them; but all plans of benevolence are carried on at their individual cost. Be assured, Eleanor, that Dr. Murray, in his ministrations, 'seeks not yours, but *you*.'"

"Ah! when people set a good example, they are very apt to expect it shall be followed, and I really cannot afford to do that."

"In one respect Dr. Murray is an exception to general rule," observed Sir Richard, rising to leave the room. "He has on all occasions shown remarkable attachment and good feeling towards this family, on account of Sir Philip having presented him to the living."

"It has been observed," said Matilda, "that clergymen often look so directly to the first Great Cause of all events, that they overlook the gratitude due towards him who is made instrumental to their promotion. But so great a moral deficiency is one instance, among many, that the best feelings of religion may be perverted. It is almost using the words of Scripture to say, 'If ye love not the benefactor whom you have seen, how can you love Him whom you have not seen?'"

Eleanor would have laughed in good earnest had she read, in the mind of Matilda, with what lively interest and expectation she watched for the arrival of her venerable visitor. No individual, in the range of that widely-extended neighborhood, could have excited the same feeling of pleasurable anticipation from the prospect of his coming to Barnard Castle; for, with the grace and dignity of a refined and highly-cultivated mind, Matilda yet retained much original simplicity of character; and it was with a palpitating heart, and a feeling of awe nearly amounting to apprehension, that she heard the library-door opened next day while sitting there alone, and Dr. Murray entered. He was an active-looking, middle-aged man, about fifty years of age, with rather homely features, and plain but dignified exterior. His high, commanding forehead and clear, intelligent eye gave promise of the bright intellect which reigned within; and, as he approached, his benevolent aspect showed at once that his was a countenance and manner to attract entire confidence, for they appeared to be external indexes of that universal charity and kindness which are the outward badge of his high profession.

"Miss Fitz-Patrick, I presume," said he, extending his hand with a cordial smile and a look of penetrating interest.

"Only her cousin," was the reply, with some embarrassment. "My name is Matilda Howard."

"Miss *Howard!*" exclaimed Dr. Murray, with a start of surprise and an increased expression of curiosity. "I have already heard of you frequently. During the last month of Sir Philip's life, business obliged me to be in Edinburgh, and most of my time was passed in his society. He spoke much of you, and I felt surprised afterwards to hear—but no matter. 'It is not in man that walketh to direct his steps.' I have frequently observed you at church, and took for granted that it was Miss Fitz-Patrick. Shall I have the pleasure of seeing her this morning?"

"I greatly fear not," replied Matilda, coloring with distress, as if she had been herself guilty of the oversight towards Dr. Murray which her cousin had shown; and with great embarrassment, but all her usual sweetness of tone and manner, she then briefly gave a candid explanation of the reason why Eleanor was absent.

"I sent previous notice of this visit, trusting, if an engagement intervened, Miss Fitz-Patrick would afford me timely intimation, that any other day might be appointed which suited her better," said Dr. Murray, with a look of surprise and of grave regret. "Let me hope it need not be attributed to entire indifference, Miss Howard, that on this occasion any other arrangement should have been considered paramount to the important mission on which I come. You may imagine how frequently it has been the subject of regret to see these splendid halls deserted; but how much more painful shall I consider it, if, throughout the whole extent of my parish, there should hereafter be spread the baleful influence of an example tending to weaken the power of Gospel truth among the many whom it will affect. I hoped much from Miss Fitz-Patrick. The careful instruction she is said to have enjoyed from one so recently departed, and the freshness of her feelings, which have scarcely yet had time to be hardened by this world's deceitful prosperities, had caused me to be sanguine. I did hope that this house might early become sanctified to the service of God, and that here there might at last be the long-desired opportunity to deliver a message of mercy from Him in whose name I come. 'We are ambassadors for Christ.'"

Dr. Murray's manner was in the highest degree impressive, and his thoughtful eye rested on Matilda with a look of anxious inquiry; but her head was averted, and her color rose, for she could not give one word of encouragement to his earnest desire and expectation, that the house of Eleanor Fitz-Patrick might ever be called on by its mistress to "serve the living God."

"There are many here who will thankfully accept the benefit of your instructions and prayers," said she, hastily rising to ring for the servants; "at some future period, let us hope that we may all learn rightly to appreciate their inestimable value."

Dr. Murray's language, in the pulpit and at all times, was classically elegant; yet in a moment he could adapt it to the most ignorant and illiterate. He never for an instant degenerated into vulgarity, nor darkened counsel by words without knowledge; but his address to the assembled domestics abounded in illustrations suited to their various capacities and was delivered with such fluency and clearness, that any child might have understood his whole remarks. Yet, though the language was simple, the truths he enforced were deep, mysterious, and comprehensive. He indulged in no fanciful explanation of texts, nor critical corrections of our English translation, by which learned men too often make plain people distrustful of their Bibles; but his discourse contained a perfect compendium of Christian doctrine, so that no one who heard Dr. Murray with attention could remain ignorant of a single point essential to salvation; while the whole was enforced with so much ardor, and addressed with such earnestness to the affections and to the fears of those around, that he really seemed to

> "Preach, as though he ne'er should preach again,
> To preach as dying unto dying men."

Dr. Murray observed, that in religion there are three essential parts which require incessant attention: Our duty to God, to our neighbor, and to ourselves, which must all be continually exercised by faith, charity, and temperance. Instead of resting in any *one* of these things, as too many do, he strongly enforced the indispensable necessity laid down in Scripture for seeking to excel in them all; and he proved in the most unanswerable manner, that each must be actively pursued in order to our being acceptable servants of that all-seeing God, who is the only master worth serving, because He alone can reward all, without disappointing any. When Dr. Murray spoke of sin, and represented its wide devastations among men, his tone was not that of a superior, who had observed in others what was foreign to his own nature, but it was that of a father lamenting to his children a deep misfortune, in which he as well as they were all partakers; while he showed that, for his own pardon as well as theirs he entertained the profoundest solicitude and the most grateful hope. "The ruin of a soul is so great a catastrophe," he observed, "that all nature trembles at the thought, and Christ himself died to avert it. Who could know so well as He did the infinite and inconceivable importance of eternity, for His own nature was eternal, while we cannot so much as imagine its endless duration; yet surely our minds might be impressed with a holy awe to think what our future misery would inevitably have been, if the Son of God saw so much to pity, that he left the glories of heaven to avert it. Shall we then dare to brave such a fate, and to reject our last hope of deliverance and of pardon while yet it may be found? That was an awful moment when Christ shed tears over the lost sinners of Jerusalem; for it seemed as if he would say to them—and may the language never be applicable to any *one* here—'My blood ye have rejected—my tears ye shall have: *that* would have saved you—these can only mourn over your hopeless desolation.'"

Anxiously and intently as Matilda listened, on her own account, to all that was said, she nevertheless became aware of a gradual change which took place on the countenances of those around. Many had entered with a look of careless curiosity, several with an expression of stubborn indifference, and some with an aspect of ignorant stupidity. Nanny tripped into the room with all her newly-acquired airs of conscious beauty, and old Mrs. Gordon seemed to have no object in coming but to watch her with looks of angry contempt. Yet when Dr. Murray began his address, with some kind and conciliatory remarks on the relation in which his professional duty placed him towards each individual present—on the deep responsibility with which he must one day answer to his and to their eternal God for the care he exercised over their consciences, and declared the interest with which, at every future period, he would be ready to hear of their sorrows, to advise them in difficulty, or to attend them in hours of sickness and extremity, the most callous heart was touched, every wandering eye became fixed, and all were ready, with heartfelt seriousness, to join in a solemn act of devotion; while Dr. Murray at length concluded his visit with a prayer, which proceeded from his divinely-instructed mind with all the eloquence of fervent hope and reverential awe. Tears started into Matilda's eyes when she heard the warmth of language, and the profound emotion with which he prayed for absent members of the family, and especially for the head of that house; while new confidence and hope seemed now to arise in her mind respecting Eleanor, when she joined her prayers to his, and thought of that promise, so unspeakably precious to the heart of all who mourn for the souls of others—"The prayer of the righteous man availeth much."

CHAPTER VII.

Where'er a tear is dried, a wounded heart
Bound up, a bruised spirit with the dew
Of sympathy anointed, or a pang
Of honest suffering soothed, or injury
Repeated oft, as oft by love forgiven;
Where'er an evil passion is subdued,
Or virtue's feeble embers found; where'er
A sin is heartily abjured and left—
There is a high and holy place, a spot
Of sacred light, a most religious fane,
Where happiness descending, sits and smiles.

POLLOK.

FROM this period a new era commenced in the life of Matilda Howard. Dr. Murray's discriminating eye had marked the animated interest with which she listened to all he said, and in the few words which she spoke he traced her deep but unobtrusive knowledge of divine truth. Before taking leave, therefore, he expressed a hope that she would occasionally visit his sister, Miss Murray, and co-operate with her as far as it might be convenient in some plans of usefulness among the children in his parish which had but lately been formed.

Matilda's welcome, on her first visit to Gaelfield, was so extremely cordial, that she did not long delay returning thither; and it soon became her almost daily walk to hasten through a shady green lane which led that way, where, under sanction of Dr. Murray, she visited with his sister the village schools, and the lowly habitations of the rural hamlet. In every house Matilda discovered traces of his active benevolence. There the desponding had been encouraged, the doubting were confirmed, the sick received the comfort of his conversation, the poor enjoyed the benefit of his purse, and the dying found the support of his prayers. Dr. Murray frequently inculcated a favorite opinion on all over whom he had any influence, that every earthly blessing is to be preserved only by active and vigorous exertion. Health, knowledge, usefulness, reputation, power, and wealth, must generally be earned throughout an incessant course of unswerving self-denial, or they can seldom be permanently enjoyed; and his own mind seemed in a continual state of energetic exercise. He possessed invincible courage, resolution, and perseverance, which were never allowed to be dormant; for indolence was, in his estimation, next to actual sin, the greatest of all enemies to human happiness. Whether in reading, in conversing, or in solitary meditation, Dr. Murray held it a sacred duty to redeem the time by keeping his intellect at the full stretch of its powers; and even his sleep was not the slumber of indolence, but the deep repose of a mind and frame exhausted by active labor and intense application. On all occasions he remembered the words of Scripture,—"If any man refuse to labor, neither shall he eat," and the example of Christ, who toiled in the vocation of Joseph, taught to others the duty of working according to our own station and ability. His personal exertions, however, were limited to Gaelfield parish, for Dr. Murray never itinerated throughout the country at the expense of charitable institutions for which a subscription was to be collected. He feared lest the language of Scripture should ever become applicable to himself,—"Mine own vineyard have I not kept!" and knowing that his utmost efforts could not adequately fulfil the sphere of professional duty, while every hour passed elsewhere must leave it neglected, he confined his eloquence entirely to the platform of his own pulpit.

Dr. Murray did not keep a diary "for the benefit of his family," or for any other pretext on which those secret things which belong only to the Lord are laid open to public view. He considered that it was introducing a snare into his own most private hours of devotion if a loop-hole were thus to be opened, through which the whole world might hereafter witness, as it were, the trials, the sorrows, and the joys of his Christian course. These were abundantly obvious in the deep experience with which he represented to his own people the struggles, the fears, and the hopes which are peculiar to every man who would estrange his affections from a present world, and fix them unreservedly on Him for whom we must be ready to sacrifice every earthly tie. Dr. Murray registered no wondering exclamations at the crowds who attended his preaching; the multitude of converts who were made by one so unworthy as himself; the extraordinary usefulness of books which he had written without a hope of their ever being read; the meekness with which he had borne the "malignity, baseness, and outrageous violence" of clergymen whose opinions differed from his own, and the surprising respect and veneration with which he was occasionally treated.

Others might speak of his virtues or his faults, but on these subjects Dr. Murray's own pen was silent. There are hours between man and his Creator which the dearest friend must not witness, for they are "hid with Christ in God." There are secret recesses in every heart, which none but an omniscient God can know; for, like the visions revealed to the Apostle, they are not for earthly utterance. There is a separated existence led by Christians in their own closets which should only be registered in Heaven, and only known on that day when all hearts shall be laid open. Self-love glimmers through many a printed confession of extreme sinfulness, but Dr. Murray's heartfelt sorrow for his own offences daily spoke in the language of prayer and humiliation to his God. The duty of self-examination was so faithfully and impartially performed, that he became conscious of many sins and many professional deficiencies; but not upon paper were they acknowledged or lamented, because he knew what it was for Christians to be vain of their humility, and had observed the perverted love of celebrity in men who would rather write of their faults than not write of themselves at all. It was by a constant, careful study of his own heart that Dr. Murray acquired a facility in reading the inmost depths of other minds. He became aware that no man writes down his thoughts and actions for himself alone. He saw, in various instances, how they became tinged with a coloring of exaggeration or partiality when recorded for the benefit of friends or strangers, and he felt that his sacred duty to his own soul would be best performed by living from day to day in the exercise of faith, repentance, and obedience. To his Great Master he frequently and solemnly committed the hope and the desire of his heart, that while his own mind was purified and taught by the Holy Spirit, he might also gain an increasing influence over those among whom he was appointed to minister; and in Dr. Murray's sympathy and commiseration for others, it frequently happened that the feeling which he showed for their sins and temptations was the first thing that made them feel for themselves.

To Matilda it soon appeared as if every step which carried her away from Barnard Castle served to lighten her of a care or a vexation, and her spirits rose with the buoyancy of former days whenever she lost sight of its gloomy magnificence, and found shelter in the cheerful parlor of Miss Murray, where she was sure that her society would be prized and that her welcome would be cordial and sincere; for there never existed a heart more open and perfectly unsophisticated than that of her newly-acquired friend, who treated her with almost motherly kindness from the first hour of their acquaintance. Miss Murray appeared some years older than her brother; but increasing age had not yet diminished her activity in doing good, nor the cheerfulness of her disposition, while she steadily pursued the even tenor of her course, knowing nothing of the politics, the fashions, or the ways of a present world. She was far from clever, and it was a frequent evidence of Dr. Murray's Christian kindness to observe the patient attention with which he listened to all she said; the forbearance he exercised in enduring her very flagrant mistakes, and the unwearied pains he took to enlighten her understanding with those profound doctrines of our holy faith which were ever nearest to his own heart.

Miss Murray's creed was simple in the extreme, yet it influenced her whole conduct, and directed all she said. Though unable, like many more showy Christians, to talk fluently, she acted on all occasions with invariable consistency. She could not give a theoretical summary of religious duty, but she was a living model of its practice. She would have failed in sketching a systematic outline of doctrine, but she existed in the exercise of prayer, and of that charity which thinketh no evil, while, with the Scriptures almost constantly in her hand, she continually either studied its pages, or meditated in her own simple way on its contents. Miss Murray had from the very first deliberately and cheerfully made up her mind to incur the odium of remaining an *old maid;* for though her manners, which were simple and pleasing, attracted an unusual portion of good-will in society, her appearance was unprepossessing, and she anticipated no probability of exciting a permanent interest in any one to whom her happiness could have been safely confided.

The conclusions of her own good sense had been hastened, however, by a family circumstance, so tragical in itself, that the lesson of experience and caution which it gave seemed to have been burnt into her mind with indelible characters. She had once possessed an elder sister, in whom her heart delighted, and who was adorned with every attractive quality in which she felt conscious of being herself deficient. Returning home one day, after an absence of several weeks, she flew, as was her custom, to Jane's room, and entered it unnoticed. There she was startled and shocked to observe her usually gay and animated companion immoveably seated in the corner of a distant sofa, with pallid cheek and quivering lip, while her eyes were fastened on a visiting card in her hand, which she seemed unable to cease contemplating. It might have appeared to a mere observer as if, in that small object, there could be little to raise intense emotion, for it contained no more than the words—"Mr. Andrew Falconar, P. P. C.;" yet these few solitary letters were the source of deep and heart-breaking sorrow. They spoke of years which had been passed in deceitful hope. They told of confidence misplaced, and they were a memorial of former pleasures, never more to be remembered without the anguish of blighted affection. Among many admirers Jane distinguished only one, whose incessant attentions and devoted anxiety to please seemed to her young and confiding heart a sufficient proof of sincerity, though no explicit declaration of attachment had pledged his honor. His professional emoluments were scarcely sufficient for competence, and he depended for wealth on the whim of a rich and aged aunt, whose tyranny and caprice sufficiently accounted, in Jane's estimation, for delay. Meantime every hour and every day bore witness to Mr. Falconar's assiduities—he was the companion of her walks—her escort at every party—he listened with intense interest to her conversation—turned over the leaves of music when she played, and sent her bouquets of flowers from his garden—whatever she read he read himself—and when she visited their mutual friends in the country, he followed her there with undiminished attention. Many years had thus passed away—the whole lifetime of her youth—and not a doubt ever occurred to Jane's mind of his attachment; when, on the previous week, he carelessly and accidentally mentioned to her brother that in a few days he was to be married. The card which he left that morning remained for hours in her hand. It was all that now remained to her of one who had occupied so long a period of her thoughts and affections. Could she have read there all that she desired to know, Jane would have asked whether any sentiment of shame, remorse, or regret visited his heart when he left it. Could she have ascertained whether he ever loved her as she had so much reason to believe, she might have been soothed by the assurance; or if, on the contrary, her existence had been wasted for one who desired only selfish gratification, then she might have been supported by indignation; but what had led him to prefer another she never now could know, for, without warning or explanation, the stroke had come silently and suddenly as death itself.

Jane Murray had what is called spirit. She speedily roused herself up to meet the occasion; called on Mr. Falconar's mother when the wedding was over, congratulated his sisters, talked of the event with her usual vivacity in every company, and apparently smiled and laughed as she had done before; but the Inverness Journal, which "advertized" the "marriage in high life" of Mr. Andrew Falconar, contained, not many months afterwards, an announcement which few would have supposed to bear any connection with so brilliant an event—the death of Jane Murray. From this time her deeply-afflicted sister, being anxious at once to establish her own mind in a state of peaceful tranquillity, gratefully acknowledged the advantage of having a brother remaining to whom all her confidence and affection might be devoted, and carefully extinguished from her mind, at the early age when this occured, all that anxiety and uncertainty which must ever attend on those who long continue to contemplate the probability of changing their situation in the world. Miss Murray considered that the game of life was played for a higher stake by those who married, than by those who did not, as the capability of happiness, or of misery, is unspeakably increased by entering on such near and sacred ties; but she looked upon it as almost impossible to preserve, in that situation, the calm tone of feeling which is peculiar to a single life, and which is so favorable to the cultivation of piety, though it requires a more than common share of good sense and good feeling to render it either happy or respected. The longer Matilda knew Miss Murray, the more she esteemed her amiable qualities, though the deficiency of her mental powers became perceptible in proportion as their intercourse increased; and occasionally the contrast forced itself upon her thoughts, between Eleanor, who was all talent without good feeling, and Miss Murray, who abounded in good feeling without a glimmering of talent. In the world's estimation, how infinitely superior was Eleanor Fitz-Patrick; but in the eye of an all-seeing God, whose thoughts are not as our thoughts, the heart alone shall be judged, and the gentle, unsophisticated disposition of Miss Murray far outweighed more brilliant gifts; for truly and sadly has the poet declared, that

> "Not many wise, rich, noble, or profound,
> Shall gain one inch of Heavenly ground."

"Matilda! I must really take a lionizing peep at your Miss Murray, for she seems to be quite a phœnix!" said Eleanor, one morning at breakfast, after her cousin had been describing, with an eloquence peculiarly her own, the good which was done in Gaelfield by Dr. Murray and his sister. "It is always desirable to see perfection in men, women, or animals."

"I do not promise you that on the present occasion," replied Matilda; "I neither think any of my friends perfect, nor wish others to believe them so. Even Dr. Murray, much as we must admire him, is merely human, after all, and would be the first to acknowledge that his sins and infirmities are numerous every day. He observed to me lately that there is scarcely one of the Patriarchs mentioned in Scripture whose faults and offences are not recorded there to show the frailty and corruption which are inseparable from our nature while we continue upon earth; and that the surest proof of divine grace being implanted in the heart of man, is when that struggle commences between good and evil, which is painfully experienced by every Christian, for, as evil continually exists within us, it can only be by quenching the good Spirit that people are enabled to say 'Peace to their awakened consciences.' Dr. Murray's being continually sensible of sin, renders him compassionate to the trials and temptations of others, for he is not one of those who can be humble before God and proud before men; therefore all his people go to him with the most entire confidence, and impart to him their thoughts and feelings. An hour every day is devoted to receiving any of his parishoners who wish to claim advice or assistance; and his invitation is without limit, whether to the evil or the good; for his sympathy extends to all without exception. He keeps a register of every family under his care, with an account of their numbers, their habits, their wants, and their religious state, so that each individual in the humblest hovel is personally known to him; and I often, in my own mind, compare Dr. Murray to a monarch benevolently reigning in the hearts and in the homes of his people."

"We shall certainly attend one of his levees," interrupted Eleanor, laughingly directing Miss Marabout's attention to Matilda's countenance, which sparkled with animation. "I have always thought that nature or fortune will make a great mistake if you are not hereafter a parson's wife. You would mend and make the family linen, prepare medicines and cheap broth for the poor; and if the good man was not particularly bright, you could even compose his sermons. Dr. Murray is unluckily *rather* too old, or he would have suited admirably. By the way, he was tutor to Sir Alfred Douglas's father, which is an additional inducement to render his acquaintance desirable, though I scarcely know why that should signify, either." Eleanor colored, and rapidly continued her sentence. "*N'importe!* we cannot live another day without visiting Gaelfield,—can we, Miss Marabout?"

"Certainly not," replied her companion in a very indifferent tone.

"Well, then! to please Miss Marabout, who seems really bent upon going, I shall drive her there in the pony carriage after luncheon, and meet you, Matilda; for, of course, some charity appointment will cause you to precede us by an hour or two in the village, where your face is better known already than the Saracen's Head. Poor Miss Murray! it is a wonder that we did not go sooner to enjoy the diversion of drawing her out, as she will be quite a study for me. I nearly died of laughing once at an anecdote of your friend's simplicity, for it was so perfectly ridiculous. Lord De Mainbury was out with the hounds, and after a capital run, they were completely at fault, when he suddenly observed Miss Murray tying up a Portugal laurel in the garden. 'Was it this way that the fox passed?' he eagerly inquired. 'Yes!' she replied, 'near that *slap* in the wall to your right hand.'—'How long since?' inquired Lord De Mainbury, impatiently reining in his horse. 'Just fifteen years ago next November!' replied she, deliberately. 'I remember it perfectly, for he carried off our Turkey cock.' It is alleged that Lord De Mainbury's rage at her stupidity exceeded all bounds, and that he gets into a fury yet whenever the story is mentioned."

CHAPTER VIII.

A primrose by the river's brim
A yellow primrose was to him,
And it was nothing more.
WORDSWORTH.

Of all the different aspects which insolent pride can assume, there is none half so oppressive to the object of it as voluble condescension, which was the form in which Eleanor occasionally delighted to assert her own importance among those whom she considered her inferiors. She entered the room at Gaelfield with an air of overpowering patronage, and with a torrent of words which completely bewildered Miss Murray's small portion of wit or understanding, while she ran on with a stream of apologies for not having called sooner and been a more sociable neighbor. Something of what she said appeared to be serious and polite, but the rest was so entirely jocular, that her simple hostess, who could scarcely discriminate between the one and the other, stole an occasional look at Matilda, with an anxious inquiring expression, which seemed to ask, "Is your cousin laughing at me or not?"

Miss Fitz-Patrick complimented her on all the good that was done in the parish, which seemed really to have gratified and surprised her; but she elicited some jests at the same time upon Matilda having been appointed "assistant and successor." She admired the garden in extravagant terms, though there was scarcely a leaf remaining in it, and professed to think her own not nearly in such good order, while six gardeners were employed continually to dress it. She fell into raptures with Miss Murray's ancient Bible, and begged it might be left to her in a legacy. She examined some scripture prints which were suspended on the wall, and after making several ridiculous blunders in guessing the subjects they represented, she turned to inspect Miss Murray's bonnet, and professed an intention to order one immediately on the same pattern. A sly look which she stole towards Miss Marabout in saying this, betrayed to Matilda how little any degree of simplicity or goodness could serve as a shield from her cousin's satirical propensities, who now proceeded to a critical dissertation on Miss Murray's knitting. "You must positively show me all the mysteries of this business, for I intend to reach a great old age, and knitting will be a valuable resource; but it requires more genius than one would suppose to accomplish it in perfection, for they tell me that any one who can turn the heel of a stocking is fit to govern a kingdom. Mine must be worked without heels, and people may draw them on the best way they can. I am convinced that no lady is ever thoroughly domestic who does not excel in some sort of work; and half our gadding about now is because we are all so intellectual, and would sooner think of lifting Cleopatra's Needle than our own. What a delightful, airy little sitting-room this is! I protest the bright yellow curtains, and the profusion of gilt frames, lighted up with that blazing fire and glowing sunshine, look altogether so gay, that it would be impossible for you ever to feel melancholy here. Such a collection of prints and pictures reminds me of the Louvre!—have you a catalogue?—I must come and spend an hour or two some day in studying them all. As for this pea-green carpet with white flowers, you must excuse me, Miss Murray, I cannot help laughing, it is so like a dish of eggs and spinach, but nothing can look better. I guess you never see a room anywhere so much to your taste as this? It certainly is quite perfect in its way."

"Very true," answered Miss Murray, with a look of placid contentment; "nothing could improve it now, since we got home the new book-cases."

"They are very handsome, indeed! I would give a fortune to transport this room by steam, or any how, to Barnard Castle."

"It would be cheap at any price, if you could purchase such feelings as are often experienced within these walls," observed Matilda. "They are what poets might fail to describe, and Christians only can know."

"Ah! here is a stray number of the Penny Magazine!" exclaimed Eleanor, in pretended rapture; "how very entertaining it seems! *Could* you lend it to me, for a single day, Miss Murray? Now don't be afraid to trust me, for it shall be honestly returned—I am a careful creature when you put me upon honor."

Eleanor seemed really enchanted with her own powers of volubility, and ran on for some time without the possibility of interruption, while Miss Murray listened and smiled in a state of helpless surprise. She had never been so perplexed in her life how to reply, but she was spared the difficulty of doing so, as not a crevice occurred for some time into which she could insert one single word, until her lively guest at length paused for a moment to take breath, and then Miss Murray instantly commenced the usual routine of what she called conversation.

"I hope Sir Richard is pretty well this morning?" was the opening question, in her usual placid, gentle manner.

"He had a cold on Thursday fortnight, but I forget whether it was better or worse to-day. Now, Miss Murray, you are just the sort of person who could furnish me with an infallible cure,—shall it be a gallon of gruel, or a bushel of lozenges?"

Like every one else, the good old lady was of course provided with a receipt, which she instantly prescribed, to Eleanor's secret diversion, who professed unbounded faith in the mixture of acids, sweets, and bitters, which were urgently recommended.

"Do you continue to have good accounts of Miss Barbara Neville?" continued Miss Murray; "I had the pleasure of knowing her formerly."

"That must have been *a pleasure* indeed! She was unluckily bit by one of Lady Susan Danvers' lap-dogs before leaving Edinburgh, and whether she died of hydrophobia afterwards or not we never heard; but I recommended that the piece should be kept to see if it foamed. Have I any more relations to be inquired for?" added Eleanor in a whisper to Miss Marabout.

"Are Sir Francis and Lady Howard continuing quite well?" pursued Miss Murray, with indefatigable perseverance.

"Not quite!" replied the heiress concealing a laugh. "My aunt has a slight attack of nervousness, and Sir Francis is extremely ill of—of rheumatism in his elbow, or gout in his little finger, it is not certain which."

"You must have made a mistake, Eleanor," said Matilda, gravely; "my father writes to me continually in the most perfect health and spirits. He has not missed going to cover a single morning this season, and often wishes there were ten hunting days in the week."

"What a keen sportsman he must be!" observed Miss Murray. "But those who like hunting are very fond of it."

"So they are!" exclaimed Eleanor, rising; "and those who like me are very fond of me, too; so I hope Miss Murray is of the number, for I am quite delighted with you—I like you amazingly. Our visit has been really a treat, and I am quite sorry that we must tear ourselves away now, though I shall often return for a comfortable chat, and to tell you how all my friends are."

"Stop a moment!—you are not going!" cried Miss Murray, whose hospitable feelings were all on fire at the prospect of any one escaping from her house, without tasting refreshment; "let me bring you some ginger-wine."

"Not for worlds!—I beg you will not think of it!" said Eleanor, turning with a clandestine grimace of disgust to Miss Marabout; "I—I am forbid by the doctors to taste wine—we all belong to the Temperance Society."

"Ah! young people never like to give trouble," said Miss Murray, diving into the depths of an enormous pocket, from whence she produced her large bunch of keys, and, hastening to a small dark cupboard, she drew forth a plate, filled with hard, massy gingerbread nuts, which looked like fragments of brick, and having placed beside them a decanter half-filled with wine, she hurried out of the room to send her maid up with glasses, and her departure was speedily followed by the distant explosion of a cork.

"No wonder you steal down here continually, Matilda, when there are such luxuries going," said Eleanor, contemptuously examining the gingerbread nuts. One would require a fresh relay of teeth every day to enjoy these properly. They were certainly baked last Thursday fortnight, when papa caught the cold I bestowed on him to-day—it is a pleasure to get my laugh out! You need not look grave, Matilda, for Miss Murray is really the best of human beings. But did ever any mortal try to pass off such truisms for good sense as your friend does? She would tell me that 'sober servants are better than drunken ones!' that 'nothing is so rural as the country!' and that 'it is more agreeable to have too much money than too little!' how is it possible to endure such prosing?"

"I can dispense with a great deal, where there is kind feeling to compensate for all deficiencies," replied Matilda. "Wit and originality are good things in their way, but not deserving of the precedence they often get in our estimation, and it is always a safe plan to be easily satisfied. I have generally tried to lower my standard of what is indispensable for enjoyment or comfort, because if we encourage fastidiousness in conversation, in reading, in music, or even in eating, we shall so much the seldomer be satisfied. You would starve, where I would be in the midst of plenty; and at this moment I could make a very tolerable luncheon on these ancient-looking gingerbread nuts."

"How delicious they are!" exclaimed Eleanor, slyly taking one up as Miss Murray re-entered the room, and pretending to eat, while she hastily concealed it in her bag; "Pray give me the receipt for making these—I never saw anything like them before, so they must be home-made. We shall cause quite a famine in the house," continued she, unwillingly accepting Miss Murray's repeated offer of more, and dropping them privately into her reticule; "you will think me a greater eater than Dando, the oyster-stealer, of whom honorable mention is so frequently made in the Morning Post."

"I never read newspapers, for fear of seeing something in them that is not true."

"What a prudent plan!—You are quite right, for truth lies at the bottom of a well, and is least of all to be found in newspapers. Good-bye for the present; but we are like a pair of scissors, parted to meet again, as I shall long to return here and to taste your gingerbread nuts another time."

"Perhaps you will allow me to send a few to Barnard Castle this evening, and also a pair of the stockings you admired so much of my own knitting?"

"Ten thousand thanks! that is precisely what I wished, so pray do!" exclaimed Eleanor, in a tone of rapturous gratitude; then turning to Miss Marabout when they were beyond the possibility of being overheard, she added, "Only fancy! my foot would look like an elephant's!—and the gingerbread nuts! who would have believed that good worthy Miss Murray was gifted with so much less than common sense? but her presents and her truisms are both inimitable. 'The French are mostly born in France! Those who spend all their money can't expect to grow rich; and health is a great blessing!'"

"Eleanor! she has done her utmost to entertain and to oblige you; but nothing makes me value Miss Murray's kindness more than to know, as I do, that if we were friend less outcasts, without any one on earth to care for us, her kind offices would be as ready, and her feelings as cordial as they are now."

"Well! well! you are right, and I, *of course*, am wrong; so a truce to lecturing!—*On sera ridicule, et je n'oserai rire!* Surely we are out of the Ashgrove trammels now!"

"Eleanor!" said Matilda, in a tone of indignant surprise; but she could add no more, for words seemed inadequate to express what she felt at so irreverent an allusion to Lady Olivia's memory; and the cousins proceeded home in unbroken silence, together.

From this time it became a favorite amusement with Eleanor to visit at Gaelfield, where she delighted to flatter and frighten the single-hearted Miss Murray, who tried to believe the intention was kind, though she could seldom follow the volubility of her visitor, and never on any occasion knew for certain whether she spoke in jest or in earnest; whether the heiress had been sincerely charmed, as she professed to be, with her society, or whether she was turning her into ridicule, and making a burlesque, as she actually did, of the whole conversation. In talking to Eleanor, Miss Murray felt the sort of apprehensive interest with which a school-boy ventures on ice which is not warranted to be safe, and which, though it affords amusement for the time, may plunge him suddenly and helplessly beneath its shining surface. The overpowering profession of deference with which it was Miss Fitz-Patrick's whim to treat her plain and unsophisticated hostess, put Miss Murray completely to the blush: and the easy familiarity with which she occasionally domesticated herself in the little parlor, caused the good old lady to blame herself on account of the constraint and distrust she unavoidably felt whenever her lively visitor entered. With Matilda, Miss Murray felt confident that she might have gone to the Palace of Truth, and not heard a single transformation in all that she said; but a lurking smile in Eleanor's eye, and the tone of gay superiority she assumed, even when her words were full of humility, betrayed to her very unsuspicious companion the total want of sincerity and good faith which pervaded all she said. Dr. Murray's presence acted for a time occasionally as some restraint upon her exuberant self-importance, for his address had all the dignity of high intellect, and his look was so penetrating that he evidently saw through all her vanity and frivolity of character, feeling a degree of pity which, in any one less imbued with Christian charity, would have nearly amounted to contempt. It is rare in society when the distinctions of this world are not paramount to everything; but in Dr. Murray's estimation she felt conscious that they only ranked in proportion as they were used to promote the glory of God and the good of others,—objects which the young heiress could not but acknowledge to herself were the very last which occupied her income, or created any solicitude in her thoughts. Neither Miss Murray nor her brother knew anything relating to Eleanor's disposition from Matilda's report, for she considered the confidence of domestic life so sacred, that not even a sigh or a disparaging shake of the head ever betrayed how fallacious she knew their hopes to be, when, in arranging plans for improving the parish, they occasionally reckoned upon assistance and encouragement from Barnard Castle.

Dr. Murray at length, one day, shortly stated some projects which it was thought might be advantageous to her indigent tenantry, and seemed confidently to anticipate the pleasure which it must give Miss Fitz-Patrick to be the means of benefiting them; but though she heard him with that respectful interest which his manner invariably excited, Eleanor now, for the first time in her life, seemed to recollect that she had guardians, and thought it necessary to consult them, though with a professed intention to entreat their co-operation in the "wise and judicious suggestions" which Dr. Murray was good enough to make. When a subject of conversation became particularly inconvenient, Miss Fitz-Patrick generally endeavored to change it, by pouring out a perfect hail-storm of words, which prevented any one from edging in a single sentence without being guilty of absolute rudeness; she therefore, on the present occasion, did so, while her auditor listened in grave astonishment to the consequential tone in which she ran on with a medley of subjects and ideas, as miscellaneous and piquant as the castors of a cruet.

"Dr. Murray! you must certainly have swallowed a concordance some day, for I never before heard so many texts quoted in support of an argument; and you make me quite ashamed of having so long remained like a Limerick merchant, 'busy doing nothing.' With respect to our church accommodation, I wish it could be made elastic, like a patent portmanteau; I perfectly agree in *all you are going to say!* Both Scripture and common humanity make it necessary to be considerate for others, and at the same time more mischief may be perpetrated by attempting injudicious charity than by doing nothing at all, so it is fortunate for me that I have such an experienced philanthropist to consult. Pray visit us often, for we shall always feel it an honor. To use expressions common in the General Assembly, never '*moderate your calls*' at Barnard Castle, where they shall all be '*harmonious*' and if ever you wish to '*hold a diet*,' let that be at six o'clock, when I only hope your dinner will be as hearty as your welcome. We have been threatening Miss Murray to drop in, and take pot-luck with her soon. She may supply the *pot*, and I shall bring the *luck*. Your sister is not very encouraging upon the subject; and I am really quite shocked at her want of hospitality, for we are all very *plain* people in every sense. I wish papa was the same, for my spirits always sink as the dinner hour approaches, he is so sure to find fault, though there are three courses every day, dressed by a man-cook, who was skilful enough to satisfy the French Ambassador. At the same time, whoever wishes to gain a point with him should come at feeding-time, for he would rather give away an estate than be interrupted. You have probably heard that an Ogre once married into our family in Ireland, so we have all been great eaters ever since. A shoulder of mutton is scarcely a mouthful to papa, and Monsieur Martigny drove the whole poultry-yard into a chicken-pie when we came here for breakfast one morning. There never was anything like the consumption of provisions in our house at present, for I have three-and-twenty servants, which you will allow to be a tolerable establishment, and——"

"A very numerous circle, indeed!" interrupted Dr. Murray, apparently determined to be heard. "With so many immortal souls, for whose eternal interest you, as their head, must be in some degree answerable, I trust that the good old custom of assembling together daily for family prayers is not discontinued?"

"Why!—all in good time! I am not sure that papa would consent," replied Eleanor, who had suddenly become very considerate of Sir Richard's inclinations.

"Did you ever ask him?" inquired Dr. Murray, anxiously.

"No!" stammered Eleanor, somewhat confused. "There

are many impediments, but—— In short, you know Rome was not built in a day, but we shall, perhaps, come to be all you wish at last. I am not one who can profess a great deal more than I feel," added she, fixing a malicious look on Matilda. "Whatever *I* do, or whatever *I* am, shall be without affectation or hypocrisy; for it would be well if every one were known as they *are*, and not as they *seem*. Tares often pass for wheat, Dr. Murray, merely by mixing with them; and those who are nearly canonized in this world will find it not so easy to stand the scrutiny of another. We may speak well, and live but indifferently here, without being known, but that will not do hereafter; and I would not for worlds appear more religious than I really am. Some people can talk by the hour in a serious way, but it all evaporates in words; and though they can speak volumes about the virtuousness of virtue, and use all the mere jargon of religion, they forget to live according to its precepts."

Eleanor had recently adopted a plan, in Matilda's presence, of inveighing against any particular fault which occurred to her fancy at the moment, until every one in the room must imagine that her cousin was addicted to the practice, though it invariably proved to be something of which she felt totally incapable. On several occasions already she had harangued on the contemptibleness of exaggeration, ill-temper, pride, hypocrisy, and even flattery, pointing the whole so evidently at Matilda, that no stranger could doubt she was guilty of those errors; while, at the same time, the expressions were thoroughly guarded, that her cousin might neither openly take the accusation to herself, nor in any way disprove it. The color mounted to Matilda's forehead from astonishment and confusion at these implied accusations, which being totally vague and unfounded, no pretext occurred for noticing; while even the excellent Dr. Murray looked at her with momentary distrust, though that feeling was instantly dispelled when, with an eye accustomed to discriminate, he marked the ingenuous surprise that animated her countenance, exhibiting abundant evidence that her conscience was at peace though her feelings were obviously hurt.

"As for acting *up* to our standard in religion, no Christian can ever entirely succeed, for it ought to be nothing short of perfection," said Dr. Murray. "We must toil up a steep ascent, seeking the grace of God to help us, while Alps on Alps arise; and none may ever pause to say that his own attainments are sufficient. Yet, in estimating the professions and conduct of others, we should judge as leniently as we hope to be judged ourselves; for, though it is easy to tell what Christianity has *not yet done* in sanctifying the characters of others, who can venture to estimate what it *has* done to improve them? It may have softened the temper that was originally violent, strengthened the principles that were unusually weak, or enlarged the benevolence which would have otherwise been extinguished by avarice; and yet the fruit may not be ripened into perfection, for if Christians could become all in this life that they ought to become, and all that they desire to be, we should certainly love them too well. There is one respect, however, Miss Fitz-Patrick, in which I have occasionally traced a great attainment in Christian forbearance," added Dr. Murray, kindly turning towards Matilda—"If, when ye do well and suffer for it, ye take it patiently, this is acceptable to God."

Few people in the world really and conscientiously desire to scatter as much happiness around them as possible, and few would afford a very large proportion of it to friends and neighbors, even if that could be done without diminishing their own share of enjoyment. It was singular that, as Eleanor's self-importance increased, so did her malicious and even envious feelings towards her cousin, whom it was her continual study to wound *à coups d'epingles;* and had it not been for the most peremptory letter from Lady Howard, desiring her daughter on no account to think of leaving Barnard Castle before Christmas, Matilda would have felt it a duty towards herself to take the earliest opportunity of returning home. Her affection could not be entirely alienated from Eleanor by any circumstances; but, with every imaginable palliation, her cousin's conduct seemed inexcusable, and she often exercised a painful degree of Christian meekness in not angrily resenting the wilful slights that were shown her, of which she sometimes thought it right openly to testify her consciousness; yet occasionally it was impossible to help smiling at the arrogance and self-sufficiency of the heiress's tone, for Matilda had a keen sense of the ridiculous, which was only restrained upon principle and right feeling. A favorite subject of miscellaneous declamation with Miss Fitz-Patrick was, on the necessity for every person being "kept in his place," because on many occasions she felt irritated and piqued, when Matilda met with the same respect on her own account that she herself did, with all the adventitious aids of fortune and property.

"There is no such word now as subordination," she often remarked. "In families, in politics, in religion, that is quite at an end, and all ranks and ages seem on a level. Children are asked their opinions as soon as they can speak, consulted about their own education, and allowed to decide upon the relative advantages of schools and professions as if they really had the power of comparing them. They are taken about to visit in country houses, too, in such numbers, that I shall have a nursery of about nine here during Christmas, each of whom is a little *wonder*, fit to associate with grown-up people. In politics, constituents dictate to their representatives; and in religion, the members of a congregation actually lecture their pastors. I wonder what it will all come to at last! For my own part, I have a certain station to keep up, and it becomes a duty to myself and my contemporaries, to preserve the dignity of it. In all situations, I consider those who hold them as being answerable to their successors for handing them down unimpaired; and the proprietor of an extensive property, like mine, cannot yield an atom of the patronage and influence it confers, without injuring every other inheritor of estates. Even Pauline owes a duty to all other ladies' maids, and must uphold the privileges and prerogatives of her office, not merely for her own sake individually, but for the benefit of Abigails in general; and I perfectly approve of her feud with Nanny about keeping the custody of my trinkets. I am no politician, Matilda; but you may depend upon it that half the democracy in this country arises from great men not submitting to the trammels of greatness as they used to do. Every pleasure on earth has to be paid for by some drawback, and it must have been a bore to the grandees of long ago that they never stirred without carriages and six, surrounded with a retinue of servants; but to vulgar eyes how *imposing* that must have been, and now, what obvious difference is visible between gentlemen of various ranks embarking in a steam-boat, except that, perhaps, one may be followed by two carpet-bags, and be attended by a servant? All are dressed in blue coats, and all very sea-sick; but even a master of the ceremonies could scarcely distinguish between a duke and his tailor—a field-marshal or the senior subaltern of a marching regiment; so that travelling is like death itself now, for it levels all distinctions. Noblemen formerly used to dine out in a blaze of orders and ribbons, but now their stars are turned into comets, which only appear once in a century; and since hoops have been abolished at court, it must seem quite an every-day event to go there. I am certain that it was a great blow to the Church of England when the bishops left off their wigs; and if the judges part with theirs it would perfectly ruin the assizes. Everything should be done to keep up the distinction of ranks; and now, Matilda, the moral of all I have said, including digressions, is to show you that, when the various visitors who assemble here next week are all collected, I shall pay them deference proportioned to their real importance, trusting that neither Charlotte Clifford nor you will feel hurt or offended at being mere pawns on the board, since I must play my part according to rule and etiquette, rather than inclination."

This pompous exordium was evidently meant to prepare Matilda for very defective attention during the ensuing festivities; and, not being anxious to encounter more of Eleanor's caprice than could possibly be avoided, she took the opportunity of announcing that Dr. and Miss Murray had invited her to spend some days with them at Gaelfield, in consequence of which she proposed going there and remaining until Christmas-day, when they had both consented, on Eleanor's urgent entreaty, to pass a week at Barnard Castle, and would accompany her back.

"Can you be serious in proposing to miss 'the gathering of the clans?'" exclaimed Eleanor, with ill-disguised pleasure. "Then, as Tilburina says to her lover—

'And must we part?
Well! if we must—we must:—and in that case
The less is said the better.'

There is no accounting for tastes, Matilda, but your choice on the present occasion certainly seems outrageously odd. I shall either come for you, however, on Tuesday morning, or send the carriage, which is a great stretch of politeness on my part, as I intend making a rule never to lend it, unless when I go a drive myself."

It may generally be observed, that when people talk of "making a rule," they invariably lay down some "rule" in which no one's comfort is studied but their own.

During the few days which Matilda spent at Gaelfield she felt more happy and at home than it had ever been possible for her to do at Barnard Castle. Days flitted rapidly by, while each as it closed left some agreeable recollection behind of useful occupation, or mental improvement, for her time was passed in a manner which might have been considered as the fleeting representation of that pure and happy state where "charity never faileth," and where prayer and praise shall forever accompany active obedience. Dr. Murray delighted to exercise his richly-illuminated mind in the familiar discussion of important truths, scattering information and entertainment almost insensibly around, while his only object, never for a moment overlooked, was to fulfil his own high vocation towards the souls of others. His extensive knowledge of the world, his deep insight into human nature, and his profound attainments in classical literature and historical lore, were all subservient to that single aim; and Matilda listened with unwearied interest and admiration to the sanctified use in conversation of such varied and remarkable talents. Sometimes a considerable degree of vivacity enlivened what he said, but yet there was a gravity of character, and a subdued tone of feeling, even in his laughter, which testified the continual prevalence of seriousness and reflection suited to his profession, and to the sacred duties it involved, which were continually present to his thoughts.

Miss Murray's constant occupation was to replenish a wardrobe of necessaries for the poor, which she frequently distributed with unsparing liberality, though sometimes clandestinely, as her brother's opinion was strongly expressed against any such indiscriminate charities as might, by possibility, paralyze exertion; and he often good-humoredly foretold that she would bring the whole parish on their hands to be fed and clothed, since the donations she bestowed were most frequently a premium on indolence and improvidence. "It has been remarked," said he one day, after detecting some of his sister's favorite protégés in a neighboring alehouse, "that in this mercantile country, whatever you cause a demand for there will be an immediate supply; and if a demand is raised for beggars, they will instantly abound. I wish Dr. Chalmers' work on Civic Economy could be rained down in thousands on the world, to show what true philanthropy means, for no science is more difficult than that of doing real good. One would be apt to imagine, my dear sister, that if a kind well-meaning person, like yourself, had a large income to spend on charity, great benefits must inevitably result; but that is not found to be a necessary inference, and the more difficulty we discover in serving the poor, the more should we turn to the great source of all wisdom, saying, 'Who will show us any good?" Above all, never furnish crutches to those who can be made to walk without them, for our prosperity depends on every individual doing as much as possible for himself. All Scotland is swarming now with hospitals, and I only hope that no shopkeeper who makes a fortune in Gaelfield will ever wish to immortalize himself by building one here. Except to shelter idiots and incurables, the maimed or the blind, nothing can be more pernicious, for they are mere hot-beds of indolence, vice, and discontent to young people; and if aged persons be the objects for which they are built, it is generally but a cruel kindness, because those who would otherwise have been carefully and affectionately attended at home are thrust aside upon public charity, where outward comfort can never compensate for the solitude of the heart."

"Indeed I have often thought," said Matilda, "that some of those poor old creatures, when conveyed from their little quiet chimney corner to the large and lofty rooms in a hospital, must feel as strange and comfortless as the oyster did in the lobster's shell. How different from the cheerful, contented poverty of poor old Janet, whom we saw to-day! I often think, Dr. Murray, how much pleasure you must have in visiting the poor of this neighborhood."

"Ah, Miss Howard, but I have not many such cases of sincere piety, and really picturesque contentment as that good old woman and her exemplary daughter. There are many anxieties and disappointments in the daily course of my superintendence here—for you know a clergyman's life must not be expected to consist in a smooth current of easy duties. Luther has truly remarked, that it is prayer, and sorrow, and temptation which makes a minister of the gospel, and daily experience proves it to be the case."

"I am aware of that now," replied Matilda, "and the labor is so much greater than I had anticipated, that you will scarcely find it possible to carry on all you do without being soon entirely exhausted."

"No, Miss Howard! I would consider it quite as wrong to be a spendthrift of my health as of my fortune. All we have must be devoted to our Master's glory; *but no more;* for He who has put limits to our possession of these blessings, has set bounds to the use we shall make of them. You blame the man who has reduced himself to poverty by unwarrantable extravagance, but he who hurries himself to an untimely grave by improvident exertion is also wrong. To study our own situation, for the purpose of ascertaining the fullest extent of our duties and opportunities, is the chief testimony we can give to our conviction of Almighty wisdom in their appointment."

"Yet I still think, as I have always done, that a country clergyman's situation must be the happiest on earth, and my visit here serves to confirm the opinion."

"Its pleasures are great indeed, but its sorrows are also peculiar," replied Dr. Murray impressively. "My own career was begun with all the sanguine expectations of youth, when in every plan of usefulness or improvement I expected unqualified good. If I preached, every eye that was fixed on mine seemed to hold out hopes of undoubted conversion—every tear that was shed gave promise of permanent repentance—every expression of gratitude was supposed to be directly from the heart. But we must not look for our reward, Miss Howard, in immediate success, nor must we be discouraged if it appear to be the divine will that 'one shall sow and *another* shall reap.' His glory must be our only object, and our highest hope to hear at last those blessed words, 'Well done, thou good and faithful servant.' One great difficulty attends our labors, which may not have occurred to you. In seeking the good of a numerous congregation, we are apt to forget that the reflections which may be useful to them are also necessary to be made on our own account; that it would not be sufficient to build the ark for others, unless we enter it ourselves, and that the teaching of the Spirit is as essential to him who preaches as to those who hear. While reading, the hope of benefiting others is continually present, and even in studying the Scriptures, I have to be watchful lest they appear to me only a fountain to refresh my people rather than a well of water springing up unto eternal life for myself. We have to think for others, to pray for others, to lament their sins, and to encourage their repentance. It is a labor I delight in, yet the apprehension is frequently occurring that I may be a mere finger-post, directing my people without advancing myself, or, in the words of St. Paul, 'lest while teaching others, I myself may become a castaway.'"

Matilda saw at once, with astonishment, how patiently Dr. Murray bore the frustration of plans and hopes from which he had confidently anticipated much success, and she admired the cheerfulness with which he instantly devised new projects of usefulness and benevolence. In the expenditure of an income which seemed ample in his own eyes, nothing was grudged but what he spent upon himself; and worldly ambition or personal luxury were so entirely unknown to him, that his only desire for wealth was to bestow it liberally, while whatever he gave was with a feeling that he had spared from *his abundance.* It was not how little might be necessary on any occasion, but how much could be done, that he endeavored to discover, and the single desire to fulfil his vocation was inseparable from every action. Fame, wealth, honor, and all that a wakensthe selfish ambition of worldly men, seemed like dust in the balance, compared with the one engrossing object of his own pursuit, while, "forgetting the things that are behind, and reaching forward to those that are before, he pressed forward to obtain the prize of his high calling."

Everything in life comes to a speedy termination, and so did Matilda's visit at Gaelfield, when, on the day appointed, Eleanor's chariot and four swept up to the little white gate leading through Dr. Murray's garden, and a peremptory message was delivered that Miss Fitz-Patrick could not wait a moment, as the horses were impatient, and she hoped to see Miss Murray at dinner, which prevented her from thinking it necessary to alight;—therefore, with a hasty glance of regret round the sunny little parlor, and bidding a hurried adieu to her friends, Matilda proceeded to seat herself in the carriage.

"Now confess that you are delighted to make an escape from that stuffy sitting-room, and poor Miss Murray's perpetual truisms," exclaimed Eleanor, taking her cousin's hand with some cordiality. "She is the most flimsy *weak-tea* sort of person I ever saw, and wearies me to death with her unalterable good-humor. The very sound of her knitting pins would drive me distracted, as well as the twaddle that she calls conversation and mistakes for good sense. Black is not *so* black, nor white so *very* white with her. Shall I ever forget being accidentally present one day when your friend attempted a consolatory address to old Janet on the recent death of her husband! Along with many religious reflections, she produced a perfect flock of little aphorisms which almost made me smile, if the occasion had not been so serious. 'It is better to lose a good husband than to be afflicted with a bad one. What can't be cured must be endured. It is not so bad as if it had been worse. Every one has his own burden,—and, none of us can expect constant happiness.' She chattered on in this way till I was in a high fever of impatience; but, if you will believe me, Janet dried up her tears and professed to feel very much comforted."

"I dare say, she did! The finest oration imaginable in well-turned periods, delivered without that appearance of sympathy, would not have had half the effect of Miss Murray's genuine, unaffected kindness. The humblest means are often used to produce the greatest ends, for there can be no strength or power in anything we do, except through the blessing of him who can bring strength out of weakness, and binds in the mighty ocean with a rope of sand."

"Very true," said Eleanor, seriously; "I must tease you no more about the good old lady who reverses Charles the Second, as she never says a wise thing, and probably never does a foolish one. But, now let me describe what an irreparable loss you have sustained by becoming an absentee during the last few days. Our party is diverting beyond measure. Colonel Pendarvis, Lord De Mainbury, and all the hunting set are here. Perhaps we may see some of them pass, for the hounds are in this direction, which was the real inducement that brought me to Gaelfield to-day. Ah! there they are, in full cry, coming down Glowrowrum Hill, and approaching us! How very fortunate! many people have hunted a whole season, and not seen more of the fox than we shall do now."

In Eleanor's eagerness she completely forgot that her young, unmanageable leaders were under the charge of a little postilion, whose chief recommendation had been his very diminutive size, while in strength he was evidently defective also. When the dogs dashed past in full career, followed by a troop of sportsmen, the noise they made, and the distant notes of the huntsman's bugle, startled her horses and in a moment they became frightfully infuriated. Every effort to check them was vain; for they kicked and plunged with terrifying violence, while the boy, who had evidently lost his presence of mind, lashed and swore with reckless desperation. Eleanor, in a voice of alarm, peremptorily desired him stop, but she might as easily have tried to make a ship stand still in a storm. She then hastily opened the carriage door, with an evident intention to spring out, but Matilda, who saw the imminent danger of doing so, forcibly prevented it, though she trembled to see that the carriage, which was now at full speed, approached towards a deep and rugged precipice, where she had just time to observe the sharp turn, over which they would probably be instantly precipitated. At this moment a horseman suddenly galloped across the fields, sprung over a wall, dismounted in less than a second, and seized the horses' heads with such a powerful grasp, that they were instantly checked, though the shock when they stopped was so sudden, that the postilion, who had already been nearly dismounted, fell to the ground. Not a moment could be lost, for the horses nearly kicked over the traces, and struggled so violently, it seemed next to impossible they should be longer controlled, when the gentleman, with a single bound, sprung into the vacant saddle, and, after a desperate encounter of skill and strength, he at length succeeded, by an exertion of masterly horsemanship, in subduing their spirit. At Eleanor's almost frantic entreaty, the traces were immediately cut and the leaders set loose, when their deliverer proceeded with perfect nonchalence to mount his own hunter; and Matilda, for the first time, recognised Mr. Grant, who rode up to the carriage window, laughingly complimenting Miss Fitz-Patrick on the high spirit and fine action of her horses, while she in return observed that his riding had never been so much admired before, as nothing could equal it except Ducrow on the high-mettled racer.

Matilda had been perfectly cool and collected in the time of danger, but now, when all was at an end, she became so overpowered with agitation and thankfulness that it was impossible for her to speak, while, on the contrary, all trace of Eleanor's terror vanished in the moment of safety; her escape seemed a matter of course, and she was at once restored to all her wonted vivacity of look and manner. She and the lively equestrian had been living in the same house for several days past, yet there were so many jests between them, and so many old stories alluded to, that Miss Fitz-Patrick evidently forgot her cousin being in the carriage, and that she had not seen Mr. Grant for a length of time, though they had been formerly intimate. Matilda had so few acquaintances that she retained a vivid recollection of all those she knew, and very naturally expected that her first meeting with Mr. Grant would be as important an event to him as it appeared to her, which turned out by no means to be the case. Having accidently caught a distant glimpse of her in the farthest corner of the chariot, he merely gave an animated bow, as if they had been in the habit of meeting every day, saying in a tone of good-humored cordiality, "Ah, Miss Howard! how are you?" Eleanor then continued the sentence he had interrupted, and Matilda felt herself at once reduced to insignificance, while a long and lively dialogue ensued, which seemed quite interminable, as her cousin and Mr. Grant frequently took leave, but always resumed it with some humorous and unexpected rejoinder.

During this time Matilda found leisure to exercise her usual penetration, and to observe with surprise and interest that there was an obvious change in the manner of Mr. Grant towards Eleanor. He had evidently placed himself at once on the familiar terms of an old friend, but no longer attempted the character of a lover. There were no traces now of that intense interest with which he formerly watched every varying expression in her beautiful features, nor of the agitated anxiety with which he once had listened to the development of her thoughts and feelings. His voice, which was always peculiarly harmonious, had long since assumed an accent of deeper tenderness towards Eleanor than Matilda could have imagined any voice to express, but that tone was wanting now. He jested with the same liveliness as before, yet it was in a vein of unembarrassed familiarity with which he might have addressed his sister; and had Matilda judged of Mr. Grant's mind only by what she witnessed that morning, she might have believed, as the world did in general, that he was nothing more than an agreeable rattle, possessing a greater command of nonsense than any man living, who threw care to the winds, "and if the winds reject it, to the waves." She knew Mr. Grant, better, however, than to suppose him deficient in feeling, though Matilda began to think that he might be capable of conquering it, and she anticipated much interest in observing a character which she always considered peculiar, but of which she had recently heard much to enhance her curiosity and to increase her esteem.

"I cut all the buttons off my coat, after Sir Colin's last story, to prevent his ever holding me by them again," said Mr. Grant, in reply to a remark of Eleanor's. "Scatterbrain would be invaluable if he were only half as *long-winded!*—So my cousin, Lady Susan, is expected this morning!—you probably thought it right on Christmas-day to deck the saloon with *evergreens?*"

"Among which, without meaning to be personal, I include *yew*—so pray come back soon to witness the debut of Lady Susan and her dogs at Barnard Castle."

"I would gallop round the world in half an hour to obey you," said Mr. Grant, with a parting bow full of grace and animation, while the wind, as he rode off, blew his hair in rich waves over his forehead, and heightened the color on his sparkling countenance.

"Poor Mr. Grant preserves his spirits wonderfully, all things considered; but it is often quite melancholy to think how many people I must sooner or later make miserable for life," said Eléanor, gazing after his receding figure as he flew across the fields, clearing every fence that stood in his way. "I dare say at this moment he is wishing it were as easy to surmount all his difficulties as it is to get over those hedges and ditches; but I must not relent, and have made it tolerably plain that his attentions are only welcome as those of an old friend. Miss Marabout is vehemently in favor of my encouraging Lord Alderby in preference, because she says the richest admirer is the most likely to be disinterested."

"Very suitable advice from a governess; but I am not at all sure of its being founded on fact. One large fortune often sets out in search of another, and I rather admire the Quakers' plan, who make wealthy girls marry the poorest lovers, and rich men are obliged to choose portionless wives; by which arrangement my intended ought to have £10,000 a-year, and *Mr. Eleanor* less than nothing."

"Excuse me there! I admire bread-and-butter-love-marriages excessively in other people, but it is the very last thing on earth I ever could fancy for myself. I take pains every day to show Mr. Grant my opinion on this subject, for, as Mrs. Malaprop says, 'I cannot afford to lavish myself upon a person not worth sixpence, and shall be obliged to *illiterate* him from my memory.' How I wish his uncle Sir Evan Grant's intentions were known, or that he possessed Lord Alderby's coronet and property."

"You remind me of a child asking for the moon, Eleanor! It was a fable long ago, which seems still to be realized, that Love and Ambition had once à deadly quarrel, and have always since been on opposite sides in matrimony. You will probably need to relinquish one or other of these requisites, and you are the only judge of which is most essential to happiness. As for the misery you are so afraid of occasioning, I am told it is as impossible to break a good modern heart now, as a plate of iron-stone china."

"Sir Alfred Douglas arrives before dinner to-day, and perhaps, after all, I may promote him, *vice* Lord Alderby and Mr. Grant cashiered. He is reported to have become more reserved than ever, but it will divert me to tame him, and I shall not dislike his singularity if he relaxes only to me. Mr. Grant is over-anxious to please, which takes away the zest of uncertainty in trying to fascinate him."

"I am not sure that he is quite such a captive knight as formerly, and indeed his motto very probably is '*Qui me neglige me perd;*' for, judging by his manner this morning, I should say that he really seems to feel what you wish him to do, no more than the kindness and regard of an old friend."

Eleanor looked startled and astonished at these words, for she entertained the highest opinion of her cousin's penetration, and was aware of her perfect candor in always saying precisely what she thought; while Matilda felt confirmed, from this moment, in suspecting that, though Eleanor's vanity delighted in conquests of superior calibre, yet her secret affections had long since been bestowed on Mr. Grant. The extraordinary vivacity of his manner had a fascination not very common in persons of such gay and eccentric conversation, on account of the high tone of feeling in his character, which became obvious even to Eleanor, for it was not always in his power to conceal the sensibility of his nature, and to make it harmonize with that reckless indifference which he usually affected towards everything but the caprice of the present hour.

"Mr. Grant must be in a strange state of suspense," observed Eleanor, absently. "It has been long conjectured, and seems now confirmed, that Sir Evan is not really married to the person who has resided at Clanpibroch Castle for twenty years past. She lives there yet in that state of wretched uncertainty respecting her children's station in life which the Scottish law unfortunately allows. Her son may either be a beggarly outcast, without a house to shelter him, without food, without a profession, without education, without even a name; or he may be raised in a moment to the rank of his father, and succeed at once to those immense estates. All this depends on the whim of that tyrannical man, Sir Evan, and upon the slavish submission with which the unfortunate woman endures his conduct to herself and to her family. It is a pitiable situation for any one with human feelings thus to witness, in silence, the degradation of those whom she loves with a mother's tenderness, while she dare not, for their sakes, on any provocation, relieve herself from the yoke of perpetual bondage."

"It seems, indeed, the most miserable state that one can well conceive, and if a single sentiment of remorse were ever, under present circumstances, to visit her heart, what a fearful struggle of conscience might ensue while she hesitated whether to plunge her children into irretrievable ruin in this world, or to continue in that course of sin which would destroy her own hopes of happiness in another. I cannot but wonder that a law which has originally facilitated the ruin of many, and kept them afterwards in a state of such prolonged endurance, has never yet claimed attention from the legislature, and been at once repealed."

"Yes! especially for the sake of nephews and cousins, who must often be many years in agonizing suspense, to know whether they may squander every shilling without reserve, and borrow to an unlimited extent on the strength of their prospects; or whether, when the old gentleman at last expires, and they fly out in a state of inconsolable grief to bury him and to take possession of the estate, a whole battalion of sons may not unexpectedly march in as heirs of entail, on the strength of some verbal acknowledgment from the deceased. It is really intolerable, because Mr. Grant, with the Clanpibroch property, might have made a very presentable paragraph in the Morning Post, and I need not have been ashamed to see myself announced as a 'marriage in high life' with Sir Thomas of that ilk."

"Would you marry for an advertisement in the newspapers, Eleanor? I think we are both above doing that; but I really admire Mr. Grant's independent spirit in declining to visit at Clanpibroch Castle while his uncle continues to live so disreputably."

"On the contrary, I think he plays his cards extremely ill, for they say he has not the shadow of a chance now; and that when any of his letters are, by mistake, directed to Clanpibroch Castle, Sir Evan returns them to the post-office, and writes on the back with his own hand, '*Not known here!*'"

"Miss Murray related to me yesterday some particulars of their final quarrel which showed an admirable instance of generous independence. Sir Evan always used to treat Mr. Grant as his *possible heir* till lately, when, by an act of extreme benevolence, he was led to incur the old gentleman's utmost rancor. Sir Evan's eldest daughter, a very beautiful girl of eighteen, had become attached to young Cameron, of Heatherbrae, who would, you know, be a most eligible match for her under present circumstances, though, for the acknowledged daughter of the family, he might not be suitable. Her father harshly forbade the marriage, without any adequate reason for doing so; and when the poor girl persevered in importuning him on the subject, he became so violently irritated, that, in a moment of uncontrollable anger, he turned her out of his house. The unfortunate mother dared not interfere, or she and all her family might have been obliged to follow; so her daughter departed utterly homeless and forlorn. It was impossible to anticipate what she could do, but Mr. Grant heard the whole circumstances, and instantly hastened to her relief. He placed her under safe guardianship with a respectable family, commissioned Miss Murray to supply her with necessaries, and after having vainly endeavored to mediate for Sir Evan's consent and forgiveness, he promised to be present at the wedding himself next month. Since then, the old gentleman has been heard to make vows of summary vengeance, which can be executed any day by acknowledging his three sons, and cutting out your friend, Mr. Grant."

"Foolish man!" exclaimed Eleanor, in a tone between jest and earnest. "He might have done the same thing in some sneaking, clandestine way that never would have reached Clanpibroch Castle; but Mr. Grant always acts upon impulse, without a grain of discretion. He might probably be heir to Lady Susan Danvers, if he would only call her young and handsome, instead of teasing her with practical jokes, and hinting continually about 'Ocean's many-wrinkled smile,' and Marshal *Blue-hair's* japan blacking for the hair and eye-brows. She is very harsh to some pretty young niece whose cause he espouses, and that is his reason for tormenting her. There is nothing half so frightful as a decayed beauty who *will not* grow old; and it used to be remarked of Lady Susan Danvers and her late sister, that the one was too beautiful to be good, and the other too good to be beautiful. I wonder if that is ever said of *us*, Matilda?"

"I shall be perfectly satisfied with the part you probably

assign to me," replied her cousin, with a smile of so much archness and good-humor that a transient doubt crossed Eleanor's mind whether her own claim to admiration could be superior, and a bitter feeling of jealousy towards Matilda, which was seldom dormant in the heiress's mind, now took entire possession of her thoughts. It seemed strange that there could be any one for a self-satisfied person like Eleanor to envy; but it was the case from her childhood, and Miss Marabout had early nursed that feeling, which grew stronger and more irritable every day. Of all the rankling pains which a human heart can experience, that of envy, is, next to remorse, the most painful. It has not the dignity of anger, it receives not the sympathy which grief excites, and it must not be acknowledged even to ourselves, for the meanest of mankind might despise himself for feeling it, and the proudest is degraded by a conviction that there lives another in whom anything appears superior to himself.

Matilda continued to talk with vivacity and humor during the continuance of their drive, though she could not but observe with surprise the peevish, consequential expression which her cousin's countenance gradually assumed; for little did she imagine that Eleanor already looked upon her as a rival for admiration among the guests now assembled at Barnard Castle, and that her mind was occupied in planning every expedient by which her companion might be kept in the background and mortified into silence and obscurity during the following week. While Matilda's heart, therefore, glowed with every amiable and affectionate emotion towards her cousin, and while her spirits were buoyant with anticipated pleasure, it was fortunate for her own happiness that she could not, on the present occasion, see "that hideous sight, a naked human heart."

CHAPTER IX.

—— "Dropping buckets into empty wells,
And growing old in drawing nothing up."

"Ah! Lady Susan Danvers is arrived!" cried Eleanor, as the carriage slowly turned round a broad sheet of gravel which expanded before the house; "there she is, as gay and fine as a perfumer's wig-block, staring out of the window. How Mr. Grant made me laugh yesterday with an account of her travels abroad, when she refused to marry ever so many ex-kings, counts, and *cardinals!* Poor Lady Susan is so frequently invited to second-rate Edinburgh parties, on account of her rank being ornamental, that he means to suggest a plan for her being *let out by the job*, and turning an honest penny by it. In ordinary dress she is worth so much —in diamonds and feathers double the price; but when she keeps her father's coroneted carriage waiting at the door, she deserves any money."

"It is said that, in Mrs. Glass's Receipt Book, or Hints on Etiquette, I forget which, you may find a prescription for assembling the most agreeable dinner-party imaginable. Get a lawyer to talk, a beauty to excite interest, a traveller to tell stories, and a peer to give it *éclat;* but, by your account, Lady Susan might serve in nearly all these capacities at once."

"So she does! For instance, Lady Montague, our opposite neighbor, gives only three dinners in a season, which take place on three days running; so my great amusement is to watch her party arriving. The first day, a coronet is emblazoned on every pannel; the second day, gentlemen's carriages arrive with only supporters; and the third day, nothing is to be seen but hackney-coaches full of poor relations; but I was amused to observe, that Lady Susan is always present at the whole of them, first to be pleased herself at the great party, and then that she may give dignity to the inferior ones."

A perfect uproar of joy took place between Eleanor and

her newly-arrived visitor when they met, and the barking of lapdogs was scarcely louder or more vociferous than the clamor of their voices while compliments, inquiries, reproaches, and protestations of regard were exchanged in rapid and animated succession. A slight bow of recognition was all that Lady Susan bestowed upon Miss Howard, followed by that deliberate stare of a cold, examining eye, which is, above all inflictions, the most formidable in society to a person of sensitive feelings; therefore, being anxious to escape from notice which was so little conciliatory, Matilda gracefully returned the acknowledgment, and quietly seated herself by the fire.

"How *very* thin you are become, Lady Susan!" exclaimed Eleanor, with well-assumed consternation, for she knew that her friend lived in perpetual vexation because her *embonpoint* was beyond what suited with any pretentions to young ladyism. "You must be fed up in the Highlands for the credit of our mountain air, and not leave Barnard Castle till you can scarcely get out at the door."

"*Bien obligée!* but you shall positively not make a prize-ox of me. I am, as you say, in very good training at present. Not quite reduced enough yet, but very little more would satisfy me."

"Why, Lady Susan! what more would you have! I declare you must be in a rapid consumption already!" replied Eleanor, undauntedly fixing her satirical eye on the broad expanse of her visitor's well-rounded figure. "I once died of laughing at the theatre, when a skeleton was brought on the stage by Harlequin, who fed it up till the figure gradually became corpulent and fattened into a London alderman; but we must try a similar experiment here without delay, or you will vanish altogether; so, ladies! come to luncheon, and if you cannot eat with an appetite, you may at least eat with a knife and fork."

On their return to the drawing-room, Matilda felt as if she had become suddenly *invisible* during a long conversation which ensued between Lady Susan Danvers and Eleanor, neither of whom seemed to contemplate the probability of her assisting the dialogue. It was chiefly carried on *sotto voce*, though such parts as she overheard amused and interested her so much, that, to prevent the appearance of being sullen or irritable, she took out some drawing materials, and resigned herself to silence, while the others sat down in that nothing-particular-to-do sort of way in which most ladies at country houses pass a large portion of their time.

"Now Miss Fitz-Patrick, pray tell me who I am to meet this morning?" asked Lady Susan, with an air of expectation. "The house, you tell me is fuller than it can hold, so there are probably *twenty odd* people at least."

"All our old set are here. Lady Montague, with Adelaide and Mary, who are dull and silent as usual; they can do nothing, you know, but look pretty;—Mrs. Clifford and her three indisposable daughters, who have set up for being an 'attached family,' which is the sort of thing I have no patience for, one sister taking you aside to praise the other *in confidence.* Colonel Pendarvis of the Blues arrived yesterday, and Sir Colin Fletcher, larger than life."

"Ah, poor Sir Colin! I was introduced to him several years ago, and we have never exchanged a syllable since, but he has the trouble of bowing to me almost every day when we pass in the street. I owe him a hat for the number of times he has taken his off to me; and if I go to ten parties in a night, he is the first person I meet at them all. It was impossible to know when one might begin to give up the acquaintance, in case of looking as if I had taken something amiss, which could not well be, seeing we had no intercourse; but now I shall either improve our intimacy, or get up a quarrel, to save the trouble of nodding my head like a Chinese mandarian every day."

"Sir Colin gives papa a great deal of additional exercise in Edinburgh, for my father invariably rounds the corner of the nearest street on catching a glimpse of his portly figure. Major Foley of the 10th came here this morning also. He is still the Beau Fribble of an old comedy in his dress and conversation, with such a look of conscious beauty that I can scarcely resist laughing. His face would do best under a bonnet, and his curls are so elaborately studied, that every hair seems to be on special duty; yet, in my opinion, your cousin Mr. Grant's head looks ten times better, which always seems to have been dressed by accident. Apropos! I am happy to tell you that he is arrived."

"Tom Grant!!" exclaimed Lady Susan, in a tone of alarm and vexation. "I shall leave the house to-morrow! What could possess him to come here at this season? If I have an aversion in the world, it is for him. The most troublesome, mischievous, and satirical of human beings, whom it is impossible to keep at a distance."

"I never heard of any one before who wished to do so! Mr. Grant is universally popular in society; and I am certain, if ladies returned a member to Parliament, he would be unanimousely elected. But," continued Eleanor, seeing that Lady Susan's observant eyes were fixed on her with a penetrating stare, "if you have any infallible prescription for repulsing forward people, pray furnish me with it instantly. I am inflicted at present with a guest in this house whom no power on earth can possibly affront or dislodge. He was an unwelcome visitor here last summer, merely tolerated as an old friend of Sir Philip's, but nothing could convince him that we were not delighted at his arrival and inconsolable when he departed. He kept repeatedly promising to return, though no one ever asked him, and here he is arrived again, with a thousand apologies for not coming sooner, and a promise to make up for that by remaining as long as possible. He is more at home than myself, and more unwelcome than a rat in a hole; but I fear that the gamekeeper, who is engaged to keep down vermin, will scarcely rid me of Mr. Armstrong."

"Sinbad's old man of the sea was nothing to this! Could you not have the door of his room locked some night, and forget to let him out?"

"I would have tried it, certainly, but you know papa is so good-natured, he hates making enemies, and Mr. Armstrong adopts a strange way of hinting as if we owed him obligations. He has a very mean, sheep-stealing look, and probably wants to impose some absurd story upon us; but it cannot be endured much longer, for there never was any one so tiresome. He sits from morning till night in that Spanish chair by the fire, whistling a tune and tattooing on the table; perfectly well dressed, with clean gloves, and so forth, but not a thing to do. He neither shoots, nor fishes, nor reads, but is forever in the way, always expecting to be spoken to and entertained. Why he comes, or when he goes away, no one can possibly guess."

"Is he a man of fortune and family?" asked Lady Susan, who was never known to omit these two important inquiries respecting any gentleman under discussion.

"Oh dear, no! Mr. Armstrong is one of the most remarkable men living, in these respects! He began the world with no visible means of existence and no connexions; yet he has lived well and frequented the best company all his life. Not a conjecture can be formed what are his resources, except that people allege he lives by a curious sort of jobbing; and Mr. Grant assures me that Sir Philip was actually *sold* by him to the picture-dealers abroad. Mr. Armstrong had mastered the whole jargon of the trade, and he showed off so much fastidious criticism, that my grand-uncle became fully impressed with his unimpeachable judgment; half the trash in my lumber-room is of his *selection;* and your cousin tells me there is not a bad picture to be got now at Florence, because Sir Philip bought them all up. Mr. Armstrong's father was a law-agent in Edinburgh, who allowed his son to travel for three years in Italy, after which it was expected that the hopeful youth would settle to the same profession; but, when he returned from abroad, with his head running on operas and paintings, no consideration could confine his soaring spirit to the desk. Accordingly his second brother, who had been more judiciously trained for business, sat down upon the vacant stool and became a pettifogging scribe, who did all sorts of odd jobs for Sir Philip, and often managed what he called '*waff cases.*' He died suddenly, about a month after my uncle, but without leaving any fortune, and his dilettante brother succeeded to little more than papers and parchments."

"But here comes my ci-devant governess, whom it is very diverting to tease, by pretending that Mr. Armstrong remains here on her account. To say the truth, she rather likes the joke, for *you know*, Lady Susan, that when ladies come to be of no particular age, they are pleased with the smallest remnant of an admirer, and after thirty we get rather into the *afternoon* of life. Ah, Miss Marabout! I was talking of you, and Lady Susan is shocked to hear what an example of cruelty is set before me in respect to my lovers. Poor Mr. Armstrong! he seemed inconsolable at breakfast this morning, and could not eat above three muffins. I observed him look exceedingly sentimental when he asked you to sweeten his tea, and there was something very forbidding in your way of offering him the toast. By the way there were some tender messages left for you when he walked out to day, whistling as usual the air, as far as I could follow it, of 'Oh no! we never mention her.'"

Miss Marabout attempted to execute a blush and a simper on the most approved boarding-school pattern, while she looked so exquisitely conscious, that Eleanor, who watched her countenance with keen enjoyment, gave Lady Susan a look expressive of satirical humor, very similar to that with which she often clandestinely imparted to her governess some jest against others which they mutually shared. Matilda's attention was in the mean time diverted from the scene before her by a perpetual annoyance from Lady Susan's three little Blenheim spaniels, which were constantly fighting or playing under the table where she sat, causing such a vibration as occasionally threatened the total overthrow of her drawing materials. till at length one of them began barking so violently that further conversation became utterly impossible.

"Excuse me, Miss Howard," said Lady Susan, affectedly, "my darling Tiny cannot bear to be looked at."

"What a modest dog!" exclaimed Matilda, unable to help laughing;—"but she is certainly a great beauty!"

"Yes!" said Eleanor, "Tiny has quite the air of a dog of fashion, and such a friendly way of putting her paw upon my arm, as if she really could speak, and had something confidential to say."

"Dear little creatures! they are very attaching! Positively, Tiny becomes so melancholy during my absence that Dentelle and I take it by turns now to remain at home from church on alternate Sundays that she may not be dull."

A long conversation ensued between the two friends on the good qualities of their respective pets, while innumerable anecdotes were told of their sagacity and affection. Dogs, long since deceased, were remembered and deplored with melancholy regret, and the infirmities and distempers of others still living were described and lamented, with expressions of interest and pity which might have been applied to their dearest friends in similar circumstances. The medical treatment of their complaints was anxiously considered, the variety of their tastes discussed, and many unpleasant endurances they each boasted of having put up with from the canine race, which would have caused a fellow-creature to be banished with disgust from their sitting-rooms. In short, it appeared as if the two ladies had formed a conspiracy to render dogs *at least* equal to mankind, if not superior. Before the endless subject seemed more than begun, the door suddenly opened, and a head appeared, exhibiting an expression of laughing animation which Murillo might have vainly attempted to copy.

"I must pay my devoirs to Lady Susan! How is my pretty cousin Mary? Have you forgiven me our last rencontre?"—cried Mr. Grant, not advancing a step. "No answer? then I must decamp, for the most agreeable personage in the world is a certain lady in *good* humor, who is the very reverse otherwise."

"Come in," replied Lady Susan; "you are not one that it is prudent to quarrel with, so we must endeavor to endure you."

"'For better and for worse?' But I dare not come *forward* yet! We are over head and ears in mud—a famous run—fifteen miles straight across the country, and killed near Dewkesbury lane."

"Do advance, and tell me all about it," said Eleanor, impatiently. "What are you afraid of?"

"A charge from the whole troop of housemaids, commanded by old Mrs. Gordon," answered Mr. Grant, approaching on tiptoe: "if she knew of my being here in this plight, her good opinion of me would be forfeited forever; and I have it upon authority that she was heard to pronounce my panegryic as a very *safe* person in the house, never elevating my feet on the sofas nor passing any one of her innumerable mats without doing homage."

"I like to see poor Mrs. Gordon's *esprit du corps*," said Matilda. "She makes as great a commotion about the mark of a footstep on the staircase as ever Robinson Crusoe did when he traced one on the sand."

"I met with a curious specimen of professional enthusiasm from my maid when we last came from London in the steamboat," said Lady Susan. "We had a perfect storm—the sea running mountains high—the sails no larger than pocket-handkerchiefs—two men lashed to the helm——"

"Yes!" interrupted Mr. Grant; "and the ladies quite fatigued working at the pumps."

"Quite sublime, and extremely terrifying, I assure you, when my maid rushed into the cabin, staggering with the motion, and scarcely able to stand, while she grasped in her hand a new cap which she entreated me to put on instantly. Almost bewildered at her earnestness, I asked why she wished it. 'Oh, my lady!' was her reply, 'we are all going to the bottom, and I wish you to be *a decent corpse*.'"

"That reminds me of our last meeting, Lady Susan! It really turned out a better joke than could have been anticipated!" said Mr. Grant with a laugh of exquisite enjoyment. "You were a little short-sighted that day."

"Now, Mr. Grant! I see you are dying to be asked for

the story, so pray give it us without delay," cried Eleanor eagerly.

"With all the pleasure in life, if I can only get leave! Your last *head-dress*, Lady Susan! The scold was enough to '*faire les cheveux dresser à la tête.*' "

"This is evidently a narrative *founded on fiction*," said Matilda, pitying the alarm and irritation which were visible in the lady's countenance. "We shall perhaps read it in the next number of Hood's Comic Annual, illustrated by Cruikshanks."

"Thank you for the hint, Miss Howard!" exclaimed Mr. Grant. "I protest it would do admirably! In the first page, I shall be represented storming with indignation at Gianetti, the hair-dresser's, because no one had appeared in the shop to supply my wants. Then my good cousin is seen slowly ascending the steps. I instantly dart round to the opposite side of the counter, throw off my hat, tie on a stray apron which happened to be there, and prepare to obey orders; but instead of being asked, in dulcet tones, for a bottle of Smith's lavender water or of Rowland's Kalydor, which were all that, in the innocence of my heart, I ever dreamt of any *young* lady wanting at a perfumer's, there burst out upon me such a discovery, and, though it was not intended for me, such a scold!"

"You deserved it, and ten times more! I never heard of anything so atrocious!" exclaimed Eleanor, in pretended indignation. "Mr. Grant, you are so fond of odd tricks, that no one ever knows, when you are in the room, whether their heads are their own or not."

"The hair on their heads, you mean," whispered Mr. Grant, aside, while his cousin was angrily endeavoring to seem occupied with her dogs. "Lady Susan, you *know* I am your best friend, and nothing promotes a good understanding among relations half so much as when they have a joke between them."

"If a joke is a good one, I enjoy it beyond anything, but there appears to me very little humor in this!"

"I see a great deal of *good-humor* in it," replied Mr. Grant, looking slyly at Lady Susan's irritated countenance. "The unfortunate *friseur* made a *hair*-breadth 'scape, and I was terrified out of my few remaining senses.

'This put Mr. Frog in a terrible fright,
He took up his hat, and he wished them good night.'

Now, pray forgive me, lady Susan, for it makes me wretched when we quarrel, considering all the obligations I owe you."

"Obligations!" exclaimed Lady Susan, in a tone of perplexity; "what may that be?"

"Have you really forgotten your kindness to me when I was a little boy? Don't you remember all the sugar-plums you gave me, and that whip with a red handle, and a whistle at the end of it?"

"I recollect nothing of the kind! You have a most fertile imagination, Mr. Grant! but if we may judge of the boy from the man, you certainly deserved the whip, whether you ever got it or not."

Mr. Grant put his hand to his face with a contortion of pain, as if he really had suffered the lash, and retreated towards a window.

"Ah! here are Dr. and Miss Murray arriving! how glad I shall be to meet them both! It does my eyes good to see such excellent people, and he is the only clever man I ever liked. One cannot expect above once in a century to see such a person!"

If Eleanor had been formerly disposed to venerate this truly good man, she felt still more impressed with a sense of his excellence, from the sincerity and warmth with which Mr. Grant expressed himself, and her beautiful countenance glowed with animation as she hastened forward to meet her guests.

"So you have ventured to see me at last, Dr. Murray! We thought you were never coming back; and if there had been no other way of prevailing on you to return, I meant to personate a rheumatic old woman, and send, in her name, an ill-spelt letter, requesting an interview, knowing how seldom you pay visits, except in charity. Miss Murray, I stopped at your gate this morning, and admired prodigiously all the improvements which are going on there. You are doing a vast deal to embellish the house and gardens."

"I see many great changes going on here, too."

"Ah! in *my small way*," replied Eleanor.

"Small!!!" exclaimed her simple-hearted visitor, in amazement.

"Yes, Miss Fitz-Patrick you are right," said Dr. Murray, who perfectly understood the pride which was veiled under an affected humility. "In scenes of such natural splendor and magnitude as these, '*what is man?*' We are but insects scratching on the beautiful face of nature."

"Or like the fly on the coach-wheel, saying, 'What a dust I raise!'" added Mr. Grant.

"A modern author gives the same idea in very striking language," said Dr. Murray. "'Take some quiet sober moment of life,' he says, 'and add together the two ideas of *pride* and of *man;* add them, if you can, without a smile. Behold him a creature of a span high, strutting in infinite space, and darting disdain from his eyes, in all the grandeur of littleness. Perched on a little speck of the universe, he is rolled along the Heavens through a road of worlds, while systems and creations are flaming above and beneath; he is an atom of atoms. Yet will this miserable creature revel in his greatness, and mock at his fellow, sprung from that same dust to which they both shall soon return.'"

"Very striking indeed!" observed Eleanor, turning heedlessly to Mr. Grant. "It is curious that we never apply any remark to ourselves, for all the time Dr. Murray has been speaking, I could not but wish that the most high and mighty Sir Alfred Douglas had benefited by such a lecture on humility. I am told that, at parties abroad, he sometimes drew up to his full height, and looked as if he meant to kick the universe from under his feet."

"Wait till you know him as well as I do, Miss Fitz-Patrick, and then you may believe all those ridiculous stories if you can——"

"I hope the state-room is ordered to be in readiness," said Lady Susan, wishing to tease Mr. Grant, who had a perfect enthusiasm for Sir Alfred. "It used to be alleged that he complained of catching cold while airing all the best beds in every house, because, somehow or other, no one ever thought of placing him in any except their principal rooms."

"I beg his pardon, then; but no such hardships are prepared for him here."

"How well I know the sort of lodgings which are reserved for stray gentlemen in some country houses," observed Mr. Grant, laughing. "If there be a cracked basin or a darned towel on the establishment, the housekeeper is heard to say, 'That may do for the bachelors' rooms!' and wherever there exists an apartment with its only window in the ceiling, or a mirror that distorts your face like a paralytic stroke, it falls to our share. At Clanpibroch Castle, the doors are all in a row, and so exactly alike, that I hung my visiting-card on the handle at last, to prevent the intrusion, by mistake, of half-a-dozen single gentlemen successively, who all lodged on the same floor, and used to catch me arranging my last *head-dress*, Lady Susan."

A lively dialogue ensued between Eleanor and Mr. Grant, during which Matilda enjoyed some interesting conversation with Dr. Murray; but Miss Fitz-Patrick at length remembered that it was her intention to fascinate her newly-arrived guests completely; so, breaking through her cousin's interview without ceremony, she called them to accompany her in the usual routine of a tour round the cabinets, conservatories, china, books, and pictures. Dr. Murray followed, with the same feeling of good-humored indulgence which would have led him to testify an interest in the toys of some pleasing, wayward child whom he wished to conciliate, but yet in his remarks there appeared that perfect judgment and good taste which characterized all he ever said.

"You have never been here since my ancesters were *all hung*, Dr. Murray," observed Eleanor, smiling defiance to Matilda, who gravely shook her head, and resumed her drawing, for the heiress had actually executed her threat by giving them new names. "Poor Sir Philip used to boast that his family never had a beginning and never would have an end; but that only reminds one now of the old epitaph—

'Here lies the Laird of Lundie.
Sic transit gloria mundi!'"

"How very unfortunate it was," remarked Miss Murray, "that he left no family."

"Excuse *me* there! *I* am far from agreeing with you," said Eleanor, much diverted. "This is Lord—Lord Dumbartonshire, who was killed at Culloden. The name seems to be written in gilt letters below the left arm. My great-grandfather, you know."

"His uniform does not belong to a Scotch regiment," observed Dr. Murray, fixing his thoughtful eyes on her countenance; "there must surely be some mistake. That inscription, too, is quite modern."

"As for the dress, artists long ago never thought of attending to that; they carried about figures ready painted, and added the head of any one who sat. A lady with shoulders up to her ears, and her waist like an alderman's wife, might choose the form of a sylph, and my great-grandfather probably preferred the uniform of the Guards to his own."

"I admire truth and accuracy in everything," said Dr. Murray, passing on to inspect the succeeding pictures.

"They are vastly genteel," said Miss Murray, in a complaisant tone. "This is Queen Mary, I suppose, or Cleopatra?"

"No! that is Lord Ben-Nevis's second wife! I cannot recollect her name."

"*Lady Ben-Nevis*, I suppose," replied Miss Murray.

"Now, who could have told you that!" cried Mr. Grant, unable to help laughing at her simplicity. "But, Miss Fitz-Patrick, there is some blunder here, for Lord Ben-Nevis was only married once."

"Indeed you are mistaken—he lost two wives at least."

"He may have lost as many as you please, but I am certain he never married above *one*."

"You genealogists are all so obstinate! This picture must have been done for somebody, and it is as likely to have been a Lady Ben-Nevis as any one else. That is old Lady Betty, who was the greatest beauty of her time, but the picture formerly served as a target for Sir Philip to shoot at when he was a boy, so one eye and the nose were gone; but when we were in Edinburgh last I sat to M'Innes, and had my own substituted, which looks just as well, so now you will allow she is handsomer than ever. Lady Betty made what was then thought a misalliance in marrying Lord de Mainbury's grandfather."

"Had he *really* a grandfather?" asked Mr. Grant, incredulously.

"So it is reported! and I have heard that when Mr. de Mainbury married my great-aunt, he desired a coach-maker to send pattern coats of arms, that he might choose what looked best."

"Two salmon rampant for supporters, of course, as all his wealth is derived from fisheries. Three sprats gules, and for the crest a cod's head and shoulders."

"How I hate people to be satirical!" said Eleanor, laughing. "Here is a picture I wish to have the public opinion upon. Lady Susan, we all know what a connoisseur you are considered, ever since that week you spent at Rome; tell me then if this is a tolerable daub or not?"

The lady in question seemed pleased at this reference,

and rolling up a sheet of paper in the form of a telescope, she gazed through it with all the air of an acknowledged critic.

"There are some *good bits of color* here, but the outline is defective, and not enough of distance preserved. These tints are scarcely forcible enough, too; but that is a very clever mountain in the back-ground, and this light is well brought out. Altogether it wants breadth."

"I see plenty of *breadth*," interrupted Eleanor, slyly directing her eye towards Lady Susan's own figure; "but there is rather a deficiency, I should say, of *depth.*"

"Do you advise Miss Fitz-Patrick to sit for her likeness to the artist who painted this, for I know she has thoughts of doing it?" asked Mr. Grant, looking so arch that Matilda felt sure he was devising mischief. "The young man is now in this house, touching up some of those portraits, and we think him a promising genius, seeing his imitation of the antique so excellent."

"Tolerable!" replied Lady Susan in a very dubious tone, "but his painting wants relief! the composition is not correct. There is no poetry here! as for genius, the less we say about *that* the better. Pray, Miss Fitz-Patrick, never think of trusting your countenance to such a mere plasterer."

"Lady Susan, you are ruined forever," cried Mr. Grant in an ecstasy of delight—"Why that is Vandyke's famous picture of the Sleeping Nymph! Did you never hear that Sir Philip paid £1000 for it? Oh Lady Susan! unfortunate Lady Susan!"

"Dr. Murray! you are admiring nature instead of art now. Is that view not magnificent!" said Eleanor, following him to a distant window. "Each of these prospects is different, and appears like a landscape handsomely framed. I have opened the plantation westwards, that we may see the sun setting every night behind that hill of Benachscrocholet. Now, do observe how completely I have mastered the Gaelic pronunciation! You will see me become quite a Highland chief! but I cannot yet get seasoned to your northern blasts. They kill me outright, and make me appear like a perfect heathen, for I can so seldom venture to church. All those country kirks are so damp that Miss Marabout and I catch cold every time we venture there. When the weather reforms, so shall I."

"Miss Fitz-Patrick!" said Dr. Murray, with mild but impressive earnestness. "Pardon me if I estimate my professional privileges too highly; but believing as I do that a sacred duty is imposed on me towards yourself, and seeing that hitherto no opportunity has been allowed me of discharging it, I venture to say a few words, trusting that they may be received as they are intended, in all sincerity and kindness. You are now in the morning of such a bright and prosperous existence, that amidst the splendors of a scene like this, it is less to be wondered at, if you are so ready to confess indifference towards those ordinances which remind us of another and a better state. We are now contemplating the portraits of those who long since lived, and felt, and acted in these very chambers, and who called those distant hills their own. Each of them has been summoned away, carrying no possession along with him but the riches which he may have wisely laid up for himself. They were stewards here, not proprietors, and they are gone to give an account of their stewardship. You are appointed for a time to the same office; but in a few short years, while yet those glorious scenes of nature continue to proclaim their Maker's hand, and to shine as brightly as before, these walls will resound with the mirth of other voices, and you and I shall each be withdrawn forever, and called to our solemn reckoning. You have been selected, Miss Fitz-Patrick, by the Master whom I serve to be an object of His peculiar bounty; and in placing you thus conspicuously, as a city set on a hill, and in gifting you with all that might add personal to family influence, He will expect of the ten talents committed to your care a very faithful and a very awful reckoning."

Dr. Murray continued to address Eleanor for some time with all that could touch her feelings, on the duties and responsibilities of the present life, and finished with a solemn appeal to the fears and the hopes for eternity, which stand in awful contrast before the Christian mind. "Consider, my young friend," said he, in conclusion, "that we perish not like blossoms that flutter and disappear in the autumn breeze; but that ours is a destiny more permanent, and, if we will, more glorious than that of the perpetual stars in the firmament above; do not then think it a trifling consideration which may be lightly set aside, whether you are preparing to spend those eternal ages in hopeless repentance, or in a degree of felicity which eye hath not seen, and the heart of man has never been able to conceive."

Eleanor's color rose while Dr. Murray addressed her in tones of impressive interest. Her look became downcast, her eyes filled with tears, the proud, consequential aspect of her countenance gradually subsided into an expression of softness, and she silently gave him her hand.

"Can you, Miss Fitz-Patrick, amongst a multitude of flatterers, suffer one faithful, uncompromising friend?" continued he, earnestly. "I feel myself the appointed guardian of each individual in this widely-extended parish; and it would be well if I might occasionally speak the words of truth and soberness to her whose influence and example will have such weight among the objects of my continual solicitude and prayers."

"I once had such a friend as you describe," replied Eleanor, in a tone of unusual sensibility. "I still need one, Dr. Murray, and though the blessing was not sufficiently valued formerly, let us hope that now I may prove deserving of it."

Eleanor believed herself sincere in saying this, and to a certain extent she was. Deeply impressed by the glowing eloquence of his manner, and conscious of Dr. Murray's exalted character, she had long desired the esteem of one whose regard was indeed an honor, since it could be acquired by nothing but personal worth. While he laid before her the utter insignificance of all earthly distinctions, she felt for the moment as if they had vanished from her affections, and as if she might yet learn to view them in due subservience to the will and to the service of her Maker. A deep conviction rushed into her mind of the inability which she had recently felt to derive happiness or peace from the fullest indulgence of every vain and extravagant inclination; and the contrast forced itself upon her thoughts between Matilda's serenity and cheerfulness in every changing scene, while her own bosom was agitated with torturing emotions of envy and worldly ambition. The ennui and weariness which she had suffered in the absence of any object sufficiently important to occupy her whole desires, now recurred to her recollection with irresistible conviction; and while Dr. Murray pursued his subject with rising energy, it seemed to Eleanor's mind as if she were gradually awakening from a stormy dream, and that peace, like moonlight on the face of the waters, had again revisited her bosom. But the world does not thus easily lose hold of its votary. Many a struggle takes place before it has been sufficiently weighed in the balance to be found wanting. Many a tear of penitence is shed before we feel that repentance which shall never need to be repented of. Many a resolution formed, before divine grace is sought to render it permanent. Who has not experienced the powerful effects of eloquent preaching on his own heart, rendering every desire and every pursuit that might seem likely to oppose the stream of exhortation like straws on the tide; but while yet only descending the steps which lead from the altar, his holy dispositions have been put to sleep, his good intentions dispersed, and the seriousness of his thoughts exchanged for all that levity and forgetfulness in which he has long indulged? It was thus with Eleanor. She seemed to have gazed for a moment through the telescope of faith, and with startling vividness to have brought eternity close to her eye, but in a moment she looked around and all was forgotten.

CHAPTER X.

Ere triflers half their wish obtain,
The toiling pleasure sickens into pain.
GOLDSMITH.

"MISS FITZ-PATRICK!" cried Lady Susan Danvers, in a tone of girlish vivacity, "do come this way and look at the sportsmen galloping home across the park. They resemble a field of scarlet poppies in a breeze of wind!"

"Strike me poetical!—what brilliant simile was that?" exclaimed Mr. Grant, taking out his pocket-book and pencil; "I must make a memorandum of it for my next publication—*puppies* did you say?"

"Well, Miss Fitz-Patrick, Sir Richard gave me a capital mount! the horse as quiet as an old cow," said Mr. Armstrong, entering with the other gentlemen, and putting himself first. "Here I am, returned on your hands like a bad shilling!"

"So I think!" replied Eleanor, dryly. "We must endeavor to *pass* you as soon as possible."

"I suppose your subscription to the hounds was paid in advance to-day, Mr. Armstrong?" asked Mr. Grant, gravely. "We generally expect it to be so from strangers."

"Subscription!!—what do you mean, sir?"

"You don't say that the master of the hounds let you join without first settling with him!" replied Mr. Grant, assuming an air of well-feigned astonishment. "Any one going out for a day is considered the same as a whole season. You are free of the pack now, but I can tell you there is no getting off without tabling the money—fifty guineas."

"But a *stranger*, who is leaving the country in a *few days*," interposed Eleanor, "could scarcely be asked to give such a sum. I shall speak to papa myself, Mr. Armstrong, and tell him that, as you go so *very* soon——"

"Ah! the sooner the better, if you wish to evade the subscription," added Mr. Grant. "It will be sent for, probably, I should think, on Saturday next."

"I shall neither leave the place, nor pay any such exaction," said Mr. Armstrong, stubbornly seating himself on the Spanish chair. No trifle of that kind would make me disappoint my friends when I have once promised to stay with them; and all the hounds in Britain will not drive me out of this snug corner, while I continue to be as welcome and as comfortable as I am now."

"Ah, Major Foley!" cried Eleanor, turning away with a grimace of chagrin; "how do you do?"

"How do *I* do!—always well when I am near Miss Fitz-Patrick."

"Colonel Pendarvis! you were reported among the killed and wounded in a desperate leap over my new enclosure at Wolfdean this morning. Did you know that Major Foley was the original Snob mentioned in the Quarterly Review?—it is an undeniable likeness, so he cannot disown it."

"I never disown anything!" replied the Major. "If you were to allege that Lord Byron's Corsair was meant for me, or the Stout Gentleman, I should be equally ready to personate either character that *pleases you.*"

"Not the Stout Gentleman! we have him already;—and here he comes; I know the creaking of his boots at any dis tance," said Eleanor, darting her satirical eye at Lord Alderby, who entered a moment afterwards. "What an admirable horse yours is, my lord, for a light weight!—he seems *very spirited* too. I have read in the Morning Post, these many years past, an advertisement for a horse to carry a 'heavy, timid gentleman.' Can anybody tell me who he is, or if there is more than one?"

"I've seen thousands at Melton!" said Major Foley; "the moment a man gets heavy he becomes timid. I ride exactly ten stone eight myself."

"In that case, it is less a compliment to you than to Alderby or Fletcher, when Miss Fitz-Patrick remarks, as she *often* does, that you are all worth your weight in gold," said Mr. Grant.

"I wish we all had it!" cried Colonel Pendarvis. "I am sure any one might read half-pay engraved on my forehead, but none of you will take half price for my hunters. Foley, it is too bad of you asking such a price for Flare-up, when everybody knows I am a soldier of fortune, meaning a soldier of no fortune at all, and that I positively cannot afford it. You should be more considerate towards a brother-officer."

"Colonel! I perceive you want to out-*General* me in our negotiation; but it won't do!"

"Are you parting with Flare-up, Major Foley?" said Eleanor, reproachfully. "I remember being so sorry last year, when Sir Francis let you have his beautiful chestnut, and to-day Lady Susan was remarking that you looked *almost handsome* upon her."

"Pendarvis! the bargain is off! she would be cheap at a thousand pounds if Miss Fitz-Patrick admires her. I flatter myself we did make a pretty good appearance on the field this morning!"

"Then you do flatter yourself prodigiously," interrupted Mr. Grant. "*Apropos* of bargains, Pendarvis, let me tell you how famously I once *did* Sir Colin out of a good mount,—he can't overhear us, does he? It is the only good story Fletcher never attempts to tell. We were out with the Galewood hounds, and I was on that slow, stumbling bay of mine that you must remember—'Dapper' we called him, on account of his clumsy proportions. Latterly it was his custom, the instant he was spurred, to drop down on his knees. Well! Fletcher was riding past on Firefly, when I stopped him and remarked what an extraordinary instinct my hunter had, for he pointed at game like a dog! Sir Colin was, of course, incredulous at first, but as I had privately observed a covey of partridges near, I turned *accidentally* that way, and when we came near them applied my spurs. Down dropped Dapper, and up rose the partridges, so the thing no longer admitted of a doubt. The old gentleman was instantly frantic to buy the horse on any terms; so I agreed to an immense price, without, of course, intending to exact it, but one condition was, that we should immediately exchange steeds. This he was delighted to do, being impatient to try the powers of his recent acquisition. Soon after we reached a stream—Dapper attempted to drink, and Sir Colin spurred him on—so, as usual, he fell on his knees, in the water, while I galloped off in triumph, exclaiming, 'Holloa! Fletcher! that's a salmon?'"

"Lord de Mainbury," said Eleanor, "how many foxes were put out of their misery to-day?"

"Only one! we set off the second time with a fine burst over the hill of Benachray, skirted Glenalpine for several miles, and lost scent at Boghill; so the hounds did not find again all day."

"They had no nose, owing to the damp ground," added Mr. Grant. "It was all that the huntsman could do to prevent them going in full cry through Gaelfield, after the little brown spaniel which followed Lady Susan's carriage."

"Surely they would not have attacked *her?*" cried she, in accents of horror and alarm. "Poor dear Tiny! impossible!"

"Depend upon it they would have discussed her in the twinkling of a bed-post," answered Mr. Grant; "hounds will attack *anything!* Did you never hear that a pack in Ireland once devoured an old woman?"

"They could only be Irish hounds to commit such a blunder!" said Eleanor, laughing

"How very sad," observed Miss Murray. "People should not hunt if such things are likely to happen."

"I hope the whole pack was hanged!" exclaimed Lady Susan, indignantly.

"Riders included? we should have all deserved it if 'dear Tiny' had suffered to-day," replied Mr. Grant, watching his cousin's angry countenance. "She had a narrow escape."

"I don't believe a word of it!—you are in jest! Now do not play upon my feelings, but tell me truly, was dearest Tiny in real danger?"

"Imminent, I assure you! Hounds are known to kill dogs sometimes, and cats often. I have observed an old woman, spectacles on nose, knitting at her cottage-door, with poor puss purring by her side—quite a pastoral scene—and the hounds have made a meal of her before we could cry 'Tally-ho.'"

"Of the old woman?" exclaimed Miss Murray, in accents of consternation."

"To be sure!" interposed Eleanor, preventing Mr. Grant from setting her right. "Nothing was left but the knitting-pins and spectacles, which I have seen frequently. Are they, by good chance, in your pocket, Mr. Grant?"

"De Mainbury! I remember well what an escape you once made at Beverley," said Sir Richard. "Having outstripped the whole field, and come in for the death, you dismounted to secure the brush, and were exercising your whip in fine style, when suddenly the hounds left the fox, and turned upon you! A minute more would have done the business! When I came up with the huntsman, two or three were already at your throat, and once down, there could have been no escape. I never desire to see any one in such a predicament again!"

"That reminds me of a story which was told many years ago," began Sir Colin Fletcher, in a slow, methodical tone, which gained little attention from the lively circle around. "It seemed, you understand, as far as I could ascertain, to be very authentic; at least the circumstances were never satisfactorily contradicted; and though I have told them frequently in many companies, there is seldom any one to be met with who has not heard the incidents already, which proves how universally they must be credited. Many of the party here may know the particulars, yet——"

"Pendarvis!" said Mr. Grant, breaking through Sir Colin's endless preface. "What could induce you to let that fat farmer ride ahead of you all day! His horse's heels must have laved the mud into your very face. I see him now, in my mind's eye, riding on the horse's neck, and pommelling his flanks with a monstrous pair of spurs. Did any one ever see such a moving mountain!"

"If a house had stood in his way, he would have knocked it over," added the Colonel. "I believe he had fifteen falls to-day."

"As for Foley," continued Mr. Grant, "he goes to cover in review order, and the first splash on his boots sends him home."

"You call yourself a sportsman, Grant!" retorted the Major; "but I appeal to Sir Richard, whether this was the proper order of precedence, as I saw it to-day: The fox first, our friend here following, and the hounds last!"

"Foley! name your place and hour!" said Mr. Grant, joining in the laugh. "But here comes Sir Alfred Douglas, Bart., of Douglas Priory—M. P. that *shall* be. The most distant roll of his chariot-wheels has something so aristocratic in the sound, that I cannot be mistaken."

"I remember once being told that Pope Clement, or Innocent the Fifteenth, issued a bull, setting forth that the American Indians were to be considered human beings," said Eleanor; "but from all I hear, it would be desirable if his Holiness were alive now, to remind Sir Alfred that there are others of the same species as himself."

"Has he really become so proud?" asked Miss Murray. "It seems but yesterday when I remember him such a sweet, clever little boy."

"Fancy Douglas a sweet little boy, with a rattle and red

shoes! That could never have been possible! He must have been *born old*," said Mr. Grant; "but never believe anything you *hear* of Sir Alfred, Miss Murray, and only half what you *see*, for there is no man on earth less understood."

"I can only say that he is the finest speaker in public, and the scantiest talker in private, that I know. He and I never *hit it* together at all," observed Major Foley, arranging his favorite curl at the looking-glass. "Nothing could be finer, or more unexpected certainly, than that burst of eloquence when he was presented to his constituents. It seemed amazing, too, how frankly he declared his sentiments, though not very prudent. Considering the divided state of the voters, I could have managed to humbug them better, with a very little ambiguity and circumlocution, which was all wanting in the speech of yesterday."

"For a ready answer I would back Sir Alfred against the field anywhere," observed Sir Richard. "He is sharp and short, like a carving-knife."

The gentlemen now gathered in a group at the window, and entered on an elaborate criticism of the baronet's four posthorses; for no quadruped that ever entered a stable is above or below the attention of sportsmen, who can trace a look of decayed grandeur in many an old, broken-down hack, and who find entertainment in discussing the points of an ancient veteran with scarcely a leg to stand on.

Meantime Eleanor stole a glance into the mirror—the three Miss Cliffords each instinctively altered the position of their bonnets—the Miss Montagues closed a scrap-book with which they had been occupied—Miss Murray put on her spectacles—Lady Susan called all the dogs around her, and an air of general expectation prevailed throughout the room, while Matilda alone remained externally still; yet her color rose to the most vivid carnation, and she bent more intently over her drawing, while past emotions rushed into her memory with such fresh remembrance, that it seemed but yesterday since she had believed herself an object of preference to Sir Alfred. A pang shot through her mind when she anticipated that now, probably, like Mr. Grant, he would meet her as a comparative stranger; and so much had been said of his pride and reserve, that she neither expected, nor very much desired, a renewal of their former intimacy, besides that she had now learnt not to hope for better memories in her old friends than the habits of society rendered probable.

When the door was thrown open, Sir Richard hastened forward, with animated cordiality, to welcome his distinguished guest. "Ha! my good friend! I rejoice to see you here," cried he, seizing Sir Alfred's hand, who patiently resigned it to be shaken. "Any news from town?"

The baronet replied in a low, confidential voice, and after making a distant bow to Eleanor and the other ladies, he continued in deep conversation with Sir Richard for a considerable time, while Matilda quietly took the opportunity to make her remarks upon the change which a year had made upon his person. Sir Alfred's dress seemed remarkable for nothing but simplicity. His appearance was dignified, but the expression of his countenance perfectly frank and open. His eyes, large, dark, and intelligent, had an expression in them of deep and serious thought, which harmonized well with the strongly-marked character of his forehead, and his clear, olive complexion had become darkened by the summer's sun of Italy since Matilda last saw him. No studied attitudes, nor affected grimaces, betrayed any vanity or littleness of mind, but he acted and spoke with a degree of calm self-possession which nothing could disturb, while his mind became evidently absorbed in whatever subject occupied his attention at the moment. Matilda looked next at Sir Richard, and was amused to observe the contrast, for such a rapid variety of expressions flitted across his features during the progress of their interview, that she even fancied it might be possible to fill up the conversation, when alternate surprise, incredulity, pleasure, and regret, all appeared successively on her uncle's countenance. The subject evidently was political, and Sir Richard seemed from the broken sentences which Matilda overheard, to be eagerly urging on Sir Alfred the necessity for still greater energy in canvassing the neighborhood. "Active opponents,"—"Unfair advantages,"—"Crush them at once,"—"Promises of no avail,"—"Public duty," &c., &c., &c. Sir Alfred's short, decided answers, though they often made Sir Richard laugh, seldom appeared to be satisfactory, for he invariably returned to the charge with growing animation. "Interests of our party at hazard,"—"Pledged to do your utmost,"—"Country at stake."

"Sir Richard, what a gentleman can do I shall; he that would do more is none! Of course public business cannot go on without dinners; but my *do-er*, as you call him in Scotland, had carte blanche to give as many at the King's

Arms as he chose. I hope, therefore, that my free and independent constituents have enjoyed abundance of the usual fare on these occasions—soiled table-cloths, steel forks, and cold lobsters. They shall hear my sentiments on all occasions without disguise or evasion, clearly and fully stated, because there is nothing in them to conceal, but I shall not on any account stand up, like a school-boy before his tutors, to be catechised."

"Well, I am thankful to have got over much of my life in better times than you will ever see again," observed Sir Richard, who was a very mournful politician, though cheerful on every other subject. "The change is great! but you young men must conform to the spirit of the age. The people require to be propitiated——"

"Trust me on that score! They are like the bear, who showed his teeth when the traveller seemed afraid, but when a stick was held up he began to dance. We who are accustomed to command, ensure compliance more certainly by preserving our tone of authority than by relinquishing it."

Sir Richard became outrageous at this reply, and Matilda heard a prodigious accession of energy in her uncle's tone, —"Anarchy in the country!—immediate revolution!—rally round the constitution!——"

"Keep all that for the hustings next Friday, Sir Richard; we shall want a little oratory there, and you are wasting a great deal of *good alarm* on me, which would do admirably for the mob. Depend upon it, no man loses in the estimation of even the lowest rabble by keeping up the dignity of that station which he is born to fill. It is scarcely worth while to be so anxious about anything in this world as you wish me to be respecting my election; but depend upon it I shall do my utmost, and moreover get up a speech upon any pattern you choose to bespeak for the occasion—either neat and appropriate, or eloquent and impassioned."

"But is there any truth in that report you told me from Downing Street?"

"I never deal in mere reports," answered Sir Alfred, strolling towards the fire. "A man who circulates false news should be put to death."

"That would cause an alarming mortality here," exclaimed Mr. Grant. "How could you furnish conversation, Douglas? for we must talk."

"*Je n'en vois pas la necessité*," replied Sir Alfred.

"In fact, a false report often suits my purpose fully better than a true one," said Mr. Grant, "because I have first the advantage of telling it, and then follows the pleasure of contradicting it."

"What shocking profligacy!" interrupted Eleanor. "No wonder Miss Murray stares like an astonished cassowary! I am glad the Doctor is not within ear-shot! We are continually hearing marriages announced which are to take place immediately, and the next day they are gone off upon settlements; but who ever guessed that they were of your counterfeit coinage!"

"Many of them are much better arranged than the matches people make for themselves! I wish no one would ever marry till they have consulted me, for I never saw a happy couple yet without thinking that one of the parties might have done better."

"I am positively resolved against a sportsman," said Eleanor, "for it must be tiresome remaining a disconsolate widow at home all winter, except during a hard frost. Members of Parliament also shall be blackballed on my list, because they annually abscond from their families during the greater part of the year."

"I shall endeavor to lose my election," said Sir Alfred, dryly.

"It would be much better if you did," replied Eleanor, laughing. "I have so often, during my long experience, been disappointed when gentlemen who had a prodigious reputation for cleverness got into Parliament, and were expected to be great orators; I generally watch for their maiden speeches, expecting a blaze of eloquence, and seldom see more than this, 'An honorable member, whose name we could not learn,—Sir Alfred Douglas, we believe,—said a few words, which were inaudible under the gallery.'"

Matilda stole a look from her drawing at Sir Alfred, and a brilliant smile illuminated her countenance, while she watched to discover how he bore her cousin's raillery. It was instantly evident that he had not been previously aware she was present, and that her appearance at Barnard Castle was no less interesting than unexpected, for he started, when her eyes caught his, made a few hasty steps forward, and actually colored with astonishment and pleasure. The next moment, however, he suddenly checked himself back again, made a distant bow of recognition, and retreated to his former station by the fire, though his eyes yet rested on the countenance of Matilda Howard, with a sort of fascination which he seemed vainly endeavoring to resist. A natural smile dimpled her cheek, and played on her lips for a moment, rendering her modest countenance more than usually lovely; for there was always a peculiar beauty in Matilda's smile. Eleanor's indicated nothing but hilarity, while hers was full of sensibility, which was not diminished on the present occasion by the emotion with which she perceived that her appearance was not a matter of so much indifference to Sir Alfred as she previously anticipated.

Matilda had not believed it was possible for any event in life to cause him so much agitation as he testified at that moment, and her own was not less. The flashing glance of his eye reminded her of former times, and raised a transient belief that he was unchanged, and that she had not been mistaken in his former sentiments. Even his sudden retreat did not entirely alter her opinion, for Matilda knew that Sir Alfred always exercised his own mind in perpetual subjection, and entertained a paramount desire to conceal his feelings from ordinary observation. Strangers might have imagined that if any person suddenly dropped down dead at his feet he would have remained as cold and self-possessed as before; but there were a few people in the world, and Matilda had formerly been one of them, from whom he sought no concealment, and to whom he revealed the inmost depths of a mind which glowed with feeling and sensibility. She had often blamed herself for wasting time on the remembrance of one whose absence was in itself a mark of indifference; and general report had led her to believe him so entirely changed, that with all the strength of a well-exercised and well-principled mind, Matilda had resolutely crushed out of her heart every thought that could endanger her peace. She had ceased to think of him except as an interesting acquaintance, in whose conversation there had been a degree of intellectual fire and vigor never equalled by any one since; and she now resolved not hastily to believe what her heart and her hopes suggested.

"You see Sir Alfred is very constant!" whispered Eleanor to her cousin, when a noise of talking prevented the possibility of her being heard.

"How!" exclaimed Matilda, starting.

"Did you not observe! when I threatened never to marry a member of Parliament, he immediately wished to lose his election. Nothing could be more decided."

"What a salutary lesson for me, to distrust my own impressions," thought Matilda, as the remembrance arose to her mind of the tears Miss Murray had often shed in describing her long-lost sister's tragical end. "I must avoid such a fate; and that can best be done by continuing to *doubt*; for no girl's affections are ever irretrievably given to another, until she previously believes herself to be loved. It is our nature to return tenfold what is bestowed, but no more to be first in attachment, than for the moon to give light before the sun has shone upon it. Many a time have I sympathized over the withering disappointments of others, who have confided their sorrows to me, but now I must be the faithful guardian of my own happiness, and allow no vain fancies to cheat me of my tranquillity."

Nothing gives us so low an estimate of our own attractions as being in the society of those we most desire to please. Matilda's mind, however, became calm in proportion as she succeeded in convincing herself that Sir Alfred's had been an almost boyish fancy, when she was scarcely yet grown up, but that now he had probably seen many superior to herself, and could not long continue to feel the interest in her which for a moment he betrayed; and being resolved at least to think on the subject no more, she again endeavored to fix her attention on the gay absurdities of Mr. Grant, who had a sort of *laisser aller* in his conversation, which rendered him infinitely diverting.

"How very handsome your poodle looks to-day, Miss Fitz-Patrick! Is it true that you have Blanco bathed every morning in eau de Cologne? His coat is really as smooth and white as floss silk! What an acquisition he would be at those taverns in London where a dog is made to walk round the table during dinner, that the company may all wipe their knives and forks on his back!"

"Mr. Grant," replied Eleanor, in a remonstrating voice, "I generally make a point of *trying* to believe what you tell me."

"Well! so you ought!—I appeal to Sir Alfred if that is not the case. Douglas! *You* have seen it done fifty times?"

"Not above twenty!" replied the Baronet, ironically, "and I always contrived to have the advantage over everybody else, because *I doubled up the tail!*"

"Now! of all the obligations in life there is none equal to being thoroughly backed out in a story. Sir Alfred, you may tell anything you please for a month to come with impunity as I shall vouch for it, even if there is a tongue thrust into every other cheek in the room."

"Very generous indeed! but I greatly fear *your credit* might be easily overdrawn; and indeed I thought it was a little shaken yesterday with your account of Sir Evan's scanty housekeeping, and the starving mice running about with tears in their eyes."

"But did I tell you of my honored uncle's favorite *egg soup?*—an egg is boiled every day for himself, and the water is distributed to the family. If a bottle of wine is ever drawn in the house, too, he has it labelled '*Poison*,' to prevent any one but himself from venturing to taste it. No wonder his daughter Mary was glad to marry anybody, poor girl."

"*A propos*, have no new marriages come out lately?" inquired Lady Susan Danvers; "they are few and far between at present."

"I refer you to Mr. Grant for the last assortment of gossip," replied Eleanor; he telegraphs Edinburgh for all the events that have or ought to have occurred there, and has a perpetual supply of the newest matches on hand."

"Every one *quite certain*," added he, in a tone of decision. "The only thing to be regretted is, that I am not on the list myself."

This was said with his usual careless off-hand tone, in which Matilda traced nothing but total indifference; yet Eleanor instantly colored, giving a little conscious laugh, and a coquettish toss of her head, which would have been infinitely amusing to any one less truly interested in all her feelings than her cousin, who regretted to observe Miss Fitz-Patrick so blindly unaware of the change which had evidently arisen in her former lover.

"I am told," said Miss Charlotte Clifford, "that there are nine-and-thirty marriages on the tapis at present."

"Suppose we make the fortieth!" exclaimed Mr. Grant, eagerly.

"Now, Charlotte, what do you say?" cried Eleanor, laughing; "this is rather a public declaration, certainly!"

"I generally propose to every young lady during her first season, if I am *sure* of being refused, because then she can boast with truth of having rejected somebody."

"But that happens to Charlotte every day! We know of at least a dozen last winter, and I only wonder what would be good enough—peers, officers, authors, travellers!—she must be waiting for a Lord of Session!"

Lady Susan now drew her chair forward and assumed an aspect of the deepest attention, while Mr. Grant, with a degree of gravity and importance suited to the occasion, drew out from his pocket a numerous collection of old letters. "Are we quite among friends?" said he, carefully turning over several papers. "The strictest secrecy must be observed. Douglas, pray step aside, because you are such a gossip, that my news will be repeated all over the country by to-morrow."

"I don't care who marries, provided nobody marries me!" replied Sir Alfred, looking *accidentally* towards Eleanor.

"I publish the banns of matrimony, then, between Miss Brown and Mr. Smith—that is positive, having been declared last week!"

"Who are they?" asked Lady Susan, anxiously.

"How should I know? very excellent people, I dare say, and extremely suitable!"

"There was a Miss Brown, or White, or Grey, or some such color, that I remember once rather admiring and bringing into fashion at Cheltenham," said Colonel Pendarvis; "but it was nearly two years ago, so she must be quite *passée* now."

"For my part I hate *new* beauties!" observed Mr. Grant, with an arch look at his cousin. "I never thoroughly admire any face till I have been accustomed to it for eight or ten years."

"Pshaw, Mr. Grant! now tell us of somebody whose name at least we know," continued she, impatiently. "What does it signify to me whether such people as these marry or not?"

"But, Lady Susan, if those in whom you are interested *will not* marry, how can I help it? Let me see—the list is only begun! A brother of the Queen of Naples, to the Grand Duke of Baden's half-sister—that is important! we are getting into high life now! Lady Susan Dan———oh! pardon me!———hem—not yet announced———hem—splendid alliance—hem—long attachment———um—magnificent settlements and jewels——"

"Ah, Mr. Grant! this is not fair! you are become a fortune-teller rather than a newsmonger," interrupted Eleanor. "There are others of the present company who might enlarge your list," added she, looking slyly from Miss

Marabout, simpering on an opposite seat, to Mr. Armstrong, who was humming the tune of "Meet me by moonlight!"

"I should like to know," said Matilda, "how long this world would last in the hands of a thorough gossip; because every person must marry immediately, and die not very long afterwards, to furnish them with entertainment."

At length a dressing-bell rung, and the whole party were dispersing to prepare for dinner, when Matilda hastily stooped down to collect some of her drawing materials, which had been scattered on the floor by Lady Susan's dogs. Supposing her to be gone, Colonel Pendarvis eagerly asked, in accents of admiration, who she was; and before Matilda could emerge from concealment, to effect an escape, Eleanor drew a sketch which evidently pointed out to her own admirers in what light she wished them to consider the original.

"A cousin of mine! quite a saint, and very blue! You have heard of my aunt, Lady Howard, who is a perfect polyglott of languages?—speaks Latin fluently—could tell if there be a dot too many in Dr. Porson's essays, and asks gentlemen whether they prefer the plays of Euripides or Sophocles. Her daughter is exactly such another—teaches Sunday schools, and is quite in the *good* line. If you ask her to dance a quadrille, she will answer with a text; and only last week I saw her *mooning* at the window so long in the evening that she is evidently trying to count whether the stars are an odd or an even number."

Colonel Pendarvis shrunk into the farthest corner of the sofa, and put up a screen, as if he were seeking protection from such a terrific being as Matilda heard herself described. Lord Alderby turned up his eyes with contempt, Major Foley shrugged his shoulders with horror, and Sir Alfred calmly fixed his penetrating eyes on the heiress's laughing, triumphant countenance.

"I deny the whole indictment, Eleanor!" said Matilda, rising when she found it impossible any longer to avoid being produced, though the necessity for coming so unexpectedly forward covered her with confusion. Her bright eyes sparkled with animation, her transparent complexion glowed with more than its usual brilliancy, and an expression of modest sensibility added a charm to her countenance which nothing could have excelled. Hastily gliding out of the room, she merely whispered to Eleanor, in a tone of gentle reproach, "Defend me from a *candid* friend! You deserve to be prosecuted for a libel!"

So completely had the heiress's suitors understood their *cue*, from what Eleanor said of her cousin, that not one in the number ventured to express the admiration which could not but be felt by them all, at her graceful appearance, except Mr. Grant, who exclaimed, with his usual independence of thinking and speaking,

"Look to your laurels, Miss Fitz-Patrick! I always maintained there was no one fit to draw in a curricle with you, except Miss Howard, and I think so still. Now, gentlemen, let me rise to explain, on the present occasion, that I like to see *the game of life* played with *fairness*, and as her portrait was rather highly colored some minutes ago, I must bear my testimony to having formerly talked to Miss Howard often without being one bit the wiser. We never discussed 'that great Roman Emperor, Pliny the Second,' nor did we quote either Dionysius of Halicarnassus on Gunpowder, or Professor Tiptoe's Essay on Greek Participles. She was always very lovely and interesting, but so improved of late, that I scarcely recognized her in the morning, and now my eyes are really quite dazzled by that beautiful apparition."

"So it appears, for you have been completely blinded," replied Eleanor, with an angry laugh. "For my own part, to say the truth, I never could see much to admire in Matilda."

"A good-humored expression, for instance?" said Mr. Grant, watching the heiress's, which was visibly irritated.

"If that be all, you might as well admire Miss Murray."

"So I do! beyond measure! A country clergyman once observed in his sermon, when I was present, that 'a good temper was *an invaluable blessing, worth five hundred a-year*;' and to those who can afford to pay for such a luxury, I really think it must be. Miss Murray seems rich in good qualities,—and ditto, I am convinced is Miss Howard."

"What an excellent plan it would be, if people's accomplishments and good qualities could be sold by auction when they are of no farther use!—Matilda, according to your way of appraising her, might acquire a tolerable income, whereas now she has none at all, and I could afford to part with several of mine."

"In fact, people are apt to do so very often when they grow rich, and to part with some that I could not dispense with, at any price. But," added Mr. Grant, resuming his usual tone of heedless vivacity, "the grapes are sour when I talk of wealth, being so poor myself that it would make me bankrupt any day, if I went twice in succession to the theatre."

"It is an infallible sign of people being rich when they talk of poverty," said Eleanor; "those who suffer in earnest, try to conceal their necessities. I suspect you must have succeeded to some large addition of fortune lately, Mr. Grant?"

"A legacy of six and eight pence; and I am trying to live upon the interest," replied he, strolling towards the door, and singing,

"How happy 's the soldier that lives on his pay,
And spends half-a-crown upon sixpence a-day."

"Pray, Grant!" cried Colonel Pendarvis, following, "if Sir Evan makes his exit from public life, leaving you £10,000 a-year, what shall you do?"

"Spend £20,000 a-year, of course!"

When Matilda had succeeded in effecting her very rapid retreat from the drawing-room, she was astonished to observe Mr. Armstrong following. "Miss Howard," said he, with a bitter smile, "you are not much more obliged to Miss Fitz-Patrick for her attention and hospitalities than myself. If you only say the word, we shall soon take the gilt off the gingerbread,—you guess what I mean,—but remember that Sir Robert Walpole said, '*every man has his price.*'"

Matilda looked at her unexpected companion with surprise, and with a transient apprehension that he might be slightly deranged; but nothing appeared on his countenance, except a prying expression in the very prominent eyes with which he seemed endeavoring to read her thoughts. "Mr. Armstrong," said she, "you suggest ideas to me which I have no wish to entertain; and, in speaking of Miss Fitz-Patrick, remember in whose house we are."

"Perhaps I know *that* rather *better* than you do, Miss Howard. If you want to open that riddle, apply the proper key. The oracles long ago never spoke for nothing. Consider what I say, and perhaps you may hereafter think more wisely of it than now. 'Better to flatter a fool than to fight him.'"

After saying these words, Mr. Armstrong walked away, singing the old Jacobite tune, "Geordie sits in Charlie's chair," words he had a constant habit of humming to himself whenever Eleanor became particularly repulsive in her manner to him, which was certainly not seldom.

CHAPTER XI.

"The graceful tear that's shed for others' woe."

Matilda did not often retire to the privacy of her own room, without devoting some portion of time to the serious consideration of all that had passed within and around her. She usually enlivened the natural cheerfulness of her own mind by a remembrance of what had pleased her taste or amused her fancy, but, above all, she carefully recalled everything that might enlighten her understanding or improve her heart; and on the present occasion, when she stirred the fire, and sat down in solitude to ruminate over the days which had elapsed since she last occupied that apartment, a variety of thoughts and emotions crowded into her mind. Mr. Armstrong's language and conduct had, during their earliest acquaintance, excited her distrust, as she saw that, from personal pique on his own part, he wished in some way to make her a tool for his revenge. She greatly doubted whether his power was equal to his inclination in working the mischief he threatened against Eleanor; and though she perfectly understood his insinuations on the subject, no possible way occurred to her imagination which could give them the slightest probability. Not a thought could be wasted for one moment on the idea of purchasing his secret, if he had one; and being more than half convinced that his hints were about as unfounded as the promised discoveries of the celebrated Mr. Ady, she dismissed them all at once from her recollection.

Matilda's next reflections were directed, with a smile of irresistible derision, to the remembrance of her own surprise and mortification at discovering the entire oblivion to which Mr. Grant seemed to have consigned their former intimacy; and she readily acknowledged that it ought to have been anticipated in one whose acquaintance was so universal, who formed intimacies every day, and might forget them as easily, and whose notions of friendship perhaps resembled those of B * * * * * l, when he once remarked, that if he lost a friend, he had only to walk down St. James' street and *take another.*

There remained but one subject which Matilda's young and inexperienced mind was unwilling to approach, even in the silence and solitude of her secret retirement, and which she postponed to the very last, because it filled her with confusion and perplexity. To a well-regulated disposition like hers, the earliest dawn of a sentiment till then unknown, and of which the depth and the influence had been as yet unfelt, must ever excite a salutary apprehension that the heart may lose that harmony and cheerfulness which have hitherto been its most precious ornaments; and therefore Matilda, with all the powers of reason and reflection, long struggled against the conviction which formerly forced itself upon her mind, that she was an object of peculiar interest to Sir Alfred Douglas. In the secure foundation and the simple structure of her happiness, love had seemed like a rich decoration, which embellished the existence of others, but which could never be meant for her; and feelings which might hereafter be the blessing or the misery of her whole earthly existence, must be cautiously entertained, lest her future life should be deservedly embittered by remorse as well as by disappointment. Delicacy and prudence prohibited her from thinking of any man as a lover, until he gave ample reason to believe that the sentiment originated with himself; but though her affections were not to be won unsought, there had been much in the manner of Sir Alfred *once* to warrant her belief in his attachment. Attentions, which in an ordinary person might have been scarcely remarkable, became conspicuous from him, on account of his singular reserve to other ladies; and he possessed a peculiar tact, by which his most trifling actions acquired meaning and expression, as if they intimated that he cared not to be understood or regarded by any one but herself. His voice had always, latterly, assumed a different tone, in speaking to her, from that with which he addressed another; his manner then testified that sensibility which he concealed from every one else, and his conversation had been frequently filled with a recollection of her favorite expressions and opinions, which seemed to be treasured up in his mind with a degree of interest and pleasure such as he appeared ashamed himself to acknowledge. There was nothing in all this which pledged his honor, and Matilda might have succeeded in persuading herself, as she resolutely attempted to do, that he merely preferred her society on account of the transient amusement it afforded him; but Sir Francis Howard by no means inclined to take that view of the subject. He constantly rallied his daughter about the crest of the Bloody Heart and the return of the Black Douglas, thus keeping up recollections which her own good sense would, if possible, have banished entirely, for hers was not a mind which could long be contented to dwell in the fool's paradise of imaginary happiness.

Matilda had been frequently warned, that it is customary, in the present day, among many gentlemen, along with the most marked attention, to make such enigmatical speeches to young ladies as may either mean a profession of attachment or a declaration of indifference, according as they are understood. She had sometimes even laughed at instances which were related to her of the ingenuity with which this can be done, but yet she became aware, that in all cases of unhappy self-deception, however justified by circumstances, the lady must bear the blame as well as the sorrow. Many of her own friends had been fatally deceived into a permanent loss of happiness by putting the construction which seemed to be intended upon such treacherous expressions and equivocal conduct; but though Matilda did not imagine Sir Alfred Douglas to be capable of the vanity and selfishness which must prevail over honor and conscience in all who would seek an attachment which they meant not to return, she felt fully impressed with the probability, from his so suddenly retiring, after the first impulse of surprise at perceiving her, that whatever his preference might once have been, it was now, perhaps, extinguished and forgotten, while she acquitted herself from having been misled entirely by vanity, as Sir Francis had made the same mistake with herself, if indeed it *was* one. Matilda could not but at this moment reflect upon an incident which deeply impressed her own mind two years before, with a consciousness of the danger there may be in implicitly trusting to any such accidental attentions as are met with frequently in society. Walking one day along Queen Street with her friend, Miss Adelaide Montague, who was then not much older than herself, they accidentally saw Colonel Pendarvis riding past on horseback; but immediately on observing them, he reined in his beautiful steed, and rode up. It was Adelaide's first winter, during which she had been a reigning beauty of the season, and the Colonel's assiduities were so conspicuous and incessant, that every tea-table in Edinburgh settled, without delay, exactly how much a-year he *had*, or expected to have, as well as the day when his marriage was certainly to take place. On the morning which Matilda now remembered, Adelaide's eyes sparkled with animation at this unexpected rencontre, and the handsome Colonel spoke in a tone full of vivacity and pleasure.

"Miss Montague! quite delighted to see you! What a charming day! I am in perfect despair! Our marching orders are come for to-morrow, and I go with the first detachment. We are all breaking our hearts, I assure you. But one consolation is, that the head-quarters are to be at Brighton! Anything rather than Ireland. *A propos*, you will be diverted to hear that our *spare* Major is fairly caught by your friend, Miss Wentworth. I'm afraid it's a lost case. Good morning! My best regards to Lady Montague and your sister."

When Adelaide had acted over all the surprise and indifference which were suitable to the occasion, she took a smiling farewell of the lively Colonel, and hastened on. Matilda felt her companion's arm weigh more heavily upon hers as they proceeded, while the few remarks she made remained unanswered, till at last she stole one single glance at Adelaide's face, and saw the consuming anguish which was painted there. Miss Montague silently and rapidly pressed her hand, when they reached home, and vanished into her mother's house; but Matilda never afterwards forgot that expression of mute despondency, and when, in society, she heard the frequently repeated "wonder" how very soon Adelaide Montague's looks had "gone off," and the constantly reiterated witticism, declaring that she now only deserved the last syllable of her name, "*laide*," that scene recurred to her thoughts, and she could neither wonder nor smile; though from that hour it became forcibly impressed on her mind how many might have fallen the unsuspected victims of a too ready belief in the apparent preference which may now be shown, in accordance with the usages of society, but the real fallacy of which she felt that it was well for herself to know. It had interested Matilda much that morning accidentally to witness the first meeting which took place between them afterwards. Colonel Pendarvis, with a polite and graceful bow, expressing his fear that Miss Montague might not do him the honor to recollect that he formerly enjoyed the pleasure of knowing her, and Adelaide's equally well-bred reply, that she perfectly remembered long ago having been introduced to him, yet Matilda could not but observe also the bitter smile which followed his retreat, when he bowed himself off; and earnestly did she now desire and pray that such feelings as those of her friend were at that moment might never be her own.

Her ruminations now painfully turned towards Eleanor, in whom every blossom of good seemed to be entirely withered beneath a blazing sunshine of prosperity. It was with an emotion of pity rather than of displeasure, that she remembered the language respecting herself which had been so recently overheard; yet with still greater earnestness than before, did Matilda wish to hasten from Barnard Castle, and she determined on speedily writing to her mother, more urgently, if possible, than she had already done, entreating to be recalled, and reiterating her request that Sir Francis would come for her without delay, though she very much suspected that her former messages to him on the same subject had never been delivered; and she was aware that he felt much occupied with the prospect of her brother returning from England for the Christmas holidays, while Sir Richard and Eleanor were also looking forward to the arrival of the two young Fitz-Patricks from Oxford, neither of whom had ever yet seen their sister's splendid inheritance.

Amidst the anxieties and perplexities thus crowding into Matilda's mind, she dwelt with pleasing recollection on the days passed at Gaelfield. They seemed like a verdant spot in the arid desert around, when she thought of the sympathy and kindness, the cheerfulness and peace, which had awaited her there, undisturbed by any apprehension of petty insults from her capricious cousin, or by uncertainty with respect to the sentiments of those around, or the conduct she ought herself to adopt. Conversation and employment were there so completely in accordance with devotion and piety, that half the difficulty seemed to have disappeared of preserving in her mind that continual desire of holiness, and that incessant remembrance of her sacred hopes and duties which are so incumbent on a Christian, and the deficiency of which, nevertheless, they have all such frequent occasion to deplore. Her thoughts and feelings on that subject were then laid open without reserve to friends who understood them, and could advise her, from long experience in every mental struggle and in every unforeseen difficulty; for all who have advanced, like them, in a Christian course, must learn, by deep and afflicting experience, to sympathize in that perpetual combat of good and evil which wars in every human heart where *any grace* exists; and simple as was Miss Murray's mind on other subjects, she could speak upon this with the knowledge and the authority of long practice, and of frequent success. The strength was not in herself, but she knew where to seek it with infallible expectation; and she spoke of her experience, and of her hopes, with the genuine eloquence of nature. When Miss Murray described her unsophisticated feeling, it seemed to Matilda like the voice of her own earliest childhood, for the hymns and the texts which first delighted her infant mind were those to which her aged companion continually referred, with unfading interest, as being the words which constantly beguiled her time, as well as directed her conduct and thoughts. The high tone of principle and of feeling which were hourly more developed by Dr. Murray, in proportion as he learnt to appreciate the cultivated mind and enlightened piety of his young companion, seemed to Matilda as if he thus led her visibly onward in a Christian course. Deeply had she lamented the necessity for leaving a retreat of so much heartfelt serenity and real enjoyment, to enter on the present scene of tumultuous amusement and artificial pleasure; and though there appeared little as yet to excite any grave disapprobation, even in the most censorious, there was a want of that *reality* in the feelings and the conversation, which would have excited her confidence and regard.

It was not a life of "cloistered indolence" which Matilda would have preferred, because few young people enjoyed society more than herself, but she desired only to see it established more upon the Christian principle of kind feeling and considerate recollection for others. Though there appeared now more of temptation to levity and forgetfulness among the gay scenes on which she seemed about to enter, than she ever experienced before, Matilda reflected that they were not her own voluntary choice, and that therefore she could confidently ask to be shielded amidst its dangers, and even venture to hope that her mind would be strengthened by the difficulties she might yet have to conquer.

Eleanor informed her guests that the dressing-bell rung only to intimate that there would be dinner in the course of that evening, though she professed to be so liberal in her hours, that it was impossible to say when; yet Matilda now discovered that little time remained to prepare for the very late period at which it was her cousin's whim to dine, and she roused herself to commence the duties of her toilette. Nanny soon afterwards entered the room, and began hastily arranging, or rather disarranging the dressing-table, while, to Matilda's surprise, she rapidly opened and closed a succession of boxes and drawers without any apparent object, and yet with a degree of nervous excitement and agitation which could not but be obvious. It had been recently reported by old Mrs. Gordon, the housekeeper, that Martha, being at last fully persuaded of her sister's indifference to William Grey, had consented to accept of his frequently repeated offer, and that their wedding was to take place without delay. This might in some measure account for a degree of incoherence and confusion in Nanny's manner, which had lately become perceptible, though she mentioned her sister's engagement some days before without any apparent surprise or emotion. Persuaded as Matilda had always been, that the poor girl was almost unconsciously attached to William, she pitied with her whole heart the misguided folly by which Nanny had estranged, and finally lost his affections. But though, in speaking on the subject to Matilda, she once confessed that her conduct towards her former lover had been foolish, and that it now occasioned regret, there seemed besides, at that time to be some unacknowledged anxiety and distress on her mind, totally unconnected with Martha and William, of which Miss Howard knew nothing, and which she appeared unable or unwilling to mention. During the drive from Gaelfield that day, Matilda now remembered that Eleanor accidentally dropt some insinuations against Nanny, and accused her of dishonesty; but thinking it was merely her usual way of haranguing against servants, as if they were all convicted thieves, or that it resulted from their peculiar good fortune if they were not, she paid very slight attention to her cousin's words at the time. Often had Matilda warned the poor girl of her imprudence in many respects; but now she thought only of her distress; yet as Nanny averted her countenance, and evidently shunned observation, Matilda proceeded to dress without immediately showing any consciousness of her presence, or of her singular proceedings in the room. Miss Howard possessed that feeling, so inseparable from sensitive minds, that affliction must not be hastily intruded upon; while no disparity of circumstances made her feel entitled to forget that delicacy, and even that respect, with which, while endeavoring to draw out the confidence of others, we must cautiously approach their sorrows. She heard with commiseration and surprise a deep sob of agony, which Nanny vainly attempted to choke back, and she felt shocked to observe the tremulousness of her hands, when there was occasion for her assistance; but desirous to ascertain the extent of her distress before she spoke, Matilda placed herself in such a position, that Nanny's countenance became unconsciously reflected in the opposite mirror.—Never was Matilda more startled and astonished than to perceive the alteration which a short time had produced on the youthful countenance which she now saw distorted with suffering. The color had entirely fled from Nanny's cheek, her very lips had grown livid, and every feature of her face seemed convulsed with weeping, so that it would scarcely have been possible to recognize her. With an irresistible impulse of surprise and sympathy, Matilda turned hastily round, and taking the poor girl's hand, she earnestly inquired what could have happened to cause such overpowering distress. A smothered, hysterical sob was all her reply, and the unfortunate sufferer seemed too much exhausted even to weep. There was always a magnetic power in the tears of others to draw forth those of Matilda, and her own eyes overflowed at the sight of such intense suffering, while she led Nanny towards a sofa, and placed herself upon it. Unmindful of Miss Howard's desire that she should do likewise, the unfortunate girl seated herself on the ground at Matilda's feet, and covering her face with her hands, she wept aloud.

"Nanny!" said Matilda, vainly trying to raise her, "tell me what has happened!—say, if I can console you!—rise and sit here—let me know everything that has occurred. I pity you from my very heart already, but perhaps we may be able also to assist you. Let me advise you, if I can; or at least let us pray together that you may find better comfort than any earthly friend can bring——"

"Oh, Miss Howard! I could not have lived till this hour if it were not for the hope that you would feel for me," cried Nanny, wringing her hands with a look of frightful agitation. "My heart must have burst, if you had not asked me to speak—oh! promise that you will not believe me guilty. You knew me from my happiest days, before I ever entered this house—do not cast me off at the first breath of suspicion. Say only once that you will remain my friend, and I may still preserve my senses." Nanny paused with a wild hys terical laugh, and looked anxiously into Matilda's countenance, while the color rushed for a moment over her face, and as instantly retreated, leaving her, if possible, paler than before.

"Trust me, Nanny," said Matilda, in a soothing tone, for she was alarmed at the sight of such extraordinary agitation, "I could not credit any stories against you; it would be a sorrowful hour for me if I did! Can I forget that you were Lady Olivia's favorite pupil—that your mother instructed you at home—that you were always a diligent and grateful girl! Oh, no! you may have acted thoughtlessly, but I could make myself responsible, without a moment's hesitation, that you have done nothing really criminal."

Nanny clasped Miss Howard's hand in hers, and buried her face on the sofa, unable to speak, while Matilda silently waited till she had sufficiently recovered the command of her voice, when, after some vain attempts to articulate, she became at last able in broken sentences to make herself understood.

"I am heart-broken, but not guilty," said she, in feeble accents. "They may destroy my good name, but they could not make me forget my duty. I can look you in the face, Miss Howard, with as much innocence now as I ever did in my happiest days: but to-morrow I am to leave this house disgraced and miserable. All that was precious in life is gone—my character has been blasted by those who wished to humble me. I have found no pity, and no help. Never shall I forget the lessons of my childhood, and they have preserved me now. I knew you would not believe their cruel stories—you are the only person in this house who will not. Oh! when my mother hears it all—when Martha is told the worst—it will break their hearts!—yet they must know it is false. And William, too! what does *he* think?—but that is no matter *now!*"

At these last words Nanny clasped her hands over her face, while large hot tears slowly coursed each other down her cheeks, and she became silent.

"Nanny! it cannot be so hopeless, surely? I believe you to be innocent of this calumny, whatever it is," cried Matilda warmly, for she saw that this assurance alone seemed to have any power in composing her agitated companion. "Tell me all, and depend upon it justice shall be done. Miss Fitz-Patrick must be informed of the circumstances without delay, and she will do what is right on the occasion."

"No! no!" replied Nanny, despondingly. "Her ears are already poisoned against me. This has not been the business of a day, and those who contrived my ruin have completed it; they convinced both Sir Richard and my young lady that I was always worthless and dishonest. Various trinkets have lately been missing in this house, especially from Sir Richard's cabinet and Miss Fitz-Patrick's jewel-box. Some of these were yesterday found concealed in a flower-stand, and I am accused of having secreted them there. It was even said that William, who came every morning to water the plants, had taken that opportunity to carry them off, and many of the most valuable are still missing. The bitterest stroke of all has been that *his* good name should be injured through me, and his place taken from him. We met to-day, Miss Howard,—he came to comfort me,—to say that he had got employment at Sir Evan's,—to know if he could be of any service,—to propose that he should break it all to my mother,—but the sight of him, after what has happened, was worse than death. Martha will make him happy, and she deserves his affection,—I never did, and least of all *now*."

"I shall speak to Miss Fitz-Patrick this very evening. You must not suffer an hour longer than can be helped; remain in my room till dinner is over, and depend upon it I shall bring you comfort; there must be some cruel mistake, and my cousin will rectify it at once."

Nanny closed her eyes, and mournfully shook her head. "You are as kind as I expected, Miss Howard! very kind! words cannot say what I feel,—but no one can help me, for the web is stronger than you think. Pauline has often been in the habit of wearing my young mistress's shawls; she went out last night in one of them,—her conduct became improper, and she was in very bad company. Stories were repeated to Miss Fitz-Patrick of what passed on that occasion; and Pauline has contrived to persuade every one that it was I, and not herself, who appeared at that hour. I remained alone in my room all the evening, suffering great distress of mind on other accounts, but that was nothing to what has befallen me since. I had lately avoided been seen, so no one can testify that I was really at home. I had found out my folly in many ways, and repented of it, but nothing can clear me now. I am bowed down to the very dust with shame and sorrow. My mother's gray hairs will be dishonored,—my sister's name is disgraced, and I dare not even ask to be laid beside my father in the grave. Oh! what shall I do, Miss Howard? The whole world is in darkness now! Will no gleam of light ever shine on me again?"

Matilda felt a nameless apprehension steal over her thoughts as she saw the wild tumult of Nanny's mind, the increasing incoherence of her manner, and the burning hectic which glowed on her cheek, and which lighted up her eye with unnatural brightness. The gong had sounded for dinner long before she left off endeavoring to bring peace and composure to the broken spirit beside her. Matilda's words of comfort fell like flakes of snow on a burning desert, so soft and so refreshing was all that she said to the suffering mind that it was her desire to cheer; and she did not leave Nanny without obtaining a promise, given with some degree of serenity, that she would retire to bed, after seeking for peace and support where alone it can never fail to be sufficient.

CHAPTER XII.

Sedentary weavers of long tal
Give me the fidgets, and my patience fails.
COWPER.

WHEN Matilda entered the drawing-room, the whole gay party had assembled, forming a brilliant contrast to the scene she so recently left. Lively groups were scattered about the room, all apparently animated by the highest spirits; and she looked around to ascertain if there was any individual with whom she felt sufficiently acquainted to place herself; but all were already engaged, or else comparative strangers, and Eleanor was so surrounded by her satellites as to be quite unapproachable; therefore, feeling very much like some person who had dropt from the clouds, and belonged to nobody, Matilda quietly glided into a chair, as near her cousin as possible, and began examining a volume of prints, to diminish the awkwardness of sitting alone and unnoticed. Meantime she stole an intelligent glance around, to observe what was passing, and felt as completely *au fait* in reading the plot of all that was going on, and as far removed from taking an active part in it, as if she had been seated in a side box at the opera. Lady Montague and Mrs. Clifford appeared to be in deep and consequential conference, probably comparing the relative prices of their milliners' bills, or else each praising her own daughter, in a confidential tone, to the other, and boasting of the brilliant talents and prospects of their respective sons. Sir Richard occupied the whole fire, which was large enough to have roasted an ox, but he contrived to spread himself entirely over it, holding by the button Dr. Murray, to whom he was eagerly demonstrating on the subject of politics. Mr. Grant had placed himself beside Miss Murray, and seemed for once to be talking gravely and in earnest, with a degree of respectful deference towards his aged companion, which, in Matilda's estimation, did him honor. Eleanor continued to be hemmed in by a cordon of beaux, each of whom seemed to rival all the others in the brilliancy of his own sallies, and in the readiness of his laughter at hers. Not far off was a contrast to this noisy coterie. Sir Alfred Douglas had retired to a distant corner of the room, externally in a state of suspended animation, though an unconscious knitting of his brow seeemed to indicate that his mind at the moment was not so inactive as his body. His eyes were half closed, and overshadowed by the dark clusters of his hair; his head was thrown back; his arms folded, and his legs stretched out to their fullest extent, so that Matilda could have laughed to see how impregnably he had fortified himself against the possibility of being invaded by any one. Before long, however, she had reason to suspect that her estimate of fashionable intrepidity was too low, for Miss Charlotte Clifford evidently intended, by a daring enterprize, to carry the outworks; and she was amused to observe, when Sir Alfred first became aware of that young lady's approach, a momentary smile that glittered only in his eyes, and the sly humor with which he observed the proceedings of his unexpected assailant.

"What an enchanting day this was, Sir Alfred;" said she, dropping accidentally into a neighboring chair.

"Indeed! I am glad it pleased you."

"Of course it did! we had a west wind and sunshine all day."

"Had we? Now who noticed all that? You never could have observed so much yourself?"

"I am half dead, Sir Alfred, this morning, with the fatigue of riding to Gaelfield."

"I can't help it!"

"Was that a new britschska you came in this morning? What a variety of equipages, I am told, you sport! Pray tell me how many?"

"I shall have them counted some day, and let you know."

"Do you mean to hunt at Melton this year?"

"No! Do you?"

"Pshaw, Sir Alfred! what nonsense you talk!"

"Merely for the sake of contrast, that I may be as different as possible from you."

"Now that is quite polite and proper! I shall repeat what you have said to every person in the house, because civil speeches are not supposed to be your forte. How agreeable it always makes people when they go to the Continent!"

"*You* have never been there I believe?"

"No! but I have a cousin-german at Paris. By the

way, one's cousins-*German* should all come from Vienna or Dresden."

"Your geography is all astray, Miss Clifford! Did you never hear that Dresden is in China? I am sure you might know better, when we dine every day off Dresden China."

"So we do! How very strange that I—— *A propos*, you will be delighted to hear that Mr. Grant, who can prove any two people that he pleases to be related, was showing us this morning, that you are actually a Scotch cousin of Eleanor's."

"How glad she must be! Miss Fitz-Patrick has something *now* to boast of."

"Yes! she will probably inscribe on her tomb-stone, 'Here lies the cousin of Sir Alfred Douglas.' Talking of that, did you admire Père la Chaise?"

"I am not very apt to admire," answered he, turning a laughing eye towards Miss Charlotte herself; "'*all seen*,' as Lord Byron says, 'but nought admired.'"

Matilda had been listening to the whole of this dialogue with infinite diversion, and suddenly looked up, while her countenance sparkled with so much archness and vivacity, that it caught even Eleanor's notice; but she hastily dropt her eyes on the album again, when she unexpectedly perceived that Sir Alfred Douglas was intently observing her.

"What have you got there so very amusing, Matilda?" exclaimed the heiress, in a tone of curiosity. "Did ever any one behold such a student? Dr. Johnson was a joke to you! but dinner waits, and we positively cannot allow of that book being brought to table, which would be done, I dare say, if you durst."

"I know of several excellent boarding-schools for young ladies, where that is actually insisted on," observed Lady Montague. "My daughter Maria, at Elysium House, was always obliged to learn her Italian exercise while she breakfasted, and her Euclid during the intervals of dinner. The girls walked out in pairs, one guiding her companion along the path, while the other read aloud from the best works on science and natural history; besides which, the French governess repeated verses to them all the time they dressed. Nothing could be more admirable than the whole system, and I only lamented being obliged to take my daughter away, because of that long unaccountable illness she had, which has never entirely left her. It is, I must say, a great mortification to me, that, with so many accomplishments, she can scarcely leave her sofa, and that, with a perfect knowledge of every language in Europe, she has hardly strength to speak even in English."

"The Manchester cotton-weavers, with their sixteen hours of labor a-day, are nothing to this," cried Mr. Grant, laughing. "When I get into Parliament, my first exploit shall be to present a petition from the distressed young ladies of Great Britain, praying to be relieved from excessive taxation on their health, their spirits, their time, and their understandings."

After a long procession had moved to the dining-room, and every preliminary arrangement was happily settled, so that no lady should be too near the door, or too far from the fire, or above or below her proper place—and after Lord de Mainbury had been called up, and Mr. Armstrong received a hint to go down, order seemed to be in some degree rising out of confusion, and Matilda found herself seated next to Sir Colin Fletcher. Opposite was Sir Alfred Douglas, but as no attempt had been made on his part to approach her, she at once determined on encouraging the conviction of his indifference, and on preserving her own by the consciousness of his.

"No one will venture into this chair between us," observed Eleanor, who never took the head of her own table, and placed herself now within one of her cousin. "Your learned reputation has caused quite a panic among the gentlemen! only think, we have been laughing for an hour at the terror poor Colonel Pendarvis is in!"

Matilda was surprised at the audacity with which the heiress alluded to her own misrepresentations, but though it did cost her an effort, she resolved to preserve her good-humor, and tried to change the subject immediately.

"Eleanor! if we enjoyed the privilege, which ladies had formerly in France, of choosing what gentleman shall sit next to them at dinner, I wonder if we could agree whom to summon now?"

"Mr. Grant, of course," said that gentleman, inserting himself into the empty space. "Are not your utmost wishes anticipated?"

Both ladies smiled a gracious assent, but Matilda soon experienced what she had previously anticipated, that it would be hopeless to attempt appropriating the smallest fragment of her lively neighbor's attention, which Eleanor claimed and entirely monopolized, while an animated dialogue instantly commenced, and continued almost without interruption till dinner was over. Having no more amusing employment for her attention, Matilda listened with great animation to what followed, though she was allowed no opportunity of putting in a single remark. Mr. Grant's conversation with her cousin seemed a complete contradiction to the proverb, "nought comes of nought," for all that passed was literally "much ado about nothing," and yet so entertaining, on account of the light spirits and gay expression of the speakers, that it was impossible not to be exceedingly amused. They did not talk absolute nonsense, though approaching to the very verge: no opinions were revealed—no sentiments expressed—no facts stated—no questions asked. The conversation had no visible object and no useful tendency, yet it never flagged for a moment; but glancing at everything, and skimming the surface, it seemed to glide along with such abundance of sail, and neither rudder nor ballast, that Matilda wondered every moment it was not stranded altogether, while they carried it on without effort, and almost without thought.

"Now, Mr. Grant, there is a laugh in your eye that tells me you are going to be satirical!—is it a droll remark or a dry observation?"

"Let me try the droll remark—hem!—what shall I say! —hem!—what a delightful day this was!"

"So I have been told a hundred and fifty times already! If that be meant for a sample of your powers, I shall turn to Lord Alderby on my other side. You shall be allowed five minutes to strike out something new!"

"I do not require two seconds! Some people are obliged to search their minds for ideas, but mine rush out like a pack of hounds from the kennel every time my mouth opens. The only difficulty is to keep them back."

"Then pray be very original and amusing without a moment's delay."

"In your company that is not difficult."

"How! do you think me so easily pleased?"

"Quite the contrary!—my meaning is, that I need only take example from yourself."

"Now, that is the only tolerable thing you have said for a century! I perceive, Mr. Grant, that your wit is a mere annual, which flourishes but once in a season. You probably live at the rate of an idea a-year! Be sure to set down that last good saying in your common-place book for future use."

"Perhaps I never write one."

"Impossible! every human being does! Did you *never* hear Mrs. Ramsbottom's advice, that we should all 'keep a *dairy* for the *cream* of what we see?' Why, even my maid Pauline, who has not three ideas, keeps her journal!"

"What a literary gem it must be! I could form a tolerably correct guess of the subjects recorded therein—a list of her true lovers, followed by a catalogue of how many gowns Miss Fitz-Patrick ought to have left off wearing."

"Now, that is a severe hit at my old black velvet! How I detest mourning!—all my cousins and relations may depend on being regretted, if they oblige me to wear black. People should mourn in white, like the Chinese. One thing I have fully made up my mind about: if ever I am in a widow's bonnet, to wear some pink bows under it, for that is the most odious dress altogether that has ever been invented!"

"So it is! How fortunate for me, that I shall never live to behold my widow in full costume!"

"Not unless you are buried alive! But tell me what you think the most becoming of all dresses."

"Black velvet."

"That is a proper *amende* to my respectable old gown. But now, seriously, Mr. Grant, and upon your veracity, what *do* you think?"

"I never was half so serious on any subject before, as in declaring that every lady might be a beauty in my estimation, if she would wear black velvet and diamonds. I give you no credit whatever for looking well in them. Lady Susan herself would be quite young and handsome in such an equipment; but show me the beauty who would be tolerable in a quaker's cap."

"I shall wear one to-morrow."

"But then, perhaps I may give out that your cap is set at me."

"No one would believe it! However, for your comfort, Miss Murray certainly intends to do so. She has been watching us all dinner-time;—what a dear old dot she is!"

"Truly excellent, indeed," replied Mr. Grant, with sudden gravity. "I do not know her equal in the world. Miss Murray, will you do me the honor to take wine? How I wish you were all like her!"

"What a dull, respectable world it would be!—why, the very art of laughing would be lost, and that is the only faculty we possess which animals do not."

"Philosophers have discovered now, that laughter is always at the expense of others, and therefore it must be a very unamiable propensity. I never have a good opinion of people who indulge in it much."

"Then take the consequences, Mr. Grant, for I shall not do more than smile at your next bon-mot, if it be ever so good."

"That would be exceedingly ungrateful, for I have laughed heartily at many of yours, when they were none of the best. But, Miss Fitz-Patrick, you are not properly sensible of half your obligations to me."

"Indeed! what may they be? You remind me of Mr. Armstrong, who frequently hints that I owe him unutterable gratitude for something or other, which is never explained. Now, pray come to particulars."

"It was only yesterday that I wore out an entire set of intellects in trying to understand some of the worst puns you perpetrated."

"Did I ever degrade myself to punning?—impossible!—your bill is protested."

"Well, then, I danced last year with two plain, elderly misses at your own ball, to make it go off well."

"Ah, that seems worth mentioning!—it is a tolerable *cheval de bataille*, so let it stand. I begin to blame myself for not having sufficiently appreciated your merits."

"Besides, I spoilt a good ear for music this morning by listening to your attempts on the flageolet."

"You are running up a perfect national debt against me! —How flagrantly ungrateful I have been! If Mr. Armstrong ever makes out as good a case for himself, I shall be covered with confusion."

"Stop a moment; you have not heard the half yet! I lamed Scatterbrain yesterday, in trying to make you admire my riding—I forced a laugh when you criticised my singing —I lost a night's rest in trying to recollect the name of that novel you wanted—I risked my life in going to the greenhouse for the sprig of myrtle you have on——"

"Not so fast, Mr. Grant! I sent you a box of jujube lozenges this morning, so your cold must be cured. It is never the sign of a generous mind to make the most of people's obligations. The new definition of gratitude is only for favors that are coming, so I owe you none at present. We must explain this to Mr. Armstrong also, if ever I vouchsafe a word to him again."

"Miss Eleanor Fitz-Patrick! will you take wine?" said the unconscious object of her animadversions.

"I wish I had fifty names, that he might give me them all!" said she, laughing affectedly, and pretending not to hear; but on Mr. Armstrong repeating his proposal, Sir Richard called her attention to it, and she was obliged to accede. "Only a single drop, if you please, Mr. Grant! I would refuse, if I durst, but papa is observing me, so we must *drop* the business in this way. Now, watch my bow, for it will be a model of repulsiveness. Ah! quite a failure! he seems as pleased as possible, so my countenance is destitute of expression."

"What a remarkable talent Mr. Armstrong has acquired for introducing into conversation the titles of all his great acquaintances," remarked Mr. Grant. "It was very diverting to hear him yesterday endeavoring to *out-peerage* Lady Montague, who goes already by the name of Lady M'Quality, on account of her adulation for rank. I am credibly informed that she puts on slight mourning for every Scotch peer who dies, because they were all her distant cousins, which assertion most people are too polite, or too indifferent, very closely to investigate, therefore she passes for being most highly, as well as very extensively connected."

"My uncle, Sir Francis, calls her the peerless Lady Montague. For my own part, I never learnt the game of 'Catch Honors;' but I fancy the conversation in that corner of the table must greatly resemble it. Mr. Armstrong first brings out Lady Ben-Nevis,—then Lady Montague trumps her with the Dowager Marchioness of Dumbartonshire, and Mr. Armstrong tables the Duchess of Cairngorum, and *takes the trick!*"

"How different that sort of vanity is from the real dignity of my friend Douglas, who never imagines he could borrow importance from any circumstance, or from any person. If he were made a peer to-morrow, or if he lost his all in this world, it would leave him unchanged. I should like to see the acquaintances, the equipages, the houses, or the estates, that *he* would think worth boasting of! But few men have such a well-balanced mind. I am *not sure* if I could even say as much for *myself!* Did you ever hear that when the late Lord de Mainbury got a title, he and his son, in order to fit themselves for London society, began with exercising each other in the peerage? and I am told it was very hard work before they both *got it up* thoroughly. 'What is the family name of Lord Inchkeith? How many daughters has the present Duchess of Cairngorum? Who is heir presumptive to Viscount Broadstairs? What title does the Marquis of Glencoe's eldest son take?'"

"Mr. Grant! you are growing satirical!"

"I can't help that, as Douglas always says,—but you know, Miss Fitz-Patrick, two of a trade never agree."

"I despise your insinuations! everybody says that I err on the side of good-nature. Even Miss Murray is much more satirical than I am; but, as the shuttlecock said to the battledore, 'you like a hit at your friends.' I begin to be afraid that you will take *me* off next."

"Pray let it be in a chaise and four then!" replied Mr. Grant, with a tone of careless jocularity which might have shown to the most superficial observer how little he expected or desired such a *dénouement*. It was evident, however, that Eleanor by no means understood his meaning in this light, for she colored deeply, and nearly pulled her bouquet to fragments, while he rattled on with other subjects, totally unsuspicious of the impression which had been produced by these few accidental words.

Tired at length of merely listening and smiling, Matilda now wished to vary her amusement, seeing she was no more expected to take a share in the dialogue between Eleanor and Mr. Grant than if it had been a debate in the House of Commons, and desiring, if possible, to have some conversation herself. The first person on whom her eye rested, in glancing round the table was Dr. Murray, flanked on one side by Lady Susan, who had turned her back upon him in the eagerness with which she spoke to Colonel Pendarvis, and on the other side, also *dos-à-dos*, by Lady Montague, who seemed engrossed with Mr. Armstrong in a conversation which appeared to be as dull as a Court Guide, or a visiting book.

"How very strange!" thought she; "the brightest talents; the profoundest learning; the truest philanthropy, and the most extensive knowledge of science, of nature, and of revelation, are all at a discount here. No one near Dr. Murray would willingly listen to the glowing eloquence with which that voice can speak,—to the clear light he can throw upon our condition and prospects,—to the plans of usefulness, of kindness, and of mercy with which that heart is teeming. Yet there is no look of angry superiority, while he listens to the development of minds so inferior to his own He does not wrap himself up in a self-satisfied elevation of intellect, but would evidently conform in a great degree to the humor of those around, if they gave him opportunity. I remember Dr. Murray saying lately, that he never was in company with any one from whom he did not learn something. I wonder if he would say so still!" Matilda's eye next caught the placid, smiling countenance of his sister, who had been for some time attempting to understand the conversation of Eleanor and Mr. Grant. Though the effort was evidently vain, she seemed pleased, nevertheless, to observe so much vivacity, and looked from one to the other, testifying the same sympathetic interest with which she might have watched the playful gambols of two lively children. Miss Murray being eminently endowed with a heart that thinketh no evil, seldom suspected any, unless something was forced upon her notice which appeared flagrantly wrong, and therefore, amidst the ebullition of frolicsome spirits before her, she still hoped there might succeed hours of serious thought and salutary meditation. There are those in the world who believe every man in the wrong till he is proved to be right; but this rule was reversed by Miss Murray. Others hear with astonishment and incredulity any favorable comment on the faith or practice of those about whom they know little, or perhaps nothing; but no traits of excellence in her acquaintances ever took Miss Murray by surprise. There is a vulgar old proverb which says, 'set a thief to catch a thief,' which is never more glaringly exemplified than in the case of those who suspect that others are hypocrites; for a true Christian, being himself incapable of deceit, will be slow to imagine it in his neighbor. Miss Murray always suspected some lurking good, where the world saw only evil. She felt sceptical about nothing but the faults of her associates, and 'shifted her trumpet' when they could no longer be defended. There had always been some perplexity in her mind with respect to Eleanor, which daily intercourse only increased. She felt occasionally a dim suspicion of being herself an object of ridicule; and she had lately lamented the heiress's gay indifference to the privations and sufferings of others; but still Miss Murray looked upon her with partial indulgence, as a child of prosperity, in whom better feelings might yet be developed, while she frequently added her prayers to her hopes, that present scenes, with all their dazzling brightness, might not permanently blind her young friend to the all-important future.

When Matilda's eye met that of Miss Murray, the good old lady nodded and smiled to her with such an expression of beaming benevolence and of natural simplicity, that her heart at the moment might have been compared to some modest wild flower amidst a collection of exotics, so artificial were the manners and feelings of those around her, amongst whom any traits of nature, or any expressions of serious recollection, would have been considered an outrage on good-breeding, and an infringement on social comfort.

About this time Eleanor, with that laudable ambition which she often testified, to raise her dogs on a level with herself, sent for a second supply of soup, which she gave to Blanco; while Lady Susan, not to be outdone, soon afterwards minced down carefully, for Tiny, a slice of Turkey which Sir Richard sent for her own consumption. The dogs being hungry, "licked the platter clean," and a footman, in haste, put Tiny's plate on the sideboard, from whence Martin, without becoming aware of any previous destination, traasferred it to Lord Alderby. Matilda, being the only person who observed this oversight, made a hasty signal for the objectionable plate to be changed; but she colored with confusion to observe the astonishment of his lordship at her unaccountable interference, which it was impossible to explain, and she could not but think afterwards that those ladies who blame a Roman emperor for promoting his horse above human nature, should *look at home.*

Nothing is half so rapid as thought, and much of this passed through Matilda's mind in the course of five minutes, when at length she observed Sir Richard's eye fixed upon her. It was his frequent remark, that vacant chairs are better at a dinner-table than silent guests, so she now determined to make an essay of her conversational powers on Sir Colin. Seeing that he was occupied in anxiously investigating the bill of fare, she ventured some leading remark upon it, by way of commencing a dialogue, but she unconsciously addressed one of those public talkers who disdain to waste their tediousness upon solitary individuals. Merely giving a hasty, constrained reply, he continued eagerly watching for the first opening into which his word and his story might be inserted, amongst a knot of joyous *bon vivants* who gathered round Sir Richard near the head of his table.

Matilda was now consigned to irretrievable silence, and she could not resist smiling to observe that Sir Alfred acted the same part from choice which she did from necessity, as he had succeeded at last in reducing Miss Charlotte Clifford, his persevering tormentor, to a state of quiescence. She now endeavored to cover her defeat by a spirited attempt at engaging Sir Richard in conversation, though he was so engrossed with his public duties, as host, that her success became laughably deficient. Of all the forlorn hopes that any one can volunteer upon, none is more desperate than that of monopolizing much attention from a hospitable country gentleman presiding at his own table, of which Matilda now saw an amusing exemplification.

"This was a charming day!" said Miss Charlotte, who seemed never to tire of praising it.

"Lady Susan Danvers! will you take wine?—port or sherry? Sir Colin calls this *vin cheri*, it is so excellent! Were you speaking to me, Miss Clifford?"

"This was a——"

"Douglas! try that salmon; it was in the river three hours ago! Alderby! send Lady Montague a paté. Pardon me, Miss Clifford: I am all attention!"

"This was a char——"

"Dr. Murray! as Mathews says, 'you are not a *soup-or-fishial* man,' I perceive! A disciple of Jephson's, evidently. Well! it is what we must all come to, sooner or later. I would rather not live at all than live on a rule-of-three diet. De Mainbury! try that *vol-au-vent.* Made on a Leamington prescription, you may depend upon it. Were you remarking anything, Miss Clifford?"

"I merely said——"

"Fletcher! that Madeira has been forty years in bottle! Excuse me, Miss Clifford!"

"My observation was very insignificant; merely that——'

"Lady Montague! pray call for a screen! you don't stand fire well!"

Matilda's countenance had been gradually kindling with animation as she watched the fate of Miss Charlotte's valuable remark, which was destined never to struggle into existence at all. She now hastily averted her eyes, to conceal a smile which irresistibly forced itself on her countenance, and, in turning another way, she unexpectedly received a look from Sir Alfred, so full of archness and humor, that she was completely taken by surprise. Often, on former occasions, the same expression had glittered in his eye beneath an external aspect of gravity, as if he wished her alone to perceive it, and now she felt almost as if a renewal had taken place of their intimacy, and that possibly he might still be unchanged from what she once thought him. "Time might have altered me also," thought she, "and a whole year may have changed all that he used to prefer. I have always thought that when people meet after a long absence, they are scarcely the same individuals who became originally attached, for years transform our sentiments, our opinions, and our spirits, as much as our appearance. If Sir Alfred ever thought as I once had some reason to believe, he may still perhaps find me the same." Matilda observed, however, that he did not ask her to take wine, nor in any way follow up their intercourse, so she again resolutely dismissed the subject from her thoughts.

Sir Richard Fitz-Patrick had now attained the paradise of hospitality, applauding his own cellar, as if his very existence depended on its being appreciated, and listening with good-humored delight to a chorus of approbation which followed the drawing of every cork.

"This hock might do for the Antiquarian Society! I dare not mention its age!" said he, in a tone of exultation. "Without vanity, I may assert that it excels anything we tasted at Clanpibroch Castle last week."

"I'll answer for that!" exclaimed Mr. Grant.

"Does your uncle not keep a well-filled cellar?" asked Colonel Pendarvis.

"I know of none except the salt-cellar. Sir Evan never gave me anything formerly but Cape Madeira and gooseberry champagne. I never can conceive where such things are bought! One day, however, I remonstrated seriously, and told him my terms, that I never dined out under a bottle of claret."

"By the way, Grant, could you give me leave to shoot over the Clanpibroch property next season?" asked Colonel Pendarvis. "Your uncle preserves so rigidly, that they tell me he has a keeper for every bird; but as I mean to Scotlandize again in August, and shall visit this neighborhood, it would be desirable in good time to secure the privilege."

"You shall have it then! but only on condition of adopting the plan that I shall suggest—otherwise there is not a chance."

"Well, let me hear it! What would I not gladly undertake for a shot over such capital moors!"

"That being the case, you must shoot Sir Evan first, and afterwards *I* can give you leave."

"How very obliging, Grant! Pray, accept all the thanks you merit for so friendly an offer, and take a glass of Burgundy with me. It turned out rather stronger than my pericranium yesterday, but no matter. If I get such another *mal de tete* again, some person must be hired to take my head off, and wear it for me till morning."

"Martin!" cried Sir Richard, turning angrily towards the butler, "you have omitted to cool this champagne! It might have been iced with the vegetables, they are all so cold."

"Talking of *sham pain*," began Sir Colin, loudly,—"the best pun in the world, except one of my own, which you shall hear afterwards, about *Cure us a'*; but next to that, the cleverest bon-mot I remember was one of Sir Jonathan Fowler's, which you shall hear, about champagne——"

"Meantime join me in a glass of it, Fletcher!" interrupted Sir Richard. "I got a supply from the Continent this month, and wish to have the public opinion. What I had last turned all at once into vinegar."

"This is inimitable and to show you how much I think of it," said Mr. Grant, "if somebody would present me with a pipe of the same, I would actually accept the offer."

"That wine is so mild, you might drink it in tumblers," continued the hospitable host.

"Then, Sir Richard, we should very soon be *tumblers* ourselves."

"Seriously," replied the Baronet, with an air of conscious merit, "I scarcely believe any one could possibly find its equal."

"Rather flat," replied Lord Alderby, with a dissenting shake of the head.

"That is a *flat* contradiction, at any rate!"

"Why, Fitz-Patrick!" exclaimed Lord de Mainbury, "your wit sparkles like your champagne!"

"Yes," pursued Sir Colin, "and the story which I was about to relate, and which you may all perhaps now be at leisure to hear——"

"Pendarvis! try that hock!—it was in bottle long before *your father* was born."

"I shall respect it accordingly, Sir Richard."

"No one venerates *a good old age* more than I do," said Mr. Grant, turning to Lady Susan, and asking her to join him in a glass of wine; "it certainly *wears well*."

"I am steady to the champagne," said Lord Alderby.

"Then you'll not be *steady* long!" observed Mr. Grant.

"As I was saying," resumed Sir Colin, looking around in desperation for a listener, "about the sham——"

"Fletcher!" interrupted Sir Richard, "we are trying a new cook to-day, and I wish you would eat down one side of the table, to let me know your candid opinion of his skill. It is intolerable to see any one wasting a good appetite on roast mutton."

Sir Colin, it was hoped, had now been effectually silenced, as the whole party were aware that he entertained no higher ambition than to be reckoned skilful in the science of gastronomy. No geologist could have understood the strata of a mountain more perfectly than he did that of a fricandeau, and his knowledge of chemical analysis was profoundly practical among sauces and seasonings. Unfortunately, however, like all superficial philosophers, he was more addicted to lecture than to study, and therefore Sir Richard's quietus did not long remain effectual, for he soon broke silence, in a tone all the more consequential, for having been thus publicly appealed to as a high authority.

"Fitz-Patrick! I have dined at Windsor—I have lived at Crockford's—and I keep a first-rate French cook myself; therefore my verdict may be supposed to carry some weight with it. You will be glad to hear that this is a very clever fricassee."

"Keep your own counsel, then, Fletcher! No good politician praises any dish till he has dined on it, and I generally make a grimace of disapprobation when most pleased, on purpose to cause a diversion in my own favor. Let us all try something different to-day, as it really hurts Monsieur Martigny's feelings extremely when any dish goes down untouched, so that I shall make it a duty to partake of whatever no one else has ventured to attack."

"How very different from me," cried Colonel Pendarvis, laughing. "My old aunt Grace, who grows every day richer and shabbier, became so saving, many years ago, that, during my juvenile visits at Yorkton Abbey, it used to be as much as my head was worth, if I presumed to be the first who opened a tart, or invaded any fortress of pastry whatever. Since then I have stormed the breach at Bergen-op-zoom, but never did I suffer more real apprehension than in once attacking such a castle of whipped-cream and almond-biscuits as this! Shall I ever forget one day, after my return from Spain, her whispering to me during dinner, 'You may take the blanc-mange, but the jelly will keep!'"

"Really," said Mr. Grant, "those rich old aunts and uncles, who exceed the age of fifty or sixty unmarried, should all retire on a pension, or be put to death in the easiest way that can be devised."

"Aunts are sometimes very respectable people too!" interposed Major Foley. "One of mine was exceedingly kind to me formerly, during the Eton holidays, and I shall never forget that day, when a letter reached me in the barracks, announcing her death. We were all sitting at the mess, when it was put in my hands, and being then quite young and unsophisticated, I instantly started up to leave the room. Our senior captain anxiously stopped me, to hope nothing distressing had occurred, and if you will believe it, the whole table burst into an explosion of laughter, when they heard me announce, in doleful accents, that 'my aunt Dorothy was dead!' you have no notion how abashed I felt; but they made me sit down again, and in two minutes and a quarter my grief was over."

Meantime Sir Colin's lectures still continued, while, with a bill of fare in one hand and his fork in the other, he prosecuted his investigations. "A cook should receive every encouragement, and be accustomed to consider himself as the most important functionary in the house, or he cannot be expected to take proper pains. I have a tray of tea-cups, filled with different kinds of soup, brought to my room every morning to be tasted, in order to judge which would be preferable for dinner, and my *chef* declares I am the only master he ever served who is really worthy of him."

"No doubt!" said Mr. Grant. "You ought also to try a plan which was adopted by the French epicures long ago, Sir Colin, to encourage exertion; they dropped half-a-crown into the sauce of any dish which pleased their palates, and thus the artist was *crowned* with approbation."

"I protest, here are woodcocks again!" exclaimed Sir Richard, in a discontented tone. "Why, Eleanor, if you go on in this way much longer, we shall have *bills growing*."

"And that would make you *bill*-ious," added Sir Colin, falling into such immoderate fits of laughter at his own wit, that he continued speechless for some minutes. "That saying of mine reminds me of the most amusing story imaginable. I have laughed at it for hours alone——"

Matilda looked breathless with expectation—universal attention was excited—and Sir Colin became at last happy in having obtained "possession of the house," which he endeavored to keep as long as possible.

"I heard the incident from Lord Ben-Nevis—who had it from Sir Jonathan Fowler—or rather, I believe, it was Lady Fowler who told it to the General's brother——"

By this time the attention of most people relaxed, and many began gradually to talk aside, while, as the circle of Sir Colin's audience perceptibly diminished, he felt obliged to lower his voice accordingly, until Matilda remained the only person whose ear he could command. The bright look of intelligence with which she had watched his promising commencement, gradually faded into an air of constraint, and in proportion as the narrator's tediousness increased, so much the more difficult did she find it to force her thoughts away from more attractive sounds of mirth and repartee which were exploding in all directions around; yet, even on such trifling occasions, Matilda had a prevailing sense of duty, which taught her not to seek entertainment at the expense of mortifying another. To spare Sir Colin any such degree of chagrin as the continuance of her solitary attention could do, after his more distinguished auditors had forsaken their allegiance, she resolutely chained her ears to his narrative, while in a dull, monotonous voice, the baronet wound his way through a labyrinth in which he soon got entangled and nearly lost. Matilda could not but privately think that her present annoyance might do admirably in a new edition of the Miseries of Human Life. At last she was called on for a complaisant laugh, as a chorus to the loud peal in which Sir Colin indulged when his story reached an end, and immediately afterwards he turned away to watch whether a larger circle of auditors could, on a future opportunity, be attracted.

When Matilda's eyes were released, she found the whole party in joyous anticipation of a proposed excursion on the ice next morning, since, to the utter discomfiture of the sportsmen, it was reported that a hard frost had set in for some hours, and that snow several inches deep was already on the ground.

"In Scotland," said Colonel Pendarvis, "people should all hunt with a pair of skates in their pockets, in order to secure some amusement for the day in so changeable a climate."

"It never snows in England," observed Mr. Grant, dryly; "and the Serpentine is to be frozen by Leslie's machinery, in future, about Christmas, that you may practice skating."

"We shall have a delightful exploit on Loch Deveril to-morrow!" exclaimed Eleanor, in an ecstasy. "Unluckily, it is too cold for gipsying under a tree and broiling chops in the open air; but we may order a picnic at the fishing-lodge, and skate about all day with a tumbler of hot negus in one hand and a biscuit in the other. I could live forever on the ice!"

"So could I, with the party you propose," added Lord Alderby, bowing and shivering.

"Is skating one of your accomplishments? I thought, my lord, your favorite aquatic amusement had been, as Dr. Johnson describes fishing, with a fly at one end and a fool at the other!"

"There is a *rod* for you, Alderby! said Mr. Grant.

"Let me tell you, Miss Fitz-Patrick," added his Lordship, "that no one knows what perfect happiness is until he has hooked a ten-pound salmon, and played it on the line for an hour. Pray try the experiment."

"Thank you! but I have other *game* quite as diverting, Lord Alderby; and sometimes I do fish in very shallow streams for compliments"

"Your only difficulty is, probably, to avoid being deluged with them."

"There! Miss Fitz-Patrick!" cried Mr. Grant. "If you were angling, that was 'a glorious nibble!'"

"I remember a laughable story of Dr. Johnson," began Sir Colin, glancing anxiously round the table for an audience, but every eye became carefully averted, and even Matilda looked inexorably away for some time, but was at last obliged, being next him, to become compassionate, and endure the endless detail of a well-known narrative, which she could have told twice as well in half the time.

"Any one who saw me to-day, for the first time, would imagine that I am dumb," thought she, when the story was ended, for Sir Colin did not wait to hear her make a single remark, before he relapsed into a state of watchful vigilance over the jovial party whose attention it was so much his desire to entrap.

"This ice is the merest snowball I ever tasted, Eleanor!" said Sir Richard, in a criticizing tone. "Could Monsieur not have thrown in a glass of Frontignac, or even a bit of brown bread, to flavor it. Send me the preserved ginger, that I may add a relish of something."

"Douglas!" cried Colonel Pendarvis, "I calculate the wine has stood with you nearly one minute and a half. Your mind seems to have been absent so long to-day, that I wish we may ever be able to bring it back!"

"The *mouton qui reve* is the worst sort of mutton I know at a dinner-table, and should be roasted without mercy," added Sir Richard. "As for circulating the bottles, I have a plan for forcing everybody to recollect that duty. They shall be made *not to stand alone.*"

"Then," replied Sir Alfred, "before long, none of your company will be able to *stand alone* either."

"When you are come to *that*, we ladies ought to withdraw," said Eleanor, rising.

"Stop one single moment, and you shall hear a most diverting circumstance," cried Sir Colin, eagerly addressing Miss Fitz-Patrick; "it can be related in very few words——"

This threat seemed only to accelerate their flight, but as the ladies were moving away, Sir Colin said to Matilda, in a promissory tone—

"You need not suffer for this precipitation, Miss Howard, because I shall tell it all to you in the drawing-room, where there will be more leisure to enjoy the details than if I had hurried them over now."

The smile which glittered on Matilda's countenance at this formidable threat was mistaken by Sir Colin for one of pleasure; but, in hastening away from table, she again caught the animated eye of Sir Alfred, whose archness and vivacity of expression seemed like a momentary gleam of lightning, revealing a glimpse of that mind which it appeared to be in general his pleasure to envelop in impenetrable obscurity, and she again felt surprised at the peculiarity of his conduct, in not placing their intimacy on former terms, or else appearing more entirely to forget it.

"Matilda! you have shown a talent for silence to-day," said Eleanor, satirically. "I think all you have said during the last four hours might be printed in a duodecimo page."

"Probably it might! I am like an echo, only able to speak when I am spoken to."

"Now I evidently perceive your intention is to set up for the reputation of *modest merit*, which is one of the most troublesome characters in society, and one of the most easy to support that can be conceived, though, let me warn you,

Matilda, that generally the vainest people affect it. Who has not been tormented, at some time or other, with that pride which apes humility among second-rate ladies, though you ought to be above it? I have had visitors of that kind here, who lived in a continual expectation of being overlooked and undervalued—who remain silent, unless particularly addressed, because they cannot presume to expect the honor of being listened to—who sit in an obscure corner of the room, unless called forward to the most conspicuous—who would pass their best friend in the street, because they would not be supposed to feel certain whether the said 'best friend' meant to notice them at all—whom no constancy of regard can teach to confide in the good-will of those who are above them in rank, and who require more anxious attention than any peeress of the party, on account of the obscurity which they seem to court, and in which, nevertheless, they would feel equally surprised and indignant to be left for a single hour."

"I am trying to trace the connection between all you say, Eleanor, and my silence at dinner, for unless I had done like the French preacher, who took up his hat in the pulpit, and held an argument with it, you can scarcely suggest any way in which a conversation could have been supported."

"Ah! your modest merit wears a different fancy-dress. When others commit themselves in conversation, you have the pleasure of silently thinking that you would never have been so caught; when others are preferred, then modest merit whispers, that if it were not for an interesting sensitiveness of disposition, you might easily eclipse all competitors; and if you condescend at any time to give out a remark, or to exhibit any little accomplishment, then comes modest merit, expecting the greatest *empressement* of attention, because it is so easily discouraged, and so seldom comes forward; therefore, in fact you, Matilda, can pass off that simple plea of modest merit as a sort of paper currency for every virtue, while, on the contrary, poor Charlotte Clifford and I frankly display all the rubbish of our minds, without a wish to pass for being more than mere every-day mortals. I would not for worlds seem better than I am conscious of deserving; but if we were all turned inside out, Matilda, some people might appear in a very different light from what they do."

"That would be rather an unpleasant experiment, certainly; but as you acknowledge its being my turn to speak now, pray listen to me for a few moments."

Matilda then related to Eleanor, in terms of the warmest feeling, all that she heard from Nanny that evening, with respect to the unfortunate misrepresentations which had taken place in the house, and entreated that they might be thoroughly cleared up, if possible, without delay; but Miss Fitz-Patrick's ruling passion had become a love of power, and one of the ways in which it appeared, was, that she never chose to act or think in the way that other people expected. If her cousin had endeavored to produce a strong feeling against Nanny, and a perfect conviction of her guilt, it would then probably have been treated as a trifle, and listened to with ridicule and incredulity; but perceiving that Matilda's feelings were strongly excited, and that she entertained no doubt of producing a similar emotion by the simple narrative of all she had seen, Eleanor, to show the independence of her own judgment, spoke of Nanny's sufferings in a tone between pity and contempt.

"Poor creature! she is the vainest and silliest mortal in the world! It has been already a most intolerable bore to have a pensive, romantic Abigail; but I was only too indulgent on the present occasion, for now she has turned out worse than you have the least idea of. Both Pauline and Mrs. Gordon have a very bad opinion of her. At the same time it is quite unnecessary to look so shocked and alarmed, for justice shall be done to all parties, therefore pray do not invariably expect that whatever I do shall be wrong."

"You mistake me, Eleanor, as you always do, *now*," replied Matilda, "but I must persevere a few moments longer in importuning you about Nanny. She is one of the last remnants of Ashgrove, and we have both known her from a child. Do, dear Eleanor, let there be no delay in trying to exculpate her. Every hour is a lifetime, while she remains under these false imputations, and nothing could possibly persuade me that they are true."

"You always had a prejudice against Pauline, Matilda. It is strange that we never, on any occasion, or even by accident, like the same people; but Mrs. Gordon's opinion ought to have some weight with you, and she gives a very indifferent account of Nanny for being extremely light-headed. Indeed, any one may see that in her whole dress and manner. I quite regret having ever had anything to do with her!"

"You may often find occasion to say so, Eleanor, if this business is neglected, for that poor girl is breaking her heart about it. Oh! think seriously for your own sake, for hers, and for the sake of our beloved aunt, who taught Nanny to value her good name as she does, and let immediate investigations be made, before she is consigned to irretrievable ruin!"

"Matilda! I know my duty in this house, perhaps, as well as you do, and have no wish to take a course of lectures upon it from any one. I wonder that phrenologists have not discovered a large organ of interferingness in some heads that I know of; but pray endeavor to practise a few of the Christian virtues you so often recommend, and then I may listen with more deference."

"She did not see Nanny's distress, as I did; she has not heard the eloquence of real suffering," thought Matilda. "Let me pardon a few hasty words to myself, and persevere, whatever be the difficulty, in trying to rescue this poor girl from her present misery."

Miss Howard hastened to her own room, where Nanny had been desired to wait for her, but she was surprised to find it not only vacant, but in the strangest disorder, while every door and window stood open to its widest extent, her flowers were all scattered on the floor, her wardrobe unclosed, and her drawers in evident confusion. Hastily rectifying in some degree what was amiss, she, meanwhile, repeatedly rung the bell, but in vain; and at length, with a vague feeling of apprehension, she snatched up her candle, and proceeded in search of Nanny to the housekeeper's room. There, no one had seen or heard anything of her for several hours, and Pauline, giving a contemptuous toss of the head, remarked, that if Miss Howard would send to inquire in the butler's hall, or the steward's room, she might probably be found, while old Mrs. Gordon shook her head, with a look of stern severity, and dryly observed, that, indeed, Nanny little merited Miss Howard's care.

"Mrs. Gordon," replied Matilda, anxiously," "I have known that poor girl since the time when we both were children. She was then the most innocent, guileless creature on earth, and if there be anything greatly wrong now, it is very recent. Let us try, then, to reclaim her. She is in a state of extreme distress, and deserves, even at the worst, our pity. Be kind to Nanny, for my sake, if not for her own, and rest assured I shall take it as a mark of personal attention to myself, if you will treat her with consideration while she so greatly needs it."

"Indeed, Miss Howard, she takes no advice from me! I never stop telling her how foolishly she has acted, and if Nanny loses her character it is no fault of mine."

"Perhaps it may be unnecessary to give counsel now, Mrs. Gordon, for Nanny's present sufferings are the strongest admonition in favor of future prudence. But do not pronounce her guilty of crime till she is proved to be so, and let her not be treated as a criminal while any hope remains that she is innocent."

"I fancy the less we say about that the better, Miss Howard, for it will soon be shown that she is little worthy of so much kind interest."

"If none of us ever got more than we deserve, Mrs. Gordon, how miserable we should all be! let us then imitate that mercy which we hope hereafter to receive, and be slow to take up an evil report. Where will it be possible to find that poor girl, for the state in which I left her was truly pitiable?"

"She has found employment, no doubt, Miss Howard, for Nanny knows how to take good care of herself," said Mrs. Gordon, maliciously looking towards Pauline. "She is not at all fit to wait on a young lady like you, ma'am."

Matilda turned away with vexation and regret, to pursue her search for Nanny, wherever there was a probability of success, but in vain; till at length, despairing for the present, and greatly perplexed how to account for her absence, she became apprehensive of remaining longer alone, knowing that Eleanor would not be sparing of animadversions; so she slowly returned to the drawing-room.

All was liveliness and vivacity there. Sir Richard and his party had joined the circle some minutes before, in a blaze of spirits and good-humor, while Eleanor might be seen fluttering about the room, like a butterfly on a sultry day, her movements were so full of animation, and her dress so *voyante* and gay. Nothing can be more just than the privilege which is given to strangers, of estimating female character at first by the test of their attire, wherein much moral principle as well as judgment may be displayed, and more of the character becomes discernible than could easily be anticipated. It is certain that accommodating external decoration to the progressive advance of years requires a degree of frequent recollection which few are willing to exercise, and some ladies never seem to *ask themselves* the question—"How old art thou?" The fortune and rank of the wearer, also, are not always sufficiently considered; and while some exhibit a lavish expenditure, inconsistent with Christian moderation, others also err in giving way to a slovenly despondency of appearance, in which the proprieties of station are overlooked. There can be no well-regulated time which does not allow sufficient leisure for personal tidiness, while, at the same time, there can be no inward delicacy of mind where anything is sacrificed to outward allurement; and in proportioning what part of an income shall be given to the needy, it is often a duty to afford them employment, as well as to afford them alms; to encourage the industrious, while we relieve the necessitous; and to have it always in view that motives to exertion should be supplied rather than premiums on idleness. Matilda's costume was chiefly regulated according to the rules of that standard work on the subject, "Mrs. Theresa Tidy's Eighteen Maxims of Neatness and Order"—being precisely adapted to her rank, and to the very liberal income which Sir Francis allowed. Though no part of her happiness consisted in dress or show, she had been taught to consider it a duty towards others, as well as towards herself, that there should be nothing in it, of which any friend could disapprove, nor any carelessness of her own to let it be supposed that strictness of Christian principle interfered with the *petites morales* of society. If she had been to pass a whole day in her room alone, still a due care would have been bestowed on personal propriety, and yet nothing she ever wore was extravagant or inconsistent. Her dress fitted well, was carefully put on, and showed to advantage the perfect symmetry of a graceful figure, while the massy folds of her smooth shining hair testified to great attention having been given to it; but from the time when Matilda left her toilette, she thought no more of dress than of the air she breathed. Eleanor's costume, on the contrary, was as capricious as her character. At one time she glittered in jewels like an eastern Sultana; and diamonds sparkled as glow-worms amidst her dark waving tresses,—but on her next appearance she might in all probability be attired like a school-girl, in her white muslin robe *à l'enfant*, with her hair simply braided, and unconscious of ornament. In the same spirit, she was muffled up one day in the utmost affectation of prudery, and the very next opportunity she ventured to the extremest verge of decency. Whatever Eleanor did, or whatever she did not, became always a subject of importance, in her own estimation, and whether the remark might be, "I always wear blue," or, "I never wear pink," it was given out as a matter of consequence which she piqued herself upon. The round white arm of Matilda was almost entirely shrouded from view, and never willingly displayed; but Eleanor's, bared almost to the shoulder, seemed only covered by the profusion of bracelets which adorned it; and her beautifully formed foot and ankle were flourished on every stool in the drawing-room, while Matilda's, of equal symmetry, was never seen, except by accident. Who has not observed the brilliant silks which are obtruded on the notice of every passenger at a shop window, till they become so wearisome to the sight, that anything less beautiful is more attractive? and thus it was with respect to the young heiress's appearance, in consequence of that vulgar-minded ostentation with which she exhibited herself, while the modest reserve of Matilda rendered her an object of watchful interest to many of whose notice she was unconscious.

"So you have taken a siesta till the gentlemen appeared!" whispered Eleanor when she entered the room. "I suppose you are annoyed because I would not fly instantly to be judge and jury at your bidding, upon this fracas between my two Abigails!—Well! with all my faults, I have rather more equanimity of temper than to sit in angry retirement during a whole evening for such trifles; and more might have been expected from one who makes such professions of religion as you do."

Matilda's color rose to its brightest vermilion at this unexpected address, and with a look of indignant surprise, almost amounting to incredulity, she was about to reply, when Eleanor, conscious that she stood on untenable ground, hastened away, leaving her cousin to ruminate with vexation and astonishment on the distorted aspect which her cousin was sometimes able, and always willing to throw upon all she did or said, while a feeling of unconquerable impatience took possession of her mind at being unwillingly detained where she was so evidently unwelcome. No distressed damsel in an enchanted castle could have seen less chance of immediate escape, for Sir Richard's outrageous hospitality, and her mother's positive determination, were more than a match for the readiness with which Eleanor and Sir Francis would have facilitated her wishes; and she could only wonder in silence what might be Lady Howard's object in forcing her to enter a scene of so much perplexity and annoyance.

Meantime, a project having originated with Major Foley and the Miss Cliffords to get up some quadrilles on the carpet, an animated discussion took place respecting the capabilities of the room for dancing; and Eleanor, having, as she hoped, obviated every difficulty, was soon in a state of almost childish glee. Her eyes glistened with anticipated pleasure, while she sung some bars of a favorite galope, and executed a few light and graceful steps towards a retired part of the room, where Sir Alfred Douglas was deeply engaged in conversation with Dr. Murray.

"What a delightful quadrille we shall have!" cried she, eagerly.

"Shall we!!" replied the young baronet, looking rather incredulous. "I hope you have prepared a tight rope for me, as I never dance on anything else."

"Now, Sir Alfred! how teasing you are! we cannot possibly make out the second set without you."

"Try that gentleman in the Spanish chair. He has a disengaged look."

"Mr. Armstrong!! I never speak to him!—and besides, he seems planted in that seat. I do believe he is like the Chinese ladies, whose feet sometimes take root in the floor. But now, Sir Alfred, do bestir yourself without delay, or I shall be obliged to give you up as a *mauvais sujet.*"

"I heartily wish you would,—but since you must know the worst, I am as immovable here as a rock."

"Then you must be blown up with gunpowder; and, indeed, Sir Alfred, if you continue to be so untractable, I shall order the floor to be made red-hot, and then you know even a bear would dance."

"Yes! and with a much better grace than I should," replied Sir Alfred, resuming his discussion with Dr. Murray, in which they both seemed to be profoundly interested.

A fatal impediment now arose to the projected amusement, as all the young ladies were ready to dance, but none of them seemed inclined to perform the music. One was "so nervous," another could do nothing without her own books, and a third had "*made a rule*" never to play for dancing. Mr. Grant jestingly offered to whistle a quadrille; and Eleanor professed her intention to order, without delay, a hand-organ containing the suitable number of tunes. Still the evil seemed without any immediate remedy, when Matilda accidentally became aware of the deficiency, and being glad of an opportunity to do something which could not be misrepresented, she hastened forward with an offer of her assistance.

"Oh! you are the best of human beings!" cried Eleanor, eagerly looking round for her partner. "Dear Matilda! how very kind you are!"

Miss Howard fixed her large speaking eyes on her cousin, and they became suddenly brightened with a tear, for her feelings had been excited previously by reflection on past scenes; and she was now reminded of the time when such words as these had been spoken frequently and sincerely, while she felt how truly they would have been deserved, at any sacrifice, if the hope and the confidence could have been restored with which she had once looked upon their friendship as that which nothing could alter.

"After all, it is a chance if you would have had a partner, and it is better to cover your retreat at the piano, as most of the gentlemen seem provided already," continued Eleanor, who had herself been the person to arrange this. "Perhaps, indeed, Sir Colin, who is dancing to cure the liver complaint, might have exhibited with you some of the 99 steps which he boasts of knowing—or Mr. Armstrong could possibly be stirred up with a pole, as the quadrupeds are in a menagerie."

"Thank you, Eleanor! two more elderly and respectable partners could scarcely have been selected. Perhaps Sir Richard also might have forgot his gout, in a fit of generous compassion," replied Matilda, taking her place at the piano, where she performed her self-appointed task with mechanical precision, while her thoughts irresistibly turned upon Nanny, of whose absence she could not but think with surprise, and whom she was anxious to form some plan for assisting. It occurred to her, at length, how thankfully Miss Murray would embrace any opportunity of doing a kind action, and as there could be no hope of retaining the poor girl longer at Barnard Castle, she resolved on requesting that Nanny might be received for a time at Gaelfield, to prevent the ap pearance of her character having been entirely forfeited Impatient to put this plan in execution, she turned hastily round, whenever the quadrille was concluded, intending to open the negotiation, when, to her infinite surprise, the quadrille party had formed themselves into a country-dance, and she saw Colonel Pendarvis clapping his hands for the music to commence. No sooner did the country-dance conclude than a waltz was called for, and to that succeeded a galope, so that Matilda thought the whole party must have been bit by a tarantula, and yet she scarcely knew how to refuse performing for those who seemed so entirely dependent on her exertions. Certainly there were no very obvious symptoms of gratitude on their part, as she neither saw nor heard any of the dancers, except now and then, when gentlemen came hastily up to her with a message from their partners to request that she would play faster or slower, according as taste or caprice happened to dictate; but it seemed to be considered a matter of course that, as music was the indispensable accompaniment of dancing, it signified little how that might be obtained, so long as it continued to be necessary.

After Dr. Murray had left the room, which he did early, Sir Alfred placed himself near the pianoforte, where it might be imagined he was listening to the music, as no other ostensible object appeared in his sitting beside Matilda. Not a word passed upon either side, and at length Eleanor came up to him, exclaiming, in a remonstrating voice—

"Sir Alfred, you really ought to *do a little popularity* amongst us, since you are canvassing the neighborhood. A dance now would be excellent practice for the election-ball, where every fat farmer's cherry-cheeked daughter will expect a quadrille."

"I would rather, at this moment, relinquish my seat in Parliament than my seat here."

"I wonder what your valet thinks, Sir Alfred, when you return from parties, night after night, without having worn out any shoes with dancing! He must fancy that you have been dreadfully at a loss for partners!"

"So I am! and therefore I never presume to ask one!"

"But did I not hear Charlotte Clifford, say, some minutes ago, when Sir Colin asked her to dance, that she was very much afraid a previous engagement to you would interfere?"

"Let Miss Clifford plead any engagement she pleases, provided I am never asked to fulfil it. Nothing on this side of Circassia would tempt me from my quiet corner."

"I wish we had the enchanted horn which forced people to dance while it was played upon, and then you should not be allowed to sit down for a year. Charlotte would be delighted to perform also for as long a time; and you have no idea how charmingly she galopes—one might suppose she was blown along the floor by a gale of wind."

"How enchanting! If your friend is really such a superlative performer, perhaps she will favor us with a specimen now. Pray ask her to exhibit a few steps here!"

"Well, Sir Alfred! since you are inexorable to Charlotte, perhaps I might be prevailed on to dance with you myself."

"It is very plain why you propose that, Miss Fitz-Patrick, because all the world would immediately exclaim, 'There is the handsomest couple in the world!' but I cannot countenance such inordinate vanity."

"It is more a matter of curiosity, to ascertain how I should feel in dancing, for once, with an unwilling partner."

"You would be as much uplifted by the honor as Abon Hassan during his one day of being a caliph; but, *seriously*, Miss Fitz-Patrick, I have got what is called in this country a sitting-down cold, and I was, besides, given over by the doctors yesterday with a sprained ankle. Pray let me settle here quietly—for life."

Eleanor gave a conscious look, and a blush, at these inadvertent words of Sir Alfred, to which Matilda perceived that she attributed as much meaning as they could carry, while she jestingly replied—

"Then I must make away with myself, since you give me no hope, for I am like time and tide, which wait for nobody; and once lost can never be recalled—Going! going! gone!"

Sir Alfred looked much relieved at the departure of his lively persecutor, and re-established himself in his retreat near the piano, where Matilda observed the inward diversion with which he seemed to watch some daring manœuvres of Mrs. Clifford to provide her daughters with partners for a quadrille which was about to be formed, and before long she had so far succeeded, that Miss Charlotte alone remained disposable.

"Mr. Grant! will you be so obliging as to help me on with this scarf?" said Mrs. Clifford, stopping that gentleman when he was about to glide past. "The room is so cold that my teeth are chattering in time to the music! How I envy you young people who can keep yourselves warm with dancing! Do you mean to join the next quadrille?"

"Yes! and if there are twenty more I am engaged for them all," replied he, hurrying past, with his laughing eyes fixed on Lady Susan, whom as usual he had been teasing. Mrs. Clifford now moved a little way on, till she caught a glimpse of Colonel Pendarvis; but when she had manœuvred herself within two yards of him, he suddenly claimed Miss Fitz-Patrick as his partner, and walked off, while the baffled lady turned round and looked for a moment at Sir Alfred, but evidently considering it a forlorn hope to attack him, she reserved her powers for what seemed possible. "Ah! Major Foley! have you not secured a partner yet?— allow me to——"

"Miss Clifford, you are quite right not to dance any more," interrupted he, hurrying off. "I am tired myself of beating the carpet all night; but really to see dancing like yours to such disadvantage quite shocks me."

"Can any one tell me where Miss Fitz-Patrick is?' asked Lord Alderby, who had been for some time wandering about with his glass at his eye. "She sent me for a camellia to the conservatory, and promised to wait here and be my partner, if I returned in time."

"Miss Fitz-Patrick went off *the instant* you left her, with Colonel Pendarvis; but my daughter Charlotte is disengaged."

"Insufferably hot rooms!" continued Lord Alderby, with perfect nonchalance; "I must positively look out for a more endurable atmosphere."

"Miss Clifford," said Matilda, who felt for the awkwardness of that young lady's situation, "here is a vacant chair which looks inviting, beside me, and perhaps you would add a note or two of accompaniment in the treble to enliven my playing."

"Thank you! but if no better partner occurs to-night, I would rather dance with a chair than sit on one. Nothing is half so dull as looking on at the enjoyments of other people! But here comes my usual *pis-aller*, Sir Colin—I wish it may never be my lot to marry him, as a last resource, for he is always so convenient."

"You might do worse, and you could scarcely do better," said Mrs. Clifford, in a jocular tone. "Young ladies have many more offers of a partner to dance, than of a partner for life, so they may afford to be much more fastidious in the one than in the other."

"Pray, Sir Colin, where is your friend, Sir Jonathan Fowler, at present," asked Miss Charlotte, arresting his steps.

"I cannot be quite certain whether he is at this moment in Rome or in Naples!" replied the baronet, looking rather surprised at so unexpected a question; "but I am searching for Miss Fitz-Patrick, to tell her such a capital anecdote——"

"Stop one single moment, then!" cried Miss Charlotte, as he was hastening past; "I would not for worlds miss seeing the effect of your story on Eleanor!—how she will laugh!—do take me with you to enjoy it also."

Sir Colin looked delighted to have his vanity so flattered; but when the young lady took his arm with an air of discontented resignation, she stole a satirical glance at her mother, and affected to suppress a yawn already, as she disappeared in the crowd.

At last Matilda heard a sudden commotion behind—hopes of release seemed unexpectedly to dawn upon her—supper was announced; and scarcely had she time to look round, before every one had rushed like a torrent to the dining-room, leaving her apparently alone at the pianoforte, where she could compare herself to nothing but a upas-tree in the desert, so completely did she at that moment feel like an alien from society. An unaccountable spell seemed over her, and though partly suspecting that it was by the manœuvres and descriptions of Eleanor, that she had become such a mute in the drama, still that only served to aggravate her vexation, and to make her long the more anxiously for home, where she would again be restored to proper consideration and respect. A moment served for these thoughts, and Matilda rose to hasten towards her own room, when she was suddenly addressed by a well-known voice, which arrested her steps, and caused the color to rise on her cheek, with surprise. She turned instantly round and saw Sir Alfred Douglas approaching, while he evinced in his manner a degree of agitation, and even of embarrassment, not less than her own.

"Miss Howard," said he, vainly trying to conquer a certain tremulousness of voice, "I have been anxious for an opportunity to express my astonishment and pleasure at finding you here! We once agreed formerly—and nothing you ever said escapes my recollection—that all great emotions shun observation. Mine certainly do, and you might judge of their extent to-day, if you could only know the effort which it caused me to control them."

"You succeeded so well, Sir Alfred, that I scarcely felt conscious till now of your having been interested at all on the occasion. I am truly glad on the score of our former intimacy, that we do not really meet now as strangers."

"I trusted that you had known me better, Miss Howard—that you had long understood me—that you never would measure *my* feelings by the degree in which they are exhibited before the world!—*strangers*, did you say?—why cannot I tell you at this moment all the injury you do me by such a supposition, and how unwillingly I would live to see that hour? But I must trust to your forbearance at present, and ask you to believe, that during the long period of my absence, it has been my—my first wish to return, and claim the place I once hoped to have in—in your recollection. Time alone can show how far I may merit its continuance, but we must begin where we left off, with *at least* being friends. More I would say, if I were at liberty to do so, but the day will come when ——— In short, Miss Howard, you well know how reserved I am to the world, but to you I would be perfectly open, and if ever I seem otherwise, ascribe it to anything rather than indifference."

Matilda's color fled and returned, in rapid succession, during these few hurried words from Sir Alfred. She bent her head to conceal the emotion which his manner could not fail to excite, and the long dark fringes of her eyelids dropt on her cheek, while he anxiously watched for the sound of that voice which was so interesting to him, and so exquisitely harmonious that all who heard it once must have wished to hear it again, but he waited in vain, for she could not reply, and a pause of some moments ensued.

This was by no means the first time that a similar warmth of feeling had been testified in the manner and expressions of Sir Alfred, and she could not but remember now the deep interest with which his former language once inspired her. Whenever they were alone, he had then always relaxed from the frozen stateliness and reserve of his general manner, and betrayed all that energy and enthusiasm of character which were peculiarly his own; but such an immediate relapse into formality took place, when there appeared a chance of being observed, that she often, on subsequent reflection, felt painfully perplexed to account for his conduct, and had even occasionally doubted his sincerity; yet it was impossible for her to do so now, when his ardent language was seconded by an expression of reality in his countenance which could not be misinterpreted.

Matilda had been frequently told by Lady Howard, that men of great conceit and little principle are in the practice of endeavoring to make a first impression on young and unsophisticated hearts, knowing that neither time nor circum stances can ever afterwards obliterate those earliest remembrances; but no one could suspect Sir Alfred of vanity, seeing the wide field he might havehad for it exercise, and that, with everything to render his attentions acceptable, he seemed careless of showing any, except to one only, who would have been as unwilling, as she was unable to suspect him of deceit. Yet Matilda felt incapable of speaking, from an apprehension of betraying more agitation than the occasion warranted, for it might appear by that means as if she attached too much importance to language which was evidently guarded, and seemed meant to be ambiguous; she therefore remained in perplexed and agitated silence.

"I have been abrupt and precipitate, Miss Howard," continued Sir Alfred; "but such an accidental opportunity as the present might not occur again. I was impatient to assure you that no change of scene has made me forget the hours we passed together formerly, and that I anticipated nothing on my return with so much ardor as the renewal of our intimacy. You know me to be a man of few words, yet those few may be implicitely relied on. But for an impediment which cannot at present be explained, my first object on reaching this country would have been to———"

A sound of voices was heard ascending the staircase, and at this moment Mr. Grant, with his usual joyous hilarity, entered the room, and walked up at once to the pianoforte.

"Miss Howard!" he exclaimed, in accents of astonishment, on observing how visibly she was agitated; but instantly afterwards, with a degree of delicacy and tact which could scarcely have been anticipated, he added in the same tone of surprise—"is it possible that you have had no supper? I see you are a more incorrigible student than was represented by Miss Fitz-Patrick, for you would rather sit here reading a music-book, than not read at all. She tells me that you think the dullest book in the world better than the best conversation; but Douglas and I must undeceive you on that point, by doing the agreeable *for once* in our lives."

Mr. Grant could not resist a sly glance at Sir Alfred, who had been examining a print to conceal his countenance, but now looked up with much of his usual calmness and self-possession.

"I have not the same happy confidence in my powers that you feel in yours, Grant. One who so continually exercises them for the benefit of every person indiscriminately, ought to be in good practice; whereas I so seldom care to please, that I scarcely deserve success, even where it is of most importance."

Mr. Grant looked with momentary surprise from Sir Alfred to Matilda; but it was only instantaneous, for he immediately reassumed an appearance of total unconsciousness, saying in his usual tone of heedless vivacity, "Miss Howard, I have not yet heard a single Latin quotation, nor a syllable about the Greek participles! Pray, if we by chance fell into conversation, how long might I depend upon its continuing in plain English?"

"You may have bail for the rest of my life," said she, trying to recover herself. "My own language is good enough for anything I have to say; but Eleanor's sketch of me was so formidable this morning, that it is to be hoped no one will ever find it bear any resemblance. I might have said on that occasion, as a Spanish officer did, who saw himself for the first time in uniform,—'With such an aspect I have even a terror of myself.'"

"Miss Fitz-Patrick's pictures are all mere daubs, loaded with color, but not in correct drawing," observed Sir Alfred. "On most occasions I prefer my own judgment to other people's descriptions."

"If every one did the same I should not perhaps be so completely under the ban of Eleanor's coterie at present; but she amused herself by giving a most ludicrous representation, which makes the boldest people afraid of me; and really, of all solitudes in the world, there is none, you know, so great as being alone in a crowd."

"I like it above everything," said Sir Alfred; "but you should imitate Miss Charlotte Clifford, whose enterprising attempts at conversation I observed you watching to-day; and certainly, Miss Howard, any one might have been envious of her success, especially considering that you were placed at dinner, where on neither side had you the smallest chance of being listened to."

"That cannot be levelled at *me* of course," observed Mr. Grant. "The fact is, that I require a great deal of *drawing out*, and Miss Fitz-Patrick, by way of doing so, talks incessantly herself, so that I really had not time so much as to give a cough all dinner-time."

"*A propos*, Grant! I always intended to ask your receipt for making young ladies conversable, because I never saw you introduced to one yet without her being instantly in a state of animated volubility."

"Keep my secret, then, and you shall hear it. Whenever I am lazy about talking, and can imagine nothing else to say, I ask my new acquaintance if she knows Captain 'Campbell?' Immediately half-a-dozen gentlemen of that name start up to her recollection, and she is eager to know which of them I mean. Of course they must all be described, and before their histories are completed, the quadrille terminates, and it is time for us to separate."

"That might do for a ball, but it will scarcely get you though the three courses of a dinner-party."

"Ah! that requires more arrangement. Begin with finding the room insufferably hot, or intensely cold; complain of being oppressed with innumerable dinner engagements, and remark how much you hate crowded parties; fall into raptures with the last concert, but disparage most of the performer's; find out a likeness for the Prima Donna, and compare the German and Italian schools, remarking, of course, that Rossini borrows from himself, and how unlucky it was that Weber died before he wrote more; then start fair with the last novel, and your business is done."

A lively dialogue ensued, which continued to be kept up with characteristic humor and animation on all sides, till at length it took a still more interesting turn; and in the interchange of sentiments and opinions which ensued, Matilda was pleased to see traits of good sense and of right feeling in Mr. Grant, for which she had scarcely been prepared, from the general care-for-nobody tone of his conversation. She could be surprised at no degree of talent or feeling that were evinced by Sir Alfred, knowing that the exhibition of both, in their highest degree, was only checked by his habitual reserve, which he seemed for the present to have laid aside; and Matilda herself, while she was delighted with the observations of others, insensibly revealed the hidden depths of her own mind, with which few would not have been captivated when it was thoroughly known, for the *naïveté* of youth were united to a degree of candor and originality in expressing her thoughts, which attracted instant confidence and regard.

At length a rush of voices in the ante-room preceded the entrance of Eleanor, leaning on Lord Alderby's arm, and followed by a numerous train of satellites; but before they appeared, Sir Alfred quietly resumed his former position on the sofa, apparently in a state of entire abstraction, while

Mr. Grant continued his sentence to Miss Howard, without expressing any surprise at this sudden desertion.

"Matilda!! I am quite petrified to find you here!" cried Eleanor, who was generally petrified or thunderstruck at least three times a-day. "Have n't you had any supper? We left some jelly below, and the drumstick of a turkey—a *ding-dong*, as Mrs. Ramsbottom calls it; so pray go down, and see what you could fancy."

Miss Howard professed an utter distaste for suppers, and gladly seized the earliest opportunity of quietly stealing to her own room, where, her heart fluttering with emotion, and her countenance glowing with happiness, which she scarcely dared confess even to herself, she hastily cast herself on a seat near the window, and began an agitated review of all that had been said by Sir Alfred. It was impossible not to become convinced of his sincerity now, and she felt that his had been the tacit declaration of a preference to which the confidence of her whole heart might be given. That some impediment prevented a more full explanation, seemed to have been implied; but she knew Sir Alfred to be gifted with an almost chivalrous sense of honor, which could not be too implicitly relied on, and she gave her mind up to the belief that he had long been, and still continued to be, attached to herself. Often before, as the guardian of her own happiness, she had called in the warning voice of prudence to remind her how many made shipwreck of their happiness by too ready a credulity on these subjects; but now she felt that not only was it justifiable to credit all Sir Alfred said, but that it would be unjustifiable any longer to doubt his professions; and, before she turned her mind upon the more serious thoughts and duties of the evening, Matilda endeavored to compose herself by a pleasing remembrance of many past scenes, which, till now, she had frequently endeavored to forget.

CHAPTER XIII.

The broad unfeeling mirth that folly wears,
Less pleases far than virtue's very tears.
GOLDSMITH.

THE silver crescent of a cloudless moon shone in solemn brightness over the distant hills, and lighted up the gaunt, bare skeletons of many ancient trees, throwing their shadows upon the grass beneath, while the deep blue sky was studded with countless stars, which were reflected in the dark, gloomy bosom of the silent waters, when Matilda looked abroad to admire the mysterious tranquillity of nature, before she prepared for consigning herself to repose. What Christian can gaze long or often on the majestic grandeur of the starry heavens, and not be lost in contemplation of its more than earthly glory, while the heart soars above those abject cares and personal feelings which belong to a present life, and is filled with the prospect of an eternal destiny? Matilda's mind expanded in the thoughts of futurity, and she anticipated that time when the remembrance of every worldly emotion would seem, in her own estimation, like the momentary ripple occasioned by a summer breeze on the fathomless ocean. A pleasing calm diffused itself over her meditations, and she was about to leave the window, and begin preparing to retire for the night, when she became suddenly startled to observe the dim shadow of a human figure, pacing rapidly up and down near the margin of the river, with vehement gesticulations, and almost maniacal energy of manner. Occasionally the person, who seemed to be a female, disappeared for some moments beneath the dark shadows of the forest, but again she emerged, and at length stooping down, where a large bundle was laid on the grass, she untied it, and drew out a quantity of shawls and ribbons, which she proceeded to hang in fantastic draperies on herself. After arranging and altering their positions in every capricious form, she heaped them all on with frantic haste, and began gazing at a reflection of her own figure in the moonlit surface of the river, as it swept rapidly past beneath the window. Matilda stood transfixed to the spot, and a thrill of apprehension ran through her frame, for it suddenly flashed upon her mind that this could be no other than Nanny, whose eccentric gestures and strange appearance caused so much terror and surprise. Still she wished to doubt, and knew not what to think or do. No one in the house could possibly be called, and Matilda remembered, not without fear, that a door which communicated with the terrace, led by a back-staircase to the large lumber-room opposite her own, and that in all probability the poor girl had gone out in that way, by which she might at any time return. While these alarming thoughts darted into her mind, a voice suddenly rose on the midnight air, in tones of wild and high excitement. Matilda listened in breathless agitation, for she traced the broken snatches of hymns and tunes which had once been familiar companions of her own childhood; a moment afterwards, however, they died away in low and melancholy cadences till the voice became utterly inaudible. Touched by remembering former times, and deeply affected by the discovery of Nanny's situation, Matilda banished at once every personal feeling, and nerving her resolution to the utmost, she instantly threw up a window, and called aloud to the poor girl, who stood immediately beneath the castle wall. A faint echo alone replied; and though she waved her handkerchief, and tried by every device to attract attention, it was all in vain; Nanny stood motionless, and apparently unconscious, till suddenly she raised a wild hysterical shriek, and Matilda heard for the first time that fearful laugh of insanity, which none who have once known can ever afterwards forget. Her courage now appeared entirely to have failed, she leaned against the window for support, and it seemed as if her heart had ceased to beat. The first suggestion of fear was to make fast her own door; but even terror could not make Matilda entirely selfish, and knowing that it would be vain to ring her bell, she anxiously thought how assistance could be most immediately obtained for securing the poor girl's safety. She looked again, and saw Nanny wildly stretch her arms towards the river, and rush down to its very margin. There she threw off her bonnet, and fell on her knees, while her long dark hair floated on her shoulders, and she clasped her hands above her head with a look of mortal agony, and of desperate resolution. Matilda snatched up her candle and instantly flew down stairs. Contrary to her usual timidity of disposition, she formed an immediate resolution, not by the loss of one single moment to spare her own feelings in a case like the present, where life or death seemed at hazard; and without an instant's pause, she rapidly glided into the drawing-room, where Sir Richard and the other gentlemen were on the point of dispersing. Matilda's steps faltered, and her color rose when she saw their evident astonishment at her unexpected presence. But personal consideration at such a time are nothing to a generous mind, and advancing straight to her uncle, she grasped his arm, and related what had occurred in a few words.

Mr. Grant comprehended the whole at once, and rushed out, followed by Sir Alfred and the other gentlemen, while Matilda remained behind, knowing that her presence could now be of no use; but she told Sir Richard, that, if Nanny were brought to the housekeeper's room, everything should be prepared for her there. She then aroused Mrs. Gordon, and several of the maids from their slumbers, and caused a fire to be rekindled in the grate; but when all was ready, and nothing more could be done, Matilda became alarmed at hearing no tidings from the gentlemen, and her heart sunk with apprehension. Every breath of wind seemed like the sound of their footsteps, and every moment that passed served to increase her fears. At length, more than half an hour had elapsed, when the door flew open, and Mr. Grant entered, bearing in his arms the apparently lifeless form of Nanny, which he hastily placed on a sofa near the fire. Matilda felt that her hair and her clothes were streaming with wet, and it became evident that she had been rescued from a watery grave, but scarcely one word of explanation was given relating to the circumstances. Mr. Grant, indeed, began a hasty narrative, apparently descriptive of great danger and exertion, which were not his own; but Sir Alfred, who stood near, gave him a look commanding silence, and, with a shrug and a grimace of humorous submission, he obeyed.

With silent, heartfelt thankfulness for the safety of every one, and a tear of pity for the unfortunate Nanny, Matilda proceeded to use every means to promote recovery; and having at last succeeded in restoring apparent consciousness, she calmly requested the gentlemen to withdraw, that the poor girl's dress might be changed for what was warm and dry. Against being left without protection, however, Mrs. Gordon loudly, and almost angrily, remonstrated, saying she would as soon be in the presence of a ghost as of a madwoman. "Bodies without spirits, or spirits without bodies, I don't know which is worst, Miss Howard! but I cannot possibly remain in the room with only you and me, and this poor *daft* creature. Her head is just turned with vanity, and I always thought she would come to no good."

"There is nothing the matter with me, but that I wish to put an end to myself!" shrieked Nanny, starting up with a sudden desperation, which caused Mrs. Gordon to retreat in terror. "I wish to put an end to myself," repeated she, deliberately, while her large dilated eyes were fastened on Matilda, with an expression which appalled for the moment, and blanched her cheek with awe and apprehension. "Why am I here? Let me go! I heard a voice that called me! I hear it now! Let me go! I am wanted! I tell you there is nothing the matter, but I want to get away from myself! Oh! I have such horrid, horrid dreams!"

"Nanny!" said Matilda, making a powerful effort to conquer her own fears, and addressing the maniac in tones of touching softness; "My poor Nanny!" continued she, laying her hand on the unfortunate girl's arm, and fixing her eye intently on hers, with an expression of kindness, though it was difficult to fasten a steady gaze on the eye-balls, glaring like living coals, which were bent on herself, with an unnatural stare. "Do you remember Ashgrove, Nanny? Do you ever think of Lady Olivia and the Sunday-school? She was very kind to you, Nanny, and she always said you would do well."

"I want to go where she is! I would have done it, but they will not let me," whispered Nanny, in a low husky voice, while a frightful wintry smile came over her rigid features. "Say nothing about it—I'll do that yet! I'll put an end to myself—there's nothing else the matter!"

"But, Nanny, it is impossible to follow Lady Olivia, unless you bear sorrow patiently, as she did. We wish to be kind to you—no one shall believe any of those foolish stories. I have contradicted them all."

At these words, Mrs. Gordon angrily drew up, with a look of injured merit, being one of those individuals who never for one moment forget their own personal feelings, even while witnessing the utmost extreme of human misery; and she considered it an impeachment of her credit, in the government of Sir Richard's household, that any person should doubt of Nanny's guilt, when she had so decidedly condemned her.

"None of us are fit for a better world before we are called to it, Nanny. You know the apple is not ripe till it falls from the tree, and you must stay your time, while the sun shines, or while the rain falls, because all is needful to prepare us. Do you remember this hymn, Nanny? Many times you said the words long ago:—

'Grace alone can cure our ills,
Sweeten life with all its cares.'"

"Yes!" said Nanny, while her eyes gradually softened into a look of recollection:—

"'Though you oft have heard in vain,
Former years in folly spent,
Grace invites you yet again,
Once more calls you to repent.'"

The unnatural fire which had glared in the unfortunate girl's eyes became suddenly quenched in tears, while large, big drops slowly coursed each other down her cheeks, and at length, clasping her hands over her face, she burst into a passionate fit of weeping, which lasted for a length of time with frightful vehemence.

"You may leave us now in perfect safety," whispered Matilda, turning calmly to Sir Alfred and Mr. Grant, who lingered near the door, and seemed still unwilling to depart. "I can manage perfectly now—more of the servants are come, and she will probably soon be composed when they have placed her in bed."

Mr. Grant looked at Matilda with a degree of grave and serious interest very different from his usual manner, and answered, in a tone of respectful kindness,—"May we feel sure, Miss Howard, that your own powers are not overtasked?—with so much sympathy as you evidently feel, this is a very trying scene. We must be allowed to remain until medical aid arrives, which Sir Richard has sent without delay to summon."

The proposal of staying was warmly seconded by Sir Alfred, and not many minutes afterwards Dr. Mackenzie arrived. Having bled his patient copiously, and prescribed a composing draught, he desired that the room might be left quiet. The whole party then dispersed, and Matilda appeared as if she were retiring also, but having contrived to elude observation, she glided noiselessly back, and gently placed herself by the bedside of Nanny, making signs to the housemaid, who was also in attendance, that she might be seated. Morning dawned, and the grey twilight dimly diffused itself over the landscape, before Matilda's prayers and watchings were ended; but at length, seeing that Nanny's eyes were closed in sleep, though her slumber was agitated and disturbed, she stole out of the room, and sought for that repose which her own frame so greatly needed.

Nothing could be more irritating to the jealous spirit of Eleanor, than next morning to observe with what interest and *empressement* Matilda was received on her entrance to breakfast by all those who had witnessed her generous exertions and heartfelt benevolence during the previous night; and nothing could have exhibited more evidently her own good sense and discretion, than the calm self-possession with which she endeavored to pass over all her own share in what had happened, by changing the subject of discussion entirely, though her quiet, unobtrusive attempts to do so did not at once succeed. Each gentleman, as he came in, renewed her embarrassment, by expressing the most anxious solicitude lest she might have suffered from her exertions; while she, with that instinctive sympathy which enabled her to read the thoughts of every one, felt perfectly conscious of her cousin's annoyance, and tried to save her feelings by retiring as much from notice as possible. Eleanor heard a distorted account of the whole scene which took place during the previous evening from Pauline, corroborated by Mrs. Gordon. Sir Richard's valet also gave a similar statement to his master, by which a prejudice had been fixed in the minds of both, and they were fully persuaded that Nanny had been equally criminal and indiscreet; in consequence of which orders were given for her immediate removal to Gowan Bank. Miss Fitz-Patrick thought she had done a great act of liberality by ordering that Dr. Mackenzie should attend the invalid, and spare no expense in the remedies he prescribed; but having done this, she felt entitled to dismiss the subject from her thoughts, and considered it an injury in any one to recall what was so disagreeable.

Eleanor, during the commencement of breakfast, was for once grave and silent. This might have been attributed to sorrow and self-reproach for the sufferings of her protégé, had there not been a shade of anger on her countenance, and of irritability in her tone of voice, which evinced anything rather than amiable feelings. Matilda resolutely closed her eyes to this, until forced at last to see it, for the color rushed unbidden into her countenance, when she heard Eleanor say, in an audible whisper, to Miss Marabout, "All got up for effect!—so fond of a scene!—some people like on any terms to be conspicuous."

"Absurd!" replied the *ci-devant* governess; "what have people in Nanny's line of life to do with fine feelings? Miss Howard has encouraged it all; and that sort of thing is as much out of its place in the poor creature's mind, as if she wore a Brussels lace dress. It is evidently done to gain some purpose, and I am glad she is to be sent home immediately. For my own part, I have long suspected the girl was a little insane, and would not for worlds live an hour in the house with any person convicted of being mad."

"There is more than one person in this house who seems to me a little mad, Miss Howard!" said Mr. Armstrong, in an undertone. "Have you not thought better of all I said to you? It is a good move on a chess-board to take the castle, and I could *pawn* my credit on the enterprise succeeding, if your own wilfulness does not check-mate the whole affair. Would it be worth while to know how *the knave* was once played to advantage already, and how you could give a Roland for an Oliver?"

"I already mentioned, Mr. Armstrong, that, if you can produce a fair and open statement of anything in which my interests are concerned, it will give me pleasure to hear it fully explained; but nothing underhand can possibly receive countenance from me, nor shall I allow myself to be made the depository of malicious inuendos against my uncle or my cousin on any occasion whatever, and especially here."

Meantime, Sir Alfred buried himself behind a widely extended sheet of "the Times," and seemed utterly insensible of all that was passing around; while Mr. Grant leaned familiarly over the back of his chair, and made a running commentary on the news of the day, which afterwards diverged into discussions of an approaching ballot at the club.

"Above all things, avoid electing any busy, legislating men," observed Sir Alfred. "There should always be a second ballot at the end of a year, to ascertain if new members may be permitted to remain."

"Admirable! I shall suggest that when our next meeting takes place. How it would thin the ranks. Poor Sir Colin, among all those he belongs to, would not survive to tell his next story at one of them. I am assured that, in London, he belongs to three or four."

"Quite a knave of clubs! I shall take my name out of White's, or the Traveller's, if they ever admit him."

"To myself and others, who are on committee at the Albion, nothing is half so troublesome to manage as a country gentleman, who has been accustomed to rule his wife, his children, and his tenantry. People who go into society, and mingle with strangers, become ten times more tranquil about trifles; but a man who lives constantly at home is in a perpetual storm about the merest bagatelles. From being accustomed to domineer without resistance, every fault he finds with our management is pronounced disgraceful, atrocious, or unheard-of at the very least; while he puts himself in a perfect uproar to know if such a thing was ever done before in any community—most likely something that everybody does every day, and which I have probably done fifty times myself."

"Ah, yes! people who live always on their own property get such an overgrown opinion of its importance, that they become like the mouse in a chest, who could not believe that there was anything larger or greater in the whole world. Society is a perfect Procrustes's bed for reducing these imaginary giants to their proper level; and it does them an infinite deal of good to be several times black-balled at a club before admission."

"How it spoils gentlemen when they begin to intermeddle with news!" said Eleanor, looking with an air of pique at the two friends, particularly Mr. Grant, whose altered manner towards herself appeared now, for the first time, to strike her. "Politics destroy conversation, and clubs ruin all the comfort of domestic life."

"I beg leave to differ from the last speaker!" cried Mr. Grant, breaking off from his studies. "Now, Miss Fitz-Patrick! argument is better than assertion; so maintain your position, and try if it be possible to convince me."

"Can you deny that a thorough club-monger is scarcely ever at home? so how can he be domestic? He bustles off early in the day, to spell over all the provincial papers, till it is time to get anxious about the London post. When that arrives, he greedily seizes one newspaper, and keeps his eye fixed upon some person, from whom he hopes to secure another. After these are concluded, he must have his pool at billiards, and probably ends the evening by playing a rubber at whist with two friends and a dummy."

"Ah! you are describing some miserable old bachelor with no attractions to take him home."

"As for that, a man who has married upon nothing, which means, you know, in London, about twelve hundred a-year, may, for the merest trifle, enjoy at his club the most splendid sitting-rooms, gilded like a lord mayor's coach, and lighted up like Alladin's palace, while his dinner is prepared by a French cook, and served up in a degree of luxury and splendor fit for an emperor. Only fancy such a man going occasionally home to a dusky parlor, in the twilight of one pair of candles—his wife and his dinner both ill-dressed—a perpetual talk of economy ringing in his ears—and probably a noisy tumult of troublesome children, throwing his room and his brains into disorder. Now, if he knew no better, the poor man might learn to call that social happiness and fire-side peace; but having a club for his refuge, he falls into a paroxysm of disgust, and exit."

"What an entire want of sentiment is ascribed to us, Miss Fitz-Patrick! Do you suppose we are insensible to the felicities of domestic confidence,—the sweet interchange of mutual affection,—the—the— In short, let us read the last chapter of any novel we can lay our hands on, which will express exactly what I mean."

"Ah! but you never see any hero of a novel who is described as being both a domestic married man and a member of White's. All stories end with the happy couple going off like a sky-rocket in a brilliant flame of love and happiness; but if we could only see the result, nothing comes back but the stick. I have already superintended the rise and fall of several very romantic love-matches, and invariably, if the gentleman was a professed frequenter of clubs, he relapsed almost immediately into bachelor habits. Mutual indifference is the consequence; and positively many married people, without any actual quarrel, have, nevertheless, so little intercourse, that I am confident, if some kind fairy offered to give each separately all the comforts they now enjoy, on condition of their never meeting again, it would be a mutual relief."

"Ah! Miss Fitz-Patrick! to a man of my exquisite sensibility, what an incredible picture that appears! Such is my idea of domestic happiness, that since no lady can be prevailed on to accept me, I have actually ordered a frame of worsted work to be placed in my sitting-room; and my parrot is taught to cry out in an angry voice, whenever I enter the room—'Where have you been all day, Tom?' merely to keep me in mind of the felicity which may one day be mine with my future better half."

"You can scarcely be disappointed, if that be all," replied Eleanor, laughing and coloring. "I hope, Sir Alfred, your standard of perfection in ladies is as moderate?"

"Mine is so high that I have never *but once* seen any one to reach it."

Observing the emphasis with which Sir Alfred spoke, Eleanor evidently applied it to herself, and dropt her eyes with a look of gratified consciousness; but had she happened to notice his intended application of the words! He merely darted one momentary glance towards the interesting countenance of Matilda, who was tying up her bouquet, and resumed his newspaper.

"You complain, Miss Fitz-Patrick, of gentlemen being too much absent from their own houses," continued Mr. Grant; "but if I were a young lady, nothing would be half so formidable to me as the prospect of ever having what is called 'an attentive husband!' A man with nothing to do,—always at home,—always in the way, and perpetually expecting to be amused;—who asks in the morning when you mean to walk, and cannot be got rid of on any terms,—equally ready to shop, or visit, or stroll in the country, and to whom, in short, no plan for the day can be proposed so odious as to make you sure to get rid of his society."

"I may certainly answer for it already, that there *are some* gentlemen who can on no terms be got quit of! Mr. Armstrong! I'll trouble you to ring the bell!—people who stay in your house, like a wasp upon a window-pane, buzzing about the table at meals, and keeping one in perpetual hot water. Mr. Armstrong, will you fill the tea-pot? It breaks my arm to reach so far."

"Those wasps you speak of are very dangerous sometimes, and can sting severely," said Mr. Armstrong, in a slow tone of suppressed rage. "I would advise you, Miss Fitz-Patrick, to beware of irritating them."

"Ah! Lord Alderby! good morning! I guess you sat up all night, in order to be down in such excellent time! Pray, give us a new idea upon the weather!"

"I always prophesy rain every morning in this country, and am sure to be right before evening."

"They tell me that this day is cold,—fine,—freezing,—likely to thaw,—likely to snow,—and likely to hold up!—how does all this promise for my skating party?"

"Eleanor! your tea will be fit to skate upon, if we don't get it soon!" exclaimed Sir Richard impatiently. "I never saw any woman yet who could make it tolerably."

"Papa! if there is an accomplishment on earth that I excel in, it is this!—but the most deserving people are generally traduced by an ungrateful public!"

"I have some *good news* to give you!" added the baronet, glancing rather dubiously at a remarkably ill-folded, awkward-looking letter, which he handed to his daughter. "Captain M'Tartan, R. N., has appointed himself to this station for three weeks, if *quite convenient.*"

"Captain M'Tartan!" cried Eleanor, faintly; "I thought he had sailed to Africa, or the West Indies, or somewhere of that kind, which would have rid us of him entirely! I had even been considering how a black velvet trimming would do on my bonnet! but Scotch cousins have been a proverbial bore *all* over the world ever since I entered it, and will probably continue so, as long as we remain."

"I consider that remark as intended to be personal, Miss Fitz-Patrick," said Sir Alfred, looking off his newspaper.

"Oh! you are enough to exculpate the whole race! But did you ever see Captain M'Tartan? Such a man!—he is my *beau idéal* of vulgarity! His face is not merely weather-beaten, but it looks as if he had been in a storm all his life!—I can't be in the room with him, he is so ugly."

"But, my dear girl! you have not seen him for ages," cried Sir Richard. "He went to the Mediterranean and to Petersburg when you were a perfect child, and no one here has been in company with him since."

"People do not improve with years, and I never forget anybody. In that respect, my memory is like the Royal Family's, and my abhorrence of Captain M'Tartan began before I was ten. He fastened my eyelids together with sticking-plaster in the school-room, when I fell asleep over my lessons, and persuaded me that I had become suddenly blind. His whole wit consisted in those sort of silly practical jokes, and *mauvaises plaisanteries*, which I detest when they are played upon myself."

"Let me tell you, Eleanor! that Donald M'Tartan is one of the most distinguished officers in our service," said Sir Richard, rather angrily. "You may be very proud of the connection, for he showed prodigious spirit at Algiers and Navarino. It is said that he has already received nine-and-twenty wounds in battle."

"Then I must take care not to wound his feelings, or that would be the thirtieth."

"And much the most difficult to bear!" added Lord Alderby, with a very asthmatic attempt at a sigh.

"He always speaks nautical language, too, as officers are represented doing in naval novels, though never heard in real life," added Eleanor. It is like dining at the United Service Club to hear him talk! He 'heaves to' when he comes up to one; 'casts anchor' when he sits down; and 'fires a broadside' of words whenever he opens his mouth. But his worst crime is yet to come! Having been intimate in our house when I was a child, he still calls me in this letter Eleanor! Nothing can be a surer test of vulgarity than that familiar way of naming to others our acquaintances, or even our near connections in their absence. I already know one or two misses professing to understand good manners, who talk of gentlemen with whom they are intimate, as 'Jack,' 'Dick,' or 'Tom.'"

"To be sure!" said Mr. Grant. "We have a right to be as intimate as we please with those who are not present to contradict us! I always speak of 'my friend, Cairngorum,' and 'that excellent fellow, Dumbartonshire,' though certainly, if they entered the room at this moment, I am not sure if either of them could recollect me, seeing we only met once."

"People of a certain calibre are not entitled to know whether I have a Christian name or not!" continued Eleanor, looking at Mr. Armstrong. "Captain M'Tartan is, in all respects, exactly like a great, overgrown schoolboy. I would rather go about with no face at all, than exhibit such a physiognomy as he does, and his laugh seems to ring in my ears already, it is so outrageous. Well! inevitable evils must be endured, and there is no perfect happiness in this world, as Matilda would say."

"You make me quite vain, Eleanor, by attributing such extraordinary originality to my remarks!" replied she, smiling. "All that has been said raises my curiosity to see your visitor, because it is interesting to be in company with remarkable people, and he certainly has a most distinguished reputation for courage."

"The M'Tartan's are an exceedingly old family," added

Mr. Grant. The whole clan was massacred several times during the ancient wars, and they got a peerage from Prince Charles."

"You will observe, Eleanor," added Sir Richard, "that he brings a foreign friend with him, which is a favor I could have excused, for you have unfortunately always been only too partial to that sort of cattle."

"Does he indeed!" exclaimed the young heiress, eagerly referring to her letter. That is really gilding the pill. A Russian, too!—Count Constantine Ecatrinoslav! I have seen that name often in the Morning Post! This is too good news to be true! Can anybody tell me what he is like?"

"Probably," replied Sir Richard, provoked at her *empressement*, "a little, dark, squinting man, covered with snuff."

"Above all things, preserve me from a squint!" cried Lady Susan Danvers, affectedly. "It makes one quite nervous when any person in company has that deformity."

"Do I hear *you* objecting to a *squint*, Lady Susan?" asked Mr. Grant, looking earnestly in her face, with well-feigned astonishment. "I certainly could not have expected *that!*"

"What can you mean, Mr. Grant! You don't intend to insinuate that *I* have one?"

"Were you never sensible of it before? What a heedless mortal I am!—how could I commit such a blunder! But, Lady Susan, many people are thought to look rather the better of a slight cast, and, for my part, I admire it excessively. With you it merely seems as if one eye was attracted by excessive brilliancy in the other!"

"Mr. Grant! you talk the most insufferable nonsense! My dog Tiny squints as much as I do!"

"How very unfortunate that the subject came under discussion at all! You know, Lady Susan, it is considered *lucky* for a man to squint, but in the case of a lady—why! —No one can become sensible of any obliquity in their own vision, because, when you look in the glass, each eye is directed straight to its own image, but when you turn away, Lady Susan——I appeal to Miss Fitz-Patrick!"

"Oh! don't ask me! I hate to tell disagreeable *truths!*" interrupted Eleanor, enjoying, beyond measure, her friend's indignant surprise. "But candidly, now, Lady Susan, did you never observe two gentlemen start up simultaneously, when you asked one of them to ring the bell? I have been puzzled once or twice myself to ascertain whether you were speaking to Miss Marabout or me."

"Of course!" said Mr. Grant, leaving the breakfast-table, and singing, as he went away,—

"There's a look that is rather uncommon,
In the flash of that very bright eye."

"Fletcher! do these words remind you," asked Sir Richard, "of a ridiculous circumstance which occurred to us when we met at dinner last Thursday——"

"Wednesday, you mean," interrupted Sir Colin; "or, I believe, on reflection, it was Friday, or Saturday!—yes! it must have been Friday, for I recollect a trifling event which——"

"Well," continued Sir Richard, impatiently; "let it be Friday, or Saturday—no matter which,—we were all sitting at the Duke of Cairngorum's——"

"Excuse me!—It was the day I went to Clanpibroch Castle," interposed Sir Colin, hastily. "You know the Duke arrived that morning for the funeral of poor Lady Anne M'Intosh——"

"At Clanpibroch Castle, then, and a gentleman happened to say——"

"I beg your pardon! it was a lady;—she wore a gold turban, and——"

"Ah!—man, woman, or child—one of them observed to Sir Colin——"

"No! no!—I first said to *her*——"

"Well! let it be so! 'Pray, Madam——'"

"But," interrupted Sir Colin, emphatically, "did you explain that I sat *next* to her?"

"You matter-of-fact idiot!" muttered Sir Richard, between his teeth. "Pray, Fletcher, tell the story yourself, since it appears that I am incompetent."

This was precisely what Sir Colin had been aiming at, and he recommenced it, telling every extraneous particular of the anecdote that could be edged in, and prolonging his narrative till breakfast was ended, and most of the company had strolled away; but Miss Howard complaisantly sat out the whole of Sir Colin's tediousness, while, in the meantime, Mr. Grant affected to fall asleep, and nodded in his chair, having previously whispered a request, to be called when it was over.

Matilda proceeded, as always had been her custom at this hour, to the music-room, which she was then sure of finding empty, and played several of her favorite songs. She excelled, without a thought of exhibiting, and had, with the most exquisite taste, a mellow, flexible voice, which was a perfect tenor, and the varied tones of which, whether in music or conversation, expressed the deepest sensibility. Matilda had begun the touching air of "Bendemere Stream," and while her thoughts reverted to Ashgrove, her notes swelled into richer harmony, and then died away, like the softest vibrations of a guitar. Before the prelude was finished, she had heard some one enter, but supposing it to be a servant come to replenish the fire, she did not look round, until, to her surprise, some low, and scarcely audible notes of accompaniment were unexpectedly thrown in, and she perceived Sir Alfred standing near, and apparently listening with entranced attention. Matilda's ready tact prevented her from exhibiting any of the astonishment she felt, but, with a heightened color, and some trepidation, she continued the air, while Sir Alfred gradually let out his voice more fully, and displayed much judgment, taste, and science, united to a manly, harmonious voice, of which the articulation was as distinct as if he had been speaking. Scarcely was the song concluded, and before Matilda had, with modest embarrassment, expressed all her pleasure at receiving such unexpected assistance, when the door flew open, and Eleanor, followed by a detachment of friends, burst into the room, full of mirth and animation.

"We heard music, but could not imagine who it was!" she exclaimed. "Sir Alfred! no one ever hinted that you were an amateur, or I should have teased you forever till we got a song!"

"That is the very reason you never heard it," said he, turning away. "I know not a note of music, and sing merely by ear, or by accident. It is the merest whim in the world when I attempt anything of the kind!"

"How very odd that nobody ever minds Matilda!" cried Eleanor. "To be sure, she is no critic, and I shall not be a very severe one. Pray, Sir Alfred, do indulge us with a cadence or two!—anything that strikes you as being suitable!"

Sir Alfred shook his head, and stolled out of the room, singing a verse of the "Charming woman," and Miss Fitz-Patrick, ever ready to fancy a compliment implied, was perfectly satisfied that the title of the song alone applied to herself; and taking instant possession of the piano, she began to play a brilliant new piece by Czerny, which had recently come from London.

"That is very *nice* music!" said Miss Murray, complaisantly. My favorite piece is 'The Battle of Prague.' Can you play it, Miss Fitz-Patrick?

A smile dimpled in the cheek of Matilda, and a contemptuous frown lowered on the brow of Eleanor at this instance of antediluvian taste, while Miss Murray, perceiving she had made a blunder, turned with an anxious whisper to ask Mr. Grant if he could explain why Eleanor seemed so irritated.

"I can't conceive! By the way," added he, seeing Miss Murray still looked perplexed and uneasy, "was not Sir Colin Fletcher wounded at the battle of Prague, or he ran away, I forget which? but you know, all things considered, it would be awkward to perform that piece before him. You are very sly and satirical, Miss Murray," added he, with an admonitory shake of the head.

"*I* am!" exclaimed she, with consternation and surprise. "You cannot surely be serious?"

"Now, Miss Murray, I shall prove it at once. Do you not always pretend to mistake my friend Foley's name, and call him, without the smallest compunction, Major *Folly?* and did I not yesterday see you hastily rise, and offer Lady Susan the arm-chair, to show, of course, that you consider her a little advancing in years, and she angrily sat down on a music-stool, by way of being juvenile? Oh, Miss Murray! Miss Murray! I am quite afraid of you myself, seeing nobody is spared!"

The gentlemen proceeded soon afterwards, as usual, to lounge away an hour at the stables in discussing, for the fortieth time, the comparative merits of their hunters, when Lord Alderby seized an opportunity to drop a few paces behind the rest with Mr. Grant, to whom he made some accidental remarks, and immediately afterwards observed, with a look of penetrating curiosity at his companion, though affecting to be solely occupied with lighting his cigar,—

"My good fellow! I mean to back you against the field yet for winning the heiress!"

"Alderby!" replied Mr. Grant, carelessly, "how dare you presume to mention Miss Fitz-Patrick's name with such a mouthful of smoke! It is a most unlover-like piece of disrespect, and would be resented accordingly if she knew it!

I observe you never think, nor speak of her but as 'the heiress;' yet even a comparative stranger, as you are, might see that her richest gifts are not in her estates. I estimate her simply as Eleanor Fitz-Patrick, whom from her earliest childhood I have known—whom I still admire—and whom ONCE I loved."

"Once!—you mean once for all, then, I suppose?" answered Lord Alderby, laughing, while he closely watched Mr. Grant's countenance. "Can I forget how you raved long ago about dark hair and hazel eyes, and an undying attachment! We were all wearied of Eleanor Fitz-Patrick's name before she came out. Every picture you saw abroad was like her—no beauty that I pointed out could be compared to her. You carved her name upon trees and tombstones—called a dog after her—and sung nothing but 'Nora Criena' forever, so that my very ears used to ring with it. That was all absurd enough at the time, but is likely to turn out well now, since it gives you the start of us."

"Alderby, you mistake me!" replied Mr. Grant, with unusual seriousness. "The revival of these stories only serves to show more strongly what a contrast there is between past and present feelings—how great, no one but myself can ever know; but that is past. You, and others whom I could name, are brought to the feet of Eleanor Fitz-Patrick by the very circumstance which places a gulf between us, and I shall never attempt to pass it."

"That sounds amazingly fine—quite chivalrous!" answered Lord Alderby, incredulously. "But, Grant, we all know what human nature is. Your estates lie contiguous—they ought to be united; your stud requires to be enlarged——"

"Alderby! whenever you judge of *me* by *yourself*, you cannot fail to be mistaken," said Mr. Grant, resuming his wonted tone of careless vivacity. "I am jealous of my independence, and shall never marry any woman whose fortune is superior to my own. It would put me frantic to hear any wife of mine talking in the way heiresses do, about 'my' carriage, '*my*' house, and 'my' establishment. I could not stand that—no, not even from Miss Fitz-Patrick! Seriously, however, there are some things changed in her already, which will make me envy less than I should have once done the man who gains her. I wish to set this subject quite at rest between us now, and therefore let me say that such an attachment as mine *was* requires to be preserved by entire approbation."

"Then, my dear fellow, if you are become so fastidious, why not retire from the field, leaving it open to us? I never could understand such Platonic friendship, which never exists upon *both* sides, you may depend upon it! Why are you carrying on such a vehement flirtation at this very hour with Miss Fitz-Patrick, that not another soul in the house can speak to her? Am I expected to believe that it is not on your own account?"

"Most potent, grave, and REVEREND SENIOR! you may believe this, that, if there be truth in man, neither Miss Fitz-Patrick nor I entertain 'any intentions,' as the usual phrase is. We have always enjoyed a little lively *persiflage* together, but there is no deeper sentiment on *either* side now."

"I am not so sure of that," muttered Lord Alderby, in an undertone.

"When any one appears, whom I think deserving of Miss Fitz-Patrick, you shall then see me retire, and act the part of a brother to her," continued Mr. Grant, in a tone of feeling and sincerity. "I know myself to be capable of it, and I *shall*. Eleanor Fitz-Patrick's happiness can never be indifferent to me, and though I seek not to be intrusted with the care of it now, I fervently desire to see it committed to one who deserves her. Excuse me, Alderby, but your motives are not satisfactory, if there were not other objections. Douglas might merit her, and I should gladly have resigned Miss Fitz-Patrick to the man whom, above all others on earth, I respect and like; but he is evidently occupied with a different object. In short, till some one starts up, who can love Miss Fitz-Patrick as I *did*, and who possesses the rank and fortune which I want, you may expect to see me act as her guardian."

"A very competent one truly!" said Lord Alderby, evidently piqued; "quite a dog in the manger. I had no idea you were bitten with sentimentality!"

"I have a tinge of what *you* would call romance in my disposition naturally, though every endeavor has been used of late to extinguish it, and, let me hope, with some success."

"Douglas!" said Lord Alderby, turning to Sir Alfred, who was lounging behind, "we were wondering that you are not more diligent in canvassing for the good graces of the heiress."

"I have more than enough of *canvassing* on my hands already, and one election will satisfy me. Some people might like to be deafened with wit, and stunned with accomplishments; but a fireside upon my plan would not suit so very brilliant a young lady as Miss Fitz-Patrick."

"She is the grand prize in the lottery of life," persisted Lord Alderby, "and unlike most girls of fortune, she is neither red-haired nor deformed, but *curiously beautiful!*"

"So she may be, but I never admire professed beauties, with that sort of 'look-*at-me*' air," replied Sir Alfred, taking the arm of Mr. Grant, and walking away. "Life is not a mere party of pleasure, or it might signify little whom we passed it with; but you know my opinions, Grant, already, and that they govern my actions in every event of life. How much more shall they do so while forming that solemn engagement in which it may almost be said, that the happiness of both worlds is at stake!"

CHAPTER XIV.

Oh, I would walk
A weary journey—to the farthest verge
Of the big world, to see that good man's form,
Who, in the blaze of wisdom and of art,
Preserves a lowly mind, and to his God,
Feeling the sense of his own littleness,
Is as a child in meek simplicity.
KIRKE WHITE.

MATILDA having understood that the unfortunate Nanny was at once removed from Barnard Castle, and carried without warning or preparation into the presence of her aged mother, felt anxiously desirous to ascertain how the good old woman had borne so sudden a shock, and she determined to lose no time in making her inquiries at Gowanbank, with a hope of ascertaining some way in which the sorrows of that once cheerful cottage could be mitigated. Having stated the case fully to Dr. and Miss Murray, they instantly proposed, as she expected and wished, to accompany her there, without delay, expressing an anxious hope that it might be possible to give assistance as well as comfort to both mother and daughter, in a case of difficulty and distress which so greatly needed both.

Nothing could be a nearer approach to perfect happiness than the feelings of Matilda, as she proceeded along the beautiful green path which led towards her destination. The glowing benevolence of her own mind, which expanded with every emotion of charity and kindness, the overflowing good-humor of Miss Murray, and the pleasing tone of intellectual elevation with which Dr. Murray conversed upon every subject which was most interesting, all combined with the bright sunshine and the varying landscape, to give her a feeling of unqualified delight; while present gratification led her to contrast it all with the artificial manners, the exaggerated expressions, the petty treachery, and the carelessness of each other's real thoughts and feelings which pervaded the party she had recently left. It was impossible to associate an hour with Dr. Murray and not feel the head and heart improved by his deep knowledge of human nature and of divine things. The more exalted might be the subject of contemplation, the more did his mind rise to explore it, for difficulties were to him like the breeze against the breast of the eagle, which only makes it soar the higher. Few subjects within the compass of human investigation remained in doubt or in darkness when he had thoroughly discussed them. His case was always clearly stated, and he brought to bear upon it, with readiness and precision, the whole mass of his extensive reading, while many things of which Matilda had desired an explanation, were given with such perfect clearness, and in such a portable compass, that they could never be afterwards forgotten or confused. Dr. Murray's knowledge seemed only estimated by himself according as it could aid him to make wise the simple. In illustrating the analogies of nature and of grace, in showing how we may discover the same almighty power and wisdom in the least and in the greatest of God's creatures, and in proving how his works and his word reflect upon each other a mutual light, Dr. Murray spoke with the mild authority of profound intellect, without pedantry, without affectation, without a thought but of recalling to his own heart, and impressing on his companions, all that might direct their affections towards the omnipotent and bountiful Creator.

"It seems strange," said Dr. Murray, in answer to a remark of his sister's, "that there really are persons who can live amidst the great and marvellous works of God, without asking themselves who created this stupendous theatre, and for what purpose we are brought to act a part in it. I have often pitied the situation of ancient heathen philosophers, who vainly speculated throughout a long and laborious life to discover whence they came and whither they were going. No doubt seems ever to have remained on their minds that our spirits are immortal, yet their wonder seems only to have been raised in order to be baffled; and how awful must have been the feeling of such meditative minds in watching the final departure of a soul, and in asking themselves on what unknown scenes it was about to enter, whither they themselves must so speedily follow!"

"Yes," replied Matilda, "I have sometimes been astonished that such persons retained their senses. Ordinary minds, to whom the every-day occurrences of life are sufficient, seem in little danger of insanity; but those who possess deep feelings and meditative spirits, without the guidance of revealed truth, must have often sustained great agitation, and it is easy to trace in the writings of heathen sages, what a state of torturing perplexity they lived in, respecting the enigma of their own existence."

"But," added Dr. Murray, "the knowledge which those learned philosophers were so darkly groping after, is revealed to us in a blaze of light, and men will scarcely attend to it. All we have to learn of our eternal relation to the great Creator, is so plainly laid down for us now, that he who runs may read,—but how few will pause one moment to reflect upon it! His majesty and power were always inscribed in the canopy of heaven, and in the glorious scenes around our path; but that which connects man with his Maker, by the ties of everlasting confidence and love, can only be found in Holy Scripture. Yet, nature and revelation are studied, as anatomists examine the body, without attending to the living Spirit which alone gives life and energy to all, and by the eye of faith only can we see what is precious and important in both. The Bible was writen not for giants in logic, but for babes in Christ, and the earth was created not merely as a curious problem for philosophers to investigate, but as a platform on which Christians are to rehearse the virtues which shall be perfected for them in a better and holier world."

"It seems melancholy indeed," observed Matilda, "that those who penetrate deepest into the wonders of nature, and into the mysteries of doctrine, are often so occupied with intellectual discovery, that they forget in all humility to adore the omnipotent Creator himself, and to recognize Him in the multitude of His works."

"Yet, if man never had been, and never was to become otherwise than he is, what a fleeting, insignificant, and painful dream would this life, at its best, be considered by those who reflected at all! But none who study the Christian revelation and their own nature, can fail to be convinced that man must have been originally created great in intellect and virtue, proportioned in dignity to the glorious universe by which he is encompassed; that we are now but a desolated ruin of what once was; and that, after a transient season of trial, degradation, and sorrow, we shall again be raised to that rank after which our fallen nature so ardently aspires. If it were otherwise,—if our hearts were vainly to pant after knowledge, happiness, and virtue, without a hope of their ever being perfected in a better st[illegible]; and if all the affections, emotions, and hopes, which support us through the sorrows of life, were in a few short years to be annihilated—then *indeed* we might envy, as Colonel Gardiner did, the existence of his dog, 'because it could neither reflect nor feel.' "

"I am sure many unbelievers must think the same," said Miss Murray; "and I remember many years ago being impressed with this conviction, when we heard of the Tom Paine Club, and were told of that remarkable circumstance, which has been so frequently since mentioned, respecting it, that both the president and secretary shot themselves."

"It is indeed a wonderful proof of our depraved nature, that men can be found who would desire to level themselves with the brutes that perish, and to argue themselves out of their own immortality; but it is '*the wish* that is father to the thought;' they prefer darkness to light, for very obvious reasons, and he who wishes to doubt may soon disbelieve anything. I read a pamphlet lately, very plausibly argued, to prove that Bonaparte never existed, and all the usual objections were stated, which infidels bring against the evidence of revelation."

"Some persons are apt," observed Matilda, "to make even the grandeur of creation an excuse for disbelieving the greatest work of all—the redemption of man. It seems so wonderful that He who made such a world of splendor should sacrifice His only Son for us, that they rashly pronounce it incredible, and therefore the magnitude of the benefit is an excuse for rejecting it altogether!"

"Yet observe what evidence we see all around of infinite care for our happiness!—the very flowers that are strewed on every bank, the joyous carol of the birds in Spring, the loveliness of landscape scenery, and every *unforbidden* joy of man's existence, speak of immeasurable love in the Almighty towards His creatures. We may confidently believe, then, that the everlasting felicity of millions is of such importance in His eye, that He mercifully planned for us what the heart of man could never have conceived. It is a mystery to be contemplated with wonder, love, and praise;—on the right belief of which our eternal hope depends, which no man can understand without the teaching of a divine Spirit,—and which we shall only comprehend in all its glory hereafter. There are depths in our holy religion which men have lost their souls by denying, and which they may lose their senses by endeavoring fully to understand!"

"Yes!" said Miss Murray! "and such religion as we shall

meet with to-day in old Janet's cottage, is often more influential on the heart and feelings than that of many a learned divine."

"True!" replied he, "there are philosophers who could speak off-hand without effort a perfect Bridgewater Treatise on the evidences of Almighty power in the structure of the universe,—and there are clergymen who can sprinkle over every page of Scripture new definitions and amended translations from the original;—but if I were to choose between the head or the heart,—though both may certainly be enlightened, I would prefer the simple belief of a day-laborer, who sees in the stars above his head nothing more glorious than in the lamps along the street, to that of the profoundest philosopher—the simple belief of a cottager, who knows only Christ, and him crucified, to the most intimate acquaintance with the Syriac, Greek, and Hebrew text."

"It was once remarked," said Matilda, "that the idea of a school-boy, who has learned to know that the earth is round, must be very inferior in sublimity to that of a wandering Arab, who believes in an unlimited world, and an unmeasurable sea. Yet I think, Dr. Murray, you must have many pleasing emotions in your own mind, to prove how much more elevated is the devotion of a cultivated intellect, amidst the wonders of creation and redemption, than the simple admiration and gratitude of an uninstructed heart. The poet says, 'an undevout astronomer is mad;' and you know better than I can imagine, how the thoughts are expanded by a knowledge of that stupendous creation, where 'worlds on worlds compose one universe.'"

"It is only where the head acts instead of the heart, and where men observe the heavens without preparing to go there, that I would deprecate learning; for a study of truth in every department of science or knowledge will but serve to exhibit its consistency and connection with the fountain of all truth; and the higher the intellect of man is raised, the more glorious will be his conceptions of Almighty power, till, like Job, he learns to say, 'The more I consider, the more I fear God.'"

Dr. Murray's eye kindled with animation, and he looked above and around him with an expression so full of devotion and reverence, that it almost seemed as if he saw the visible presence of Him who shall be know in His works, and whose power may be traced in the light that shines on our path, and in the very air that we breathe. "Yes!" added he, "there are hours of holy meditation, which appear like a foretaste of the joy that shall hereafter be revealed ;—but there are seasons, too, of sorrow and humiliation, to remind us that the tempest-tossed vessel is yet at sea, and the haven only in sight."

"I have often thought," said Matilda, "how very different must be the anticipation of heaven formed by various individuals, according to their habits and capacities of thinking. We each hope at some time to be admitted there, and few have passed through many years without attempting in some degree to conceive that state to which all are hastening. Bishop Hall remarks, that an impenitent sinner would feel as much out of his element in heaven as a toad in a king's palace; yet every one expects to go there, and probably most minds form an idea of what might be anticipated in that state of perfect happiness. A laborer, worn out with the toils of his daily task, will meditate most on the promise of eternal rest, where there shall be no more labor, nor sorrow; while the man of science could scarcely imagine any gratification apart from mental exertion, and will joyfully anticipate the time when 'increase of knowledge' shall no longer be 'increase of sorrow'; for he shall live with Him in whom are hid all the treasures of wisdom, and whose perfections will flow on before his adoring contemplation, like a ceaseless stream. And those who are now delighting in the pleasures of benevolence, or in the intercourse of friendship, must be desirous to believe that in a state of unclouded joy, such blessed feelings of the heart will not be absent."

"I think we are warranted in Scripture to conceive as vividly the happiness of heaven as the terrors of hell, and to exercise our minds in seeking a knowledge of what is revealed on that subject, though not positively to conclude that we are infallibly right."

"Many Christians feel satisfied," replied Matilda, "with that important text which declares, that 'eye hath not seen, nor ear heard, neither have entered into the heart of man the things which God hath prepared for them that love Him.'"

"Yet," said Dr. Murray, "we must not forget the verse which comes next: 'But God *hath revealed them to us*, by His Spirit.' The passage which follows enjoins Christians to 'know the things that are freely given to them of God;' and I am convinced it engenders a feeling of indifference not to realize in some degree the conception of that life which we shall one day enjoy, and which we now desire. In attempting to give precision to our thoughts on this solemn subject, let us pray for understanding to know as much as is revealed, while we are preserved from prying into more, for 'secret things belong unto the Lord'; but at the same time 'He has brought life and immortality to light.'"

"It appears," observed Matilda, "as if the Bible presented a map of heaven, on which are drawn in distinct outlines what shall be enjoyed hereafter; and Christians may confidently anticipate, that on entering the New Jerusalem, we shall be ready to say, as the Queen of Sheba did when she heard the wisdom of Solomon, 'The half was not told me.'"

"If a full revelation of Heaven in all its glory were made, how could any one endure a present life?" said Dr. Murray. "We should feel like a man who fixed his eyes on the blazing sun, and then attempted to look at the scenery around. The whole would appear dim and distorted. But though it be a presumptuous and an impossible attempt to realize *all* that is promised, and often difficult in Scripture to distinguish what is allegorical from what is real, yet many things are told of that 'place' which Christ has gone to prepare."

"I often think," said Matilda, "that much of the indifference which prevails in this world about a future state may be traced to the vagueness of our conceptions respecting its enjoyments, for few people fully consider how much is implied in the promises of revelation, with which our natures, even as they are now constituted, can have sympathy and connection. I remember, as a child, when any of my juvenile indulgences particularly delighted me, I frequently asked the nursery-maid if there would be pleasures similar to these in Heaven; but her invariable answer was, of course, in the negative; yet she might have added much to fill my mind with joyful anticipation, instead of the blank disappointment which her unqualified 'no' occasioned me. I think Christians often treat men of the world in a similar way. They tell, what is really true, that no sinful pleasures shall be there, but they forget to add those blessed hopes for hereafter which our Bibles hold out to all whom the Spirit shall fit and prepare."

"True," replied Dr. Murray. "It is impossible to speak or to think of them too much, for they are described contin-nally as motives to our love and obedience, which we ought to see and to appreciate, in order that we may pursue them diligently. The grateful and adoring contemplation of perfect holiness, and of infinite glory, will be the first and chief theme of every Christian's delight, when seeking to join in that eternal anthem of praise which St. John, in his mortal state, could not learn, though he heard it, and which St. Paul, when caught up into the third heaven, declared that it was not possible for man to utter. In a form such as our own, we shall then behold the merciful Author of our Redemption, and feel, in His presence, that the gratitude and love which are now but faint and occasional, can be continually exercised without effort, and without fear of diminution. Our praise, too, will be unmingled with sorrow, and uninjured by any remaining consciousness of sin, to mar that confidence and joy with which we shall stand before a benignant Saviour. The reunion of sisters, friends, and brethren, when we are '*gathered to our fathers*,' will be a meeting of unalloyed delight; for then every eye will be kindled with the same feelings of adoration, and every look will be one of sympathy and love. We read that St. Paul expected his converts to be 'a crown of joy and of rejoicing' in the presence of their Saviour, which gives a blessed confidence that the minister and his people shall not then forget their mutual ties. As St. Peter knew the glorified spirits of Moses and Elias, we may hope at once to distinguish the patriarchs and saints whose memory we reverence now; and as St. Paul forbade Christians to grieve like those who have no hope, who can doubt that it was because our lost friends were to be restored to us? David also comforted himself for the departure of his child by the prospect of going to him, and Dives is represented as recognizing Abraham. We read, too, that the rich man in Hell wished to save his brethren from so wretched a fate, and if there be brotherly love even there, what must it be amidst the society of just men made perfect; for who can question that the graces and virtues which we are commanded to exercise now, will hereafter find an abundant field for exercise? Those who have been faithful over few things shall be rulers over many things, which is a promise that implies active employment when men become, as we are told they shall, 'kings and priests unto God.' The bodies which we now wear shall then be restored to us, and in the new heavens and the new earth which are to be our blessed abode, how often will men look back, with distinct recollection, on their past existence, and acknowledge, with adoring admiration and gratitude, the infinite wisdom which caused every event of life to work together for their good, and which led them, blind, and faint, and wilful, as we all are, safe through the dangers and temptations of a thorny path, to the green pastures and the still waters of that better country, where the sun always shines, and where the joy is without measure and without end!"

Dr. Murray walked on for some time in silence, and Matilda did not interrupt him. There are thoughts too solemn for utterance, and there are emotions too profound for the ear of another. It became evident that his mind was delivered up to the boundless contemplation of futurity, and that his heart bore testimony to the language of his lips when he spoke of its incomparable importance, and of the grateful delight with which a Christian can forget every intermediate care of an earthly existence, and satisfy himself with the confident hope of a sinless and tearless eternity. When they approached within sight of Gowanbank, however, he seemed at once to call his mind back from the pleasures of meditation to the business and duty of the present hour.

"Mine has been a life of unusual peace," said he, "with none of those nearer ties which produce the keenest emotions of joy and of sorrow. Those few real afflictions which have fallen to my lot are so tempered by consolation that they scarcely deserve the name; but I have seen enough, in my sympathy for others, and in such worldly grief as Providence, in His wisdom, has ordained for myself, to prove that it is, indeed, better to visit the house of mourning than the house of feasting, and I trust that in administering comfort here we shall still find cause to say so."

Matilda could not but think how differently Dr. Murray's society would be appreciated in the house which they were now about to enter, from what she had seen it previously at Barnard Castle; and as she considered how he had been forgotten and overlooked amidst the gay revelry of those whom they had recently left, while she knew how his presence was hailed as the harbinger of consolation to many a desolated heart, she almost thought that such estimation as the servant of God received in these contrasted scenes of prosperity and adversity, might fairly illustrate the comparative importance in which they teach men to hold that Great Master whose cause Dr. Murray felt continually desirous to promote.

Old Janet met Matilda at the door, and made a faint endeavor to assume her usual smile of hospitable welcome, but the words she would have spoken died on her lips; and turning hastily away, with a faltering step she preceded them into the cottage, where Martha sat, with her sister's hand in her own, and her eyes despondingly bent on the ground.

If ever there lived a heart which vibrated to every tone of human suffering, it was that of Dr. Murray, who only showed he had inwardly felt what grief is, by the deep experience with which he could talk to others of its consolations. Yet, accustomed as he had long been to scenes and sights of wo, he paused, in silent pity and astonishment, when they entered and beheld the desolating effects of mental agony. There is a fable of Niobe having been turned into stone by extreme anguish, which seems true to nature, whenever we behold the consequences of sudden calamity. Tears characterize a gentle feeling, but the blanched cheek, the sunk eye, and the parched lip of Nanny, mournfully testified that grief, like an ice-bolt, had entered into her heart, and paralyzed her senses. She crouched on a low seat, motionless as death, her hair dishevelled over her face, and her eye fixed on vacancy, without the slightest evidence of observing what passed around. It appeared, indeed, that "her beauty had consumed away," and as Matilda looked at her, with speechless emotion, it seemed as if years must have passed since she had beheld that haggard countenance in all the bloom of youth.

After many vain efforts to attract her notice, Nanny at length looked up, with a strange ghastly smile, at Matilda, until, after some moments, a dawn of recollection seemed struggling into her mind, and beckoning her forward, she whispered in a low bewildered tone, pointing to old Janet—

"Speak to *her!*—Tell her it was untrue!—We'll not let Martha know that I cared about him!—Who put all those things in the flower-stand? Oh! don't say it was me!"

"Nanny!" said Dr. Murray, in a tone of mild authority, which attracted her instant attention, "there is a day coming when the secrets of all hearts shall be laid open. Those who are unfairly accused will then be acquitted, and any one who has told a falsehood against his neighbor shall be known and punished. I believe, when that hour comes, that your mother, your sister, and all of us who believe you to be innocent, will then rejoice in hearing the real truth. But there are many unfounded stories, and many evil reports in this world, and we must not break our hearts if they rise up against ourselves. You should be comforted when unjustly accused, by feeling in your own heart that it actually is untrue, and that you were never really tempted to do what is said. We commit sins every day, which are known only to God, and not to man—how much better it is if the Almighty sees we are not guilty, when man suspects that we are. Every sorrow in life is light and easy to endure in comparison of remorse: but a wounded spirit who can bear? We must value our good name and character in the world more than any mere earthly blessing; but still even that may be taken from us by the wisdom of Him who knows what is good for every one. Let us then be ready to suffer, though it were worse than death itself, not considering the loss as an accident, nor as the fruit of malice, but as the merciful correction of a Father, who knows what is best. It would be better, certainly, to weep for a short season and live forever, than to rejoice in that mirth which is as the crackling of thorns under a pot, and ends in quick destruction. By the loss of friends, and the treachery of enemies, or in any way that may be surest, oh! who would not desire, on whatever terms, to be fitted for that country where no enemy ever entered, and from whence no friend shall ever go away!"

Dr. Murray continued his address, from time to time, in the soothing accents of kindness and pity, while Nanny seemed to listen; but it was difficult to say how far her mind followed his meaning, for she appeared stunned and stupefied, without the power to express emotion, or to reflect on anything but the weight of her own sorrow. Old Janet watched her countenance with intense anxiety, till at length she shook her head despondingly, and turned away, while tears started into Martha's eyes; but when Dr. Murray at length proposed that they should unite in prayer, Nanny looked around with sudden recollection, and then slowly, with an air of deep solemnity and devotion, sunk upon the ground, and buried her face on her mother's knee, while she clasped her hands together with convulsive energy.

CHAPTER XV.

I'll introduce you: Gentlemen! my friend.
CRABBE.

"ELEANOR!" cried Sir Richard, entering next day, when the whole party were gathered merrily round a blazing fire, and fixing a look of sly humor on his daughter, "I have charming news for you!—My good friend and kinsman, M'Tartan, has met with an accident on the road; and whether it be a spring broken, or a fractured limb, is, I am aware, all one to you, since it must inevitably postpone his arrival here. But," added the Baronet, drawing a long breath, and trying to assume some appearance of gravity, "he has very stupidly forwarded this foreign Count of his, who may probably arrive in an hour. It will be an unspeakable bore, because my French is not in good repair now, and he speaks no English."

"Delightful!" exclaimed Eleanor. "You know, papa, how I doat upon foreigners, so make him over entirely to my care. It wanted but this to make me completely happy!—how enchanting it will be to have him for a partner this evening!"

"I have no objection, provided you don't take him as a partner for life!" replied her father, with a look of irrepressible glee, which seemed quite unaccountable to Matilda. "These foreigners are all so handsome, and so insinuating, that they invariably carry off our heiresses now; and if I had foreseen that you were to become the *laird* here, your honor should never have been allowed to learn one syllable of French!"

"Oh! how barbarous, papa! I would rather relinquish my mother tongue; and if the Count speaks only Italian, that would be irresistible."

"I always feared this," continued Sir Richard, trying to look very serious; "we Englishmen have no chance in a drawing-room, when foreigners, with nine syllables to their names, like Count Constantine Ecatrinoslav, arise and shine in our hemisphere. I must ring for Martin directly, to give him a lesson of pronunciation, that he may announce our visitor properly. It will take some hours' practice at least, to make him perfect; and Monsieur le Comte will arrive immediately, for, as Shakspeare says,

> 'By the pricking of my thumbs,
> Something wicked this way comes!' "

"What is he like?" asked Major Foley, turning towards the mirror, and pulling up his neckcloth. "You have seen him, I suppose?"

"Why, no. I never was in company with Count Constantine; but his description is set down here with a degree of accuracy, that might have done for a passport. Tall, dark hair, florid complexion, grey eyes, and so forth."

"Has he mustachios?" exclaimed Mr. Grant, clasping his hands, and assuming a look of agonizing suspense.

"Prodigious!" replied Sir Richard, laughing.

"Then we are all undone!" continued Mr. Grant, giving a glance of condolence to the other gentlemen, and sinking back on the sofa, in an attitude of despair.

"I am the last man on earth to be at all illiberal," said Lord Alderby, in a pompous tone; "but at the same time I hate all foreigners, and consider them most dangerous people in society."

"I wish the Count, had staid in Siberia, for it freezes my very blood to think of him!" added Mr. Grant, laughing. "Remember, Miss Fitz-Patrick, if he cuts me out of my seat next to you at dinner to-day, I shall be seen wandering round the table, with tears frozen in icicles from my eye-lashes, according to the fashion of his country."

"A very *melting* sight indeed," replied Eleanor.

"My hair would grow grey in a night with distress of mind!" continued Mr. Grant.

"Ah! that happens to every person now, once in their lives!—we never hear of any one becoming grey in the regular course of nature, but always some romantic history of its coming on in a few hours."

"I dare say this Count that shall be nameless, because it really fatigues me to pronounce his endless designation, probably travels with a bear inside the carriage," added Mr. Grant; "a monkey on the dicky; smokes cigars all along the road; and brings a hamper of the best train-oil with him to flavor M. Martigny's sauces."

"Eleanor has such a passion for everything foreign," observed Sir Richard, "that I doubt if she will even object to that."

"Not at all!" persisted she eagerly. "My penchant for foreigners is incurable, they are all so agreeable. It is the only rule I know without a single exception."

"He will play the pianoforte for you on Sundays," continued Sir Richard, slyly watching the effect of all he said; "and the Count performs charmingly on—on the Russian horn."

"There must surely be some mistake here!" said Sir Alfred, who had been listening for some time past to the conversation with an air of perplexity and surprise. "I once met Count Constantine Ecatrinoslav abroad; and though *he* had not the honor of being introduced to me, yet I have a dim recollection ——"

"Very *dim* indeed, I dare say," cried Sir Richard, with a degree of *brusquerie* and eagerness which astonished Matilda not less than it evidently did Sir Alfred. "He is amazingly altered of late, I am told, and that reminds me that I wish to consult you about the—the—the new kennel I am building, so let us waste no more time in foreign affairs. By the way, we have not discussed the state of your canvass this morning yet," added Sir Richard, hastily beckoning Sir Alfred aside, who rather unwillingly followed. The two gentlemen continued in close conference for some time, while Matilda observed that the former seemed to be explaining something which infinitely diverted himself, while the handsome and expressive countenance of his companion indicated a vain attempt at good-humored remonstrance, which ended in his giving a smile of unwilling acquiescence, and silently resuming his place amidst the joyous party round the fire.

Eleanor's impatient curiosity to see her foreign visitor was not destined to be of long duration, for Sir Richard entered the drawing-room about an hour afterwards, rubbing his hands with glee, and announcing that Count Constantine's carriage had come in sight. "It is extremely like the one you arrived in lately, Sir Alfred," added he "but only *much handsomer*."

"He copies me, I have no doubt," replied the baronet, dryly. "There are a number of people who do, which is very inconvenient. The moment I get a new equipage, or even a new waistcoat, everybody starts one in imitation."

"Pray come to the window and look at him," continued Sir Richard, eagerly.

"You had better bring *him* to look at *me*," answered Sir Alfred, rising as he spoke, and strolling up to his laughing host, who continued whispering and talking, until the door flew open, and Count Ecatrinoslav was duly announced.

Sir Richard hastened forward with surprising cordiality, and Eleanor thought it the strongest proof she had ever witnessed of her father's unbounded hospitality, that, with all his prejudice against foreigners, he welcomed their illustrious visitor with a truly English shake of the hand, expressive of the warmest cordiality. Not a word passed on either side, but he instantly led the Count all round, introducing him with great ceremony and respect to each individual of the assembled circle, while the newly-arrived stranger followed up these presentations by performing a profusion of bows. At every repetition of his name, he struck his heels together and clashed his spurs, while his hat was clasped to his heart and then waved to the very ground. Sir Alfred vouchsafed to give only a very slight inclination of the head in reply, but when Mr. Grant's turn came, he completely excelled Count Constantine in the number and profoundness of his salutations, till Matilda could scarcely refrain from laughing outright, to observe how rapidly the two gentlemen flitted from right to left, and from left to right, before each other.

Eleanor's eyes followed Count Constantine round the room with an expression of delighted approbation, because nothing could be more outrageously foreign than his whole dress and appearance. His face was let out through a parenthesis of enormous whiskers, while mustachios and patches were scattered over every part of his countenance where they could be supposed possible. A greatcoat, completely lined with splendid sables and covered with frogs and tassels, was what he wore, with boots that seemed to raise him on tiptoe, the heels seemed so elevated, and several scraps of ribbon which were visible on his inner coat, appeared to indicate the existence of corresponding medals and orders, when he chose to make a display. After Eleanor had concluded the ceremony of receiving him, with all her natural grace, and more than her natural dignity, she turned to Mr. Grant, whispering in an undertone, "The Count looks quite like a hero!"

"Rather *mock*-heroic! He is the very model of what would be admired among nursery-maids and boarding-school misses. Those Russians always wear ribbons of more various colors than any tailor's pattern-book, but your visitor must have distinguished himself in every battle that ever was fought, and acquired all the medals and orders that were ever invented. Shall I pierce my last shilling to-day, and hang it on a blue ribbon to my button-hole, in order to keep him in countenance?"

Eleanor now resolved to lose no time in making an entire monopoly of the interesting foreigner, and entered immediately upon a discussion of all the subjects which appeared most suitable, speaking at random, in French, with such rapidity and fluency, that scarcely an interval was allowed for the Count to give more than a bow and a shrug of reply. Upon her favorite principle of adaptation, she chose every topic in the most distant degree connected with Russia. The Emperor Paul, St. Petersburg, Countess Dashkoff, bear's grease, sledges, palaces of ice, Marshal Blücher, Elizabeth of Siberia, the state of Poland, and a panorama of the burning of Moscow, which she asked her guest if he had seen in London.

Putting his hand suddenly to his forehead, the Count turned away, and Matilda could not but think, for one moment, that the convulsive working of his features looked almost like laughter, till Sir Richard stepped hastily forward, and whispered to his daughter in a tone of indignant remonstrance, "My dear Eleanor, how can you be so cruelly thoughtless?—ladies never have any reflection! The Count lost on that occasion a splendid palace, plate, jewels, pictures, books——"

"An old Russian-leather writing-case," added Mr. Grant. in an undertone, "and several very valuable pair of *Russia ducks*, which have never since been replaced."

"How exquisitely agreeable he is," exclaimed Eleanor, affectedly, when Count Constantine soon after sent for his foreign servant and left the room to see his baggage arranged.

"I am not sensible that our friend has spoken above one or two monosyllables," replied Sir Richard; "but that shows, my dear girl, the power of prejudice."

"Not at all! I never saw a more romantic-looking man—such an air *distingué*—such perfect self-possession—so much grace in his address——"

"I would rather not be asked my opinion of him," said Mr. Grant. "It may be prejudice, from the description we had of the personage who introduced Count Ecatrinoslav here; but there certainly appears something very M'Tartanish about him. I know a thorough-bred foreigner by instinct, and this is evidently some *valet de place*, who has murdered his master, and stolen his letters of recommendation."

"How very malicious! when we all know that you are dying to be like him."

"The last man on earth that any one could wish to resemble, except in his power of pleasing you."

"All envy and detraction! I must positively leave the room, Mr. Grant, if you become so very censorious. In fact, the world is getting extremely ill-natured of late, and will soon be unfit for me to live in."

"And if *you* were to depart, I am sure it would be fit for nobody else," added Lord Alderby.

"Eleanor, can you be serious in thinking so much of the Count?" asked Sir Richard, stooping over a newspaper, so as to hide his face. "My old *protégé*, Donald M'Tartan, used to be fully better looking, were you only to see him with the same eyes."

"If I became blind, there might then be no visible difference; but, papa, your favoritism of Captain M'Tartan was an old grievance ages ago, and I am sorry to see it reviving."

"If my good cousin had been handsome and agreeable, like this new importation from Petersburg, would you have received him as graciously?"

"Quite! I have actually no preference for foreigners, when our own people can learn to be equally agreeable," replied she in a tone of lively *persiflage*. "Let me announce, however, papa, to complete your horror, that this Count bids fair to become a special favorite of mine."

"It is only to be hoped that the partiality is mutual," said Sir Richard, dryly.

"Undoubtedly, as all Miss Fitz-Patrick's partialities must be," observed Lord Alderby, with a sigh that might have driven a man-of-war from its anchorage.

"Surely the Count has lost his way," continued she, anxiously. "Mr. Armstrong's baggage had to be moved up another flight of stairs. I really am sorry not to have a better room at my disposal, for, though it might do very well for Captain M'Tartan, yet——"

"Eleanor, you have exceeded my hopes," exclaimed Sir Richard, slapping his hand on the table, and rising, with an explosion of laughter, which he seemed totally unable to control, while the whole party looked on in silent amazement. As soon as he could command his voice, however, he added:

"I knew that it was impossible to expect a tolerable reception for my friend the Captain, so we planned together a little agreeable *coup de théâtre*, which has outdone my utmost expectations. Count Ecatrinoslav was unexpectedly detained for several days by an invitation to Windsor, but mean time allow me to introduce my cousin, Count Constantine M'Tartan! I did not intend to betray our secret for a month, but this opportunity becomes irresistible."

Sir Richard hurried, in an ecstasy of delight, to the entrance-hall, and produced the *ci-devant* foreigner, who looked precisely as he did before, but with a laugh in his eye, which showed Eleanor at once how completely she had been imposed upon.

Matilda felt alarmed to anticipate what her cousin might say or do, for anger flashed in her countenance, and she was evidently irritated in the highest degree; but before the sentence which rose to her lips could be uttered, she suddenly caught the calm, observant eye of Sir Alfred fixed upon her, and instantly became silent; while Miss Howard, to fill up the pause, observed, in a soothing tone—

"We have been all completely taken in, Eleanor. Sir Richard can claim little credit for imposing on me, but it really must be allowed that the joke was excellently got up when it deceived you."

"I know," began Sir Colin, "a very curious circumstance of the kind which occurred to myself——"

"So do I!" interrupted Eleanor, instantaneously recovering her temper, and giving way to a hearty fit of laughter. "Papa! for this once I forgive you, and shall, moreover, generously add my congratulation on your success. Captain M'Tartan! so you are as fond of masquerading as ever! Now observe! when you have been translated into English, I hereby retract all that was said after you entered this house, either in favor of the Count, or in disparagement of yourself. At the same time allow me to request that you will remain at Barnard Castle till your spirits have recovered the loss of your palace at Moscow, and of all the plate, pictures, jewels, and writing-cases. How could I be such a dupe; but that was not the case either, *for I guessed it all the time!*"

When Matilda had dressed for dinner, and was about to re-enter the drawing-room, she heard a new voice, and a ringing laugh of such uproarious vulgarity, that it puzzled her for a moment to conjecture who could perpetrate sounds so out of keeping with the harmonious tone of the party in general; but immediately afterwards she perceived Captain M'Tartan, who had hitherto appeared only in dumbshow, standing upon the hearth-rug, in a perfect blaze of spirits, and addressing every one familiarly, whether he knew them or not.

"You've been in India, I suppose, Sir Colin? One may guess it by a little tinge of the pagoda in your complexion; but six weeks at Cheltenham is infallible for the liver."

Sir Colin's feeble attempts to deny this imaginary trip to the East, and the consequent aspersion on his liver, were drowned in the stentorian voice of his new acquaintance.

"I've seen officers come home that you might have coined their faces into gold; and it was quite a benevolent pleasure to watch every day at the Wells, how they gradually cleared up. Fine Indian-looking city Cheltenham is; by the way, you would suppose every Nabob had brought his own bungalow from Calcutta and set it up there with verandahs and balconies complete—the walls, too, such a delicate color, they seem to be built of cream-cheese. *A propos*, Fitz-Patrick, the yellow-fever broke out on board of us at Jamaica, and nearly sent me off to a *foreign station*—officers were dropping like nine-pins. Since then, we never saw a sight of land—forgot my geography entirely, but I've at last remembered my way here. You must teach me, Eleanor, to know a cow from a camel, and a man from a monkey."

"I see very little difference myself sometimes! but among all other oblivions, I perceive, Captain M'Tartan has *not yet* taken the trouble to forget my Christian name."

"Ah! for that matter, I know your name and date pretty correctly, Eleanor!—we'll not say how much twice nine makes, for I can keep a secret as well as another. Ladies never like their ages to be published, Lady Susan Danvers, so I ask no questions, that we may hear no untruths. Did I ever see any girl rise above twenty! and old ladies stick at nine-and-forty for ten or a dozen years always! For my part, as the Irish lady said, 'I'm just the age of other people.' So my old acquaintance Sir Alfred is here—he's not a bad fellow, Douglas! I really feel a regard for him—a little brusque or so occasionally, but has some very good points, when you know how to manage him—rather too shy, perhaps. Ah, my good friend! speak of any one, and he starts up directly. How goes all at Douglas Priory?" said Captain M'Tartan, advancing with extended hand to the Baronet, who entered at that moment, and assuming that patronizing air of encouragement which is always exhibited towards those who have the reputation of shyness.

"Did you wish to see the Courier?" replied Sir Alfred, holding out some newspapers which were in his hand, and making a distant bow.

Captain M'Tartan shrunk back, provoked, but not abashed.

"Tell me, Eleanor, how shall we amuse ourselves this season? I am your man for anything. A *tableau of all work*, or whatever pleases you; but come what may, for better or for worse, I have hung up my hat here for three weeks at least!"

"I wish you would change places with it."

"No! no! I'm not come to *that* yet! You will never make a victim of me! We've known each other too long, Eleanor, so there can never be much love lost between us, though let me tell you that a certain gentleman, not many miles off, was *immensely* admired by the Russian ladies."

"Every person is supposed to be admired who leaves home," answered Eleanor. "When any young lady goes to England, we are invariably assured by all her relations that she has been considered the greatest beauty in London. If she gets as far off as Rome, there are no bounds to what may be said;—we are then generally told she is taken for Raphael's Madonna, and mobbed wherever she appears. But when you talk of what people admire in Russia, I should imagine that Medusa might pass there for one of the Graces. *A propos* of those frozen regions, I hope we shall enjoy an arctic climate for my skating-party to-morrow, when there must be no clouds either on the sky or the earth."

Next morning a bright, joyous, laughing sunshine, and a clear, hard frost, fulfilled Eleanor's most sanguine hopes, and for once a party of pleasure assembled, unanimously declaring that the weather was beyond criticism. Loch Deveril glittered, like a broad expanse of mirror, in one resplendent field, and the whole surrounding country was clad in a winding-sheet of snow, when the cavalcade of britschskas, phaetons, pony-carriages, and riders, drew up along its margin, and the whole *cortége* alighted in a tumult of joyous excitement.

Sir Alfred wrapped himself in a large cloak of sable fur, and leaned against the trunk of a tree, while several other gentlemen impatiently launched themselves on the ice. There is something characteristic in every action of a man's life, whether it be his manner of sitting, standing, walking, dancing, entering a room, or even skating, and Eleanor felt amused for some time with watching and criticizing the different conceptions of that art which were exhibited by various performers.

Captain M'Tartan displayed tremendous powers of velocity, which contrasted well with the graceful evolutions of Mr. Grant, whose light and buoyant figure skimmed along as if he scarcely touched the ice, while Lord Alderby appeared, by his weight, to shake the whole surface of the lake.

"This is already marked down as one of the *white days* in my life!" cried Eleanor. "Ah! there goes Sir Colin! slow, deliberate, and vascillating, like one of his own stories. Mr. Grant's manœuvres remind one of the maze at Hampton Court, where so many doublings and windings have been contrived, that we are always moving, but never advancing. I see he is waiting for us. Captain M'Tartan looks like a Dutch hulk in full sail! Now, Sir Alfred, what shall you and I do?"

"One vowel at a time, if you please, Miss Fitz-Patrick, for that is all that either U or I ever profess to take care of."

"You must be the Scandinavian bear escaped from the Zoological Gardens, Sir Alfred, for that was precisely the answer he once made me on a similar occasion. Any one else in this world would have had his head turned forever, if I had so much as hinted that his escort might be acceptable."

"We are both spoilt by adulation, Miss Fitz-Patrick."

"Will nobody take down your vanity! Positively, Sir Alfred, you grow more intolerable every day!"

"Do I?—that is the very thing I desire!"

"Now, tell me, seriously, if one may venture to ask—are you supposed to have complete possession of your senses?"

"I know only one or two people who have!"

"Mine would very soon be distracted with listening to such incredibilities, so good-bye, Sir Alfred! I shall never see you again! It is scarcely worth while to be a 'lady in waiting' for any one, while there stands a lord in waiting not far off." She pointed to Lord Alderby, and slipping on her skates, proceeded to join some more active members of the party, who were already at some distance, in gay and lively emulation of each other's achievements.

"As Ophelia says, 'What a noble mind is there o'erthrown!'" observed Sir Alfred, watching Eleanor's departure, and addressing Matilda. "Your cousin always seems to me like a pianoforte *all treble*, with no full, deep tones in her character at all."

"Perhaps you might think otherwise, Sir Alfred, if Eleanor were in circumstances to call them forth. At the time of her poor mother's death she suffered deeply, and no one would have thought her deficient in feeling then; but amidst such scenes of festivity as she has lately enjoyed, there is little opportunity to judge of the heart, or to know whether people have any heart at all."

"Your zealous defence of Miss Fitz-Patrick, for instance, is no evidence whether judgment or feeling is the strongest," replied Sir Alfred, smiling at Matilda's warmth. "But could a mind of any sensibility be satisfied with mere amusement, in which every serious reflection, and every kind impulse, is for the present laid aside! Could *you?*" asked he, at once resuming a tone of confidential intimacy. "No, Miss Howard! I read the answer in your countenance, for we are both convinced that there is a sphere of thought, of feeling, and of enjoyment, which the world knows not of, and which, nevertheless, no one can be happy without having tried, in a way that your brilliant cousin has never yet done. Nothing amuses me more than her air when she enters the room, which looks as much as to say, 'Here is Miss Fitz-Patrick, of Barnard Castle, who can neither think, say, nor do a single thing that should not be watched and admired.' One might fancy, from her look sometimes, that she expected to be received with three rounds of applause."

"Sir Alfred!" replied Matilda, archly, "if we were to judge of every one from appearances, I have heard something very like that said of somebody else."

"I dare say you have! The truth is, Miss Howard, for I wish to conceal nothing from *you*, that my reserve seems unconquerable, except towards the very few whom I trust entirely; and I care for no familiar intercourse with any one whose sentiments are not in some degree similar to my own. As most pleasures appear to be greater when clandestine, so, in my deepest emotions, it often gives them a profounder zest to think that they are known only by those friends who have my most sacred confidence. I shall never be slow to acknowledge opinions and principles, where it seems right to do so, for they are my highest honor; but in proportion to my reverence for holy things, is my apprehension of hearing them hackneyed in ordinary conversation, as a subject for mawkish sentiment or idle gossip."

"I quite agree with you, Sir Alfred, in disliking a superficial interchange of unfelt truths, and all that mere jargon which people sometimes talk in society now; but yet it appears to me a matter of duty, openly to acknowledge such convictions as are inwardly felt, that we may not seem ashamed of them."

"I certainly do encourage rather a morbid sensibility in that respect, but the moment any man publicly declares his attachment to serious religion he becomes liable to a thousand deceptions. All those who have any object to gain by pleasing him, adapt their conversation to his supposed inclinations, so, that in the forming of friendships, and of all nearer ties, he is apt to be misled and disappointed. Religion is the fashion now, rather than an object of persecution, as formerly, and my friend Leicester warned me once of what he had to undergo, after it became generally known that he withdrew from the world, on Christian principles. Each lady or gentleman who wished for his confidence, professed an inclination to do likewise, but for some cruel necessity which prevented it. They all agreed to his opinions, were convinced by his arguments, felt all he had felt, read what he recommended, subscribed to his favorite charities, and, in short, made him their counsellor and confessor. Every one can talk so fluently, and read so much, that he seemed to live in an atmosphere of profession without principle, and my good friend soon had really little else to do than listen to the eloquence of those whose practice was entirely inconsistent with that knowledge they were so ready so display."

"It is certainly singular what a general familiarity prevails in every company, with the doctrines and feelings of religion. You never encounter any one in society now who is not able and willing to discuss that subject in an interesting manner; and though there are not many to whom it is the *first* object in life, scarcely an individual I ever converse with, does not make it the *second*, to be promoted at some future time to its proper place."

"There is pain in associating with those who are entirely ignorant of religion, but still more in hearing those who know their Master's will, and evidently do it not. I have seen your cousin talk like a bishop to Dr. Murray, when the whim takes her, and if it were understood that the subject is one of more than common interest for me, even my friend, Miss Charlotte Clifford, might get up a few suitable questions and remarks."

"By allowing yourself to become so fastidious, may not many opportunities be lost, Sir Alfred, of usefulness to others, and gratification to yourself? I have often felt agreeably surprised in talking to friends, on finding that the subject excited more interest, and that their sentiments were really more serious than might have been anticipated. With respect to Eleanor, she had early advantages, of which, I trust and believe, we shall yet see the fruits."

"No one can be otherwise than amused by her vivacity; but Miss Fitz-Patrick's entire want of sympathy and kindness towards one who deserves both in their highest degree, has, perhaps, prejudiced me too strongly. For all that gives worth or interest to the female character, I long since looked elsewhere, and found more than my most sanguine wishes could desire, without having been ever on any single occasion deceived or disappointed. I am naturally gifted with a keen perception of character and motives, which, in a world like this, is seldom an agreeable instinct to possess. With me it seems like an additional sense, the clear light in which I can read thoughts and intentions carefully veiled from ordinary observation; and it is only when in company with Miss Howard, and a very few others, that I have never felt cause to regret this habitual penetration."

Scarcely had Sir Alfred done speaking, when a loud and piercing shriek, which seemed to rend the very skies, arose on the ice, and was repeated again and again, while Matilda, with clasped hands and straining eyes, gazed in the direction from whence it came, vainly seeking to ascertain any cause for so much terror and alarm; but a moment afterwards her utmost fears were exceeded.

In gay emulation of each other's skill, the party of skaters had careered about Loch Deveril for a considerable time, wheeling backwards and forwards, cutting spread-eagles, and trying races in proof of their pre-eminent grace and velocity. At length Eleanor, unthinkingly, started with her utmost speed towards a point which none of the party had ventured to approach because of a rapid stream which fell from the neighboring hills, and was known to flow across the ice, rendering it at all times extremely unsafe. A loud cry of apprehension from her companions was uttered in vain, for Miss Fitz-Patrick seemed determined to out-dare them all; and, delighted with the notice she excited, as well as ignorant of her danger, she seemed in the act of lightly skimming along the surface, and gracefully kissing her hands to the group of alarmed spectators behind, in laughing defiance of their warnings, when in a moment she disappeared.

The instant Matilda became conscious of what had happened, she uttered a cry of grief and despair while rushing forward to the margin of the lake, and hastily proceeding onwards, almost unconscious of what she did, when her arm was firmly grasped, and her progress arrested by Sir Alfred Douglas.

"She is lost!—let me go!—let me try to save her," gasped Matilda, in breathless agitation; "I must help her, or perish with her!—oh! Sir Alfred, do not stop me, as you value the life of the person dearest to you on earth."

"That is my reason for detaining *you*," replied he, in a tone of such emotion that even her present terror and distress could not make Matilda entirely insensible of it. "Promise me that you will remain here, whatever happens, and I shall instantly go in your place."

Scarcely had Matilda given the required assurance before Sir Alfred darted off, and proceeded on the ice at a rate which seemed more like the flight of a bird than any mere human effort of velocity, while she remained fixed to the spot, with straining eyes and beating heart, watching his progress, and uttering many an inward prayer for Eleanor, herself, and him.

No sooner did it become obvious into what very imminent danger Miss Fitz-Patrick's fool-hardiness had betrayed her, than, with the most eager recklessness of danger, she was instantly pursued by one whose courage and presence of mind were equal to every emergency, while his very life seemed never worth a thought when an opportunity occurred of risking it with spirit, or of losing it with honor. Captain M'Tartan appeared to outstrip the wind, he flew forward with such incomparable fleetness; and all the anxiety with which he was followed by Mr. Grant could not afford the smallest chance of his being anticipated or overtaken. Instantly plunging into the gulf where Eleanor vanished, he seemed scarcely to have left his native element, and grasping her with a powerful arm, he buffeted his way up the course of a torrent, which had broken through the ice, and a moment afterwards placed Miss Fitz-Patrick safe, though nearly insensible, on the shore, amidst the loud acclamations from the surrounding spectators, who instantly crowded to the spot.

Miss Marabout was at once sufficiently recovered from her recent fright to wish for a little bustle and importance on an occasion when she felt entitled to assume the lead. She caused Eleanor to be instantly conveyed to the fishing-lodge where, after banishing Matilda and every one else from the room, she prepared to place Miss Fitz-Patrick in bed, when Eleanor suddenly roused herself, to make a decided protest against any such arrangement. No persuasions on the part of Miss Marabout could induce her to take any precautions, except changing her dress for one which was purchased from the fisherman's daughter; and thus equipped she soon rejoined the party, with all her usual animation of manner, and with more than her usual beauty, in consequence of recent agitation having heightened her color, and given additional lustre to her eyes.

When Matilda saw her cousin once more restored to life and safety, she forgot for a moment everything but the joy with which her heart was filled, and clasping Eleanor in her arms with an exclamation of thankfulness, she burst into tears.

"My good cousin!" said Miss Fitz-Patrick, in a tone of more kindness than usual, "you are a perfect Niobe, and will dissolve altogether some day, if we do not look after you! My danger must have been greatly exaggerated, and besides, every one is immortal till his hour is come. Depend upon it, I am not to be drowned in Loch Deveril, so you should never anticipate the worst, but remember there is no evil so bad as that which never happened. I recollect nothing of the accident now, except a strange sensation from having nothing to stand on."

"As for Miss Howard's alarm, that could never be compared with mine!" said Miss Marabout; "but it is not my way to say much. Every one must see how pale I look! My heart still beats like a clock, and my eyes are perfectly dim with the fright. Really our obligations to Captain M'Tartan are incalculable, and if he were only in the room——"

"Don't speak of him!" interrupted Eleanor, impatiently. "If I was destined to meet with an adventure, would nobody be the hero of it but Captain M'Tartan!"

"You *must* end in being married to him at last," said

Lady Susan Danvers, in an oracular voice. "Whenever any gentleman saves a lady's life, that is the certain *dénouement*, however unlikely at the time."

"Yes, every impediment will, of course, give way," added Miss Charlotte, enjoying Eleanor's visible irritation. "How delightful it was, long ago, when no young lady seems ever to have embarked in a boat, mounted on horseback, or staid at home, without being rescued from imminent danger, as you were to-day, by some hero like Captain M'Tartan, who married her three volumes afterwards!"

"I am trying to calculate," said Eleanor, gravely, "whether it would have been most advantageous to the world, that Captain M'Tartan and I should have been *both saved* or both drowned—whether he would not have been as great a riddance to you all as I am an acquisition."

"He has done more for you," said Lady Susan, looking maliciously at Mr. Grant, "than many people who make finer speeches."

"Poor Foley! We must not be too severe upon him," replied her cousin, turning away the sarcasm from himself. "I was sure you thought the Major too complimentary this morning, when he discovered such a family likeness between us, but I really forgave him at last, knowing how completely it is his foible, wishing to put ladies on good terms with themselves."

At this moment Captain M'Tartan entered from an inner room, where he had been engaged in performing a hasty toilet, having contrived with extreme difficulty to squeeze on the Sunday clothes of a young man who seemed on a moderate computation to be about half his size. The coat appeared in imminent danger of bursting, and the sleeves were so short and so tight, that his elbows could not be bent, and his wrists remained totally uncovered. A pair of white trowsers, which were meant to be long and wide, scarcely reached below the knees, his face and hands looked purple with cold, and his hair stood on end, as if frozen in an upright position. Bowing rather uncouthly to the ladies, he would have hastened past, when Miss Marabout, who was on all occasions very attentive to middle-aged beaux, hastily intercepted his steps, and began an oration which was meant to be long and eloquent.

"Captain M'Tartan, let me take the first opportunity to express our admiration and gratitude——"

"Pshaw!—nonsense, Miss Marabout!—I hate palaver,"

interrupted he, trying to hurry on, but she skilfully intercepted him, and proceeded,—

"We really do consider ourselves under the deepest obligations, and Miss Fitz-Patrick feels most grateful as well as myself. A pretty story it would have been, Captain M'Tartan, if the heiress of these wide domains had been drowned in sight of us all, without any one affording her the least assistance, which would have been the case, but for your gallantry and heroism."

"One would think we were at a public dinner, Miss Marabout," replied Captain M'Tartan, impatiently measuring the distance between himself and the door, with evident intentions to make a spring at it.

"Indeed, many people have had public dinners given them for less," persisted she.

"It would take a man several bottles of claret to stand such a broadside as this," muttered the captain, angrily attempting to escape, but still in vain, for though Miss Marabout could not well take him by the button. she contrived to make it almost equally impossible that he should elude her vigilance.

"I only speak what Miss Fitz-Patrick thinks, and she would have expressed her own sentiments on the occasion, but unfortunately, you will perceive, she is still rather hysterical."

The truth was, that Eleanor had been for some time convulsively endeavoring to restrain a burst of laughter with which she nearly greeted the entrance of her heroic deliverer, and she dared not yet venture on a second glance at his strange-looking figure.

"This is too much for the shilling gallery," whispered she to Mr. Grant, seeing a servant enter to announce the carriage, who was obliged to turn away unable to speak, when his eye caught the grotesque costume before him.

"There is a great difference between empty professions and spirited actions," continued Miss Marabout, warming into eloquence; "and it will be seen that Miss Fitz-Patrick can appreciate the true value of both."

"Hem! if the coat fits put it on!" said Mr. Grant, good-humoredly coming up to the relief of Captain M'Tartan, whom he perceived to be really annoyed at his detention; "Stultz, of course," continued he, slipping his arm into the captain's, and walking him away. "My good fellow, as we say in Persia, may your shadow never be less!"

"Captain M'Tartan," said Sir Alfred, offering him his hand with the warmest cordiality. "You must pardon a little malice and envy from us all. Fortune has favored you already with so many opportunities of gaining distinction, that your laurels might have been spared this morning to those of us who needed them more."

The grasp of a vice could scarcely have been more powerful than that with which Captain M'Tartan seized the extended hand, but Sir Alfred returned his friendly greeting with scarcely less *empressement*, while Eleanor was restored to instant gravity by the surprise of observing what passed.

"To be well shaken when taken," said Mr. Grant, offering his hand also, and contriving to give Eleanor a hint to do likewise, in consequence of which she felt, *bon gré mal gré*, obliged to come forward. Lady Susan, perceiving how the tide set, next advanced, followed by Miss Charlotte and the whole party, who crowded round the Captain with such a chorus of congratulation and praise, that his stock of patience became completely exhausted. "Ladies and gentlemen," said he, breaking through the thick array, and escaping out at the door, "I wish you would observe a rule made in the Laird of Macfarlane's family long ago, that not above nine of them were to speak at once!"

"I could tell you a much better story than that"—began Sir Colin, in a slow methodical voice, which instantly cleared the cottage of its inmates, and drove them all for refuge into the various carriages which were waiting to convey them home.

"Matilda," whispered Eleanor, taking her cousin's arm, in a tone of friendly confidence, "there certainly is something of the sublime and beautiful about Sir Alfred very different from other men, and you will allow that we can feel very little doubt now of his preference."

"For whom?" asked her cousin, starting and coloring.

"Nonsense, Matilda!—you must have observed it. Miss Marabout tells me his efforts to reach the place where I fell into Loch Deveril were perfectly superhuman, and his speech to Captain M'Tartan was made with prodigious feeling. All this is quite unlike his usual indifference about every one else, and makes the affair perfectly plain to me. Besides, it is unprecedented, his remaining so much in the saloon as he has done lately, for Mr. Grant told me that his friend used to have an utter contempt for any mere drawing-room man. Indeed, he asked me, with a particular look this morning, if I had never yet guessed what caused the great change in Sir Alfred's habits, and would certainly have mentioned something interesting at the moment, but he gave a cautionary glance towards you, as much as to say that we might be overheard."

"Eleanor," replied Matilda, trying to steady her voice, while a very inconvenient blush stole into her cheek, "there is some mistake—I am almost certain—that is to say—I think it right to mention———"

"You don't mean to profess any doubt!" exclaimed her cousin, with a laugh of angry surprise. "But I see how it is—you may talk of vanity, Matilda, but I know some young ladies who never can think enough of any trifling attentions which are shown to themselves. Girls who are unaccustomed to much notice become so conscious of any little civility, that their color flits like an aurora borealis or a shot silk whenever they are spoken to. I have had some little experience now in these matters, Matilda, and let me tell you, that when a gentleman has any serious intentions, his external devoirs are all paid to some aunt, or cousin, or grandmother;—even the lap-dog and piping bull-finches come in for a share; but it is to be hoped none of the parties will ever make the mistake of supposing they are preferred."

"Eleanor! there are limits to what I can feel justified in submitting to from you," said Matilda, with gentle firmness. "You put old friendship and my sense of our present relative position to a very trying test; but it would be neglecting my duty either towards myself or you, not to explain the strong reasons I have for believing ———"

"Pshaw, Matilda! I shall never laugh at Charlotte Clifford again, for all young ladies are alike. I did think you had been above those sort of missy-ish confidences; and, to say the truth, I am tired to death of them. Sir Alfred scarcely ever speaks to you; but if he ever makes a formal declaration let me know,—meantime I believe nothing that I am told on these subjects, and only half what I see."

Matilda could not resist a smile when she perceived how clear-sighted Eleanor was respecting the self-deception of her friends, while she so blindly flattered herself; but anxious yet to put Miss Fitz-Patrick on her guard, she took her cousin's hand before they parted, saying, with a look of frankness and affection,—

"You may say some hasty words in a moment of anger,

Eleanor, but it is impossible seriously to doubt the integrity of my intentions, or the warmth of my friendship; so, without being overanxious about your good opinion at present, let me only hint that I have reason to believe Sir Alfred is not yet attached to you; that, moreover, I seriously think you prefer Mr. Grant, who would suit you better; and that while you are amused with attracting attention from the one, merely because he piques your vanity, the other will be lost forever, if he is not so already, and I scarcely know any one whom you would have equal cause to regret. Now, Eleanor, after all that has passed, I know what you will think of me for venturing this opinion, but I am resolved at least to *deserve* your confidence."

Matilda sprung into the carriage, where Lady Montague and Miss Marabout waited for her, and felt unable to speak for some time from agitation on account of the effort it had cost her to persevere in being candid with Eleanor. At the time when she had thus openly given an opinion of Sir Alfred's sentiments, she considered how painfully difficult it was fully to understand them herself, and how gratefully she would have listened to any friend who could have acted towards her as she wished to do towards Eleanor. Matilda knew but little of the world and its ways; she placed entire reliance on Sir Alfred's honor and integrity, but still he had said nothing which a brother might not have done; and the more she felt inclined to think of him, the stricter seemed that vigilance with which she ought to watch over her own peace of mind. His eye had been the first to mark Eleanor's want of kindness towards herself, his voice had been the first to speak of sympathy in a sorrow which had so long distressed her, and it would have been a pleasing indulgence to let hope and imagination picture a secret attachment on the part of Sir Alfred, which for some inconceivable reason he could not at once declare. Almost every young man has a tyrannical uncle, or father, or aunt, whose wealth and caprice might be supposed to afford plausible impediments to any decided *eclaircissement*—but Sir Alfred entertained no expectations from any one: he was, according to the modern phrase, "his own father," and quite independent of any one's opinion, so Matilda determined to suppose nothing meant unless distinctly expressed. It was now that she felt the benefit of having been early practised in commanding her own thoughts. No romantic visions of imaginary happiness were allowed to flit through her mind; no exaggerated recollection of past professions, nor any fancied meaning given to words or actions which she could not entirely forget; but after calmly and dispassionately considering all that had passed, she became able to satisfy her heart with the reflection that her happiness had been long since implicitly consigned to the care of Him who ordered all things well. In praying that every event may be ordained for the best, *we know not what we ask*, unless that petition distinctly pledges us to suffer cheerfully the disappointment of every earthly hope, if necessary to our future well-being, for it is seldom that the enjoyment of our desires in a present world is consistent with our safe and speedy preparation for a better and more enduring inheritence.

CHAPTER XVI.

When I was yet a child, no childish play
To me was pleasing; all my mind was set
Serious to learn and know, and thence to do
What might be gen'ral good; myself I thought
Born to that end, born to promote all truth,
All righteous things.

MILTON.

WHEN Matilda re-entered the drawing-room, before dinner, she perceived Dr. Murray and Sir Alfred engaged in deep and earnest conversation, in which they had both the appearance of being profoundly interested, while she observed with pleasure, her venerable friend's rising animation of manner, in proportion as he felt himself understood and appreciated by the young Baronet, who delighted to take every opportunity of drawing him aside to a private conference.

Matilda had not the slightest intention of joining them, but before she was seated, Sir Alfred rose, and placed a chair, apparently anxious that she should partake in the same pleasure which he enjoyed so much himself, while, to his no small surprise, Eleanor accompanied her cousin as a volunteer in the little coterie. Miss Fitz-Patrick had such a happy confidence in herself, that she felt, on all occasions, sure of being an acquisition; and whenever she saw people intently conversing, her first impulse was to become one of the party, though generally rather with an intention to lead than to follow. On the present occasion, however, she listened with unusual deference to the conclusion of Dr. Murray's discussion respecting the subjects for meditation, which are most to be cultivated by the Christian mind; and, though what he said had not been at first intended for so many listeners, he continued, without showing any apparent consciousness of their augmented numbers. In describing the wide field of thought, and the refreshing streams of pleasure which are thus opened for the heart of man to rejoice in, his own extraordinary powers of reflection, and his impassioned eloquence of expression, became strikingly obvious, and had their usual impressive effect upon all who heard him. Even Eleanor experienced the influence of a heart and understanding so truly elevated; but wherever the feelings ought to be touched, hers were seldom exactly tuned up to *concert pitch;* and as she always spoke out the first thought that occurred, without a doubt of it being right, she could not fail to betray the nature of her own reflections. Pleased with all he said, and judging from herself that praise must be always acceptable, she exclaimed, in a tone of real admiration, "Dr. Murray! how completely you must feel lost in this little country parish!"

"Lost! did you say, Miss Fitz-Patrick?" asked he, with a look of surprise and perplexity. "In what respect?"

"Why, there is no opportunity here of distinguishing yourself,—no public meetings,—no platforms to make speeches on!—and you ought to have the largest church in the kingdom, instead of the least."

"Little as you think it, the responsibility is more than sufficient, Miss Fitz-Patrick; and could I alter the extent of this parish at all, my first wish would be to diminish it; but the bounds of our habitation are appointed for us; therefore my only desire is to have strength given me in proportion to what is a sacred duty towards the four thousand persons for whose welfare I am in a great degree answerable."

"But your learning and talents are thrown away upon people who cannot possibly appreciate them."

"My parishioners estimate me precisely as I wish," replied Dr. Murray, with a benevolent smile, seeing that for once he must talk of the person who was generally least in his thoughts or conversation—*himself.* "I trust we all experience, that there is no happiness in life equal to that of promoting the happiness of others; and in watching over that of so many, my greatest ambition is to be regarded as the friend and counsellor of each individual. I would not have one of them imagine me above sympathizing in their cares and sorrows, and even in their ignorance, for it has often occurred to me that much of the dissent throughout this kingdom is occasioned by the wide disparity in rank and intellect between the established clergy and their parishioners. It must seem to these poor people as if we could never have suffered like themselves, and could scarcely enter into their ideas, which might account for their being enticed by the ministrations of those who do not intimidate them by a show of superiority. Nothing pleases me more, Miss Fitz-Patrick, than to perceive the perfect readiness with which my people come to me, and the entire confidence with which they ask my opinion in every emergency. Poor Donald M'Intyre consulted me yesterday, about the price of his cart-horse, and I was quite flattered to observe the interest he expected me to take in his purchase."

"But then, Dr. Murray, what pleasure can there be in composing your sermons so beautifully, and delivering them with such eloquence as I know you do?"

"Miss Fitz-Patrick, never poison your friends with praise,—it is dangerous diet for any one to live upon; but if there be a single individual to whom the mere composition and delivery are of importance, then no pains should be spared to improve both. We must be 'all things to all men, that by *any* means we may win *some*.' Yet, give me a congregation who listen profoundly, and disperse to their houses in silence, impressed with the awful truths which I come to promulgate, rather than one who could be moved to a tempest of emotion, and then follow it up, as people of education too often do, with a critical disquisition on the style, on the train of argument, and on everything except the effect intended to be produced on their own life and conduct."

"That reminds me," said Matilda, "of the panegyric which Louis XIV. pronounced on Massillon, for I am sure you would prefer it, Dr. Murray, to any other praise: 'many preachers make me think a great deal of *them*, but this one teaches me to think *think little of myself*.'"

"So, Dr. Murray, being myself a member of the parish," observed Eleanor, "I am glad for the sake of Gaelfield, that you have no ambition for a higher sphere."

"It would scarcely be possible for me to enter on a happier one. Miss Fitz-Patrick, those who were young when I first came here, have grown old under my care. I have rejoiced in the blessed progress of the just, and mourned over the sins of the profligate. Many parents and many children I have buried, and I married most of those who are now smiling in prosperity around me. It has been my duty to soothe the sorrows of all, and to know, in every separate house, the hopes and fears, the temptations and afflictions of my people. Could anything ever unite me as closely to another congregation? These are, in every sense, my own family, and no promotion could compensate for dividing me from all that has hitherto engrossed and interested me in existence. It is strange,—it is deeply impressive, to be a spectator of life so long as I have been. To look back upon the lapse of years, and remember it like the flitting pageantry of a theatre. The bloom of youth has now faded on many a healthful cheek—the spring of hope has dried up in many a sanguine heart;—the smiling infant, the cherished bride, and the aged patriarch, have each and all been torn from their weeping families, while I am *yet* left to declare that there has been but one anchor of hope, both sure and steadfast. They have passed away, as it were, in a mournful procession, and I wait till my summons comes, to follow. Then, when dust returns to dust, my desire is to be laid in the grave beside my own people, and beneath the shadow of those walls where we have so often assembled together."

There was silence for a moment, as no one could reply; and Dr. Murray seemed anxious to proceed, though unable at once to do so; but having considered for some time, he added, in a tone of great feeling,—

"Miss Fitz-Patrick! I have laid open my mind the more clearly at present, from an anxious desire to speak once again on the subject which we discussed yesterday, that by revealing the deep interest I take in all my people, you may appreciate the extent of my solicitude respecting one who suffers so severely. I might tell you that many sorrowful scenes have already fallen to my share,—that I have seen the laugh of frolicsome youth suddenly change to the cry of despairing anguish,—that I have seen hearts alienated forever, which once were linked by the strongest ties of earthly affection; and that, stranger and sadder than either, I have watched over the bright intellect of man becoming gradually darkened beneath the infirmities of age, while the senses and the affections were sunk into a living grave; but never, oh! never before, did I see all these united in one overpowering calamity, and a mind, yet in the vigor of youth, struggling against the undeserved imputations of guilt, and against the inroads of insanity."

"Dr. Murray!" replied Eleanor, starting and coloring. "it was impossible to hear all you told me yesterday without being deeply affected, and I lost not an hour in sending my housekeeper, Mrs. Gordon, to Gowanbank. She says Nanny has greatly recovered since your visit, and is urgent for her sister's marriage to take place without delay. She talks of the wedding incessantly, and her eyes were perfectly lighted up when she spoke of it to Martha; but she has merely requested that William Grey shall never enter the house till he becomes her brother. The cold Nanny caught, with being out so late and so improperly in the evenings, brought on a slight feverishness and delirium, which Mrs. Gordon assures me is perfectly cured, and I have desired no expense to be spared in making her comfortable at home. We shall send again, in a few days, to inquire if she continues well."

"No messenger will be necessary to-morrow, as I shall call there myself, on our way home, to tell Nanny of the promise you made me yesterday, Miss Fitz-Patrick. It will be the poor girl's best consolation to feel assured that this whole business shall be thoroughly sifted. Her character must not be left at the mercy of vague suspicion any longer; and for my own part, I have a perfect confidence in the result of your investigations."

Eleanor looked exceedingly annoyed at this unexpected appeal to her memory, respecting a promise which had been given in haste, and repented of at leisure. She foresaw a world of trouble which it would involve to disturb the harmony of her household at present, and it had appeared such an easy way of temporizing with the whole affair, to get rid of Nanny, and let the blame rest with her, that she fully persuaded herself of the justice, as well as the convenience of this measure; and now, with a peevish exclamation about the "plague of servants," she turned hastily from the observant look with which Dr. Murray regarded her, for it was evident that, upon this subject, he had resolved to be persevering and decided.

"Well, Dr. Murray," said Eleanor, adopting her usual plan of altering disagreeable topics, "if this country were the Happy Valley of Rasselas, I should still feel in your place the same misery that he did, about the impossibility of ever getting away, for I begin to dislike it already, with respect to Barnard Castle."

"There is much truth in the French proverb," said Sir Alfred. "'La félicité est dans le goût, et non pas dans les choses, ou les places.'"

"True indeed," replied Dr. Murray. "My neighbor at Clanpibroch Castle is poor and discontented on an almost boundless income—and old Janet used to think herself rich and happy with scarcely enough to purchase the necessaries of life. Many a lesson I have received in that cottage, of cheerful self-denial, for truly our best school of practical divinity is often found in the homes of the pious poor."

"You must frequently wish for a larger income, in order to relieve their wants?" said Eleanor. "It might extend your sphere of usefulness."

"I have quite a sufficient one for all professional purposes. We have long been happy on little, and might be miserable on a great deal; therefore, neither for my people nor myself do I desire an increase. Their habits are simple, and their wants are few."

"I do wonder, then, how people manage to keep down their necessities," said Eleanor, with a consequential look round her splendid rooms. "Mine seem to increase every day."

"You should never let them grow," said Mr. Grant, joining the circle. "No man is poor unless he thinks himself so, and I live upon a straw a-day without ever feeling the want of more. You would admire, Miss Fitz-Patrick, the superlative dignity with which I can pay off my last guinea, looking as if thousands more were ready to follow."

"But with respect to Dr. Murray, he must really give us a chapter like Dr. Johnson's, 'On the wants of a man who wants nothing;' for he is the first person I ever met with who had not some good presentable reason for wishing to be rich."

"Unfortunately, you must perceive, Miss Fitz-Patrick, that our friend here has no expensive taste to serve as an outlet for this imaginary large income. Dr. Murray feels but little ambition to collect china or pictures—he dislikes a carriage, has no *penchant* for a French cook, nor the slightest desire to set up his yacht. Besides which, if all his friends are like me, they would rather dine with him on a plain joint and a bottle of sherry, than with any other person on champagne and turtle. Therefore, having settled to your satisfaction the impossibility of his spending, I believe he would still more dislike to hoard, which reminds me of a plan I once invented for enriching the government, to be proposed by some able legislator like Sir Alfred. Whenever it can be legally proved that any man has, during ten years, not lived up to his fortune, let the surplus be confiscated on behalf of those good people who positively cannot live within theirs; and anything that is over, to go for the relief of taxation."

"Very good," said Eleanor; "your uncle might be kept

very cheaply at the public expense, with the old gig, the old horse, the old butler, and the old grey coat, as usual, and what would he lose? I estimate every person's wealth by what he spends; and an avaricious man, whatever money may be in his name at a bank, is born a beggar, and dies a beggar!"

"I consider every one more or less insane in proportion as he hoards or does not hoard," observed Mr. Grant, laughing; "yet to those who thoroughly enjoy the pleasure of saving, it is a perpetual amusement. The richest of us cannot be always giving or spending money, but the miser finds incessantly recurring pleasure in every pin he picks up, or in every scrap of paper he saves; but certainly those of modern times enjoy less happiness than their predecessors, because a banker's book cannot be half so interesting an object of contemplation as the chests of gold and the bright guineas which they are represented as perpetually counting in old pictures."

"Sir Alfred," said Eleanor, soon after, when Dr. Murray was called away by Sir Richard, "I see you understand canvassing better than one would suppose, by your paying attention to our parish clergyman. He has unbounded influence over all the farmers and people about the district, if you only persuade him to exert it."

"Can you possibly imagine, Miss Fitz-Patrick, that I am biassed by self-interest in associating with Dr. Murray!" replied Sir Alfred in momentary astonishment. No, believe me, that is an honor which I appreciate for its own sake. We never touch upon politics together, and, except where they are immediately connected with his own profession, he generally avoids the subject entirely."

"*A propos*, Douglas," said Mr. Grant, "I have been doing a bit of popularity for you to-day. Our old adversary, Jones, the farmer at Bannockfield, has lost a quantity of cattle lately, so I rode over, and asked, at a venture, for his brown cow. By good fortune there were a dozen of that color, one of which had been complaining, so he was prodigiously pleased at the attention. We went all over the stock, and I praised his pigs, poultry, and children most zealously, besides talking big about the landed interest. His parting looks promised me a vote, and, if you will believe me, Miss Howard, nothing could exceed old Jones's disappointment when he discovered that I was not the candidate myself!"

"I dare say that, for in his place I would certainly have capitulated."

"Now, Sir Alfred's conception of canvassing is such a contrast to mine! He rides up to the door of every farmer or shopkeeper, with his well-mounted groom behind, and sends for the voters. Out they come, hat in hand, and he strokes his horse's head, tells them his opinions have been fully stated, and asks for their votes in the sort of commanding tone with which I would order a pair of boots or a few tons of hay. It takes amazingly, for he looks as if no one had ever refused him anything, and that it was quite impossible they should."

"There are occasions when I could be diffident enough—perhaps more so than you. Grant; but that is only where there is much to be asked," said Sir Alfred, fixing his eyes for a moment on Matilda, with a look of anxious interest, which brought the ready color to her cheek. The tone in which these few words were said, appeared so full of sensibility, that Eleanor felt how much meaning was attached to them; but supposing that, of course, they must be meant for herself, she turned away with a conscious smile, satisfied that nothing could be more undoubted than his devoted attachment.

"Sir Alfred," said Miss Charlotte, joining the party, "I am positively assured you were so exclusive on the Continent that you would not make a single acquaintance, and cut all those who knew you already."

"On the contrary, I behaved particularly well!—answered almost everybody who spoke to me, and endeavored to endure them. But, Miss Clifford, pray write my travels, and depend upon it I shall vouch for whatever you like to assert."

"It is a great advantage to begin the world, as you have done, by establishing a reputation for being 'odd,' as one must never be surprised or offended at anything you say or do," continued Miss Charlotte. "I often tell people the strangest stories about you, Sir Alfred, but they invariably reply, with a laugh, 'That is so like him!'"

"On the same plan, every lady at the head of a country mansion," said Mr. Grant, "should set up for having 'a way' of her own, and then whatever habit she adopts is above all criticism. If any visitor complains of remaining a whole day in the house without her noticing him, as Mr. Armstrong did yesterday, the ready answer of every one is—'Ah! that is *her way!*' If another remarks that she kept dinner waiting an hour, those who are more intimate reply, with a look of contemptuous superiority, 'I perceive you don't know "her way"!' and if she sits a whole evening in a remote corner of the room with one friend, to the exclusion of all the others, still nobody could be so unreasonable as to take offence, if it is 'her way.' So, the moment any lady establishes *a way*, she is at perfect liberty to be as capricious as she likes, though, till then, I do not know a greater slave to the whims of others than one who is determined to make her country house agreeable."

"Well, then! here is Martin to announce dinner, and it is 'my way' not to wait till Lord Alderby comes to hand me in," said Eleanor, looking at Sir Alfred, who felt obliged to take the hint, and with an almost imperceptible glance towards Matilda, who could not but observe it, he offered his arm to Miss Fitz-Patrick, and silently conducted her to the dining-room. The young Baronet had often maintained an opinion that it was much more tolerable to live with those who talk too little than with those who talk too much, and he never felt more perfectly confirmed in any assertion than on the present occasion. Eleanor's spirits were excited beyond even their usual pitch; and being resolved to complete at once her supposed conquest, she spoke incessantly, and made Sir Alfred's eyes, ears, and whole attention perfect prisoners, so that he could scarcely snatch a momentary interval to eat, and sent the greater portion of his dinner away untasted. It would have been more tolerable to him if the dinner-bell had continued ringing in his ears during as long a time; but there being no escape, he composedly resigned himself to his fate, and assumed an external aspect of deference and attention, to conceal the want of real interest in what she said. Upon this Eleanor became more than ever confident that he must be charmed with her vivacity; and, little guessing how different was the style of conversation he preferred, she rattled on with immeasurable rapidity, regretting only that Matilda seldom looked her way, or she could not have been otherwise than convinced how fallacious had been her own opinion of Sir Alfred's indifference.

Meantime Miss Marabout began entertaining Dr. Murray, at another end of the table, with a most sublime and terrific edition of Eleanor's adventure that morning on the ice. Her account might have sufficed to bring Captain M'Tartan a medal from the Humane Society, she enlarged upon it in such glowing terms; and being seldom much listened to by any one, her eloquence rose as she proceeded, and seemed likely to become endless. The object of this panegyric, who sat near, was evidently annoyed almost beyond endurance; he writhed about in his chair, colored, talked of other subjects, and at length, perceiving that it would never terminate, as she appeared evidently to think praise must be secretly gratifying to him, Captain M'Tartan exclaimed, in an irritated voice,

"Miss Marabout! I would rather go into the pillory at once than be held up in this ridiculous way!—one would imagine I had leaped into the whirlpool of Corryvrekan!"

"Come! my good friend! take a glass of wine with Eleanor!" said Sir Richard. "I fancy you both had water enough for to-day."

"Why really, my cousin's white poodle might do all I did to-day; and Blanco would have answered the purpose better than I in one respect, that I fancy she is very much preferred!"

"I remember hearing a remarkable instance of sagacity in a Newfoundland dog," began Sir Colin, eagerly.

"Fletcher! a glass of Madeira?" interrupted Sir Richard.

"With pleasure!—in a Newfoundland dog, and——"

"Sir Colin! send Miss Clifford a slice of turkey," interposed Mr. Grant.

"Take my advice, old gentleman! and when you want to spin a yarn in this house, clap on all steam, or else wait till after dinner," said Captain M'Tartan, good-humoredly.

"The dog was given to my friend, Sir Jonathan Fowler, by Captain Hargrave," persisted the Baronet, "one of these Leicestershire Hargraves, a Captain in the 33rd infantry, who distinguished himself in Spain.—Poor fellow! he lost both his legs there———"

"The *dog!*" exclaimed Mr. Grant.

"No! Sir Jonathan Fowler," replied Colonel Pendarvis.

"You are all wrong! it was Captain Hargrave of the 33rd."

"Rather awkward for a Captain in the Feet to lose both his legs!" added Major Foley.

"Pray," asked Miss Murray, "how do *officers* travel in an infantry regiment? Do they take post-chaises?"

"Always in hackney-coaches," replied Mr. Grant. "But I am told every regiment is to have its own omnibus now."

"In fact," pursued Sir Colin, "the courage and sagacity of those animals might often put men to the blush, and———"

"Very true!" interrupted Miss Marabout, "and had it not been for Captain M'Tartan's admirable boldness and presence of———"

"Miss Marabout!" interrupted he, "if you mention this affair in my hearing again, I shall instantly leave the room."

"M'Tartan! will you take wine?" said Sir Alfred, in a tone of friendly regard with which he seldom addressed any one; and if the gallant Captain had been knighted on the spot, he could scarcely have looked more surprised and pleased than at this unexpected attention.

"As I was saying," continued Sir Colin, deliberately, "about this dog of Sir Jonathan's——"

"Fletcher, I am told you make it a rule never to tell any story twice the same, because that would show such a want of imagination," said Mr. Grant. "I like the plan amazingly, for it is so much more entertaining than those dull prosing people who have everything stereotyped on their brain, and never can bring out a new edition. Now! last time you told that story the dog was a poodle!—yes, decidedly, a black poodle!"

"People with luxuriant imaginations should really try to curb them," added Eleanor. "One must keep to fact, Sir Colin, for there is nothing of so much consequence as to be quite correct in the minutest details. I like even to know whether you sat on a person's right hand or his left."

No inducement could bring either of his accusers to hear Sir Colin's indignant protestations of rigid accuracy—the laugh was universal, and, in despair of receiving common justice, he turned angrily to Matilda, who compassionately lent her eyes for half an hour, though her ears were more amusingly entertained in listening to the lively sallies that were passing all round the table. Sir Colin's voice sounded like a bee buzzing at her ear, until his final titter recalled her attention in time to take a part in the laughing chorus with which he always wished to conclude.

When the gentlemen re-entered the drawing-room at a late hour that evening, Mr. Grant stole round behind a large sofa where most of the young ladies were engaged in an animated discussion, and leaning over the back of it, with a coffee-cup in his hand, he fixed his laughing eyes on Eleanor and Miss Charlotte, who had both been talking at once, but paused suddenly on observing him near.

"Mr. Grant," said Eleanor, slyly, "listeners never hear good of themselves. If you could adopt invisibility, and know all we are saying, it would make you hold up your three hands with astonishment!"

"Then it is as I guessed, and you were talking of me. I was certain the subject must be more than commonly interesting. Few nerves can stand the reception we meet with on coming up stairs after dinner. The ladies all pause, and look disconcerted at our entrance, which really puts a shy, diffident man like me quite out of countenance."

"Every person living professes to be shy!" exclaimed Miss Charlotte; "but I certainly had an idea that you were thoroughly bronzed, Mr. Grant."

"How little you know me, Miss Clifford! I really am the shyest man in existence, and often wonder that young ladies never have the charity to pay me more attention. You should try to draw me out, and give me confidence. I have one small merit which obscures many greater ones, and that is modest merit."

"Matilda made precisely that remark on you five minutes ago," said Eleanor, archly. "My cousin is always rather censorious, and she was wondering you ever went into society, seeing how dull and silent it made you; but she thinks Sir Alfred's chatty pleasant manners must render him the life of every tea-table."

"You have my free permission to believe this, if it be possible, Mr. Grant," added Matilda; "my cousin seems to have mistaken her own opinion for mine."

"You would never do for the heroine of a novel, being so ready with an answer," cried Eleanor, laughing. "Now a thorough-bred heroine ought to appear continually speechless with emotion. Another deficiency, let me take this opportunity of remarking,—Whenever a gentleman attempted being civil to a young lady formerly, she was all on fire to repress his hopes and to punish his presumption; but, on the contrary, my *good* cousin is really forgetting her duty towards poor Sir Colin. He has twice handed you a cup of tea to-night, so it is full time *at least to look* repulsive; this morning you got up a smile at his favorite *bon mot* about Sir Jonathan Fowler calling his fallen postili*on* a postilli*off*; and you are the only young lady he knows who can laugh at his *stories*, and not at *himself*."

"You are maliciously bent on making mischief between Sir Colin and me, Eleanor, but I shall not be your dupe, having resolved to avoid all Missy-ish airs of that kind. You may have the most perfect reliance on his indifference, and I find great advantage from the attention he shows me."

"Well! well! we shall all see what you will bring on yet. Mr. Grant, only imagine what a proposal it would be;—two sheets of foolscap, with six or seven postscripts at least."

"Imagine!" exclaimed Mr. Grant, with animation. "If it be supposed possible for him to have so much presumption, I could write down every word he would say; beginning with——"

"Hush! not now!" exclaimed Eleanor, with sudden eagerness; and Matilda looked round expecting from her cousin's manner to perceive Sir Colin within ear-shot: but she saw only Sir Alfred sitting near, and the old Baronet himself, at a great distance, haranguing to Lady Susan, who had assumed a look of animated attention.

"How I do like to see *young people* happy!" said Mr. Grant, following the direction of Matilda's eyes. "Their united ages are exactly a hundred and sixty."

"Now hear me, Matilda!" continued Eleanor, gravely. "I know the world, and you do not, so it is quite presumptuous to set up your judgment in opposition to mine. Depend upon it, Sir Colin is not a man to trifle with. I once knew an old gentleman, nearly his age, who died of an apoplexy from disappointment; and poor General Anderson has had the gout ever since Adelaide Montague refused him. If you hear a story out once again, observe, I shall not be answerable for the consequences. Go now, like a good girl, and give us some music, after which you—you might dance us a few of your steps."

Matilda plainly perceived that Eleanor wished to monopolize the conversation of Mr. Grant, so she strolled to a distant table for her work. Scarcely had she drawn out a needle, however, before, to her infinite annoyance, Sir Colin approached, and was instantly plunged into the labyrinth of his most interminable narrative, from which nothing short of rudeness could have disentangled her. A transient smile passed over the features of Sir Alfred, when he caught Matilda's eye wandering round the room for a pretext to escape, while she also saw her cousin and Mr. Grant watching her with the most undisguised diversion. It seemed evident that they were talking of her; and the subject became productive of extreme amusement, which was testified by frequent laughter. Nevertheless, Eleanor found intervals to cast many satirical glances and reproachful looks at Matilda, shrugging her shoulders, and turning up her eyes to intimate what an unpardonable flirt they both considered her. Miss Howard felt a shrinking apprehension of ridicule; but having resolved on all occasions, whether trifling or important, not to be biassed by it, but to act, as she believed at the moment, to be right, without indulging too much her own natural sensitiveness, she determined now to remain stationary though annoyed by her cousin's bantering looks, and inwardly intent on escaping from the thraldom of Sir Colins ANECdotage at the first opportunity when politeness and good feeling rendered it possible. At length Eleanor hastily rose, and gravely shaking her head at her cousin, she walked towards the library, followed by Mr. Grant. No sooner had they departed, than Sir Alfred approached the place where she sat, and made an immediate diversion in Matilda's favor, by asking Sir Colin for his friend Sir Jonathan Fowler, and assuming an attitude of attention to the very elaborate reply which followed, while she gladly hastened towards the pianoforte. It was now that Miss Howard, for the first time, fully estimated the prolixity of Sir Colin's style, when she observed Sir Alfred enduring it on her account, and that his eye became fixed on a vacant chair near herself, which he seemed evidently anxious to seize the first opportunity of occupying. It was obvious with what impatience he bore Sir Colin's tediousness; but at length, having hastily terminated the interview, by making a short concluding remark, in his own peculiar style, Sir Alfred proceeded a step towards the seat he had so long been preparing to take. Matilda colored and smiled as he approached; and nothing seemed likely to impede the pleasure of the evening, when suddenly, and most unexpectedly, the empty place became occupied by the very last person in the room whom she expected to see there.

Mr. Armstrong had been for some time humming to himself the airs in *I Puritani*, while sitting near Eleanor, in the library, when all at once he started up, after something she said to Mr. Grant, and hurried in obvious irritation to the drawing-room. It was evident from the glitter of Miss Fitz-Patrick's eye, that her wit had been levelled at him, and that she had put in what was considered a successful stroke, for the excited and furious expression of Mr. Armstrong's dark sallow countenance showed how it had told. Placing himself beside Matilda, he remained for some moments silent, but his compressed lip and flashing eye spoke of the storm that raged within. To the disappointment of seeing Sir Alfred withdraw and join Dr. Murray instead of herself, Matilda had the additional grievance of being placed beside the only person against whom she ever entertained an unconquerable aversion; and there was a sternness and malignity in his eye, which, united with his meanness in remaining under a roof where he appeared so obviously unwelcome, made her gentle nature recoil from his approach.

"Pray, Miss Howard!" said he, abruptly, "did you ever hear of an Irishman who sawed off the branch of a tree on which he was sitting himself? Your cousin may some morning encounter such another fall as he had, and be equally surprised."

"Indeed!" replied Matilda, seeing she was expected to speak. "I should be sorry for that!"

"Perhaps you may have cause to rejoice, and I shall be the first to light a bonfire on that occasion. If you were told all Miss Marabout repeats of your cousin's observations on us both, you would know better what to think upon this subject."

"I am shocked to hear of Miss Marabout's treachery! but, Mr. Armstrong, no man need expect to be discussed in his absence as he would be if present, and we must make allowances for lively spirits. I could not trust the misrepresentations of any person who openly violates the mutual confidence on which all society depends, and I am sorry that the friend my cousin so entirely relies on should be unworthy of her kindness."

"There are secrets, Miss Howard, in the best regulated families, and if you could find them *all* out, I know one which would be worth a trifle. Pay your best respects to me, and if I choose to do all that *could* be done—but I say nothing."

"So it appears!" replied Matilda, laughing good-humoredly. "Do what is just and right, Mr. Armstrong, but never expect that I shall pay attention to any one from sinister motives."

"What is *just!*" exclaimed he, twisting his features into a tremendous contortion, expressive of mysterious caution. "You may be rather surprised, Miss Howard, to hear what strict justice might involve. How should you like to have £12,000 a-year?—answer me that! What would you say, if with a single whisper, I could bring Lord Alderby, and all Miss Fitz-Patrick's admirers to your feet, instead of hers?"

"Why! neither she nor I could desire it!"

"You know the old proverb, Miss Howard, '*point d'argent, point de Suisse.*' It would be a friendly thing to drop a hint of that to Miss Fitz-Patrick. Perhaps, if I am not better treated, her lovers may be put to the test," added Mr. Armstrong, with a look of malignity towards the next room, where Eleanor sat laughing, with Mr. Grant, but his voice became nearly drowned by a brilliant prelude with which Matilda began an air of Rossini's, in order to terminate a conversation which she considered unpleasant and incomprehensible.

"Miss Howard," said he, with increasing irritability, "your music may be good, but your *cards* are very ill played."

"How can I do otherwise, without knowing what the cards are?" replied she, pausing in the midst of a cadence, and turning her bright ingenuous contenance full upon him. "Seriously, Mr. Armstrong, you perplex and annoy me with hints and inuendoes which it is impossible to understand, and which direct my thoughts toward apparent impossibilities; therefore, let there be an end to such discussions, and, believe me, I am perfectly satisfied with the present state of affairs, which are all more wisely ordered than either you or I could have done. If any alteration ever comes, it shall not be of my seeking."

"Then allow me to say but one word at parting," answered Mr. Armstrong, with a look of intense cunning, "and take time to consider what you would *give*, Miss Howard, to have the mystery cleared up. I could make you mistress of Barnard Castle to-morrow, with a snap of my fingers," and, suiting the action to the word, he suddenly started up, and hurried out of the room.

Matilda was bewildered and amazed at his strange language, and extraordinary manner, though the more she considered, the less she thought it possible that such power could be in his hands, as he seemed to intimate, nor did she feel that it could have added to her happiness, if the revolution had been produced which he threatened. Miss Howard saw the evil effects of extreme prosperity on her cousin, and she would have feared it for herself. She observed, also, in no very inviting colors, the unnatural position which any young lady must hold in society, who is very richly endowed; and she perceived Eleanor often so encumbered with the adventitious importance of her situation, besides being viewed by every acquaintance so differently from what she would have been without it, that Matilda sometimes remembered the fable of the peacock which asked Jupiter for a splendid tail, and afterwards found himself so unable to fly, and so beset by other birds of inferior plumage, that he would gladly, at last, have dispensed with his brilliant appendage, to be placed on an equality with the rest.

Matilda had been completely abstracted for some moments, till she perceived that the ladies were about to withdraw, and was surprised to observe that Mr. Grant and Eleanor were still apparently engaged in a secret conference, which ended by his rapidly glancing round the room, and clandestinely slipping a letter into the heiress's hand, who received it with a smile of animated pleasure, but at the same time, with an equally apparent desire of concealment, for when she suddenly looked round, and caught her cousin's eye, the color mounted to her cheeks with perplexity and annoyance, while she hastily secreted the document in her reticule.

What it could be, Miss Howard had scarcely time to conjecture, before her cousin hastily beckoned her to follow, saying she had something particular to communicate. Matilda had been seated for some time afterwards beside the dressing-room fire, before Eleanor seemed conscious of her presence, for she continued nearly ten minutes in an anteroom with Pauline, giving some very lengthened directions and explanations, which were concluded with the most earnest injunctions on her Abigail to be speedy. When all was over, and Miss Fitz-Patrick at last sat down, her cousin had too much good breeding to testify any impatient curiosity respecting the object of her being summoned, but made a trifling remark in hopes that the business would soon be opened on which they had met; but whatever that might be, it seemed for the moment entirely to have escaped her friend's memory, who caught hold of any subject which might be suggested, and pursued it eagerly, as if that alone had any interest. At length it seemed necessary to recall her cousin's attention to whatever she had been so anxious to communicate, therefore Matilda determined to lead the way.

"You wished to speak to me this evening, I think, Eleanor?"

"Oh yes!—to be sure I did!—what was I going to say?

—Now, help me, Matilda, for you can always guess what I would be at."

"Perhaps it was about that letter which I saw Mr. Grant give you?"

"A letter!—oh no!—that was only a—a copy of a new song. Have you seen the—'The charming woman?'"

"You had the words of that song some time ago; but I shall intrude on your confidence no farther, seeing you do not wish it at present; only, dear Eleanor, beware for your own sake, as well as Mr. Grant's, how you encourage his intimacy without a definite decision as to what influence it may have on the happiness of either. He suffered all the sorrow of unrequited affection once; so it would be your turn next." This was said in a jocular tone by Matilda; and yet there appeared more of sincerity in her remark than Eleanor liked, and a pause of some moments ensued. "Perhaps," added she, coloring and hesitating, "you meant to allow me one more opportunity of pleading for poor Nanny; and at all events, I must risk your anger for this once to preserve us both from all danger of future self-reproach."

With all the eloquence of nature and feeling, Matilda now represented Nanny's situation, and entreated Eleanor to judge for herself, and not to be biassed by the misrepresentations of any one, so as to deny her an opportunity of being speedily reinstated in the good opinions of all around, by a strenuous investigation of the whole business. It was too late now to restore the poor girl's happiness to what it might have been, for she understood that by Nanny's own desire, her former lover was to be married the very next day to Martha, according to their previous engagement; but at least her reputation was still within the reach of justification, and ought if possible to be cleared. Where there is a total vacuum, the largest bell is rung in vain, and Matilda's efforts called forth no answering look from Miss Fitz-Patrick, who seemed entirely pre-occupied with some other subject, while an unconquerable smile played about her mouth and lurked in the corner of her eye.

"Well! I shall think of all this, Matilda; but now good-night, for you must be tired of talking so much, and of listening to Sir Colin also—could you not give him the same hint that Gil Blas did to the Archbishop of Grenada about his homilies? Don't you talk of flirting, for I never went on in my life as you did this evening! after having been fairly warned, too, so take the consequences! Be careful not to lose your way through the passages, for all the lamps must be out; and Pauline once spent an entire night on the staircase, in consequence of having been benighted there. Poor creature; she is terrified at every turn after dusk, expecting to encounter one of our Highland ghosts in full kilt."

CHAPTER XVII.

Grace, that with tenderness and sense combin'd
To form that harmony of soul and face,
Where beauty shines the mirror of the mind.
MASON.

MATILDA took leave, and rapidly proceeded towards her own apartment. As she traversed the large gloomy entrance-hall, silence reigned throughout its wide extent; and at every door a draught of air threatened to blow out the light she carried, which flared up in her eyes, when she ventured to quicken her pace. At last a sudden gust of wind extinguished her taper, and Matilda was left in total darkness. Perfectly acquainted with the way, however, she groped along, feeling entire confidence, and had begun slowly ascending a steep winding staircase which led through the turret exclusively to her own apartment, when suddenly she became startled and astonished to hear the distinct sound of footsteps coming downwards. Matilda paused and listened. No one slept near, nor could there be a possible cause conjectured why any person should be in that direction; yet the noise of steps descending was distinctly audible, accompanied by the sound of rustling silk. Scarcely a single individual is entirely free from superstition; and though Matilda's well-poised mind and enlightened understanding had never before yielded to supernatural fear, yet the sudden remembrance thrilled through her frame of Eleanor's stories connected with this ancient staircase, in which it had been stated that during more than two hundred years there had been the report of sounds such as these being unaccountably heard on the spot where she stood. For one moment a cold shudder passed through her frame; but hastily dismissing these apprehensions, she regained her self-command, and nerved her resolution by the thought that she must act for herself, as no one could possibly be summoned to her assistance. Matilda now called out as loudly as she could, to know if any one was there; and as her voice became feeble from terror, she repeated her words again. The sound echoed upwards in harsh hollow tones, when instantly afterwards a noise of whispering seemed audible above, a light gleamed there for an instant, and the rush of footsteps followed in an opposite direction, after which all was still.

Matilda stood transfixed to the spot with amazement and fear, her heart ceased to beat, her limbs quivered, and she remained motionless, as if she had been turned into stone, while listening with intense attention to catch the smallest sound. Her hearing seemed to be sharpened by apprehension, but she waited in vain. Resolved at length to brave the worst, she summoned a degree of desperate resolution, and proceeded as rapidly as the darkness would permit towards her own room, where she intended to obtain a light. In passing the dreary lumber-room opposite to her own, she again saw a momentary gleam in the distance,—a slight rustling noise called her attention to a white figure flitting out of sight in the gloomiest recesses, and instantly afterwards a loud crash took place which startled and bewildered her, so that, unable to hazard another glance around, she rushed into her own room, and with a fluttering heart and unsteady hand bolted the door. Matilda could not but remark that it was wide open as she entered, though the housemaids invariably closed it, and that her fire bore traces of having been recently and violently stirred, though not a servant on the establishment would have ventured up that staircase after dusk; she therefore still trembled with nervous apprehension to find herself thus alone, and so completely unprotected. All the theories of apparitions which she had ever read or could remember, failed to compose her agitated nerves. She trembled at ever crack which the old wainscot gave in her room, the rattling of the window-frame startled her, and a mouse in the wall would have almost made her faint. "What poor weak creatures we are!" thought Matilda, trying to imagine some plausible explanation of all she had seen, and to compose her mind for the solemn duties of the evening. "But yesterday I should have been the first to laugh at such a story as this, yet no human being can foresee how he will feel or act under any circumstances, until he is actually placed in them." Impatient for the first peep of daylight, she opened the curtains, and looked out upon the pale, cold moon; the deep shadows cut upon the grass, the glittering stream rolling beneath her window, the massy clouds careering along the sky, and the bright stars shining in perpetual beauty. There is something which speaks peace to the heart amidst a scene of such majestic stillness; and Matilda now began in some degree to forget her alarm. The agitation which she had witnessed in Nanny's state of mind during the previous night, forced itself on her thoughts, accompanied by a feeling of melancholy at remembering the callousness with which Eleanor had treated those distressing circumstances which followed, though she was consoled by the hope, that her cousin's judgment had been in some degree perverted by the misrepresentations of Pauline and Mrs. Gordon. The remembrance next succeeded, of all that Mr. Armstrong had said,—or rather, according to his own phraseology, what he had *not* said; but the whole was so indefinite and unpleasant that nothing remained on which she could have any desire to rest her meditations, except those pleasing words of Scripture,—which are consoling in every period of similar perplexity—"He shall choose our inheritance for us." But Matilda found it more difficult to banish from her mind the increasing uncertainty she felt respecting Sir Alfred's conduct. It was impossible to have any hesitation in believing that she was an object of peculiar interest to him; he always betrayed a consciousness of her presence; while the most trifling remark she uttered evidently acquired importance in his eyes when she made it, for at whatever distance he might be off, it always seemed to reach him, and to arrest his attention in preference to every one else. His favorite position in the room was near her, and she could not but be aware how anxiously he had desired an opportunity of speaking to her unobserved during the evening. Yet when Matilda reflected that Eleanor was equally confident of Sir Alfred's regard, she felt how prudent and desirable it must be, under whatever circumstances, to maintain an uncertainty of that which was not yet declared. Nothing cures people so surely of their faults as to see the very same errors exaggerated in the conduct or feelings of others, for we then become conscious of their danger and deformity. Miss Howard, therefore, being unable to avoid the conviction of her cousin's vain and unwarrantable expectations, found it easier to diminish her own. Had she been addicted to amusing self-deceptions, Matilda might even have begun to flatter herself that the gay and lively Mr. Grant was becoming conscious of her charms, as there had been much in his manner to her of late, which tended to that conclusion. From the moment when he observed her soothing kindness to the wretched Nanny, and her unaffected indifference to the interest which she herself excited on that occasion, he adopted a new tone towards Matilda, full of respectful deference, while his attentions were frequent though unobtrusive ; and the conversation which he addressed to her became often so superior to his general character and style, that during dinner that day she had been surprised and flattered at the change. Eleanor might often have remarked, if vanity did not lay observation to sleep, how different seemed the manner of gentlemen in general towards her cousin from what it was towards herself. A gay tone of easy familiarity they all assumed in suiting themselves to her, and it appeared often no better than the lively *persiflage* with which they were willing to amuse a wayward child, whom they perfectly understood, and whom it was their interest to humor and indulge in every capricious whim ; but when Matilda entered unobtrusively into the room, a look of interest became obvious in the manner which they adopted towards her, and of pleasure in observing one who seemed so unconscious of attracting notice, and so indifferent to admiration. People are usually most desirous to acquire that of which they are uncertain, and while all felt secure of amusing Eleanor, many had become anxious to please Matilda, whose remarkable richness of mind, united with her graceful turn of expression, her fertility of thought, and her tone of sensibility, gave a charm to her society quite unrivalled. With Eleanor many gay effusions of wit and vivacity sparkled under the influence of excitement, but when once her spirits flagged, the game of conversation "was up." But Matilda, on the contrary, had a quiet under-current of knowledge and observation which varied the occasional vivacity of her ideas; and Mr. Grant had been heard to declare, after sitting next her for nearly an hour, in apparently serious discussion, that "he did not know her equal at '*a two-handed crack.*' "

Unable yet to feel sufficiently composed for retiring to rest, and finding it unusually difficult to banish from her thoughts those subjects which perplexed while they interested her, Matilda rose to procure a book, and was surprised, in passing the toilet-table, to observe a letter laid conspicuously on her dressing-box. Snatching it hastily up, she examined the handwriting, which was unknown, and the direction, which was certainly for herself. Matilda then turned it over, to inspect the large and consequential-looking seal ; but she became startled to observe that it bore the impression of a tortoise carrying the globe, which, being somewhat of a herald, she at once recognized as the crest of Sir Colin Fletcher. Two monkeys, with *long tails*, for supporters, had often been the subject of wit among the Baronet's friends, and the motto " *Je Fuis*," was always quoted as particularly inappropriate. Eleanor's warning now flashed into Matilda's memory—she had lately heard proposals spoken of as an every-day occurrence, without apprehending any danger of meeting with one herself; but, ignorant of the way in which these events took place, she felt a pang of self-reproach for having acted entirely on her own judgment, and for having allowed herself to believe that her cousin's prophecies were merely in jest, when they ought at least to have produced some caution. Sir Colin's advanced age had prevented Matilda from ever imagining the possibility of his marrying, but Eleanor had recently assured her, that no multiplicity of years could be any security. Coloring with vexation, as these recollections crowded into her mind, Matilda's trepidation increased when she broke the seal and read as follows:—

" Dear Madam,

" Many letters begin with the use of a possessive pronoun, which is wanting here, seeing that I am not *yet* entitled to use it towards you; but the very great encouragement with which I have lately been honored, entitles me to believe that before long I shall have acquired the privilege of doing so. My friend, Sir Jonathan Fowler, who is one of the cleverest people to be met with in society, and tells a story better than any man I know—with a single exception—for no rule is without one—indeed, I believe the present company is always *ex*cepted, and I trust in this instance will be ACcepted too, which is a *bon mot* of which you may not discover the merit till my letter is finished—My friend, Sir Jonathan, I say, who had a story for every occasion, or who made an occasion for every story, as few people had a better art of introducing them, or told one better when he set about it—I have actually seen him entertain a circle from breakfast-time till dinner, without stopping to take breath, when he could find an audience, which is not easy in these talkative times, as people have all got into an unpleasant habit of holding forth incessantly themselves, especially young ladies, which I particularly disapprove of, being still of the old, exploded opinion, that they should be seen and not heard. Even my own narratives are not listened to as they used to be in former days, which is perfectly unaccountable, since I now relate them with much more accuracy than formerly, when many essential preliminaries were carelessly slurred over—as Mr. Grant does, who tells a story worse than any man I know—he has such a trick of dashing out the point at once, and setting people in a roar of laughter, without keeping them a moment in suspense. I really wonder that Mr. Grant receives so much attention in company, when others, greatly his superiors, scarcely obtain common civility. This very circumstance, however, has made me desirous to secure the constant society of one who has penetration and taste to understand good conversation, and discretion also to abstain from monopolizing too large a share of it herself, which is an undoubted proof of the soundest good sense. Therefore, to make a long story short—a practice by no means to be recommended in general—let me ask a plain question, though, by the way, we are losing sight of my friend, Sir Jonathan's story, which nevertheless, you can have ample leisure to enjoy hereafter, as we shall probably be much together, and I prefer telling a story to writing it, because of the pleasure it affords me to watch your increasing anxiety during the progress, and the animated satisfaction with which you at last reach the conclusion. Few people are more competent to appreciate your fascinations than myself, having always kept the best cook that France could produce, and entertained personages of the highest rank and distinction at my table, besides having travelled in Sweden, Spain, America, and the Orkneys; yet I never saw any young lady more highly gifted, and with whom I would prefer to spend the rest of my life. Hoping and believing that this good opinion is reciprocal, and that you are desirous, like myself, of an agreeable companion during our joint lives, I shall willingly take you for better or for worse; and should no answer reach me before breakfast to-morrow, I shall consider the whole affair to be favorably arranged, which will save you the trouble of a reply, and enable me to write, without delay, to Sir Francis, as well as to announce the joyful event instantly to our mutual friends here. Meantime, I am always and entirely yours,

"COLIN FLETCHER."

Matilda read over this strange farrago of nonsense several times, with renewed astonishment and confusion. Her mind had been agitated and bewildered by the previous events of that evening, so that she now felt perfectly incompetent to fix her thoughts with deliberation on anything; but Sir Colin's style of writing was so complete a specimen of his conversation, that on each revisal of his letter she felt as if he was speaking to her, and could not resist laughing, in the midst of all her annoyance, at the perfect certainty with which he evidently anticipated an acceptance. The first idea of its being possible for Sir Colin to marry, had been broached in her presence some days before by Miss Charlotte Clifford, who never received the most accidental notice from any gentleman without at once coming to a conclusion as to his suitableness for herself; and she had remarked, in allusion to Sir Colin, that it would be much more tolerable to marry a really old man than one who was merely middle-aged; after which she had proceeded to deliver an elaborate panegyric on his house, which she had once seen, on his pictures, his furniture, his china, *cutlery and damask*, ending the whole by observing—"And as for the man himself, he really is *passable enough*." It had been then very evident that Miss Charlotte would have required no long time to deliberate before accepting an offer which so greatly shocked and annoyed Matilda, whose most prominent desire at the moment was that neither Eleanor nor Mr. Grant should ever know it had taken place. Alarmed at the threat which was contained in Sir Colin's concluding paragraph, that the whole affair should be divulged without delay, she instantly sat down to compose a polite and peremptory refusal. Matilda began with expressing her conviction that if he had a little longer delayed the declaration of his sentiments, Sir Colin must have discovered that the qualities he had supposed her to possess, which might render her a suitable companion, were entirely the result of his own imagination; which conviction might have prevented his feeling any regret on being assured that no circumstance could ever render it possible for her to accept his addresses. With many expressions of regret that her own inconsiderate conduct should have unintentionally appeared like an encouragement of his preference, and with sincere good wishes for his future happiness, though she was not herself capable of contributing to it, Matilda then hastily concluded, and folded up her important despatch.

Daylight had dawned before this "heavy task" was done; and, happy that her adventures for the night appeared at last to be terminated, she felt so utterly exhausted by the complicated feelings which had successively assailed her that she instantly retired and fell into a broken and agitated slumber.

The first sound which awoke Matilda next morning, was the gong giving notice that it wanted but half an hour to breakfast; and being accustomed to employ more than double that time in her morning duties, she hastily arose, and hurried through her toilet, having first rung for a housemaid, to whom she intrusted the care of instantly conveying her letter to Sir Colin's valet, adding the most urgent instructions for its being delivered without delay. Matilda hastened down with all possible despatch to breakfast, where the whole party was already assembled in its usual state of joyous excitement. No place remained vacant, except a chair between Sir Alfred Douglas and Sir Colin, of which she reluctantly took possession, feeling the more unwilling to place herself there, because it was precisely opposite to Eleanor and Mr. Grant, whose satirical eyes were instantly fixed on her, with looks of sparkling animation and humor, after which they exchanged a momentary glance of intelligence, as Matilda took her seat, and broke off a conference in which they had been previously engaged, and which was so suddenly terminated on her entrance that she could not but feel a vague apprehension of having been its object.

"The *late* Miss Howard!" said Eleanor, reproachfully. "Has anything *extraordinary* occurred to detain you so long? We were afraid you had *eloped* this morning; and Sir Colin, too, has only this minute appeared."

Matilda's countenance instantly assumed its deepest hue of pink, and she tried to avoid further notice, by making no reply.

"You were probably writing letters," observed Mr. Grant. "That is a favorite excuse with ladies."

"I envy your correspondent, Miss Howard," said Major Foley.

"Ah! perhaps, poor fellow! he may be more deserving of pity," sighed Mr. Grant, sentimentally.

"You should not leap at conclusions!" cried Eleanor, with marked emphasis. "But I really wonder that Mr. Grant is ever listened to, when others, greatly his superiors, can scarcely obtain the slightest attention."

Matilda started when she recognized these well-known words, and again her color rose to crimson; but she remained silent while suffering from a feeling of embarrassment greater than she had ever known before. A pause ensued, which appeared endless, while she was conscious that

Eleanor's laughing eyes were maliciously bent on her with a look which she dared not venture to encounter. The case seemed desperate, for an alarming conjecture flashed into her mind, that Sir Colin's letter, and her own, had been seen in some way by her cousin, and she wondered he did not already feel conscious of these allusions to them; but, on the contrary, Matilda saw, with increasing surprise, that her self-satisfied admirer was composedly stirring his tea, and scarcely attending to what passed.

"You seem all to be spell-bound, like the seven sleepers!" exclaimed Eleanor, delighted with the sensation she had occasioned. "The first who speaks dies! Matilda, do you know the game of 'What is my thought like?' Pray favor us with yours!"

Before Miss Howard could reply, she was surprised to find a new direction given to the conversation, by Sir Alfred, who rarely addressed any except the person next him, and that generally in an undertone, but who now broke forth in a voice which attracted general notice.

"There is a purpose of marriage between Henry Douglas, commonly called Marquis of Dumbartonshire, and Lady Emilia Arundell! If any one here present knows any just cause or impediment ——"

"Nonsense!" interrupted Eleanor, eagerly. "You must be quizzing, Sir Alfred! I never saw you indulge us with a bit of gossip before!"

"That cuts you out of a very good thing, Douglas!" said Mr. Grant, laughing. "While your *Most Noble* cousin was cruising in his yatch, many a sleepless night you must have *enjoyed*, thinking how easily a single blast in the Bay of Biscay might make you a marquis! I should have rehearsed my maiden speech for the House of Lords pretty frequently before now, in your place."

"I know it cannot be true," said Lady Susan; "because Lady Emilia told me, last time we talked of him, that he looked like a monkey just escaped from his chains; and when I said that most people thought him rather fascinating, she replied that he might do, then, for most people, but not for her. It is certainly some mistake!"

"If his own hand and seal can give authenticity to the report, my intelligence is credible, but signatures are sometimes taken great liberties with, Miss Fitz-Patrick. My cousin was quite as decided in his denial of the marriage to me ten days ago; but not from any apprehension of an im pediment on the lady's part, as Dumbartonshire often declared that he would be accepted by any girl in London, if he merely wrote her a note."

"How I admire modest merit! But let me tell you, Sir Alfred, there are instances recently on record, where gentlemen equally confident of success, have been told that 'no circumstances can ever render it possible for their addresses to be acceptable!'"

Matilda stole an alarmed look towards Sir Colin, hoping to bespeak Eleanor's forbearance on his account, if not on her own; but she was astonished to perceive him insinuating his butter-toast into his mouth with perfect *nonchalance.* "How well he carries it off!" thought she. "What would I not give for the same enviable command of countenance!"

"I am much entertained," continued Eleanor, in a tone of pique, "at Lord Dumbartonshire's assurance! I know nothing of London yet, but his *note* would have been protested in Scotland *often;* I can answer for that!"

"Gentlemen must speak in this confident tone to each other," observed Major Foley, bowing; "but it is a mere flourish of trumpets to cover their retreat, as we all know that, nine times out of ten, they are refused."

"Yes! of course," added Eleanor, laughing. "I have always fancied, Sir Alfred, that you were born to sing through life the gay old song:—

'I care for nobody,
And nobody cares for me.'"

"That remains to be proved," replied he, in a low tone, which seemed only meant to reach Matilda, who instinctively colored when he looked at her; but Eleanor's ready ear at the same time caught the tone of manly feeling in which these few words were spoken, and she dropt her eyes, with an air of gratified vanity.

"Douglas!" cried Mr. Grant, "positively this morning I begin not to despair of seeing you, some rainy day, what I have always ardently wished, 'desperately and hopelessly in love!'"

"Thank you! there is no saying what we may all come to at last; for I think," said Sir Alfred, still contemplating his letters, "some bridegroom has gone mad, and bit all my acquaintances."

"Pray indulge us with your budget!" exclaimed Miss Charlotte, eagerly. "My whole crop of London correspondents has failed this year, like Sir Richard's turnip-field, and I am most wretchedly in the dark about what goes on in the matrimonial world."

"You should apply to the clerk of St. George's, Hanover Square," answered Sir Alfred. "He is better informed than most people on these subjects."

"Present company EXcepted!" interrupted Eleanor, with an intelligent eye on Matilda. "And I trust they may be ACcepted also, which is a *bon mot* of which you cannot yet perceive the merit."

"That puts me in mind of a case in point," began Sir Colin, deliberately. "My friend——"

"Sir Jonathan Fowler!" interrupted Mr. Grant. "He is one of the cleverest men on earth! Did you meet him, Fletcher, during your residence in Sweden, or the Orkneys?"

"I never visited either of these places, and am much too comfortable at home to think of travelling now."

"Or of changing your situation in any way?"

"Why, there's no saying!" answered Sir Colin, with an encouraging nod to Matilda. "Marriage is a lottery, and——"

"You and I have always drawn blanks as yet, Fletcher!" added Mr. Grant, in a condoling voice. "We have both been very ill used by the ladies."

"Speak for yourself!" replied Sir Colin, indignantly. "I never yet put it in any lady's power to refuse me, so I must not complain of their cruelty."

"What an inexorable bachelor you are, Fletcher!" exclaimed Sir Richard, laughing.

Matilda's eyes were gradually opened, during the progress of this dialogue, and she plainly perceived that Eleaner had taken advantage of her being so completely unsophisticated in society to impose upon her credulity with a counterfeit letter. From the moment that an idea of such a thing being possible dawned upon her mind, the whole became so obvious that she wondered at her own stupidity in not detecting the imposture at once; but she had never before heard of such a trick being played, and the borrowing of any person's seal and signature was rather beyond the limits of what she would have considered a legitimate hoax. But still she could not help being amused at the ingenuity with which it had been done; and feeling almost as if she deserved to suffer for not having detected the conspiracy. During an *éclat de rire*, occasioned by a lively sally of Mr. Grant's. Sir Alfred said to her, in an undertone, "Miss Howard, you will easily believe that I had no share in this legerdemain of your cousin's, but it will be an incessant annoyance till the jest is worn threadbare, unless you brave it out boldly."

Matilda gave Sir Alfred a grateful smile for his timely hint; and as the opposite party still levelled all their strokes of humor at her, she resolved to show him that it was not thrown away.

"Mr Grant," said she, in her usual animated tone, "you should have got my epistle franked last night, instead of ruining me in postage! Unluckily this morning I omitted to put the answer under your cover; but fortunately it seems to have reached the proper destination; and, though 'private and confidential' was not marked on the outside—you must have perceived that it ought to have been. I therefore appeal from Mr. Grant in a laughing mood to Mr. Grant in a serious one, whether it would be quite right to make my blunder more public, or to let it reach the person who is chiefly injured by this inadvertence of mine."

The gentleman thus addressed held up his plate, in imitation of a fan, assuming at the same time a comical expression of dismay, while his accomplices covered their faces with their handkerchiefs, and burst into a peal of laughter.

"Well! in my whole life I never saw people so easily amused," observed Sir Colin, with a bewildered look; "that seems to me a very sensible remark of Miss Howard's. I have known very unpleasant blunders made about letters often, and could relate several remarkable instances of the kind. You may laugh, Grant, being not much *a man of letters* yourself, but———"

"Capital, Sir Colin!—capital!" echoed the whole party, glad of an excuse to indulge their irresistible inclination to laugh, and feeling confident that he would be surprised at no excess of risibility after a jest of his own.

"I envy you that brilliant sally, Fletcher!" said Mr. Grant, recovering his gravity; "it is new and original! Pray, allow me the use of it for a week or two—I shall sport *the man of letters* on the hustings to-morrow, and establish my reputation as a wit on the spot."

"The story I was about to relate," continued the Baronet, in his usual persevering tone, "is very remarkable, and not at all generally known——"

"Ah, Sir Colin!" interrupted Eleanor, "we all consider

you a perfect *Arabian Knight*. Everybody allows you to be *the greatest story-teller living*."

"I shall trace its origin," continued he, "to show how authentic the particulars are; but they must only be mentioned among friends, so let me beg these circumstances may go no farther."

"We are all quite upon honor," replied Mr. Grant gravely, "and if you will believe me, Fletcher, I never do, by any chance, repeat a story of yours. At the same time, it does appear unlucky that no one has ever yet acted Boswell to your Johnson. What an incredible loss it would be to the world if we finally lost all record of the innumerable 'laughable circumstances, remarkable incidents and authentic facts,' with which the lumber-room of your memory is stored!"

"Very true; and it seems astonishing to me how authors contrive to get so much leisure," replied the Baronet, in a tone of superiority; "for my own part, I have sometimes intended to write such a book as Boswell's Johnson, but the only difficulty is to find *time*."

"Only fancy! 'The Diary and Recollections of Sir Colin Fletcher!'" said Eleanor, laughing.

"Edited by his disconsolate widow!" added Mr. Grant, with a sly look at Matilda. "That is the fashion now, Sir Colin. You must marry, and then we shall have the gratification of knowing, that a month after your decease, Lady Fletcher will be seated at her writing-desk, in deep mourning, correcting the press, with a pen in one hand, and a pocket-handkerchief in the other."

"What a remarkably good hand you write, Matilda!" observed Eleanor, looking archly at her cousin, as they rose to leave the breakfast-room. "I took a copy of your letter this morning, that it may be ready for the next baronet who presumes like Sir Colin."

"Notice, to all whom it may concern," said Sir Richard, "what is all this nonsense you are talking to-day, Eleanor?"

"Only that your niece has refused a certain gentleman, with the most barbarous cruelty! I wonder how you could be so hard-hearted, Matilda, for it really is not in my nature, and if Sir Colin had only proposed to me———"

"Eleanor, this subject does not admit of discussion. My foolish credulity has brought his name into circumstances where he never would have placed it himself, and let me entreat that the mistake may now be forgotten. You have had quite as good a laugh as the joke deserves, and you owe me a little forbearance, after all my sufferings last night. A proposal and an apparition, both in one afternoon, form an accumulation of horrors more than any ordinary brain could have stood, and I really do not promise to survive such another night."

"An apparition!!" exclaimed Eleanor, with breathless eagerness, "what can you mean! tell me about it instantly! I know nothing of this! Sir Alfred, pray close the shutters, that we may enjoy it in perfection."

Matilda now gave an animated and amusing sketch of her midnight progress from Miss Fitz-Patrick's room to her own, embellished with a retrospect of the traditions with which Eleanor had prepared her mind to be superstitious; and she ended by candidly acknowledging the nervous fears which had at last so nearly got the better of her.

"And after all!" said Eleanor, in a tone of disappointment, "it was only Pauline, who stupidly lost her way, after depositing the letter. She had been charged, on pain of death, not to let you see her. How provoking! that a commencement which might have done for Mrs. Radcliffe ends in so paltry a manner. By the way, I am surprised that it never occurred to me till this instant, that we might attempt a ghost upon you, Matilda. It might be admirably got up in the old lumber-room."

"Pray never try so dangerous an experiment on any one, Eleanor! The result has sometimes been worse than death, and entailed endless regret on those who attempted it. I could not be answerable for my own nerves, because there is a degree of latent superstition in every mind, which may be excited by circumstances."

"I make no rash promises!" answered Eleanor, with a mischievous laugh.

"Miss Fitz-Patrick!" said Sir Alfred, "if I thought that we were liable to such terrifying visitations as has been described, nothing should induce me to remain here after dusk; and I must obtain a solemn assurance that no one *more supernatural than yourself* shall be exhibited while I remain, or we must take advantage of what little daylight is remaining to hasten homewards. I am particularly afraid of ghosts!"

There was a humorous expression in the dark eye of Sir Alfred when he made this assertion, which showed Matilda that what he said was on her account, and she felt gratified at the unobtrusive attention with which he seemed constantly on the watch to assist her in the many little embarrassments which she frequently encountered.

"If I abstain from an apparition, then, Sir Alfred," asked Eleanor, "will you escort us this morning to the Fairy Bridge? It is well worth seeing, on account of its extraordinary beauty, being the highest single arch in Scotland."

"Indeed!" replied Sir Alfred, sitting down to write a letter. "I shall try to recollect the loftiest arch I ever saw, and add a foot or two."

"But you have not heard the most important part of my story," continued Eleanor. "Thomas the Rhymer once prophesied that any gentleman who ventures to throw himself over, shall find below the richest and most beautiful young lady in the world, glittering with jewels."

"What temptation could there be to take such a leap, while *you* remain at the top?" replied he, continuing to write; "Unless we go over hand in hand, I could have no security for the prophecy being fulfilled." Eleanor gave a triumphant glance at Matilda, as if to ask whether a doubt could remain on her mind of Sir Alfred's partiality.

"Now, Sir Alfred! do bestir yourself and come while the morning is so bright. We shall offer you a carte blanche as to terms—a cigar and the privelege of total silence—my footman to carry a camp-stool, and I intend to hand you over the stiles myself."

"Thank you," replied Sir Alfred, continuing to write; "I am like the Frenchman who said when he reached the summit of a misty hill, '*Aimez vous le beautés de la nature? pour moi, je les* abhorre!' As far as the eye can reach, from this window, I am ready to admire anything you please; but unless this ottoman could be metamorphosed into a palanquin, I do not mean to leave it, till the world is better aired. Pray take my good wishes along with you, however."

"As much as to say, What a happy riddance you all are!" said Eleanor, retreating towards the door.

"Not *all*," replied Sir Alfred, looking for a moment at Matilda, but Eleanor heard only the tone of sensibility in which this ambiguous sentence was uttered; and turning to her cousin, as they crossed the staircase together, she said, "Now, Matilda, can you doubt his sentiments any longer? Did you observe what Sir Alfred said about leaping over the bridge?—That was very decided."

"But, Eleanor, his rallying tone evidently showed that it

was merely in jest!—I shall never again volunteer my opinion upon this subject; but when you ask it now, let me assure you of my candid and conscientious belief, that his sentiments are entirely misunderstood."

"There are none so blind as those who will not see! You were always very obstinate, Matilda, but I shall convince you some day, and that will be one of my greatest pleasures, when Sir Alfred declares himself. How delightfully odd and eccentric he is!—but I cannot make up my mind whether he would suit me or not."

"Then try, if possible, to think that he would not!" said Matilda, earnestly. "My dear Eleanor, I appeal to your own knowledge of me, whether I would deceive you, or prefer my interest to yours, if both were at stake; but it would be unlike our *former* friendship, not to tell you fairly my real opinion, that in appearing to prefer Sir Alfred to Mr. Grant, you are mistaking your happiness, as well as your real feelings."

CHAPTER XVIII.

What spirits were *theirs*, what wit, and what whim,
Now breaking a jest, and now breaking a limb—
Now wrangling and grumbling, to keep up the ball—
Now teasing and vexing, yet laughing at all!

GOLDSMITH.

DURING their walk to the Fairy Glen, Eleanor contrived that her cousin should again fall a victim to the prosing propensities of Sir Colin, while she proceeded at some distance herself, with a numerous train of attendants. Matilda had little notice to spare for any one, as her thoughts were pleasingly engrossed with tracing the almost imperceptible attentions by which Sir Alfred contrived to testify how continually she occupied his mind. It filled her with surprise, at the same time, to consider how greatly he seemed embarrassed after any unusual exhibition of his feelings towards herself, and how instantly he became reserved when there was a chance of his being remarked. "What can it all mean?" was the question which forced itself upon her thoughts in a thousand different shapes, as she proceeded along the path in deep, though agreeable meditation.

Meantime, Sir Colin's voice flowed on in an uninterrupted stream, while, *à propos* to an accidental remark on the extreme coldness of the day, he gave Matilda an elaborate description of all the greatcoats he had used during many successive winters; and by the time they were nearly worn out, the subject happily diverged into a dissertation on coughs and colds, when the Baronet treated her to an account of a violent rheumatism which he had *very nearly caught*, about twenty years before, owing to a window having been left open at night, though he fortunately discovered the mistake in time to have it closed before retiring to bed.

Sir Colin was charmed with the silent interest which Matilda manifested in the dangers he had passed. Her large, bright eyes were intently fixed on him, and he was not aware that their usual intelligent expression was wanting, for when ever he appealed to her, and asked whether what he related was not "wonderful, fortunate, or remarkable," she almost unconsciously echoed his words, with a preliminary adjective, giving additional emphasis to his expression. Matilda had on no previous occasion thus completely lost the command of her attention, but Sir Colin was filled with admiration of her good sense. He had never before met with so judicious a young lady! so conversable! so companionable! so easily amused, and so highly intelligent! "How superior to her cousin!" thought he, "whose flippant manner spoils conversation entirely! If Miss Howard continues to play her cards as well, there is no saying what may be the consequences! She knows what she is about!"

But Matilda was very far from "knowing what she was about." The varied scenery of her extensive walk was, for the first time, unmarked by her eye, the impediments in her path were now mechanically surmounted, and the incessant hum of Sir Colin's voice became only obvious to her senses when he paused for a reply, while she rapidly traced over her whole intercourse with Sir Alfred.—The peculiar interest he had testified on their first meeting at Barnard Castle,—the deep attention he paid to all she said,—the assistance and protection he was constantly on the alert to afford her in Eleanor's society, and the ambiguous expressions, either of love or of friendship, which he had long taken every opportunity of addressing to her. There was lately even a tone of diffidence in his manner of speaking to her, far different from his aspect of cold indifference to others, which rendered the contrast only stronger; and as this change occurred to the remembrance of Matilda, her color became brighter, and she walked with a more elastic step than before. "But Eleanor has observed nothing of all this!" thought she, with a sudden revulsion of feeling; "and who is so observant as she is, if there had been any truth in all I have fancied! No! I will not plunge myself into the dark abyss of disappointed affection and unavailing regret, by allowing vanity, even for this one hour, to deceive me. The customs of society warrant all the attention Sir Alfred has yet shown me, and I must not imitate Eleanor in misconstruing his meaning."

Matilda's reveries were interrupted by the party in advance suddenly coming to a dead pause, and she was instantly restored to the consciousness of Sir Colin's presence, by hearing him conclude his long oration with a remark which was intended to be quite new and original.

"So, you see, Miss Howard, nothing can be more dangerous than a draught of air."

"What is it that gives a cold, cures a cold, and pays the doctor?" asked Mr. Grant, wheeling suddenly round. "Do you give it up, Fletcher?—a draft!"

"As for curing a cold," began Sir Colin, deliberately "there's nothing equal to——"

"Leaping over a three pair of stairs' window! That is what I always recommend to my friends, for it saves such a fortune in lozenges."

"Now, good people! here is the cottage of old Janet, which I brought you to admire," cried Eleanor, rounding an angle in the glen, and displaying, with evident exultation, a scene which nature and art seemed to rival each other in embellishing. The sunbeams played gaily through the inmost depths of a lovely valley, and streamed along the bright edges of every tree and bramble, which glittered with the silver whiteness of a clear hard frost. The distant mountains were covered with patches of snow, varied by the dark face of many a rough gigantic precipice. The river danced merrily along over a bed of granite, and after rushing and tumbling through massy blocks of stone, it suddenly shot over the highest pinnacle of the rock, and fell in one vast arch of foam into the dark and fathomless basin beneath.

Contrasted with the bolder features of this gorgeous landscape stood Gowanbank, a lovely rustic cottage, which seemed formed to become the abode of peace and contentment. It crowned a sloping bank, which rose from the margin of the stream; a little white paling surrounded the garden, which was fancifully planted with groups of evergreens, the varnished and sombre leaves of which were tipped with golden light, and edged with fringes of snow. Every bough, and every rock, was hung with wreaths of sparkling icicles, which were illuminated by a thousand prismatic hues, rivalling the tints of a rainbow; and the deep overhanging roof of the cottage had so sheltered the southern wall, that it still bloomed with the scarlet blossoms of the pyrus japonica.

"Now for a sonnet, or a fugitive piece of some kind, Mr. Grant!" said Eleanor; "you ought to be an eloquent *improvisatore*, having resided so much in Italy!"

"Indeed, Miss Fitz-Patrick, I possess the finest poetical vein in the world! It has but one little defect, that the moment feelings should be put into words, the whole evaporates! I have a thousand times seized a sheet of paper, feeling precisely like Byron or Moore, but invariably, after writing a large emphatic OH! at the top of a page, I have been obliged to desist."

"How very unlucky! for I was planning what a good amusement it would be, if our large party were to set about writing a Christmas Annual. You must each send a contribution, and I shall sit for the frontispiece myself. Sir Colin's story must be limited to twenty pages; Mr. Grant may throw in a few comic sketches; and Major Foley shall court the muses."

"I can be at no loss for a subject," said he, with a gratified bow.

"That is precisely what I intended you to say! Captain M'Tartan must toss up some good shipwrecks for us, and be sure to invent a splendid storm."

"If a leaf of my log-book can be of any service, you are welcome; but otherwise, I never *speak of the ship* upon shore, and would rather *wave* the subject. Besides I may perhaps publish a volume myself, to be called 'Dulse and Tangle, or Yarns at Sea,' dedicated to the first Lord of the Admiralty, whoever that may be."

"Colonel Pendarvis! we shall accept any of your adventures which have not already enlivened the United Service Journal. By the way, I must make an exception of your trip to Calcutta, because nothing new can ever said be about India. My receipt for a book upon that subject would describe them all. Begin with a tiger-hunt, then follows a suttee; a visit to a rajah, two or three serpents, plenty of currie, and an escape from an alligator."

"One might quite as generally characterize all descriptions of savage countries, which are invariable repetitions of the same thing," said Mr. Grant. "Whether the subject be New Zealand, Polynesia, Greenland, the South Pole, or the North, you may bind them up in alternate pages without being found out. Describe the universal outcry for glass beads and knives, the filthiness of the natives, their thievish propensities, their wonder at first seeing a ship, some detestable particulars of the food they eat, and a great deal about the author's gentlemanlike horror at observing them use their fingers, as if these poor creatures ought to starve until they had silver forks—and the whole is wound up with a tremendous picture of cruelty, depravity, vice, and superstition."

"There is but one use in reading such representations,"

said Matilda, coloring, for she felt it an effort to say anything out of keeping with the general tone of the conversation. "They render us more anxious to encourage those who visit distant lands, and encounter all that misery, in order to substitute knowledge for ignorance, virtue for vice, and the light of Christian hope for the darkness of vain superstition. It is a noble endeavor, and should be nobly encouraged."

"Now for a subscription book!" cried Eleanor, satirically. "I like the new fashion of penny collectors best. This is not the first time, I assure you all, that my cousin has been reduced to beggary; for she attacked me two days ago to assist in making out a *trousseau* for the daughter of that old woman who lives at Gowanbank, and who was married, I believe, this morning. Her sister Nanny may supply Martha with ornaments, for I am sure she has taken plenty of mine!"

"You are *not* sure, Eleanor," whispered Matilda, indignantly. "No one *can* be sure; and till it is proved we have no right to say so. They are in great distress," added she, with emotion.

"Ah! that is her best apology," said the heiress; "she was very pretty, and very poor; so it was, as Mrs. Gordon said, a great temptation."

"I did not allude to her poverty, Eleanor! she is poor, but I could be answerable for Nanny's honesty, as well as for her mother's; and they yet hope to see these calumnies refuted. With respect to pecuniary difficulties, they have nothing now to complain of, for old Janet told Dr. Murray that a gentleman from Barnard Castle, who accidentally heard their story, called yesterday on horseback, and after remaining there some time, left a very liberal donation, which will enable Martha and William to begin the world in some comfort."

"Now! who could that be?—from Barnard Castle, did you say? A charitable incognito! how very romantic!—Mr. Grant do not assume that look of amiable consciousness, for I never even suspected you!—Colonel Pendarvis? no!—Major Foley? impossible!—Ah! Sir Colin! you are precisely the sort of person to do good by stealth, and 'blush to find it fame.'"

"I have not gone near a cottage for seven years, except to light my cigar, Miss Fitz-Patrick! but there was a curious incident that occurred to me in the village of Nettleton, which may enliven us while we stand here——"

"Stop, Sir Colin! we must investigate Matilda's story before you gain a hearing. One at a time, gentlemen, if you please, as the countryman said to a quack doctor, when he and his donkey both brayed at once."

"Miss Fitz-Patrick! you have rather spoilt that circumstance; it was——"

"How dare you say so, Sir Colin!—Tell me that I have improved or invented a story, and still hope to be forgiven; but to hint that I can possibly spoil one is an unpardonable affront. I shall not listen to a word you say for three weeks, so now consider yourself in Coventry."

"Eleanor," whispered Matilda, slipping her arm into Miss Fitz-Patrick's, and drawing her aside—"dear Eleanor! your laughter at this moment goes to my very heart; for it would be difficult to conceive the state of heart-breaking grief in which that poor old woman has lately been weeping beside her once cheerful fireside. Give the subject a moment's serious thought. I cannot be so near without stealing over for an instant to inquire about Janet. There is a confused report that something very distressing occurred at their wedding to-day, but I cannot understand what it was, for the ceremony was to take place at Dr. Murray's, where neither Nanny nor her mother intended to be present; and the young couple went immediately afterwards to the village of Clanpibroch. I shall never be missed by the party here; but let me take a kind and compassionate message from you, Eleanor, to cheer their hearts, for they greatly need it. May I say that your judgment of Nanny shall be suspended till a fair, candid, and open investigation is made into her conduct? for that is what Dr. Murray promises to bring about without delay, and to which he says you consented."

"Did I? The less done in that way the better for Nanny, I suspect! but she has completely hoodwinked that good excellent man, by her plausible stories; and we must really get him to hear the truth from Mrs. Gordon and Pauline."

"Eleanor!" said Matilda, taking her hand, while the tears gathered in her eyes, "you were not always so reckless of other people's misery as now! I remember the time when we wept together, because Nanny was thought to be dying, and our dear aunt Olivia could scarcely console us.

It would have been better for that poor girl to have been cut off then, if her future years are to be darkened by disgrace and misery."

Matilda spoke with all the eloquence of intense feeling; and she had touched the right cord at last. Few people whose hearts are recently hardened by worldly prosperity can recall the tender emotions of their own childhood without sentiments of regret, and without having their benumbed feelings softened for a moment by observing the contrast of former and present character.

"Matilda, you are right! I begin to fear that my conduct has been rash and hasty in this business. Poor Nanny! everything most precious in life to her is at stake. She certainly was a good, excellent creature long ago. I dare not think of it all at present though. I see it now, as I ought to have done from the first. She *may* possibly be innocent, and then indeed I have been criminally careless. Ah! Matilda, you are always the same, and if our dear aunt could look back, she would see you unchanged, but oh, what would she think of *me?*" Eleanor walked rapidly on for a few steps, and seemed scarcely able to refrain from bursting into tears. "These thoughts sometimes shoot across my mind, Matilda, but I dare not let them remain. Do what you like for poor Nanny; take all the responsibility from me if you can. Bring her back to Barnard Castle when you like, and tell her we shall thoroughly and heartily investigate the whole affair. Miserable as it would make me in one respect to find her innocent, I shall most truly rejoice at it, and do all that money can do—which is not a little—to make up for what she has suffered."

"Thank you, dear Eleanor,—a thousand thanks," answered Matilda, accompanying her cousin, who hastily rejoined the party, as if afraid to trust herself longer on the subject, which had evidently affected her more than she wished to acknowledge. A moment afterwards she was talking in her usual tone of careless vivacity.

"Mr. Grant, I see you are trying to imitate the Irish beggar we met last night; but, as papa's valet said, when he saw the eclipse of the sun, 'it is quite a failure, sir;' even with all my love of giving alms, you would never beguile me of a single sous."

"Allow me to differ from the last speaker! I could bet any sum on being able to maintain myself for a month, with no other resource than the credulity of a benevolent public. What do you say, Miss Howard?"

"Your tone is much too whining and professional. I have an instinctive perception of impostors, and could almost pledge myself to detect one anywhere. The Irishman, for instance, whom you describe, seems to be half knave and half fool, but I should certainly not like to meet such a *fortune-hunter* on the road when I was alone, for if ever he got anything from me it would be fear rather than charity that extorted it."

"Ah! Matilda is easily moved, and not a bit wiser than other people," said Eleanor, laughing; "you would have parted with half-a-crown, as I did yesterday, if you had seen poor Paddy—though I am certain it went straight to the ale-house, or assisted to buy lemons for his fillet of veal."

"If I had thought so, neither force nor fraud should have got a shilling out of me," replied Matilda, smiling, while she gradually slackened her pace, and dropt behind the other pedestrians. At length, having caught a favorable opportunity, she left them entirely, and hastened over a rustic bridge which led to the cottage.

CHAPTER XIX.

"The bursting heart, the tearless eye,
The cold and torpid frame,
The smother'd groan, the broken sigh,
The grief she dare not name."

When Matilda swung open a little white gate, which led through the garden to Gowanbank, and saw the whole landscape brilliantly lighted up with a sheet of sunshine, she remembered her first visits there in autumn, when the placid old woman always met her with a smiling welcome at the door, and Martha used to suspend her labors, with many expressions of pleasure and gratitude for the kindness she showed them in coming. Often formerly had Matilda lingered on that threshold, to breathe the fragrant air, as it wafted the perfume of various flowers which then profusely decorated the little enclosure; but the wind had passed over them, and they were gone as though they had never been, while thus it was also with the peace and cheerfulness which once reigned within those walls.

Sad as were Matilda's anticipations of the scene which awaited her in the cottage, she was far from being prepared for the sight of such utter desolation as that which caught her eye when she entered. Old Janet was alone, seated upon a low stool, with her face buried in her hands, and bowed down almost to her knees, the very image of feebleness and misery. Her spinning-wheel, the busy hum of which had seldom before been silent, now stood idle and neglected; the furniture, usually so clean and polished, looked dusty and disordered; the fire had nearly gone out, and her breakfast, which seemed to have been long since prepared, lay untouched by her side. How impressive is the silence of extreme grief! Matilda stood for a moment immovable at the door with surprise at the sight of such unexpected distress, and then gently advancing to the old woman, she took her by the hand, which was cold as death. Janet feebly returned the pressure of Miss Howard's fingers, and looked up with an expression of momentary wonder, showing a face so haggard, so shrunk, so cold and disconsolate, that Matilda started with astonishment; but seeing her unable to speak, she postponed all inquiries for the present, and, with characteristic activity, gathered the remaining embers of the fire together, and relighted them into a cheerful blaze. She then boiled the kettle afresh, and after preparing some tea, tried to rouse once more the old woman's attention, by entreating her to take some.

There is a magnetic power in the accents of real kindness which reaches to the inmost recesses of mental suffering; and the voice of pity and commiseration in which Matilda addressed old Janet spoke instant peace to her mind. She looked at first bewildered and faint, but gradually revived to a greater appearance of consciousness, while her sympathizing visitor continued to administer refreshment to her exhausted frame. Matilda could not but wonder to find old Janet so entirely deserted; but seeing her still unable to speak, she at length insisted on supporting her tottering frame to bed, which with some difficulty she succeeded in doing. Having now done everything for her bodily comfort, Miss Howard ventured to begin a cautious and tender inquiry into the cause of such unaccountable distress.

"Janet, I fear you are very unwell to-day?"

"Almost in eternity," replied the old woman, feebly, while she turned on Matilda a countenance as perfectly white and as rigid as if she had been already dead.

"You seem very poorly, indeed, Janet; I never saw you unfit to work before; and why are none of the neighbors here—or Nanny?"

"They are all gone to look for *her*," replied she, in a hoarse deep voice, and speaking with great effort, for the old woman became frightfully agitated. "Oh, Miss Howard," added she, covering her face with her hands, "have you not heard yet? My poor Nanny! we thought she had not known the hour of Matty's wedding—that she did not wish to see it—but when all was over, and they came out of Dr. Murray's house, she suddenly appeared. Her mind was gone, but yet she gave them her blessing. She wished them happiness—she spoke to them both, and then rushed out of sight. No eye has seen her since. They tried to stop Nanny, but she fled as if a spectre had pursued, and none could speed like her. I saw her bonnet brought home from the river, but that sweet face, which was the pride of my heart, we never shall look upon again. Oh! why did she ever leave me!"

A burst of grief choked the old woman's utterance, and she sobbed aloud. Who can look upon the tears of helpless age and not weep also? Matilda's whole heart was melted with pity for the afflicted mother, and she shuddered to think of Nanny's probable fate. Even Eleanor had a place in her thoughts at this moment, when she reflected on all the remorse that might await her for causing so much wretchedness. Matilda's tongue seemed to be chained when she gazed on the intense agony of old Janet, and tried to think what might be said to console her. She longed to fly for Dr. Murray, whose words would have more experience and authority than her own; but yet she could not go, without first using her best endeavors to soothe and alleviate such heart-rending sorrow. She did not now take that tone of admonition and superiority with which most people in the height of prosperity can teach others how they ought to bear sudden calamity and anguish of spirit. She did not deal out sentences nor attempt the slightest exhibition of good sense—but Matilda had a heart to feel, and she felt and knew what would be the effect of every word on the suffering mind she desired to comfort. She did not forget that it was to an *aged Christian* she spoke, whose afflictions might obscure the brightness of her hope for a moment; but who needed only to be reminded of the inheritance which awaited her, rather than to be taught a due estimate of its unspeakable worth.

"This is a sorrowful hour indeed, Janet," she said in a tone of heartfelt sympathy. "You may well say, like Naomi, 'the Almighty hath dealt very bitterly with me.' I trust, however, that instead of being like Rachael, who refused to be comforted, you are spared to be an example of that power which can support us under the severest calamities. I weep myself, Janet, to think of your affliction, and what must *you* feel—oh! how great are the sorrows that this world can bring!—but we are sinners, and have cause to be thankful, whatever is laid on us, so long as we are not eternally condemned. Think how short a time any of us have to mourn and how soon you will be in the presence of that Great Being in a better world, who has always been with you on earth."

"Yes, Miss Howard, death seems neither so strange nor so distant as it used to do, and oh! it will be welcome now. I am in the dark strait, when grief has struck me to the heart, and resignation has scarcely yet been granted. Age and grey-hairs, sickness and infirmity, have all been gathering round me for years, and my heart was still supported and cheerful—but my child—my poor Nanny; she has destroyed herself, and how can I ever know peace again! My sorrow is the only one that religion does not cure, because the more I think, the worse it seems, that she should have died in a way which religion forbids. Every step that approaches my door this day seems to bring me the last awful tidings, or perhaps to be the sound of those who are bearing in her lifeless body."

"We are not certain of the worst yet. She may possibly be saved. Let us cling to hope, and remember that Nanny was quite unconscious of what she did—her intellects have certainly been wandering for some time past."

"She was deeply tried, Miss Howard; she was disgraced and desperate. Oh! it comforts me to hear you still speak of hope. No one would say this morning that they had any. She flew straight to the river, which is deep and rapid. If I could but see Nanny once again—if I could but hear that she was cleared of all the evil that has been said, my eyes would close on every earthly concern in thankfulness and peace."

"We may trust, Janet, that her former companions who raised these stories, will now be shocked at the mischief they have done, and repent sufficiently to make them confess her innocence. Miss Fitz-Patrick was already resolved to investigate the whole affair, and though justice is sometimes reserved for a better world, still I hope that even now your daughter's character will be cleared."

"You are right, my good young lady—either now or hereafter the truth will be known, and why should I be impatient! My days on earth will be few, and they must not be wasted in vain lamentation. That dear child is taken from me, probably to make life less desirable, when its close is so near—and death less a subject of regret. I have a great work to do, for I must prepare to suffer and to die, *not* as those who have no hope; and though nature feels, and my heart seems broken for Nanny, yet the Christian may believe, in such an hour of extremity, that this sorrow is the last which shall come throughout an endless eternity."

Matilda thought, from Janet's altered appearance, that indeed she had not long to endure, whatever the result of her suspense might be; and having extended her visit to the utmost possible limit, she now prepared to withdraw, especially after having been relieved by the entrance of a neighbor, who had hastened back from his unsuccessful search. Before departing, however, she read the twelfth chapter of Hebrews, which has been for ages the consolation of successive generations, while they have mourned and wept in this world of changes. An expression of resignation and peace gradually stole over the old woman's countenance as Matilda proceeded, far different from the ghastly and haggard look which it had worn when she entered; and at the conclusion, Janet slowly and solemnly raised herself in the bed, and pronounced a devout blessing on her young and lovely visitor. "Now," added she, "I shall endeavor patiently to await the time, when it shall be my turn, like the grass, to be cut down; and though she, who was as the flower of the grass, is fallen before me, yet the word of the Lord endureth, and shall be my portion forever. It comforts the heart of a poor, helpless being like me, Miss Howard, that there are rich and precious blessings which my prayers may bring down on one whom I have no other way to serve, and many and constant shall they be for *you*. Farewell, my kind young friend; you leave me as well as I shall be on this side of eternity; and probably our next meeting will take place where uncertainty and sorrow will be forever at an end. Grief and sickness are our best apprenticeship for death."

CHAPTER XX.

I am unable, yonder beggar cries,
To stand or go. If he says true, he lies.
DONNE.

A HEAVY fall of snow had come on while Matilda remained at Gowanbank, but the weather now cleared up into the very *beau idéal* of a winter day—bright, cold, and clear. The air was like ice, the pure, unsullied snow lay thickly over the buried fields, and a cloudless sunshine threw the broad shadows of the overhanging branches along her path. She looked upon the glittering landscape around, and experienced that rapturous pleasure of existence, which, independent of every other cause, often exhilarates the spirits amidst such scenes of natural beauty, and gives a sensation of happiness which can scarcely be traced to its source. Everything seemed new and delightful. The blue ethereal sky, in its matchless splendor, proclaimed the glory of Him who has stretched the heavens as a span, and the pure, untrodden snow reminded her, by its dazzling whiteness, of those garments in which glorified saints shall at length be clothed. It would be as easy for our bodies to exist without the beating pulse within, as for our minds to live in a religious state without meditation; and Matilda now reflected, in astonishment, how much her thoughts were lately occupied and almost engrossed, with the amusements and petty interests of the little circle in which she had recently mingled. Excepting Sir Alfred, and, she could not but add, with a smile of partial indulgence, an exception also in favor of Mr. Grant, the visitors then at Barnard Castle seemed in their conduct, to resemble a number of spoilt, and not very amiable children, in their continual necessity for restless excitement, their exaggerated views of every little vexation which interrupted present gratification, their total regardlessness of each other's real feelings, and their almost undisguised desire of pre-eminence and distinction. The Miss Cliffords gloried in testifying openly an abhorrence of Captain M'Tartan and Mr. Armstrong, as if they had been themselves the highest caste of Brahmins thrown into contact with a couple of Pariahs from the desert; while Colonel Pendarvis and Major Foley lived in a perpetual horror of Miss Marabout and Miss Murray, whom they pricked their ears and shyed at, as one of their own hunters would have done at a donkey on the road, and whom they classed together as a couple of undistinguishable old maids. Lord de Mainbury at the same time, looked down on the Major and the Colonel, as mere soldiers of fortune, who could scarcely keep a tolerable stud; and Lord Alderby despised Lord de Mainbury, as a man of yesterday, while he constantly whispered some old family tradition about his Lordship's grandfather having once been butler at Alderby Forest. Matilda wondered to think that all this was considered the highest refinement of good breeding, and she could not but reflect how inferior the dancing-master and the school of fashion are to that school of the heart which taught how the feelings of the most insignificant are to be treated with respect, and how each should consider another better than himself; but religion is intended to eradicate entirely that selfishness, which it is the utmost effort of mere good manners *to conceal*, and which many who profess to be perfectly well-bred do not even attempt to hide. Matilda had often remarked that many people will treat such as are decidedly their inferiors with kindness and condescension, while the whole weight of their exclusiveness and repulsive *hauteur* is reserved for those who approach the nearest to themselves in rank and station, because then comes the struggle for that pre-eminence which they are anxious to assert; and even with some who affect to act on Christian principle, it becomes a salvo to their own consciences if they stoop gracefully to encourage those who are far removed from themselves, and, at the same time, rudely *elbow off* such as they come in immediate contact with.

Something similar is the feeling of Christians in respect to the doctrine and conduct of those with whom they associate—the nearer that any one approaches to their own standard the more narrowly do they scan deficiencies; and while they can look with pity and indulgence on many who are near the threshold, there is a feeling of rivalship which too often steals into the sentiments with which those are observed who seem as far advanced as themselves. "How trifling all those vain competitions appear, now that I am removed from the scene of them!" thought Matilda; "and it is probably with such feelings as I here contemplate the last few days, that, in a future life, we shall all look back on the scenes and the pleasures which are now so enticing! The most important events in life will then appear to have been insignificant, except in so far as they served to lead us on in our Christian course, and the greatest pleasures we have ever known will seem but a dream of folly, except such as were consistent with religion."

Her steps seemed as light as the falling snow, while Matilda advanced speedily homewards, and rapidly entered a long, narrow lane which led towards the approach. A few foot-marks in the centre pointed out the path, and showed that others had preceded her there during that morning, or else the air of profound solitude which pervaded the whole scene might have made it appear as if there were not another being in the world but herself. The massy stems of the beech-trees, like a long colonnade of pillars, rose in majestic dignity on each side, throwing their long branches out till they met overhead, and were curiously interlaced in the distance, like a Gothic window of some ancient cathedral. The resplendent snow, glittering like sunshine on marble, stretched as far as her eye could reach, and the dazzling beams of a setting sun reposed on the far distant mountains, and shed a glow of ruddy light over the horizon. The air was perfectly still, and not a sound could be heard but her own footstep on the crisp, unyielding frost, until Matilda was suddenly startled from her agreeable meditations by the loud rough voice of a beggar, who emerged from behind a hedge, and, to her no small alarm, addressed her. His appearance, which seemed by no means prepossessing, answered completely to the description she had already heard from Eleanor.* He was dressed in a long, loose greatcoat, such as is usually worn by the country people in that neighborhood; a large handkerchief, which covered his ears, was tied over the rag of a hat with which his head was adorned. His face seemed begrimed with snuff, and one of his eyes was fast closed up, which gave a strange, unnatural contortion to his whole features. He looked athletic, though evidently very lame, and his accent was Irish.

"Och! long life to your honor, and many of them, madam," said he, coming up to her, in a tone of humor, which called an irresistible smile into Matilda's countenance. "Sure you'll be after giving something to a poor distressed cratur, who has nine starving childer, besides myself, and not a drop of comfort for any of us! Give me a tinpenny, and, by your lave, you'll never be a farthing the poorer."

Matilda could not help being amused at the *dégagé* air with which he addressed her, and the look of Irish humor which glittered in his only eye; but she hurried on without answering, being a determined enemy to imposture.

"It's you that have the face of charity and goodness, ma'am! sure you'll not belie such looks!—winter would turn to summer at the sight of ye! Indeed, Miss, we are in very indolent circumstances."

"I can give you nothing at present," replied Matilda, trying to look very stern and decided. "Call at Barnard Castle to-morrow, and perhaps Sir Richard may have your case inquired into."

"But a lady like yourself wouldn't be after walking without a purse entirely! and you'll give something as a token of respect. A poor boy such as I wouldn't be after returning empty-handed as he came out; and throth, it's not an hour since I dreamt that one like yourself came by. Didn't I see you, as plain as my staff, take a shilling out to give me, and return the purse into your bag?"

"You know," answered Matilda, hurrying rapidly on, "dreams go by contraries."

"Then it's the purse you'll give me, and the shilling you'll keep! och, but that bates the world. By the stick in my hand, I'd cut a throat any day for half as much?" cried the beggar in an ecstasy of gratitude; "you're a lady, every inch of you! The purse then, if you plase, ma'am, and thanks t'ye!"

He held out his hand with an air more like command than entreaty, and Matilda began less and less to like her persevering companion. "We must examine into your claims," said she, hurriedly; "I never give to people who beg on the high road."

"Och, honey! is it into your parlor that I must come? And for character, I'd refer you to Paddy O'Connar from Kilkenny. No!—he's been in jail this month past—the drink makes fools of us all. Then there's Jerry Sullivan, but he's gone beyond seas; just a trifle of money he lifted! We're all tarred with the same stick; but you'll hear the very best of me from myself, and who knows better? I'm *mortal sober* always, and haven't tasted above three glasses to-day; but I'll drink your health this afternoon with the two shillings you're going to give me; and may you never die while you live."

Matilda really wished it had been less against all principle and conscience to bestow something on the poor man, whose reckless audacity had a degree of humor along with it, which diverted her in spite of considerable alarm which she felt at their being so completely alone.

"Troth, ma'am," added he in a piteous tone, "you don't know what I may be reduced to, if something is not given me soon."

"To what?" asked Matilda, rather relenting.

"To *work*, ma'am! Bestow a trifle on me any how, for I wouldn't wish to *rob you.*"

There was something sinister in the villain's eye when he said this, which greatly intimidated Matilda, who expected the next instant that he would snatch away her bag, or perhaps even produce a pistol. She quickened her steps, but became more and more alarmed on discovering that he walked faster also; and his lameness, which had been at first so conspicuous, became scarcely perceptible. If he had been walking for a wager, it would have been impossible to keep up better with her accelerated pace. At length a sharp turn in the lane disclosed another long, straight path, of nearly half a mile in extent, about the centre of which Matilda descried the distant appearance of a gentleman. Instantly, with the speed of thought, she darted forward, and knowing that few people could ever keep up with her rapidity, she flew on for protection towards the figure in advance. No sooner did the Irishman observe her intention to take flight, than he started forward, evidently desirous to impede her progress, and when she quickly eluded his intention, he loudly vociferated for her to stop. Terror now gave wings to Matilda's feet, which scarcely touched the ground, so that long after the beggar had ceased his pursuit, she continued to fly, thinking she still heard the sound of his footsteps, and his loud calls on her to return. She even fancied, for a moment, that her own name was reiterated in the distant air, and that a noise like laughter echoed behind, but all this only gave fresh impetus to her speed. The next moment, panting, breathless, and faint, Matilda overtook the person whose form at a distance had encouraged her to attempt an escape, and grasping his arm with convulsive energy, she could not articulate a word, but stood for some moments gasping to recover herself. At length, having raised her head to look at this unintentional deliverer, she suddenly encountered the astonished gaze of Sir Alfred Douglas. If fear had already deprived Matilda of utterance, agitation now completely overpowered her. The scene she had lately gone through at Gowanbank, the panic which had seized her about the Irishman, and the confusion of having intruded so unexpectedly on Sir Alfred, altogether combined to agitate her nerves so powerfully, that every attempt to articulate only ended in a convulsive quiver of the lips. She pointed backwards on the path which had so lately been the scene of her flight, but not a trace was left of the miscreant who had alarmed her, and, overcome with the shock, she leant against a tree and burst into tears.

After anxiously surveying the surrounding country, where nothing appeared visible but a wild waste of snow,—and after pausing some moments in the evident hope of an explanation, which Matilda's increasing agitation rendered every moment more improbable, Sir Alfred at length turned to her, with a look of respectful interest, but at the same time he spoke with good-humored raillery, while still gazing all round, in obvious perplexity and surprise.

"Pray, Miss Howard, what planet have you dropt from? It is said that *talking* of friends always brings them into one's presence; but if *thinking* had the same effect, you would never be absent from me. I am concerned to observe how much you have been frightened; tell me what I can do. Show me any tangible foe to exercise my valor on—I am ready to shed the last drop of my blood, and so forth—but rub my eyes as I may, there is really nothing to be seen. It can scarcely be our old enemy, the ghost, in such broad daylight? Above all things, do not treat me to a fainting fit, as I have no turn for nervous complaints, and could scarcely find a drop of water within three miles at least!"

Matilda could not help smiling, and made a vain attempt to speak, but her voice died away in inarticulate whispers. Sir Alfred now became seriously embarrassed and distressed. He took her hand, with a look of real sympathy, and anxiously watched Matilda's countenance.

"It is only a trifle," said she, attempting to laugh, but still unable to finish her sentence.

"Can anything be a trifle that relates to *you?*" replied he, in a tone which only increased her confusion: but at length, by a powerful effort, she so far recovered as to begin some hurried explanation in broken sentences, of all that had occurred during the morning, when, having accidentally looked round, and giving a sudden exclamation of alarm, she pointed to a neighboring hedge, over which the beggar's head had for a moment become visible, though he instantly afterwards vanished. Sir Alfred did, however, catch a momentary glimpse of him likewise, and rushing forward, he sprung over the fence, and seized the Irishman by the collar. Matilda's first impulse would have been to resume her flight, but terror chained her to the spot, an agitated spectator of the scene. She felt amazed at the agility and strength of Sir Alfred, who usually appeared so inert; and temporary suspense terminated in the most animated sensation of pleasure, when she saw her unexpected champion wrest the miscreant's stick out of his hand, and at once overpower him.

"I'll bet ten to one you don't do that again, Sir Alfred!" exclaimed a voice that seemed familiar to Matilda's ears. "You took me at a complete disadvantage, for I was more overcome with surprise than even by your extraordinary prowess. Do indulge me with another round, Douglas, and let Miss Howard be bottle-holder!"

"Grant, your idea of a jest is rather different from mine!" replied Sir Alfred, with as little appearance of surprise as if he had known him all along. A distant laugh was immediately afterwards heard approaching, and Eleanor appeared rapidly advancing with the rest of her party, and exclaiming in a tone of triumphant pleasure, "Well this is really beyond my hopes! Matilda is such an easy dupe that there is no glory in imposing upon her! but *you*, Sir Alfred, who could have expected it! Mr. Grant, I give you infinite credit for executing my plan so admirably. The giant has turned into a wind-mill. It is the best joke, without exception, that ever I saw!"

"Then you have been unfortunate, for I never knew a worse," replied Sir Alfred, looking at the pale countenance of Matilda, who was doing her utmost to get up a laugh. "Some people will sacrifice more for a bad jest than I would ever do for a good one. Miss Howard, let me hope that you have not suffered materially from this amusing little *jeu d'esprit?*"

"Not at all!" answered Matilda, in a tremulous voice, while her limbs shook so that she could scarcely stand. "I shall recover in a moment. How stupid of me not to see the whole at once! I am quite well now."

"Allow me to differ!" said Sir Alfred. "You are still very nervous, and I must insist on your taking my arm."

"With great pleasure," replied she, coloring and smiling.

"I wish it had been *my hand* that you are so willing to accept," added Sir Alfred in an undertone; and when Matilda looked up for a moment, his eyes were fixed upon her with a look of penetrating interest. "Miss Howard," added he, in an altered voice, "I trust you will believe me incapable of lightly alluding to a subject which is of sacred importance to me, and in which my whole future happiness may yet be at stake. I know not what interest it may hereafter have for you, but it involves the earthly hopes of my own existence. Time will enable me to explain the circumstances which have involved me for the present in a situation of embarrassment, in which my conduct has been such as might have been misconstrued by any one less candid and generous than yourself. I could not even dare to say so much as I have done, were it not for the fear that you may attribute that reserve to inclination, which is only the result of temporary necessity."

Matilda suddenly recollected at this moment what Miss Marabout has said respecting a promise of Sir Alfred's to his mother, on the subject of at least postponing any declaration or engagement; and without pausing to analyze the emotions to which this remembrance gave rise, she made a hurried and agitated reply. Sir Alfred then led the conversation into a new channel, involving an interesting discussion of various subjects, wherein that similarity and diversity of opinion was elicited between the parties which gives its highest zest to conversation, leading them on insensibly to the development of those sacred principles and engrossing interests in which both were so deeply versed.

"Mr. Grant!" said Eleanor, looking sarcastically after Matilda, "my cousin has got up a perfect scene on this occasion! You should really assist in supporting her home!"

"No! no! I have performed my part to please you, but it went too far. When once I get into the spirit of anything there is no stopping me. I once acted Mad Tom on the summit of Dover Cliff, and if Douglas had not seized hold of me in time, would have fairly leaped over in the enthusiasm of the moment. But positively, Miss Fitz-Patrick, I am afraid of your cousin, she is so very fascinating. Such perfect *naïveté* and good humor, with so much talent and principle, have altogether captivated me, and I would propose to her to-morrow, if you can give me a single peg to hang a hope upon."

"Indeed!" said Eleanor, changing color, and with a look of angry surprise. "It was scarcely necessary to tell me this! I thought you had known the world better, Mr. Grant, than to entertain one lady with a rhapsody on the charms of another!"

"Ah! Miss Fitz-Patrick! we understand each other now, and you acted very fairly long since, by putting me on my guard in good time against presumption. You know very well that I went through all the agonies of death for you last year, and how hard a struggle it cost me to fly away on the wings of disappointment. As Don Whiskerandos says, however, 'One can't stay dying here forever!' and I should not have ventured to your enchanted castle at all if there had been the least apprehension of troubling you with a relapse. My present case is equally hopeless, unfortunate man that I am! for every one may see how completely Sir Alfred is devoted to Miss Howard, and there probably exists not a man living who presumes to imagine he could rival him."

"You are in jest, Mr. Grant!" exclaimed Eleanor, angrily, for every word he had said spoke daggers to her vanity. "Sir Alfred cares no more for my cousin than for Miss Marabout."

"Pray convince me of that, for I shall be most willing to believe it. Indeed, Miss Fitz-Patrick, there are not two Matilda Howards in the world, or I might be happy; but as it is now, my friend Douglas deserves her, and you may depend upon it they understand each other."

Eleanor walked rapidly on, in evident agitation, and preserved an unbroken silence for some time, while Mr. Grant endeavored to seem unconscious of it, and sung, in the most beautiful cadences of his melodious voice, the air of "One struggle more!" suiting the tune to the words, for it gradually deepened into melancholy, till the sound at length died away entirely, and, for the first time in their lives, Eleanor and her *ci-devant* lover pursued their course without speaking. Mr. Grant had long wished for an opportunity of communicating to Miss Fitz-Patrick his conjecture respecting Sir Alfred's attachment, because, in his anxious solicitude for her happiness, he observed the increasing interest she took in his friend's society, and could not but apprehend that it might be dangerous to her peace; for, greatly valuing, as he did, the high character and brilliant talents of Sir Alfred, he thought it impossible to overestimate the admiration and attachment which he *ought* to excite.

Nothing could be a greater mistake, however, than the conjecture of Mr. Grant with respect to Eleanor's real feelings. Her vanity would have become deeply wounded, could she have been convinced that Sir Alfred viewed her with indifference; but to imagine for a moment that he also preferred Matilda, was so revolting to her wishes, that she could not allow it to be possible, though the suggestion renewed in her mind that rankling feeling of jealousy which had long burnt fiercely within her breast, and occasioned actual misery to herself, while it destroyed every emotion towards her cousin but dislike. Painful, nevertheless, and corroding as was the state of her mind on this subject, Mr. Grant little imagined how greatly he erred in attributing to disappointment, on account of his friend, the sudden paleness of Eleanor's cheek, and the unnatural hectic which succeeded it. No one could appreciate more highly than Miss Fitz-Patrick did the noble appearance and high reputation of Sir Alfred. That which gave its richest embellishment to both, his unswerving principle and his deep devotion of mind, she could neither know nor value,—yet she saw him the object of universal respect and admiration; she knew him to be gifted with everything that gives grace or dignity to high station; and she had long considered it as a triumph which she must one day achieve to see Sir Alfred at her feet. To gain such a victory Eleanor never paused to consider how far her own happiness or his might be involved in the enterprise; but her feelings were in reality no more than many young and enthusiastic minds must frequently experience in the presence of any one whose distinguished conduct has gained him pre-eminence in the world. The sentiment of profound interest and admiration with which she regarded him might have been transferred, almost unaltered, to the first celebrated poet, or applauded orator, or successful hero whom she accidentally met;—it was even with a modification of the same feeling that she admired and endeavored to please Dr. Murray, for vanity alone rendered her desirous to gain a supreme interest with one whom every other person was seeking to attract. But there was a deeper sentiment in the breast of Miss Fitz-Patrick, which had long been smothered, but which now made itself heard with a voice that could not be stilled. Never till this moment had she doubted the constancy and the fervency of Mr. Grant's attachment, nor that the day would come when she should be called on to choose between him and his friend. If ever she became wearied and disgusted by the officious assiduities of her self-interested lovers, who, she was conscious, were admirers more of her estate than of herself, she had long been accustomed to recur with her earliest feelings of regard to Mr. Grant's unalterable affection, for it was impossible to know him, and to doubt its entire disinterestedness. The frank and open-hearted disposition of her former lover, his graceful manners and high tone of independence and good feeling, had long since made an indelible impression on her heart; and there had been a degree of considerate kindness in his tone and manner of late, partaking more of the friend than of the lover, which she had attributed to diffidence, while it pleased and gratified her. Unaccustomed to restraint or to self-examination, Miss Fitz-Patrick went on recklessly following the bent of every wayward and fantastic caprice, but forgetful that the destiny of her whole future life might be involved in the impression which her conduct conveyed at a time when she was thus thinking only of instant gratification. While Eleanor felt surprised and shocked to discover Mr. Grant's estrangement, she could not but remember now a thousand instances in which her own careless indifference and heedless vivacity must have given him a full conviction that the alteration was mutual. Whatever Eleanor actually possessed she became indifferent to, and saw only its defects,—but uncertainty always brought forth its real worth; and above all, her lover now appeared to the utmost advantage in her eyes when he was irretrievably lost; every evidence of his altered feelings enhanced beyond measure the merit and the value of her liberated captive; and when he spoke of his former admiration in a careless tone, which showed how entirely it was considered as a "tale of other times," she no longer thought of his small property and uncertain inheritance, but she felt the inestimable value of his long-tried attachment; and she for the first time became fully aware of the place he occupied in her affections.

To conceal these thoughts from every one, and especially from Mr. Grant, became now Eleanor's first object; and no one who observed her brilliant spirits during that evening and the following day, could have suspected the aching void which she felt within her heart, the loathing with which she viewed all that had hitherto dazzled or delighted her, and the melancholy depression which she vainly endeavored to conquer. Life seemed to Eleanor for the time like a dreary farce, in which she must act her part with spirit, on account of the spectators, to whom her own private feelings were indifferent and unknown. Mr. Grant alone perceived the change, which he attributed entirely to the discovery of Sir Alfred's previous attachment, though Eleanor still entirely disbelieved that, and saw nothing in his conduct towards Matilda to disprove her own opinion. She had no conception of strong feeling which was not displayed; and in the silent interest with which Sir Alfred attended to all Matilda said, and in the unobtrusive attentions which accidentally fell under her notice, she acknowledged no apprehensions to herself of a deeper sentiment than the most ordinary civility.

Mr. Grant redoubled his assiduities to Eleanor, with a friendly desire to divert her thoughts from Sir Alfred, whom he fancied that she observed with a degree of anxious interest, the motive for which he entirely misconceived. There was more of gravity and feeling than usual towards her, on account of his consciousness that she was suffering,—he blamed himself for not having sooner put Eleanor on her guard; and never did his powers of entertainment and fascination come out with greater effect than on the first evening when Miss Fitz-Patrick became conscious that she had lost him forever.

CHAPTER XXI.

At church, with meek and unaffected grace,
His looks adorned the venerable place:
Truth from his lips prevail'd with double sway,
And fools, who came to scoff, remain'd to pray.
GOLDSMITH.

"No muffins—and cold rolls for breakfast!—that is a sure indication of its being Sunday," cried Eleanor, next morning, with a forced attempt at vivacity. "I am always more hungry to-day than any other day in the week, one has so little to do. If anybody proposes going to church this bleak snowy morning, I must order the carriage at twelve, and our pew may be recommended as the best of all places for cultivating coughs, colds, rheumatisms, influenzas, and all the ills flesh is heir to. Lady Susan! No, by the way, this is your letter-writing day. I always know when to expect a line, if you are in my debt. Lady Montague! with that cold, it is out of the question. Young ladies! Charlotte Clifford! your weekly headache has come on. Well then, the *noes* have it, and we may read prayers in the library, with Miss Marabout for chaplain."

Miss Fitz-Patrick cautiously shunned looking towards her cousin, who felt conscious of the intended omission. Her color rose, but she carefully avoided appearing to notice the oversight, and continued calmly conversing with Mr. Grant, who had previously addressed her.

"Stop, Miss Fitz-Patrick, *we* have not been polled yet," said he, turning hastily round; "here is one vote, I am certain, on the opposite side."

"Oh, no," whispered Matilda, anxiously, for she already anticipated the pleasure of stealing off and proceeding alone to Gaelfield. "I have a conveyance of my own which takes me always to church and back again. It is the safest and most wholesome diligence in the world, which Eleanor knows I constantly use from preference, in all weathers and on all occasions."

"You don't mean to walk!—it would be impossible to get through the snow without stilts to-day."

"And yet many who are much more delicate than I am will make the effort. You have no idea, Mr. Grant, what frail old creatures will come tottering to church this morning—what numbers will rise from beds of sickness to go there, and what hundreds have learned from Dr. Murray to forget present inconvenience, while seeking to avoid future misery. If I had not a paramount interest of my own in frequenting church, I would even go to-day for the pleasure of sympathizing with others in the joy it gives many to attend. Poor old Janet said yesterday that it was the only remaining happiness which she could feel it possible to enjoy in this world; and for my own part, I hope and be lieve it will survive all others."

"This is the first time, Miss Howard, that I ever thought you had a tolerable opinion of me," replied Mr. Grant, in a voice between jest and earnest. "You only speak seriously to those who are in some degree to be trusted, and in whom you take an interest. I must have always appeared a mere Tom Fool in your eyes, for I deserved nothing better, and yet when we are together I have occasionally felt ——; but it is no matter now," added he, in a tone of agitation, and, turning suddenly round, he looked at Sir Alfred for a moment in silence. "No, I would make no change if it had even been possible. I do not wish it. With all my faults, let me never be selfish."

"Grant, my good fellow, what were you soliloquizing there for with such a tragical look?" said Sir Alfred, taking his arm as they left the breakfast-room. "I hope it was the rehearsal of such an oration for the hustings as shall resound throughout the universe next Tuesday?"

"I was thinking, Douglas, of a different election, in which your success is still more to be envied; but on both you shall have my warmest and most hearty congratulations."

"Do not feel too sure of my requiring them on either occasion," said Sir Alfred with emotion. "You are aware, Grant, that I have no concealments from a friend like yourself, and that I am still bound to remain in uncertainty with respect to Miss Howard's sentiments."

"Can you seriously mean to express any doubt of success?" asked Mr. Grant, in a tone of incredulity. "It is not like you, Douglas, to affect such a thing."

"If my acceptance were an affair that rested merely on the ordinary calculations of prudence and eligibility, I might be as confident as you expect; but where principle and inclination are alone likely to be consulted, you might feel, Grant, if you were as deeply attached as I am, what suspense and diffidence mean."

"Say what you will, I only wish my prospects were as happy and as securely founded as yours, Douglas; but it is enough to have a friend whose prosperity is as dear to me as my own. Many an hour of good counsel you have wasted on me, but the day has come when I begin to perceive its full value, and to think that my time, talents, and opportunities, such as they are, might be put out to better interest than they have ever brought me yet."

Sir Alfred clasped his friend's hand in his own with emotion, while he looked earnestly and seriously in his countenance. "Grant, there was but one thing wanting to the perfect unity of our friendship. I always believed that this hour would arrive. Let us talk together alone, for I have much to say. Perhaps you will walk with me to church?"

"If it rain icebergs I will."

Matilda paused before entering the church, to admire, as she had often done before, a degree of neatness unusual in country churchyards, which often gave her pleasure as she passed. Miss Murray had once described the disorder in which she originally found it, with long rank grass, and nettles waving in neglected luxuriance over the departed fathers of the congregation; a few wretched, unwholesome sheep pasturing amidst the graves, while the broken and dilapidated wall admitted children and dogs from the village to play their noisy gambols amidst broken and ruinous tomb-stones, which it was a favorite amusement with the boys to deface. Dr. Murray often saw occasion to lament such irreverence for the dead in other places, but it was one of his earliest acts at Gaelfield to assert that respect which is due from human beings towards each other, even in their last stage of humiliation and decay. He considered that the universal feeling, even among savage nations, of veneration for their deceased friends and parents, was one of the few natural impulses which is really respectable, and ought to be encouraged. He could admire no enlightened wisdom that raised men above those little sympathies and tendernesses of nature, and without long delay he abolished the use of churchyard mutton in his parish—repaired the wall, mowed down the grass, re-erected many prostrate tomb stones, and restored to the whole scene that air of silent and solemn dignity suited to the awful habitation of the dead.

Matilda was seated in church for some time before the service began, and watched with agreeable interest the gathering of a very numerous congregation, whose countenances wore an expression of salutary seriousness which harmonized with the reflections of her own mind, and made her conscious that the pleasure of sympathy is indeed a welcome auxiliary to that of devotion, while our prayers are mingled with those of others in the public worship of God. Her heart expanded with joy and peace when she considered herself placed there to enjoy the rich moral and intellectual feast, to which all who are willing may consider themselves invited guests; and Matilda could not but think what infinite wisdom there is in the appointment of a stated period, when the busiest, the most ignorant, the most careless, and the most diffident may, in a moment, without effort, without difficulty, without being ashamed, or even conspicuous, enjoy the advice and the entire concentrated knowledge and experience of such a man as Dr. Murray, whose whole existence was devoted to seeking out those truths which could be told them in an hour; and Matilda reflected with what despair men might have often dropt down on the threshold of religion, if their own unassisted efforts had been the only human means by which the powerful convictions of conscience must be followed up. Day by day Dr. Murray repeated over the simplest truths to his people. Like a mother teaching her child his simple hymn, which she rehearses again and again without making perceptible progress, till at length he is found to be thoroughly, though gradually, versed in his lesson, so the venerable pastor constantly reverted to first principles. He varied his explanations also by a profusion of apt illustrations, by the mention of appropriate incidents, by allusions to circumstances of general interest in the congregation, and by quoting largely from other theologians; at the same time, Dr. Murray never mentioned from the pulpit any names, however eminent, which are not recorded in Holy Scripture, for he considered that no authority should be so honored, from the seat of ministerial instruction, except such as are divinely appointed.

When the service was about to commence, Matilda heard a step advancing along the gallery, which proved to be that of Sir Alfred, who placed himself in an opposite corner of the pew, and without giving even a transient glance around, he opened the large Bible which lay before him. Mr. Grant followed, and, with characteristic rapidity, threw himself into a seat, instinctively passed his fingers through his hair, looked at his watch, and then folding his arms, he fell into a profound and evidently very serious meditation.

Dr. Murray's deep, melodious voice broke the solemn silence which prevailed, and as he proceeded in the service, intense attention might be traced in every countenance. So absorbing was the interest with which Matilda listened, that she at once forgot there was another individual in the sacred edifice but herself and the preacher, while every word seemed to be directed immediately to her own conscience. The energy of Dr. Murray's address, which seemed always skilfully aimed at the heart, consisted not in vehemence of gesticulation, or in rhetorical display, but there was an impressive dignity in his manner, and a power in the modulations of his richly-toned voice, which enchained the most wandering mind, while his profound vein of thought, his forcible arguments, and his awful views of life, in all its hopes, its fears, and its responsibilities, evinced that a full conviction rested in his own mind of the tremendous importance attached to those subjects on which he treated, and that, whether he described the terrors or the hopes of the Gospel, his language was that of a heart filled with reverence towards God, and with love towards man. Dr. Murray made a rule to avoid prolixity in his sermons. Everything he did was upon reflection and principle, rather than from impulse; and as his object was "by any means to win some," he considered that infirmities of age, restlessness in childhood, and languor from indisposition, limited the power of attention in many; while, even to the most devout of his people, ample leisure was desirable at home to digest what they had heard by meditation and prayer. Many unskilful attendants on the sick have imagined that if, by administering a small dose of medicine, they diminished the evil, an unlimited application would produce instant recovery; but, as Baxter says, "It is safer to feed your flock like chickens than to cram them like turkeys." Dr. Murray, therefore, was never heard to boast of having found it impossible to stop, because, on all occasions, he avoided vain repetitions, and never grudged the additional trouble which Paley complained that it cost *him* to "make his sermons *short*."

When the numerous congregation at Gaelfield silently dispersed, without having dissipated their serious impressions by any whispered gossiping, or irreverent criticisms of the sermon, Matilda rose also to depart, and found Sir Alfred, with his companion, waiting for her near the church door.

"You evaded us in coming here, Miss Howard," said Mr. Grant, reproachfully. "I could scarcely have overtaken such rapid movements at a gallop; but there is no chance of escape now unless by taking actual flight in the fashion of yesterday."

"No inducement shall make me do that again, Mr. Grant, because it is only an old friend with a new face that I would avoid," replied Matilda, giving him one of her sweetest smiles. "We have all enjoyed the pleasure of hearing such important truths to-day that it would be impossible to think on other subjects, and there could be no greater gratification to me than in discussing them as we go homewards."

"It would be difficult, indeed, I may add almost sinful, to estrange our thoughts from what has been said. The impression should last forever," replied Mr. Grant, beginning a conversation which continued, with increasing interest, until the party at length reached that long green lane where Matilda met with her adventure on the preceding day. Sir Alfred then paused in the middle of a sentence, and looked at Mr. Grant. "Miss Howard," added he, "we visited a friend of yours this morning, who is very desirous to see you soon. I made a rash promise, perhaps overestimating my own influence, in venturing to engage that you would accompany Mr. Grant and myself to see her now."

"A friend of mine?—It must have been a mistake for Eleanor!"

"I rather believe not," replied Sir Alfred, smiling to Mr. Grant. "We know of several, but the one in question was praising you with great eloquence to-day."

"Ah! then you need not add another word! It must have been good, excellent Miss Murray, who has a kind opinion of every one."

"Still wrong! I should never have remembered the panegyric of such an indiscriminate admirer. 'They who dare not censure scarce can praise.' Our friend to-day was one who experiences little cause to think well of the world in general, but she said much of you, and more than you would wish any one to believe."

"Sir Alfred, you are infected with Eleanor's genius foi passing a jest upon me, but I am become very cunning and suspicious, particularly as friends and admirers of mine are not very abundant anywhere."

"Not even in the village?" asked Sir Alfred, archly. "Are you going to deny being on visiting terms at the house of that unfortunate old woman whose daughter disappeared so strangely?"

"I guessed right, then, yesterday! It was *you* who acted so generously towards poor Janet!" exclaimed Matilda, with a brilliant look of surprise and pleasure.

"Your own experience testifies, Miss Howard, that there is no happiness on earth equal to that of promoting it in others, and therefore we cannot allow you to monopolize a privilege which all ought to share. Let us, then, accompany you now, and though this is the first time we have gone to such scenes together, I trust it will not be the last."

CHAPTER XXII.

Nor those blest hours on idle trifles waste,
Which all who lavish shall lament at last.
HYMN.

"WHAT untidy weather this is!" exclaimed Eleanor, next morning, after breakfast, while she flitted from window to window in the library, as if she hoped at some one of them to discover more sunshine than the rest displayed; but each presented an unbroken winding-sheet of snow, which looked as if it might defy a summer's heat, while an incessant fall of large downy flakes were to be seen, lounging lazily down, as if they meant to settle for weeks. Some of the largest were eagerly pointed out by Lord Alderby and Colonel Pendarvis, who traced their slow, dignified descent, and betted largely on the relative rapidity of their fall, while Major Foley acted as umpire.

"Are you trying to discover, my Lord, whether that red spot on the sky means to pass for the sun or the moon?" asked Eleanor, looking wearily out; "or perhaps watching to take a lesson how winter powders his wig, in case of *ever growing old*, and feeling obliged to wear one?"

"I was thinking rather of becoming young again, than of getting old, Miss Fitz-Patrick, for we are trying a new pastime. One of my favorite amusements in travelling, is something on the same plan. We have generally a bet who shall see the greatest number of living animals upon his own side of the carriage. A donkey counts *four*, a turkey-cock *two*, a peacock *five*, and a cat looking in at a window is always game! Pendarvis and I once amused ourselves the whole way to London with no other resource, when we were going up to attend our duties in Parliament!"

A transient expression of contempt passed over Eleanor's beautiful countenance, and with a look of unconquerable dejection she dropt into a seat. The gentlemen instantly gathered round her in evident certainty of being entertained by her lively sallies and amusing caprices, but the young heiress felt for once incapable of exertion. To conceal the spiritless tone of her mind, she immediately opened a large box, containing innumerable alphabets printed on little squares of ivory, and spread them out on the table, desiring each individual to select the letters which formed any word, and having skaken them miscellaneously together, to exchange them with some one else of the party, who must exhibit his talent by the quickness with which he discovered what was meant. Matilda watched Eleanor transposing and puzzling over the letters EDISARP, which had been presented to her with such a sentimental sigh by Major Foley, that it would not have been difficult to guess from his countenance he intended to express Despair. Sir Colin and Lord Alderby were in agonies of uncertainty over a handful of letters, which Miss Fitz-Patrick had laughingly reached them, while Sir Alfred continued perseveringly, though with a look of sly humor, to decline many importunate invitations to join in the amusement.

"Amusement! that word must have a different meaning in the dictionary from what I had ever imagined."

"Do try, Sir Alfred! You are afraid of being thought stupid, but we shall be very indulgent at first. It would entertain you beyond measure; and I do enjoy a little diverting nonsense occasionally."

"I rather prefer diverting sense," replied he, looking at Matilda for an instant, and then resuming his book.

"Here is a very easy word, and exactly characteristic of yourself! Now let us see a laudable curiosity to ascertain what that is!"

"Excuse me; I have really no genius for spelling; it is an accomplishment that never could be taught me. If you will believe it, Miss Fitz-Patrick, I always spell philosopher beginning with F, and capricious with a K."

"That is the more surprising, since the last word is so appropriate to yourself; but it would be unpardonable to lose this opportunity of improvement. I shall undertake to teach you unimpeachable spelling in six lessons."

"Indeed you have no conception how desperate the case is. I was always of opinion with Sir William Curtis, who hated the three R's in education, Reading, *Riting*, and *R*ithmetic."

"There are no symptoms of your antipathy to reading," answered Eleanor, looking with an air of pique at Sir Alfred's book. "I shall write a volume to-morrow, if you will promise to sit dozing and *mooning* over it all day, as you do often with that little volume, which seems to live in your pocket. I have the worst opinion of books bound in white parchment; they are all as old and dry as a Herculaneum manuscript. I only wish they were equally inaccessible."

"Then, pray, Miss Fitz-Patrick, if you were condescending enough to undertake the regulation of my studies, what would be prescribed?"

"A very light diet at first, to clear your brain from the clouds of Greek and Latin, with which it is at present darkened. But *à propos*—that reminds me, Sir Alfred, what a very untoward pupil you were formerly. I recollect once, at Douglas Priory, making you positively promise to read Lady Ashton's new novel, 'The Marchioness,' and being actually so obliging as to find it for you in the library. Afterwards, whenever we called on Lady Amelia, I used to discover the first volume, with your mark still in it; and though I several times slipped it a few pages backwards to tease and puzzle you, I question whether the trick was ever even suspected."

"That accounts for its having appeared so insufferably tedious. The very recollection of that book puts me to sleep. It was the only novel in fashionable life that I ever travelled through; and luckily for myself, I never knew originals for any one of the characters. It was full of false sentiment, bad morality, and ideas only fit for milliners' apprentices."

"You forget, Sir Alfred, that I recommended the work as an especial favorite; but there is no improving your taste."

"Very true; it is an absolute waste of time to attempt it. You may say, Miss Fitz-Patrick, as my old tutor used to do, that I must be allowed to 'hang as I grow;' but perhaps Miss Howard will exercise her spelling instead of me. It has been rumored that her education, like mine, was deficient on that score. As Dogberry says, 'reading and writing come by nature.'"

Matilda had been almost unconsciously standing beside Eleanor, with an air of graceful negligence, while she listened to the preceding dialogue; but as her cousin had constantly shunned for the last three days having any intercourse with her which could be decently avoided, she therefore colored and looked confused at being thus unexpectedly brought into prominent notice.

"Are you there, Matilda?" said Eleanor in a tone of marked indifference; and, without adding another syllable, she instantly busied herself with the alphabets, and pushed towards Lord de Mainbury a confused miscellany of letters which ought to constitute the word DISINTERESTED. His Lordship instantly assumed an attitude of deep attention; but though he sat for nearly an hour, bestowing upon the subject his undivided observation, and such intense study as might have solved a problem in mathematics, or revealed what is the square of a circle, he never was able to ascertain the oracular word with which Miss Fitz-Patrick had favored him.

"I wish some fairy, as bright as yourself, would give these a touch of her wand!" said he, looking completely bewildered. "But all their enchantments have been stolen away by one fair lady who shall be nameless."

Matilda thought she had never witnessed such an outlay of time bringing in so small a return of entertainment in proportion. She looked round to ascertain what resources might be adopted by others of the party. Lady Susan was rushing through the last new novel. The Miss Montagues were exhibiting their graceful figures in a game at battledore and shuttlecock in the entrance hall, where frequent exclamations of interest were made, evidently to attract notice. Miss Marabout was lounging in an attitude on the ottoman, near which she had drawn a large table, surrounded by a wreath of the newest annuals, while she tried, with all her might, to laugh at the one commonly called "Comic!" Her seat commanded an excellent view of two splendid mirrors, into which she stole hasty glances whenever a smile had been called up, because it gave her an opportunity of studying expression, and of seeing her teeth, which were still tolerable. Miss Charlotte Clifford, with an air of great importance, placed herself at the pianoforte, and opened her small miniature music-book, decorated with a gold lock, in which were four "treasures" of songs. The words seemed much as usual, and the air nothing particular, but still they were *new*—not another young lady in the world had a copy—and they *could not be had!* So terrified was she for their becoming common, that none of her friends might even be allowed to turn the leaves over when she sung, from an apprehension that the words might be stolen, and Mr. Grant now made her adopt a redoubled degree of watchfulness. He had contrived, with great quickness, when she was performing the day before, to pick up a verse, from one which she particularly prized, and while Miss Clifford was arranging a music-stool, he stood at the fire with his newspaper, carelessly humming the words, and singing it in such an audible key as to attract her immediate notice.

"Where *did* you get 'Tears and Smiles,' Mr. Grant?" exclaimed Miss Charlotte, in a voice of alarm.

"I really forget; it's an old thing. Was it my groom who sung it? or the dairymaid?—I can easily obtain a copy for you, however, or write something else quite as good. You know, Miss Clifford, it is a proverb, when anything is totally worthless, that it might be sold for an old song."

Sir Richard strolled about the room, fretting and grumbling at the weather, while he prophesied that this heavy snow-storm would stop the post for three weeks at least. After having exhausted every advertisement and paragraph in the *Times* and *Morning Post*, he turned to his daughter, saying, "Eleanor, I once observed, in some of the uninhabited bedrooms, newspapers dangling in front of the grates, to keep off dust, but I beg you will have them all carefully collected for me now. In this remote corner it is necessary to husband our resources of information and amusement."

"To the curious in newspapers! Well, papa, your idea is ingenious, and there are several well-lined trunks up stairs, which shall be added to your store."

"Life is a poor affair at best, but quite unbearable in the country without a billiard-table! We must order one immediately, Eleanor. All the green meadows in Inverness-shire are not equal to a smooth field of green baize, fenced in with mahogany."

"Ask Alderby to stoop in a horizontal position—his green coat is an acre in breadth, and with the pockets would do admirably," whispered Mr. Grant to Eleanor. "We can easily provide cues, and make Sir Richard happy at once, for his Lordship would do anything to oblige *you*."

"My windows rattled all last night like an old post chaise!" pursued the Baronet, fretfully, "and to-day, I would literally have to be dug out of the snow, if we ventured near the stable. The ministry may be changed and restored again before our post arrives, and Parliament dissolve sooner than the snow. Gentlemen, would any of you like to have the shutters closed, and a bowl of punch! I wish, Fletcher, that Harlequin's wand could transform your inkstand into one—the sealing-wax might be metamorphosed into cigars also, and day into night."

Matilda, seeing Sir Colin clear his throat for a long story, determined on stealing off to the solitary enjoyment of her own numerous occupations, and was amused as she left the room, to hear Lady Montague ask her daughters, in a tone of importance, whether they had any message for a numerous constellation of peeresses, whom she announced her intention of writing to that day, while they returned the usual unsatisfactory answer on such appeals being made, "nothing but our kind remembrances." It often astonished Miss Howard to observe a rational being, whose whole thoughts and actions were concentrated on one object so entirely as those of Lady Montague. In her intercourse with her own family, or with strangers, even with shopkeepers and servants, the desire never was absent, for a single instant, to "keep up *her own* consequence!" To this every domestic pleasure, every exercise of her affections, and every amusement was made subservient "If I could but acquire the same singleness of purpose in seeking for higher attainment in holiness!" thought Matilda, with a feeling of self-reproach, as she drew in a chair at her own fireside, and thought over the whole scene she had quitted with sentiments of surprise at that listless ennui which most of the party had exhibited. "How truly Dr. Murray observed, that nothing desirable can be obtained without vigorous exertion, for I perceive than even those who seek merely for amusement must fail, if they pursue it indolently. The effort is the actual pleasure on all occasions. If a sportsman could be supplied with as many brace of birds on the 12th of August as he chose to name, where would be his enjoyment? If an author saw his books ready made to his wish, what satisfaction would they give him? I can imagine myself placed suddenly in possession of every earthly blessing that could be named, and if they be granted without limit and without difficulty, they could confer no happiness. Let the keenest collector of pictures be told that he shall receive them in cart-loads whenever he desires it—let the greatest miser be told that any number of thousands he chooses to name shall be found ready at his bank,—or even those who follow the nobler pursuit of fame, let it be supposed that every eye is fastened on them when they pass, and every ear listens entranced when they speak, still the certainty and the abundance of all these gifts would render them disgusting. We must have suspense, uncertainty, and difficulty, as a zest to success; and, like Alexander the Great, who gave away every worldly possession for the pleasure of exertion and the promises of hope, I think the Christian must feel that not only is hope the best part of every temporal object, but the worthlessness of all present possessions without it is a strong emblem how little we should gain if the whole world were our own, without *that hope* which reaches beyond it, and can never be fully realized here. There is an aching void in every heart until the love of God be implanted within, and then every affection and desire has an ample field for exercise."

Matilda resolutely detached her thoughts from any subject of immediate interest which would have naturally engrossed them; she felt how true it is, that "*en songeant qu'on doit oublier, on s'en souvient;*" and being accustomed to exercise a despotic government over her own mind, she opened some of her favorite books, the gifts of Lady Olivia, and became so completely absorbed in the study, that it caused a start of surprise when the gong sounded some hours afterwards for luncheon. When Matilda hastened into the drawing-room, Miss Clifford had reached her final cadence, Miss Marabout performed her parting smile over the Comic Annual, the Miss Montagues replaced the little ornamental purses which they were working into small mother-of-pearl work-boxes, and the whole party seemed reviving with the prospect of at last finding something to do. Sir Alfred stood at the window, discussing with Sir Richard and Mr. Grant some arrangements for his election on the following day, when Eleanor, who thought herself privileged to interrupt any conference, joined the trio, and exclaimed, looking out at the snow, which was now falling in almost a solid mass, and undulating in graceful wreaths along the park—"What a *delightful* day this is, Sir Alfred!"

"Charming indeed!—suppose we try a walk!"

"Agreed.—I have the greatest mind to take you at your word."

"I shall certainly venture as far as the stables soon; so if you choose to come I can't help it."

"How very pressing! It is impossible to resist such importunity, therefore my Esquimaux boots and ermine pelisse shall be in requisition after luncheon."

"Before, if you please. My horse always expects me

precisely at three, and I would not disappoint Vesuvius on any consideration."

"But luncheon has been already announced, and this is the only time of day when I ever feel hungry," replied Eleanor, who, according to the etiquette of young ladies, professed always a ravenous appetite in the forenoon, and an utter incapacity of eating at all other meals. "I should die of exhaustion in an hour without taking something to support nature."

"Then our engagement is broken off," replied Sir Alfred, escaping towards the door; "I am not a good *waiter.*"

"But, stop a moment. You ought to remain, for papa has ordered his favorite dish this morning—a pie of singed sheep's head!"

"Can you suppose, Miss Fitz-Patrick, that I would remain in the house with such a thing!" replied he, affecting a look of disgust, and accomplishing his retreat. Sir Alfred was soon after seen proceeding from the stables, where he scarcely stopped a moment, and walking rapidly over a neighboring eminence, clothed in a large Mackintosh cloak, boots in which he might have waded dry-shod through the Spey, and his hat already covered with a canopy of snow.

"Now, where can he be going?" cried Eleanor. "Sir Alfred must have mistaken his way, for that road leads only to Gowanbank, and one or two wretched little cottages. I shall certainly have my jest upon his visiting acquaintances at Middenditch, and his leaving a card for Mrs. Muckleraith."

"Well, Miss Howard," said Mr. Armstrong, approaching Matilda with an appearance of easy and rather patronizing familiarity, "it would be bad policy to lose your ship for a pennyworth of tar. Have you thought better of what I dropped lately?"

"Not more than could be helped," replied she, dryly. "I neither wish to consider nor to discuss a subject that is without remedy."

"But there is a remedy in my power, *if you make it worth while* to produce certain documents which might be forthcoming."

"Mr. Armstrong! if it is not worth while to act honorably for conscience' sake, you shall have no inferior inducement from me. A man who could suppress papers which ought to have been produced, might also be capable of counterfeiting them."

"You'll repent of this, Miss Howard. I only wish that it were possible to be revenged on Miss Fitz-Patrick without serving you," said he angrily, leaving the room, where he had been entirely unnoticed all the morning either by Eleanor or any of her visitors.

The day of Sir Alfred's election was at length ushered in by such a continued snow-storm, that the gentlemen had some difficulty in reaching the scene of action, and Eleanor was unwillingly obliged to relinquish her hopes of seeing the member chaired. As a dinner was to be given at the neighboring town, from whence Sir Richard and his party were not expected home till late in the evening, the ladies dined early, and dispersed to their rooms, having agreed, by way of variety, to have good appetites, and to take *a severe tea* at ten o'clock, when their friends from the hustings promised to attend also.

On Matilda's coming down at the appointed hour, she was surprised to find a brilliantly illuminated room, decorated with a profusion of blue ribbons and flowers, while all the ladies were ornamented with the same color. Some of them wore scarfs, and others had large conspicuous bows mingled with their hair, while each carried an artificial bouquet of blue convolvulus and forget-me-not. Eleanor was radiant with animation, pouring out the tea, and singing with great vivacity,

"He promised to buy me a bunch of blue ribbons,
To tie up my bonnie brown hair."

"Ah, Matilda!" said she, carelessly, "did not I tell you our intention of doing honor to Sir Alfred by wearing his colors! But the omission scarcely signifies, because you are sure at any rate to be in *blue stockings*."

"No, Eleanor," replied Matilda, "I only wear that color in my eyes, which you do not."

"I see what you mean," cried the heiress, laughing. "Mr. Grant was talking a great deal of his nonsense to Sir Alfred this morning about his choosing blue in compliment to some fair lady, and, of course, you have since been comparing '*les yeux bleus et noirs*,' to the no small disadvantage of the latter."

Nothing could be more rapturous than the congratulations with which Sir Alfred and his friends were soon after received, when they entered the room, announcing complete success. The carriage and four had driven up to the gate covered with favors and surrounded by outriders, most of whom were constituents from the neighborhood, who accompanied him to testify their respect, and who now dispersed. Mr. Grant instantly proceeded to give a picturesque and amusing description of the whole scene, commemorating all the jests cracked, and the glasses broken, with infinite humor, while he took off most effectively the oratory of several spokesmen who had that day professed themselves, with every appearance of veracity, "unaccustomed to public speaking." Matilda forgot her own indignation at Eleanor's malicious remarks and omissions, in the amusement with which she now listened to Mr. Grant's lively sallies, who gave a diverting account of a deputation which he had headed to the opposite party, on which embassy Colonel Pendarvis mentioned that he had been forcibly detained to enliven a very dull circle. On his return to do duty for Sir Alfred, Sir Richard laughingly related that an unaccountable ommission having been made in the list of toasts, where "The Croupier" was entirely omitted, Mr. Grant got up, and after a long and appropriate panegyric, proposed *his own health*, which had been immediately drunk with enthusiasm.

It was universally whispered that Sir Alfred made an appearance brilliant beyond example, but no one felt at liberty to venture the remark within his own hearing, because every individual present knew his unaffected desire to shun observation, and that, pre-eminent as his talents were when occasion offered for their exercise, yet he chose to wear them almost constantly *under a domino* in general society. Sir Alfred, however, entered into the humor of this evening with more liveliness than he had ever before displayed; and his dry, sarcastic remarks, and ready wit, formed an enlivening accompaniment to the diverting nonsense of Mr. Grant, and the playful vivacity of Eleanor, who seemed inspired with an extraordinary degree of amusing repartee for the occasion.

Though the eyes of Sir Alfred were lighted up with animation, yet Matilda could not but be conscious that they softened into a look of interest whenever he addressed herself, and though his voice had now assumed a new tone of vivacity, it became subdued into an expression of sensibility when he spoke to her. The sensitive feelings of Matilda told her of an obvious change, and that, for the first time, Sir Alfred adopted the same manner before others which he had so long done when they were alone. He no longer seemed desirous to conceal the preference which had formerly been but hinted. His first eager look when he entered the drawing-room searched for Matilda, it was to her that he at once advanced with frankness and animation to claim her congratulations, and to her he now invariably turned with a desire to ascertain how she felt interested by all that passed, while he looked with evident admiration at the sparkling smile and dazzling color which a secret consciousness of his own attention called into her countenance.

Eleanor at length proposed music, and played, by way of commencement, the "Blue Bells of Scotland," while Matilda proceeded, as had been her usual custom lately, to the library with Sir Richard, where, with the door open to catch a distant sound of the piano, he liked her to read the *Times* and *Standard*, as she had long ago insisted on supplying the place of his spectacles occasionally, and he now preferred hearing her always to the use of his own not very available eyes. On this occasion, however, his niece had scarcely been seated, and begun a few preliminary remarks of her own, when Sir Richard looked restlessly round, and then started up, saying, with a good-humored laugh and an air of exquisite enjoyment,

"Many thanks, my dear girl, for your obliging intentions, but we must be better employed to-night. I have promised to relinquish my seat this evening, and not to hear one word, because a friend of mine is impatient to obtain an audience himself."

Matilda scarcely looked round before Sir Richard had vanished, and Sir Alfred Douglas stood in his place. There was agitation and embarrassment in his manner, but yet the expression paramount in his countenance seemed to be pleasure, which might be traced in his heightened color and animated smile, when he seated himself beside Matilda, whose cheek became pale and red alternately with surprise and agitation.

"You have not honored me by wearing the true blue, Miss Howard!—It is most appropriate to my own feelings at this moment, being the color of hope, and also of the uncertain sky," said Sir Alfred, looking earnestly at Matilda. "Must I consider you as an enemy?"

"Oh impossible!—that is to say, at least,—I—I was not aware—no one told me it was customary,—or—or expected ——"

"Miss Howard, I never read any novel yet which could

have held together for a single volume, if the parties had only stated their grievances with ordinary candor, or if some trumpery secret had not been kept, which ought to have been told; allow me, therefore, to mention, that Miss Fitz-Patrick herself suggested the idea of sporting the *blue* cockade or I should never have presumed to ask it, and she even permitted me the honor of ordering from one of my principal constituents in the borough, his whole *assortment* of scarfs and ribbons, which she assured me should be worn by all who were friendly to my cause. The natural inference, therefore, on this occasion might have been very unfavorable to my hopes; but yet, Miss Howard, I did *not* allow myself to be discouraged. Was I wrong? Would you have refused to wear my colors had you known that the greatest pleasure I looked for on returning has been to see *you* in them?"

Matilda hastily drew off her glove, and, with a modest smile, pointed to the torquoise-ring which she usually wore.

"That emblem, is, indeed, sufficient," said Sir Alfred, suddenly seizing the beautiful hand which she had uncovered, and carrying it to his lips. "One small token of goodwill from Matilda Howard would be more dear to me than that of all the world besides. Do not withdraw this precious hand till you have promised to bestow it upon me forever."

Matilda started in astonishment, and gently drew back, with involuntary confusion, at a declaration so instantaneous, but no reply was necessary, for Sir Alfred continued to speak with agitation and rapidity. "No heart can conceive, Miss Howard, with what impatience this moment has been longed for, when I might at last divulge my whole feelings, and ask if they are returned. Sir Francis knew my secret long since, but I had been surprised into a promise that for one year these hopes should be hid from yourself. My fortune was ample, but the wealth of Crœsus can scarcely satisfy a parent's ambition. Mine saw only one external difference between you and your cousin—she imagined it *possible* I might *change!* She did not know that there is nothing transient or capricious in my attachment, which principle and inclination have rooted with a depth and firmness never to be altered. Aware that this election must bring me into your cousin's society here, my mother made it her last request that the contest should be finished before my heart became known to you. Could I refuse?

She meant it in kindness, yet who could conceive the difficulty it entailed on me! I did not even foresee it myself! The apprehension never entered my thoughts, that we might be in the same house,—that I should see you continually, an object of admiration to others,—that I should be obliged to veil my own heart, and pursue an equivocal line of conduct, and that, with the perpetual fear of being misinterpreted, I should still be obliged to keep silence. But *such silence as mine* could scarcely be mistaken for insensibility," added Sir Alfred, with a conscious smile. "I can scarcely claim the merit of having preserved it,—you must have understood me. You must have seen that from the very first day we met, my honor was pledged,—that time had not effaced the impression you once made on my heart, and that absence could not diminish it. Let me hope, since I was not then repulsed, you will listen to me favorably now. I do not ask you to speak. I see you cannot; but my desire is to be allowed an opportunity,—an *early* opportunity to plead my own cause,—to explain myself more fully,—to tell you that my utmost endeavor in life would be to merit your affection."

Sir Alfred paused a single moment, and then added, in a voice of persuasive eloquence—"Yet, Matilda, if you could but grant one word or look, to assure me that I have not loved in vain,—that every cherished hope of my heart shall be realized,—that you consent to double all the joys of my future life, and to share in all its sorrows, let the suspense of months be terminated now,—let hope be changed into certainty, and promise that you will at least endeavor to love me,—that you will one day consent to become mine forever."

Matilda looked up for a moment, and words could not express more tenderness and ingenuous modesty than did her young and lovely countenance. With all her natural frankness she placed her hand in Sir Alfred's, and covered her eyes, overpowered with agitation, while she hung her averted head, and tears coursed each other down her cheeks, Sir Alfred clasped Matilda's hand in his own, and there was deep and solemn emotion mingled with the tenderness of his manner, for language would have been feeble compared with the eloquence of silence. He kept the hand which had now become his own, while a pause of some moments ensued; and he had the delicacy and consideration not even to look at Matilda, while both knew that their feelings were mutually understood. A union of confidence and affection was now established between them, more than that of friendship or love, which time could never dissolve, and which death itself might suspend, but not finally terminate.

"What are you two about here?" exclaimed Eleanor, hastening unexpectedly into the library, while Matilda, at the same moment, darted off in an opposite direction. "Sir Alfred, I am come to secure your first frank as a trophy, which my correspondent shall return immediately, that it may be framed and hung up in the library, or form the commencement to a splendid collection of autographs."

"You shall have all the other nine, Miss Fitz-Patrick, but my first frank is previously engaged to go on an embassy of great importance," replied Sir Alfred, rising, while he endeavored to conceal, by a rallying tone, his own extreme emotion. "Having claimed the kind congratulations of our friends this evening already, I cannot deny myself the pleasure of saying, Miss Fitz-Patrick, that, before long, it is my fervent hope and expectation to receive as many good wishes on an occasion of still greater importance, in which the happiness of my life has long been involved."

Eleanor gazed at Sir Alfred with surprise, and observing how much he seemed agitated, she colored and looked down with an air of expectation, not entirely devoid of embarrassment.

"You must have been long since aware of my ardent attachment," continued Sir Alfred, hurriedly. "It has been obvious to others less interested. Sir Richard mentioned the subject to me this morning, when I was happy enough to obtain his concurrence."

"Rather premature," said Eleanor, blushing.

"My friend Grant also discovered my sentiments long since, and therefore I cannot but wonder that they should have entirely escaped your notice, because it appeared as if every moment must have betrayed me to such penetration as Miss Fitz-Patrick's. All necessity for concealment, however, is now at an end, and it is with pride and pleasure I announce that your cousin has this moment pledged her affections to me. Need I say that not a wish of my heart remains ungratified?"

For an instant Eleanor turned pale as death. Her lips became compressed, her eyes fixed and dilated, her whole countenance seemed to undergo a momentary convulsion.

She passed her hand over her face, and remained silent. At length pride restored her presence of mind, and making a strong effort of self-command, she turned to Sir Alfred with her usual company-smile, saying in a slow-measured voice, "I wish you both all the happiness that this world can give to any one, but that, I fear, is not much."

"*We* expect *more*—far more," replied he, with an expression in which joy seemed to be chastened for the moment by serious reflection; "who would not pity any man for gaining the whole world, if he could be satisfied with that! No, Miss Fitz-Patrick, let us hope that you and I and my own Matilda, have a better portion in view than any earthly blessing can supply."

Eleanor looked at Sir Alfred with surprise. She had sometimes before seen reason to suspect his religious principles to be deep and influential, but her conjectures were carelessly considered, until now when fully confirmed. After Eleanor that evening found shelter in the solitude of her own dressing-room, a pang shot through her mind as she recalled these words of Sir Alfred, and compared what she had once been herself in principle and feeling, contrasted with what she was now.

The early impressions of childhood, so long extinguished, were for an instant revived while, breathing a deep sigh of humiliation and regret, she retraced the past. Many a thought which had slumbered unheeded in Eleanor's mind for years, now forced itself into remembrance, and wrung her heart in solitary anguish. Religion actually appeared in a new light, when she saw it viewed and acknowledged as the first object in existence by a person of such distinguished consideration as Sir Alfred, for it is singular what powerful effect is produced by personally meeting any one highly gifted, and yet under the influence of Divine truth. Eleanor always knew, like every one else, that the greatest as well as the best of men had been Christians—that Milton, the first of poets, Newton, the chief of philosophers, Addison, the most elegant of moral writers, Johnson, the profoundest of scholars, Bacon, the most learned of statesmen, and a thousand other illustrious names, derived their greatest eminence and their only happiness from the profession of a deep and holy veneration for Christianity; but it was new to her when she beheld one who possessed everything in life to render it attractive, and whom she had been accustomed to see the object of universal admiration and respect, considering the whole as an idle dream, except inasmuch as he was preparing to leave those fleeting objects, and to awake in eternity.

Miss Fitz-Patrick hastily tore out the camellias from amidst her clustering curls, and sat for hours before a dressing-table, with her fingers passed through her hair, and her eyes and throbbing forehead pressed upon her hands, while her mind strayed in a wild wilderness of tumultuous emotions; but still, as she tried to collect her scattered faculties, the young heiress could not but recollect with what incredulity she once listened to the heartfelt opinion of Lady Olivia, that, even in this life people are happy, whatever their circumstances may be, exactly in proportion as their thoughts are devoted to God. Those affectionate admonitions of her first and kindest friend had long been overlooked; and while she thought with bitter regret of them, she also remembered her subsequent treatment of Matilda with keen self-reproach. Memory seemed to have become an enemy which would do nothing but upbraid her, while for a moment she became conscious that had such ingratitude and unkindness been foretold in former years, her exclamation would have been like that of Hazael, "Is thy servant a dog?" Her thoughts reached back into the long vista of past days, when nature, feeling, and principle all combined with the exercise of natural affection to render her happy and to lead her on in a course of devotion and peace. Eleanor's heart was smitten by the contrast, and a crushing sense of misery weighed down her spirit. The rich gifts of fortune appeared now in their native insignificance compared with those of nature; for friendship, affection, peace, contentment, and cheerfulness seemed all to have been sacrificed in a mere delirium of vanity, while she felt what a mirage of the desert had misled her. "Oh! that it were with me as in the days that are past!" thought she bitterly; "but more easily might I gather the scattered leaves of this fallen flower, and restore them to life and beauty, than hope to become the same simple, unsophisticated girl I once was. Nature intended me for better things, and providence blessed me with peculiar advantages, but all is madly thrown away, and I will not—*for I dare not*—reflect or attempt to retrace my steps."

CHAPTER XXIII.

"Hearts are not flint, yet flint is rent,
Hearts are not steel, yet steel is bent."

Next morning, before breakfast, Matilda entered Eleanor's room, and, with all her usual tact and delicacy, announced her own happy prospects, as if they had indeed been like sisters, and that it formed a subject of mutual interest and confidence between them. Not a trace seemed to remain in her memory that her cousin had mistaken the nature of Sir Alfred's intentions, nor did she seem to entertain a suspicion that anything could arise but sympathy and good wishes from the friend of her childhood. Miss Fitz-Patrick was melted and overcome by her cousin's considerate kindness; but pride still prevailed, and rather than show any emotion liable to be mistaken for regret or disappointment, she answered, during the few moments that Matilda remained, with coldness and constraint, which rendered it a mutual relief when the interview was terminated.

Miss Howard started with surprise to discover, during breakfast, how universally Sir Alfred had announced the news of their engagement, for the usual reserve of his character had apparently vanished, while Sir Richard was evidently rehearsing all the sly allusions, hints, and inuendoes which abound on such occasions. It seemed on this day as if the whole party had changed characters. Eleanor was pensive and silent, her spirits were evidently forced, and a slight nervous quiver of the lip gave evidence of internal agitation. Mr. Grant seemed also grave, and glanced occasionally at Eleanor's countenance with an expression almost amounting to pity, so fully had he been impressed with the idea that Miss Fitz-Patrick was secretly attached to his friend. There appeared a degree of *empressement* in his attentions now, beyond what he ever testified formerly, but yet Eleanor became thoroughly conscious, that these cares were for her sake entirely, not for his own—that the cloud which agitated his spirits was one in which she had no share, and that, while anxiously desirous to promote her happiness, his feelings were no longer dependent on her caprice. It seemed to Eleanor as if everything in life had been transformed around her, and when, after breakfast, Sir Alfred led Matilda into the library, she hastily retreated to her own room, and in solitary retirement gave vent to every bitter emotion which was at war within her breast, where not a single source of comfort presented itself, to which she might turn for relief, in brooding over past events and present circumstances. It would have been difficult for any one, and impossible for Eleanor, to analyze her complicated sensations; but there arose an intense and prevailing sense of wretchedness in her mind, while silently weeping such tears as are seldom shed but once. For a moment she acknowledged, that Matilda merited happiness, while she was herself unfit to be the chosen companion of one so singularly gifted as Sir Alfred, and Eleanor felt humbled by the contrast of her own mind and heart with her cousin's. Yet, while conviction struggled for the mastery over envy and mortified pride, there rankled a feeling deeper than all, which pierced to the inmost recesses of her spirit, when the belief became inevitable that Mr. Grant also had learned to view her with indifference. It always hitherto appeared certain to her imagination, that at some time or other there would be a necessity for choosing between Sir Alfred and her former lover, whom she fancied that no circumstances could alienate. Though grander features of character in the one had dazzled and almost captivated Eleanor for a time, yet in all the suppositious scenes with which she frequently beguiled an idle hour, it invariably happened that the preference was given to Mr. Grant. She generally caused him to suffer agonies of imaginary suspense, and made the concession of accepting him an obligation which could never be sufficiently appreciated; but still an interview had been so frequently rehearsed, and arranged on her own pattern, that it seemed incredible to think it might not perhaps take place in actual reality. If anything more trying than another could have been added to present mortification, it was the consciousness of Matilda being preferred; and in remembering her own ungenerous conduct to her cousin, she thought of it all with shame and contrition, while the very possibility of making any acknowledgment or reparation seemed now out of the question.

Eleanor's mind was thus tortured by vain regrets and

temporary remorse, when these painful ruminations were interrupted by the announcement that Dr. Murray had called, requesting to see her immediately, and alone. Anything seemed to promise relief from the wretched state of her present thoughts, and she desired that he should be ushered into her own boudoir, where they had occasionally met already on parish business.

There appeared an unwonted expression of melancholy gravity in the eye of Dr. Murray as he entered Eleanor's presence, and his step was lingering and slow, as if unwilling to hasten the time when he must speak. Having observed, after a friendly greeting on both sides, that Miss Fitz-Patrick seemed unusually languid and pale, he took her by the hand with a look of benevolent interest, saying he feared she had suffered materially from her recent perilous adventure on the ice.

"Oh dear, no! It was scarcely worth mentioning. I might be in danger for a few minutes, but with so many friends near, and such prompt assistance, there could be little cause for serious apprehension."

"Miss Fitz-Patrick!" replied he, still preserving a look of unwonted seriousness, "the issues of life and of death are in the hands of Him by whose providential care you were then preserved. Had that alarming accident been foreseen, without its merciful conclusion also becoming known, think how fervent would have been your prayers for that safety which now seems a matter of course. It is seldom that our thankfulness, after any interposition of this kind, bears a due proportion to the anxiety which we previously felt; but as the servant of Him to whom you owe every hour of existence, and the many blessings which render it precious, I should claim and expect to see the most heartfelt gratitude. There is much to make life enticing to you, Miss Fitz-Patrick, but there is yet more to make death alarming, when we consider how readily you acknowledge that the rich bounties of Providence have only served to estrange you from the Giver. I could have wished, I had almost believed that, when snatched, as it were, from the borders of the grave, you might have considered seriously that important purpose for which a new lease of life had been granted. Of that, however, let us speak hereafter; but the business on which I come this morning calls for urgent haste. You are aware, Miss Fitz-Patrick, that the unfortunate young girl who was a short time in your service is now no more——"

"Dead?" interrupted she, turning pale, and sinking into a seat. "Surely, Dr. Murray, you cannot mean to say she is actually dead?"

The venerable clergyman mournfully shook his head, while Eleanor sat for a moment transfixed with amazement, and then, burying her face on the arm of the sofa, she remained silent during several minutes.

"She is supposed to have drowned herself some days ago," added Dr. Murray, in a subdued voice, and with evident emotion. "We may trust that the poor girl was not a responsible being at that time, for there is unquestionable evidence of her mind having been in a state of frightful delirium, brought on by distress. It is deeply to be deplored that more caution was not used before her being abandoned to such extreme suffering; and, on the part of Nanny's aged mother, who seems now at the point of death, I come to you, Miss Fitz-Patrick, this morning. The only remaining wish of old Janet's heart is, that her daughter's character may be cleared before she expires. The poor woman clings to her belief of Nanny's innocence, but she wishes to die in the knowledge of it. Her last request then is, that you will now investigate those accusations against her child, in the hope that I may return, before her eyes are closed forever, with the consoling assurance that all is done that *can* be done to clear the memory of her departed daughter from infamy."

"Dr. Murray," said Eleanor, rising, and speaking with great effort, "it appears to me this morning, as if, in the language of David, I might say, 'My sins have found me out!' Never till this moment did I duly reflect upon my conduct to that girl—but now—I see it as you see it. I dare not take time to consider that, nor any one of the thousand things which are crowding into my mind. To you, Dr. Murray, who would not speak with confidence? I shall do so hereafter, when you will be benevolently interested for one who little deserves it from you, or from any person. Of all the tortures it would be possible to endure, I believe the greatest might be to read over my past life as it was, and to be told by my own heart and conscience what it *ought* to have been—to see the unnecessary perplexities I have plunged into—the friends I have alienated—the unknown miseries I have occasioned—and the opportunities of doing good that I have missed. Oh! Dr. Murray, I cannot but think, when in a future world all this is revealed to us at once, how the very best will stand speechless and amazed. Through infinite mercy it is never too late for repentance here, and certainly it can never be *too soon.* I shall at least show one proof of readiness to make any reparation in my power to the unfortunate mother. Poor Nanny! she is beyond the reach of all that compunction and sorrow can suggest; but I shall accompany you to Gowanbank myself. Meanwhile this is no time to speak, for I must act. Let us consult my father what immediate steps shall be taken."

Eleanor instantly rung the bell, and sent a message for Sir Richard; but on being informed that he had gone out, she requested to see Mr. Grant, whom, as a justice of the peace, she at once resolved to consult. No sooner did he obey her summons, than with perfect candor, and no extenuation, she hastily recapitulated every circumstance relating to Nanny, taking upon herself the whole blame, and ending by an earnest entreaty to both gentlemen, that whatever plan occurred for immediate investigation, might be instantly put in action. A hectic spot burnt on Eleanor's cheek, while the rest of her countenance remained pale as marble—there was the hurry and rapidity of nervous excitement in her manner,—her lips were strongly compressed to conceal emotion, and her eye spoke a language of grief and anxiety so unknown there before, that Mr. Grant felt surprised and affected to observe such a sudden change.

Dr. Murray first suggested that Mrs. Gordon might be desired to assemble the servants, which was done without delay in the library, where they had on a former occasion been summoned to family prayers, and therefore all attended without hesitation or uneasiness. Eleanor then hastened into the drawing-room, and passing by Miss Marabout in silence, she advanced to her cousin, who was standing at a window with Sir Alfred, and, unable to speak, she took Miss Howard by the hand and made a sign for her to follow. Matilda asked no questions; she did not even express by a look the astonishment which it was impossible not to feel at observing Eleanor's agitated manner, but assuming an external appearance of composure, she took her cousin affectionately by the arm, and accompanied her in silence to the library, where they sat down together in an obscure corner, while she looked round with wonder and apprehension to ascertain the cause of Eleanor's distress.

Dr. Murray then approached to where the servants were placed, and passing his mild benevolent eye along the line in which they stood, he fixed it with penetrating earnestness on Pauline, and a solemn pause ensued. It now became evident to all, that they were assembled on no ordinary occasion, while the increasing agitation of Eleanor, and a look of grave and anxious interest on the countenance of Mr. Grant, confirmed their conjectures, and caused a general impression of awe."

"I am come, my friends," said Dr. Murray, "with a message to you all from the chamber of death. A fellow-creature, now laid in the last agonies of expiring nature, whom each of us has known, asks for one last gleam of earthly comfort from *you*. Age and infirmity, sickness and grief, are doing their worst upon her, and yet I would rather at this moment take her place than be the person who could willingly cause such affliction, and who would withhold consolation. All the sorrows of life, and all the sufferings of death, are as nothing compared with *remorse;* and if repentance be delayed for a few hours it may come too late. That young and blooming girl who so lately stood amongst you is now no more. In desperation and sorrow she has hurried to that awful tribunal where we shall speedily meet; and I would ask, whether in that hour, when the secrets of all hearts shall be laid open, none of you will see cause to lament having occasioned the wretchedness which has ended thus fatally. If it be so, you must either repent of it in this world, or repent throughout a hopeless eternity. Nanny is beyond the reach either of malice or kindness—our very prayers can no longer avail her—and the place that once knew her shall know her no more. Yet the broken-hearted mother seeks for peace, and would find it, were she only assured that her child never became the guilty criminal which has been said—that she did not forget the principles of her early days, and that before she lost her reason, she was incapable of flagrantly violating conscience. That her heart had been allured into vanity—that her mind was unstable, and that her last act is one which every Christian must shudder to contemplate, the dying woman feels ready to acknowledge; yet she cherishes a hope that you might exculpate this poor girl's memory from any more aggravated crime. Is there one amongst you, then, who will say whether the most trifling circumstance can be mentioned which might give peace to her expiring parent? If you are moved by the thought of a mother's agony—if you are touched by the remembrance of her young and lovely daughter, brought at once to shame, insanity, and death—I solemnly adjure you to confess whether private malice, or personal guilt, induced you to blast the good name of this unfortunate girl, or whether you believe any one else to have done so *falsely?*"

Silence reigned throughout the room for some minutes, while every eye instinctively turned on Pauline; but though she trembled and became pale at the mention of Nanny's death, it seemed evident that nothing which had been said reached her feelings. Unable to look any person in the face, she stole a furtive glance around, and fixing her eyes on vacancy, preserved an impenetrable obduracy of appearance.

"If confession were made now," continued Dr. Murray, "we might deal leniently with those who gave such voluntary evidence of repentance—but when legal measures are once resorted to, as they *shall* be, we owe it to public justice, that the law, in all its terrors, be fully enforced. Many articles of value belonging to Miss Fitz-Patrick are still missing. Mr. Grant is ready to give a warrant that the house shall be searched—and before a single individual leaves this room it must be done. Let me now appeal to each person separately, whether anything can be remembered or confessed to bring out the real truth."

Dr. Murray then began with Mrs. Gordon, and went regularly along the line, patiently and perseveringly asking every individual what might be remembered which bore upon the subject in question, and whether, as far as her knowledge extended, she believed Nanny to have been guilty of stealing the articles in question, or not.

"Pauline!" said he solemnly, when her turn came, while his eye seemed to read her very thoughts, "you, who ought to know most on this subject, say nothing! Tell me truly, and you shall never have reason to regret the confession, was Nanny falsely accused?"

With a strong effort Pauline looked up, but her eye fell beneath his penetrating gaze, her voice quivered inaudibly, and in an instant more, she fainted. Measures were immediately taken for her restoration, while Dr. Murray proceeded with his inquiries. One of the housemaids had twice seen Pauline, late at night, near a flower-stand, where some of the missing ornaments were afterwards discovered; while at that untimely hour, she professed to have been sent by Miss

Fitz-Patrick to cut the geraniums. Sir Richard's valet, with many expressions of contrition for having maliciously concealed the circumstance so long, acknowledged that he had met her dressed in the shawl which Nanny was accused of wearing on that evening; and another maid produced a skeleton key which had been found on the floor of the lady's-maid's room, a short time previously, and it tallied exactly with that of Sir Richard's cabinet. Still, on recovering Pauline strenuously denied all knowledge of the robbery, and even smiled when the threat was repeated of having a strict search immediately instituted. Not a doubt could remain on the mind of any one present that she was guilty, but Matilda almost despaired of the truth being elicited at this time; and Eleanor covered her face with her hands in agonized conviction of her maid's criminality, and yet completely at a loss how to proceed. Dr. Murray himself paused in silent perplexity, when Mr. Grant unexpectedly walked forward, assuming in his countenance an expression of tremendous import.

"Pauline!" he said, with grave severity, "I am a magistrate of this county. If immediate confession is not made where those jewels are concealed, I shall make you disgorge your ill-gotten gains, like a leech on a plate of salt."

This oration, so suited to the capacity of his audience, had an instant and powerful effect. The guilty woman rushed for protection to Mrs. Gordon, who sternly threw her off with angry reproaches, hoping she might be instantly consigned to justice. Alarmed and overcome, she then requested that some person would accompany her to an old tool-house in the garden, where, beneath several sacks of seeds, appeared a small box, containing not only all the trinkets which were missing, but a quantity of money in silver. Pauline afterwards confessed the perfect innocence of Nanny and her own criminality, declaring that her first irresistible inducement to steal originated from Miss Fitz-Patrick's carelessness, who left money frequently loose in her dressing-box, or carried it in a reticule, to which any one could have constant access.

No sooner was Eleanor convinced of Nanny's innocence than she insisted on accompanying Dr. Murray and Mr. Grant to Gowanbank. It seemed a relief to act rather than to think; and leaning on Matilda, she walked there in silent meditation. No sooner did Miss Fitz-Patrick reach the cottage, than, without losing a moment, or in the slightest degree palliating her own conduct, she shortly and hurriedly related to Martha, and to the aged sufferer herself, all that had passed, earnestly and repeatedly assuring them that Nanny's character seemed fully exculpated now in the eyes of every one. Matilda felt alarmed to observe the convulsive workings of old Janet's countenance while she listened, and the death-like hue of her cheek; but Eleanor, invariably the creature of impulse, could not be stopped, until, having reached the conclusion of all that could be said, she sat down by the bedside and burst into tears.

"Now, Janet," added she, in a faltering voice, "Nanny can never grant me pardon in this world,—but *will you?*—I have caused her death,—I have hastened yours,—and embittered the remainder of my own days,—but still, as a Christian, forgive me,—pray for me,—ask that I may receive such mercy as I never showed,—that my whole heart may be changed, until I abhor myself, even more than I do now. Speak without delay, and give me the only consolation which a remembrance of this hour can ever afford."

The old woman feebly moved her hands, and a prayer trembled on her lips, which seemed to be one of thankfulness and praise."

"All is peace now!" she said in a voice of calm resignation. "My sight has failed,—my strength is fast departing,—and my voice will soon be heard no more; but I would speak comfort to you while breath remains. There are no distinctions now,—worldly honors, and worldly afflictions accompany us to the borders of eternity, but they leave us *there.* O think, Miss Fitz-Patrick, when this hour shall come, will all the enjoyments of life prepare you to meet it, as sorrow has prepared me? Then do not regret that my cup of trial has been full,—nor that an event like this makes you pause to reflect. What are we all so busy and anxious about?—This is the end of all!———"

Janet now raised herself on the bed, and held out her hand, apparently intending to give Eleanor her blessing, when a deep sob stopped her utterance, she shuddered, and suddenly her jaw stiffened, her eyes fixed, and in the very act of supplication she expired.

When it became evident that all was over, Mr. Grant led Eleanor, overpowered by the shock, into another room, where, after some time, Dr. Murray followed, leaving Martha and William to pay the last duties. Ever ready to take any opportunity of impressing on his people how short a passage this life is to eternity, Dr. Murray proposed, before leaving Gowanbank, that they should all unite in prayer; and seeing that Eleanor's conscience needed not now to be awakened, he carefully avoided whatever might be peculiarly painful to her feelings. It was his rule, in addressing the hearts of others, never so much as to remember what were their individual offences, but to set before all men alike the guilt and danger of every human soul, as well as the absolute necessity of repentance, faith, and sanctification. On this occasion his prayer and address were deeply affecting so that Eleanor, unable to speak, took the arm of Mr. Grant and left the cottage in melancholy silence. Observing, when they reached home, the setting sun shedding its refulgence on distant clouds and hill-tops, she paused, and for the first time addressed her companion.

"On such an evening as this, Mr. Grant, my mother died: and it would have been well for myself and others if I had not survived! There was sorrow then, but it was without a sting of self-reproach. She departed in the blessed hope of rising again, and pointed to that glorious sun as the daily memorial of our death and resurrection. Many a day it has shone brightly on me since; but *you* know, and have seen, what a change it has witnessed on me, and that, forgetful of every serious thought, I have lived for the present hour as if this were my eternal home. I could wish, even now, that my sun had set like that old woman's, with the same certainty of rising again in glory."

During that evening Matilda kept close beside Eleanor, and vainly tried to engage her in conversation, for she answered absently and indifferently, though with none of the harshness or sarcasm of manner which had appeared there formerly. A cloud seemed to have come over all the party, most of whom were to disperse next morning, and Miss Fitz-Patrick rose at last, with undisguised satisfaction, when she found it was time to retire. Unwilling to dwell on all the painful subjects which assailed her mind, and having never been accustomed to hold serious communion with herself, she dismissed her maid, and hurried to bed, eagerly seeking for that repose which might bring temporary oblivion from self-reproach; but sleep was denied her agitated nerves.

After having tossed in feverish restlessness for several hours, Miss Fitz-Patrick struck her repeater, for the twentieth time, and found that it was three o'clock. The smoul dering ashes were expiring in the grate, and a dim rush light feebly sent its checkered shadows around—all was still and silent as the grave, when Eleanor's attention became suddenly and fearfully attracted towards the door of a distant closet. It seemed to be slowly opening, and a tall female figure appeared there. Emerging from the obscurity, she noiselessly approached towards the fire, where, silently stooping over its dying embers, she extended her fingers above them, as if for warmth, while her hair fell in large, dishevelled masses upon her face and shoulders. Petrified with horror and amazement, Eleanor seemed neither to move nor breathe, but became stiffened with fear. Half-raised on her elbow, and transfixed to the spot, her eyes were fastened on the strange apparition with more than mortal apprehension. It seemed to Eleanor's alarmed imagination as if a lifetime elapsed while she gazed with awe at this mysterious and motionless figure. Unable to endure suspense any longer, she at length, by a powerful effort of resolution, stretched out her hand to the bell, and rung it with almost frantic violence. Instantly a fearful shriek arose, while the object of her terror sprung forward towards the bed, and, bursting into a wild, hysterical laugh, she fell on her knees before Eleanor, who recognized, with astonishment and dismay, the haggard countenance of Nanny.

When, in reply to a loud and repeated summons from Miss Fitz-Patrick's bell, several servants rushed into the room, they found her stretched on the bed in a fainting fit, while, fixed and motionless as a corpse by her side, stood the unfortunate maniac, her hands clasped, her eyes glazed, and her features sharpened with suffering. How she had stolen into the house, or where she had subsisted during the period of her disappearance, could never be afterwards discovered, but her wasted figure and emaciated countenance bore melancholy testimony how greatly she had endured.

Nanny was instantly removed, and medical attendance summoned, while Matilda devoted herself to the care of her cousin, whose feverish pulse and agitated appearance were such as to cause extreme solicitude. Miss Fitz-Patrick lay for several hours with her eyes half-closed, and every effort to soothe or restore her seemed vain. She sighed often and deeply without speaking, and only once turned feebly to Matilda, and took her by the hand, whispering, in accents of emotion, "Let us be thankful that, at least, she is not dead!" Miss Howard pressed her hand, and kissed her cheek, in token of sympathy, but she again relapsed into painful, and evidently affecting rumination.

On the following day, Miss Murray, who had heard of Nanny's unexpected restoration, arrived at Barnard Castle, and obtained leave for her being immediately conveyed to Gaelfield, where, under careful superintendence, she entertained a sanguine hope of bringing her back to composure and recollection. Meantime, Eleanor requested to see Miss Murray, and a long conversation ensued. Miss Fitz-Patrick then felt the influence of a mind which, though feeble in itself, had been strengthened by Divine teaching, and by Christian consistency. She wondered to think that her aged companion could have ever appeared otherwise than venerable, and deserving of the highest respect, while she listened to her clear views of Gospel truth, and to her gentle, admonitory hints for the future. Her heart seemed to be melted with sorrow and remorse, which were expressed with a degree of freedom and candor, which could not have been shown to any one less experienced, or less indulgent, and Miss Fitz-Patrick found relief from having any friend to whom her mind might be so unreservedly opened.

At length Eleanor suddenly announced an intention of rising to join her friends in the drawing-room, though every imaginable persuasion was used to prevent her. She seemed actuated by some powerful influence, and merely said, in answer to Matilda's entreaties, "I shall exert for to-day—many of our visitors are to leave this house—and after that, nothing will remain for me in this world that is worth a thought. I may then reap all the misery that I have sown, and *even you* must allow it is deserved."

There was fever in Eleanor's eye, and hectic on her cheek, when she appeared, and it seemed vain to attempt any disguise of the deep despondency which weighed on her spirits. She neither eat nor spoke during luncheon, while her visitors seemed at a loss how to act. Lady Montague and her daughters were now about to take their final departure, and Mrs. Clifford had an engagement to be absent for some days. Sir Richard, meantime, stood at the fire in vehement altercation with Colonel Pendarvis, on discovering that his britschska had arrived at the door to carry off himself and Major Foley. Their leave of absence was within a week of being out, but still the hospitable Baronet tried to drive a hard bargain for that additional period, gradually letting down his demand on their time, like a Dutch auction, till he promised at last to be satisfied with one day more; but even that was denied him. Eleanor seemed scarcely conscious of what passed, but the gallant Colonel had offered her, on the previous evening, to settle at Barnard Castle for life, and finding that the proposal was not duly appreciated by the heiress, he could not remain another hour. For a somewhat similar reason, Lord Alderby also eluded Sir Richard's vigilance, and, feeling exceedingly ill-treated, left Barnard Castle during the previous day, without assigning any reason, or even taking leave, which gave the Baronet a shrewd suspicion of what had occurred, and extended that conjecture throughout the minds of all who observed his Lordship's sudden exit.

Mr. Grant stood at a window alone, watching the process of packing Colonel Pendarvis's carriage, and humming the tune of "Go where glory waits thee," when Eleanor rose from table, and joined him.

"I understand," she said, "that you also leave us to-day! and my father mentions, Mr. Grant, that you have some idea of returning to the Continent!"

"Yes! I intend exploring Greece once more, and getting up a little sublime melancholy there, after the pattern of Lord Byron.

'Dejected, sad, and lone, and blighted,
More than this I scarce can die!'"

"It is well, Mr. Grant, that you can jest upon grief, for then it must be lighter than mine. I have lately caused such suffering as it makes me tremble to contemplate, and whatever be my own share now, is deserved. I cannot, however, take leave of one who has so long continued my ——my friend, without saying, that if ever we meet again, such a change will have taken place as all who knew me lately, and could yet continue to feel any interest in me must have desired."

"Let me candidly acknowledge, Miss Fitz-Patrick, that in some respects I have thought you spoilt by prosperity, but when our cup is full it is very apt to intoxicate the strongest head. I dare not even answer for my own, if Sir Evan were to give me a step. Concerning the alteration you threaten us with, why, long before my return you will probably, like all young ladies, have changed your situation for better or for worse; therefore, as an old, and very sincere friend, my fervent hope is, that whoever may be happy enough to obtain the preference, shall prove himself deserving of you—not on account of his rank, his wealth, or his property, but for his disinterested attachment to *yourself*."

"No, Mr. Grant, that can never be *now*," replied Eleanor, in a tone of deep emotion, which it was impossible to misunderstand. I long since alienated the only person on earth who might have answered your description, or who could have ever been truly preferred. While I live, no other shall supply that place."

Before Mr. Grant could answer, or look round, Eleanor vanished, and, while he was yet retracing with surprise the few words she had said, and the undisguised agitation with which she had spoken, Sir Richard impatiently beckoned him to join in an excursion to the stable. There, for the fiftieth time, an elaborate discussion ensued upon martingales and patent bridles, fast-trotting and leaping, spavins and broken knees.

"I'll tell you what it is, Grant!" cried the Baronet, seeing his companion's eye vacantly fixed for several minutes on a dead wall opposite, "you are calculating the height of that fence, but Mad Tom could clear it perfectly! As for your own chesnut, Harum Scarum, he would go over with his legs tied; and I'll lay a bet that any bullock in my park could do the same. For a standing-leap, we might back one of those clumsy animals against the most thoroughbred hunter in your stud."

It is wonderful how ignorant people remain of what is really passing in the minds of their associates. Sir Richard concluded a long interview with Mr. Grant, and set out for his ride of some hours, perfectly satisfied that his companion's whole heart had been in their recent discussion, while the other slowly and thoughtfully returned towards Barnard Castle, to prepare for immediate departure.

Meantime Eleanor re-entered the drawing-room, having, by a great effort, rallied her spirits sufficiently to bid adieu to her departing guests. She was conversing with Miss Charlotte Clifford on Mr. Grant's entrance, and though the color rushed into her face, and receded as instantly again when he approached, she resolutely conquered all external agitation, and affected a tone of extraordinary vivacity.

"Really these incessant leave-takings are too much for human nature," said she, forcing a laugh. "Poor Sir Colin's last farewell nearly overset me. His old story about Sir

Evan telling his guests that visitors are like fish, good the first day, tolerable the second, and not to be endured the third; which served as the preface to an elaborate apology for having paid so long a visitation here, while I was evidently expected to answer, as of course I did, that he had been the life of the company!"

"Fletcher's existence at home must be very strange," observed Mr. Grant. "I never yet called at his house without being shown into the drawing-room, where he is to be found, seated on a chair, with his back to the window, his arms folded, his legs crossed, and not a thing to see or to do. Not a book, nor an inkstand, nor a newspaper—neither dog, cat, nor bird, to enliven solitude."

"His thoughts must be less intolerable to himself than those of some people I know," replied Eleanor, mournfully; "but, after all, such a life reminds one of a wild beast in a menagerie, more than of a rational being, who has talents and affections to exercise. It is wonderful to what a level men sometimes degrade themselves, not merely to animal, but actually to *vegetable* life."

"Yet in society no one is more sociably inclined than Sir Colin, which causes one to wonder the more how he makes it out alone!" said Mr. Grant. "Everything that passes through his mind must be spoken to the first listener, for he has no power of mental reflection. If he has met an acquaintance, or mislaid a letter, or been annoyed with his valet, or traced a figure in the clouds, or a face in the fire, it must all be communicaied at our club to the nearest person. One of Sir Colin's most unbearable inflictions, however, remains to be noticed. When any person, on whose good-nature he can entirely depend, happens to be particularly busy, perhaps scribbling some troublesome letter of condolence or congratulation, or reading a book of more than ordinary interest, his great delight is, on these occasions, to plant himself close by, newspaper in hand, while he intrudes little paragraphs on their notice perpetually. I watched Miss Howard suffering under the infliction this morning, in passing through the library, and it might have made an owl die of laughing. She seemed writing against time to catch the post—we all know that her letters are not of every-day interest, and she had evidently secured a swarm of franks from Sir Alfred, who was writing also. Sir Colin began with calling your cousin's attention to an alarming fire in a gas manufactory, where happily no lives were lost—then followed the particulars of an unfortunate climbing-boy sticking in a chimney, and of an Irish murder, with all the usual circumstances,—he next proceeded to several advertising panegyrics upon new books, and was in full career through the prospectus of a Newcastle railway, when Martin paraded in with the post-bag for letters. I observed Miss Howard hurriedly seal the only cover she had time to fill, while Sir Alfred quietly stole away the remaining franks, altered their dates for to-morrow, and silently replaced them. Nothing could be more brilliant than your cousin's smile of surprise, when she found the covers all transformed so unexpectedly."

It was a strong proof of Eleanor's being greatly changed, that she neither seemed piqued nor displeased at the termination of Mr. Grant's narrative, but spoke of Sir Alfred's engagement to Matilda with an appearance of such real satisfaction, that it became obvious how mistaken any conjecture must have been which supposed that she had been herself attached to him. Lady Montague and Mrs. Clifford now successively bid her farewell, but as the hour of Mr. Grant's intended departure approached, Eleanor's countenance became paler, while she still kept up the farce of remarkable vivacity.

"Quite a small select party!" cried she, entering the library with Mr. Grant, to join Sir Alfred and Matilda. "We are reduced now to a mere whist party!—If ever *a dummy* is wanted, I shall be sure of Mr. Armstrong, who seems as stationary by our fireside as the fender, and fully more inanimate. We hear often in Scotland of a *self-contained house*, but he is the only instance I know of a self-contained man! It is astonishing, that in the inventory of fixtures belonging to this house, he was omitted! I often wonder what brought Mr. Armstrong here, and still more, whether anything will *ever* take him away!"

"A chaise and pair shall this very night," said the gentleman in question, emerging from the deep embrasure of a window, in which he had been reading; "but, Miss Fitz-Patrick, it will be one of the darkest days in your life when I leave this house."

"Then I shall have little reason to lament a want of sunshine," replied Eleanor, sarcastically. "Mr. Armstrong, you have been in the habit of using expressions towards me lately which are entirely unwarrantable. As the friend of Sir Philip, and as my father's guest, I regret that you should have heard remarks which it would give me pleasure to recall, but not on account of any threat or insinuation of your own, because nothing you say or do can be of the slightest importance to me."

"No!—indeed!" cried Mr. Armstromg, ironically; and then changing his tone to one of intolerable anger, he added, grinding his clenched teeth together, "perhaps, Miss Fitz-Patrick, I could alter your opinion upon that subject. Possibly you may not be a *fixture* here very long yourself!"

Eleanor eyed him with a look of cold incredulity and contempt, then sitting down to the harp, she carelessly sung a few bars of Rode's variations, apparently forgetting the very existence of her infuriated guest. Mr. Armstrong looked at her for some moments with rising fury. Suddenly wheeling round, he then darted out of the room, and as quickly returned, carrying a large packet in his hand.

"There!" cried he, hurling it on the table with frightful vehemence, "you *will* have it so, and you deserve it! My brother was your uncle's agent, employed to draw up that will. He did so only two months before Sir Philip died, and it was written in order to cut *you* off, Miss Fitz-Patrick. Your satirical wit had not even spared him, and he found it out. That deed was dictated in a whirlwind of passion. Sir Philip forgot to insert those legacies to friends which he certainly intended, and which were recorded in his previous settlement. My brother produced only that will which was to benefit himself and me. On returning from the Continent, I was unwilling to stain his memory by revealing this. It seemed probable, also, that Miss Howard, who now succeeds to everything, would have engaged to compensate my own losses in doing so, but she played her cards better. And now, Miss Fitz-Patrick!" added Mr. Armstrong, with a look of bitter vengeance, which seemed an ample repayment for the disgrace of his previous confession, "I know from Miss Marabout all you have said of me. She, too, abhors your satirical temper, and suffers from it. I told her that an ample revenge was in my power. Are you satisfied that it is so?—read that, and say whether I can do nothing of importance to *you?*"

"Silence, Mr. Armstrong!" said Sir Alfred, rising with an air of authority, while lightning flashed in his eye. "This must not be!—you are in no state of mind to address Miss Fitz-Patrick!—leave the room instantly!"

Saying these words, he calmly proceeded towards the door

with an air of commanding dignity, and throwing it open, made a signal for Mr. Armstrong to depart.

"Give me my papers, then," cried the enraged man, rising however, to obey a mandate which he saw it would be impossible to resist; "I must take back that packet!"

"No!" replied Eleanor, with a look of stern resolution, "these papers belong to *me.* Come what may from them, justice shall be done, and it is not in your option now, Mr. Armstrong, either to bestow or to withhold it. There are witnesses enough here to my having retained this packet; and, Mr. Grant, I consign it to you, requesting instantly, and without a moment's delay, to be apprised of its nature and contents."

"Surely not *now*, Miss Fitz-Patrick? wait till Sir Richard returns. Let your father's agent communicate with *this person.* It is no fit business, apparently, for us to enter upon."

"I never could endure suspense," answered Eleanor, with a slight hysterical laugh, as Sir Alfred closed the door on Mr. Armstrong. "When once resolved to undergo anything, if it were the amputation of a limb, every moment seems an age till it is done."

"Miss Fitz-Patrick," said Sir Alfred, preparing to leave the room, "let me advise you to postpone all investigation at present. Be not rash or imprudent; you have a parent and guardians to act for you, and in all probability this may turn out to be some malicious fabrication to serve the purposes of immediate revenge."

"No, Sir Alfred, I fear it is not. On various occasions hints and inuendoes have been dropt by Mr. Armstrong, which leads me to suppose that he fully believes his own statement. Neither my father nor I could understand his meaning, but now it has become plain enough. Let me entreat you to remain."

"Not if you intend to proceed without Sir Richard's presence. It is due to him, as your father and guardian, to be apprised of the circumstance before those seals are broken. I need scarcely remind your cousin, too, that as a party whose interests are apparently involved in this business, she would do better not hastily to enter upon it."

Miss Fitz-Patrick answered only with a gesture of impatience, and eagerly tore the envelop asunder, while Sir Alfred withdrew, accompanied by Matilda, as she felt the propriety and delicacy of his suggestion, though sympathy for Eleanor would have otherwise induced her to remain.

"Mr. Grant," said the heiress, unfolding an enormous sheet of parchment, formally drawn up, and methodically sealed with several signatures crowded at the bottom of every page, "what am I to think of this?"

"Do not ask me, Miss Fitz-Patrick," he replied, looking away with an expression of grave regret.

"It would have been well for me, Mr. Grant, and you know it, if I had never succeeded to this property," said Eleanor mournfully. "No one can ever imagine all that it has cost me! my peace of mind, the affection of those who loved me most, and every better disposition that I once possessed. Can you fear, then, to say that I must lose it? The wretched girl Nanny, who is now perhaps dying, scarcely felt more misery than I do, for she was free from self-reproach—but when I look at her—when I see Matilda, and—and—think of others who have loved me, whom I might have made happy, and who are deservedly estranged, I *do* feel reckless of any future evil, and it almost appears as if I wished to see justice dealt upon myself. Perhaps when sorrow and humiliation are heaped upon me, I may merit them less by bearing them aright. What can any external privation be *now*, when I can say, from the agonizing experience of my own inward feelings, 'a wounded spirit who can bear!' You saw the old woman expire with words of forgiveness on her lips, but could I forgive myself! You watched her daughter delirious with grief and shame, and while my senses remain can I forget it? You observe every day, every hour, my generous cousin's considerate attention, but does not that only heaps coals of fire on my head? These are sorrows!—yet those which strike the deepest can never be told to any earthly friend! Time, talents, opportunities lost!—all the impressions of my early days!—all the better hopes that might have cheered me now! It seems strange, Mr. Grant, why this should be said to you, but old friendship may justify confidence, and my feelings could never be either concealed or controlled. If there were a Protestant nunnery in this country, my state of mind would fit me to enter it now, and abjure the world forever."

"Miss Fitz-Patrick!" said Mr. Grant, looking up, from a state of profound reflection, "I have heard your sentiments with the deepest emotion, and let me trust that, in return, you will listen to mine. We have known each other from the time when, as a lovely and playful child, you appeared to my youthful fancy like a bright vision of almost celestial beauty. I have contemplated your gradual progress with rising interest, though often, I will acknowledge, of late with feelings of regret. Who would not have lamented the destroying influence of flattery and indulgence on such talents and dispositions as have seldom been equalled? It is impossible to say, Miss Fitz-Patrick, when I first began to love you. It was my misfortune to do so then, with a degree of ardor and enthusiasm which made your very faults become dear to me. You know all. You know that though my attachment had never been declared, it was deep and strong as any earthly feeling has ever been. Your sudden acquisition of wealth raised for the time a barrier between us, because, young and inexperienced as you were, I would not take advantage of our previous intimacy to establish any claim upon your affection. What my sufferings were in departing, no heart need attempt to conceive, for that would be impossible!—where honor and principle are at stake, they must be preserved, though life itself be the sacrifice! I returned, Miss Fitz-Patrick, and found you, as might have been feared, the spoilt child of fortune, whom, as you then were, I could view with indifference. My spirit is proud and independent. I would not be obliged *even to you.* Miss Howard was ill-treated, and it appeared unquestionable that the heart which could be so ungenerous to such a friend might be equally so to a lover. It is impossible for me to know whether, under any circumstances, I could have ever become acceptable to you. I do not even ask the question now, for what has been said is premature; but were that change to happen which may render others indifferent, it might revive many feelings of former days. The chief source of your altered disposition will then be removed—the barrier which first divided us would fall—and then, Eleanor Fitz-Patrick, I would ask to hear my fate. As we are at present, I know it already."

He was about to withdraw, and had reached the door, when Eleanor, in a scarcely audible voice, called him back.

"Mr. Grant!" said she, coloring deeply, and extending her hand towards him, "I would rejoice in the loss of every earthly possession if it restored your affection to what it was."

"Be mine, then, Eleanor!" said he, suddenly clasping her in his arms; "and come what may, we shall be happy."

Meantime Matilda had proceeded with Sir Alfred to the enjoyment of a walk by the river side; and as nothing increases the power of pleasing so much as a consciousness of success, her conversation never before appeared so richly embellished with the rare fascination of deep feeling, united to right principle, while she spoke, without effort or disguise, every passing sentiment of her mind.

"Matilda!" said Sir Alfred, after many mutual anticipations of happiness, "I have purchased lately a small addition to my property near Douglas Priory, to which it is my impatient desire that you shall accompany me soon. Try if it be possible to guess where I thought you could be most easily induced to go?"

"Can you mean Ashgrove?" exclaimed Matilda, coloring with eagerness and animation. "Oh! what happiness!" added she, observing the smile with which Sir Alfred betrayed that her conjecture was right. "My utmost wishes are indeed fulfilled, and that place will be doubly dear to me now, as a remembrance of your considerate attention."

"Let us hope that I shall always be able to read your wishes, and to anticipate them as successfully. I know your love for Ashgrove so well, Matilda, that if I had brought a bottle of water from the rivulet that dashes past the windows, or even picked the mud off my chariot wheels there, you would have preserved it as a relic."

"Yes! our earliest associations are always delightful! I have travelled in many lovely scenes since the happy days that I passed there, but at Ashgrove and Douglas Priory such remembrances are connected with every shrub, and every tree, that, in my thoughts, the sun is brighter, the air is purer, and the birds sing more sweetly amidst those woods than elsewhere. In the words of your own favorite song—

'The last rays of feeling and life must depart,
Ere the bloom of that valley shall fade from my heart.'"

"It pleases me to think, Matilda, that we shall visit together the early home where all those amiable qualities were first implanted, which shall form the happiness of my future life. This world has much to give us now,—it may have much to take away hereafter, but we shall not forget under any circumstances to prepare for a happier state, where friendship and affection, founded like ours, shall at last become perfect in its nature and unending in its duration."

"The desire of my heart is, Sir Alfred, to be indeed all

that you think me, and all that you can continue to love, but after having so long accustomed myself to banish you from my thoughts, how strange it seems that what was always so difficult, and sometimes impossible, is no longer necessary."

"And yet, Matilda, with every pleasure of life there comes a duty; and for my own part, I now feel that in the purest and holiest affections of our nature, there may be a danger of excess. It seems, as if in every future hour even sorrow itself might be banished by your presence; for I need scarcely say that my attachments diverge into few channels, and are all the deeper where they flow; but while mutual confidence and love are strengthened by the lapse of years, let it still be our care to live not only for each other, but for the best interests of all around us, and for the glory of Him to whom our whole hearts belong."

CHAPTER XXIV.

"Yet ev'ry sorrow cuts a cord,
And urges us to rise."

"SUDDEN joys, like griefs, confound at first." Thus it appeared in the experience of Matilda, while seated at the window of her own room, in agitated and pleasing meditation respecting the happy prospects which had suddenly brightened on her path; for still she had that feeling always attendant on great and unexpected events, that they can scarcely be real. It softens the blighting anguish of recent sorrow when our hearts refuse to credit what our senses have too surely announced,—and it moderates the first intoxication of pleasure when the fulfilment of hope seems yet but a dream of fancy. It is long before even happiness itself can make us happy; but for the first time Matilda now felt at liberty to think, to hope, and to feel as her heart directed, while the expectation of present happiness was sanctified and enhanced by many serious anticipations of duties and trials, in which she should no longer have to act or to suffer alone, and of the mutual confidence and sympathy with which she might hereafter hope to give and to receive encouragement in the difficult and dangerous struggle of Christian attainment. The remembrance of her probable succession scarcely crossed Matilda's mind; for nothing seemed worth a thought connected with woredly objects, but the consciousness of Sir Alfred's attachment, and the recollection of all he had said during their recent interview, while he traced out the origin and progress of his affection, showing how justly he all along appreciated her motives of action, and how thoroughly his preference had been founded on principle, and confirmed by perfect esteem, added to youthful enthusiasm.

Matilda's mind was yet agitated by emotions unlike the glassy smoothness and tranquillity of its ordinary state, when her attention became slightly attracted by a gentle tap at the door. Before she could speak, it was slowly opened, and Matilda, looking hastily round, beheld Eleanor standing near the threshold. Her cheek was pale, her eyes were downcast, her whole countenance convulsed; and while her lips quivered with a vain attempt to speak, it was evident that she had not voice to articulate the words which died away inaudibly on her lips. Matilda rushed forward and threw her arms round her cousin, embracing Eleanor with the most fervent and heartfelt expressions of affection and endearment, while tears fell thick and fast from the eyes of both.

"Matilda!" sobbed Eleanor, "I repulsed your affection, and insulted your feelings, while you were in my power; and now, when it can never be repaired—when it should have been *your* turn to retaliate, I come for pardon. Will you believe that my repentance is sincere? Can you forget the past, and love me as formerly? I know your generous mind, and that you will neither say a word, nor think a thought, that could hurt my feelings. Oh, Matilda!" added she, burying her face on her cousin's shoulder, and weeping without control, "say that you forgive me—that you do not suppose the discovery of this day causes my distress—that all your injuries are buried in oblivion—that for the sake of our early attachment, and of the departed friend who blessed us both, you will believe my repentance, though late, to be sincere. Our situations are changed—let me learn from your kindness a continual lesson how I ought to have treated you—let me humbly endeavor to acquire the same spirit with which you bore every trial, and let our future lives teach *me* in what way I might have better deserved your friendship."

Eleanor spoke with such rapidity and vehemence that all Matilda's attempts at interruption were vain, but she still riveted her arms round her cousin, and wept like herself.

"Dear—dear Eleanor," said she warmly, "if there are any trifles in our past intercourse, which either of us might wish to forget, we must think and speak of them no more."

"*You* may forget—but I never shall!—oh no, Matilda! let me remember them forever! Any bitterness which may be mingled hereafter in my cup of sorrow, must be received with a humble remembrance that I was tried by prosperity, and that it would have corrupted and destroyed me."

"Indeed, dear Eleanor, that is a dangerous test to us all! and while we mourn for the insignificant oversights which may occur in an earthly friendship, how deeply should we both lament to think of our Omnipotent benefactor and friend, who has loaded us with so many benefits, and whom we are still so prone to forget. Towards him *only*, dearest Eleanor, you can never overestimate the penitence that we owe."

"True, Matilda! and all has been done as you wish. I made confession to God before another thought was permitted to dwell in my mind, praying that he would grant me that true, deep, and influential repentance which shall never need to be repented of. Once already I experienced the deceitfulness of my own heart when my mother died, and a few tears of penitence seemed then an undoubted evidence of conversion,—even yet, Matilda can I hope that, though pierced to the heart with a consciousness of sin, better feelings will arise? Alas! perhaps the weeds may be rooted out, and only a blank remain."

"Eleanor! we were both often taught that every soul which shall be saved is twice created,—first with the love of this world supremely governing our hearts, while it produces an aversion to every devout feeling,—and afterwards the Holy Spirit changes all this into penitence, belief, and obedience. We might wonder sometimes at the wide devastation of sorrow in every house and in every heart, were it not evident that affliction is the most ordinary means by which grace is ordained to sanctify nature. Moses entered a cloud before he was permitted near access to God. David confesses that *before* he was afflicted he went astray; the prodigal son would have lived always estranged from his father's house but for sorrow; and as Elijah was carried to Heaven in a chariot of fire, it seems generally some fiery trial by which our hearts are first elevated above this world. I remember hearing of a good divine who said, on his death-bed, that he never attained to perfect peace until he felt thoroughly convinced that there was 'no happiness for him in this world.' While building upon any mere worldly foundation, we do but build upon a wave; how thankful then should we be for any chastisement that shows its real instability!"

"Yes, Matilda! it is the privilege of *established* Christians to know for certain, that all the gifts bestowed upon them are a blessing sent from God; and all that are taken away are likewise an advantage, for they are given or withheld by Infinite goodness, as well as Infinite wisdom.

'Who sees not Providence supremely wise,
Alike in what he gives, and what denies?'

Now, Matilda, tell me, for the time is fitting, what was that message from our beloved aunt which you once so affectionately importuned me to hear? She first taught us, that God's mercies do not flow most on the shallow, sparkling channel of prosperity, and how truly it has been so with me! I did experience yesterday that prodigious capability of wretchedness which lives within the corrupted heart of man while seeking rest and finding none; but now the iron band which chained my better feelings appears to have suddenly burst, the cloud has passed from my eyes, and, by the shock of many events which have crowded on me, I seem at once restored, and in my right mind!"

"Then, indeed, the prayer of Aunt Olivia is answered, and you are happy, Eleanor!" said Matilda, again embracing her cousin. "How often we are enjoined to 'watch and pray!' but those who *pray, and watch for the answer*, cannot long continue to doubt how greatly the intercessions of the righteous prevail. We are both living evidences that the effect of His people's supplication is not limited to their own individual happiness, nor to the term of their lives, but that, in the experience of devout Christians, that promise shall be realized,—'I will bless you, and ye shall be a blessing.' Above all things, Eleanor, we must persevere in prayer, which is so essential and so powerful an assistance in life, that it was truly remarked,—'We cannot possibly both continue to pray and continue to sin.' The strength of our earthly attachments will also be an additional motive to ardor in the cultivation of holiness. Every thought and feeling of our hearts should originate in one common source, and return, like the sun's rays, to one glorious centre; for what does our frail, transitory life possess, to give it interest or dignity, but that only object which should be dear to our hearts—the glory of God, which leads us, as our sole means of promoting it, to be diligent and persevering in our desire for the salvation of ourselves and others? Dr. Murray once told me, that if ever he indulged a momentary carelessness respecting the salvation of his people, he had but to imagine, for one moment, the day of judgment, and the look of mute despair with which a condemned soul shall hear the sentence of his Maker. An expression of speechless anguish then seems turned on himself, and he feels as if to rescue one single fellow-creature from such unending wretchedness would be worth the sacrifice of every earthly joy. It was this feeling of compassion, carried to a Divine extent, which caused the Son of God to pity our lost condition, and to die that we might be enabled to shun such anguish; and there is not one human soul among the thousands in Heaven who had not sinned beyond all hope of pardon, except through that sacrifice and propitiation of our crucified Saviour."

CHAPTER XXV.

"How vainly, through infinite trouble and strife,
The many their labors employ!
Since all that is truly delightful in life,
Is what all, if they please, may enjoy."

"MATILDA," said Eleanor, taking her cousin by the hand, when their interview was nearly over, "I trust we shall both live to see the permanence of my present feelings and resolutions, though it is easy to feel a desire for holiness, and, oh, how difficult to attain it! During the next year I have resolved to live in retirement and meditation, while pursuing such a course of reading as our adviser and friend, Dr. Murray, may suggest. Meanwhile," added she, losing the paleness of her cheek in a deep glow of carnation, "it is Mr. Grant's intention to travel on the Continent. He has been urgent with me to accompany him there, but my heart must not yet be trusted with happiness. You know, Matilda, how truly he was preferred to all others; and my father having consented, I shall soon exchange the gilded misery which lately cheated me of real peace, for a moderate fortune. and as much earthly happiness as can exist along with the remembrance, which shall remain forever, of past follies, and of worse than these, ingratitude, selfishness, and sin."

When Matidla proceeded on her way to the saloon, before dinner, she was called by Sir Richard into his sitting-room, and her heart sunk with apprehension respecting what he might say of the recent discovery by Mr. Armstrong; but he held out his hand to her with an expression of kindness, though of extreme gravity.

"My dear girl, this has been a surprise to us all! You need not be told that it is as great to me as to any one. I shall, of course, defend your cousin's claims with all the energy in my power; but if Sir Philip's subsequent settlement be found good, then I shall yield without regret to one who is scarcely less dear to me than Eleanor herself. You deserve my affection, but prosperity tries us all, and no doubt your head will become as giddy on the pinnacle as your cousin's. We must allow, *entre nous*, that she became *rather* spoilt. Be ready to start with us for Edinburgh to-morrow, and in every sense, I think your father will meet with a *surprise*."

On the following week, Mr. Armstrong's packet being put into the hands of counsel, all the ingenuity of man could not discover a doubt of Sir Philip's last will being valid. For once there seemed no occasion to complain in Scotland of "*the law's delay*." Matilda Howard was not destined, like many, to grow old in seeking for her rights, and after lingering in weariness and suspense till she outlived the possibility of enjoying them, to receive *what is called justice*, in being allowed to bequeath for others the possession of that which ought to have embellished her own existence. After a short period of uncertainty, she received a visit from Sir Richard, to announce, in terms of affection and kindness, that Eleanor's claim was, by the concurrent advice of the Solicitor-General and many other legal advisers, finally relinquished.

Every event happens unexpectedly, and even those which we have daily considered for years, come when least anticipated, and cause the same astonishment as if they never were supposed possible. Mr. Grant had been thinking rather less than usual about the state of Sir Evan's health, when one morning, about this time, he received letters sealed with black, to announce that a sudden fit of apoplexy carried him off one day while sitting after dinner. As he had been struck speechless at once, no opportunity occurred of acknowledging any marriage to the mother of his children, a manœuvre which he always proposed to execute at the last moment, thus intending to continue her dependence on his humors while he lived, and still to enjoy his cherished desire of vengeance on his nephew. Mr. Grant could scarcely be expected to drop a tear over his uncle's memory, before he blotted him out forever; but he hastened to pay Sir Evan's remains all the decencies of respect, and to make a liberal provision for his numerous and dependent family, each of whom were subsequently established in a profession.

Before setting out to attend the funeral, Mr. Grant requested an interview with Miss Fitz-Patrick, and pleaded his own cause with impassioned eloquence and genuine good feeling, till he at length extorted from her the promise he asked. Eleanor consented that the retirement and privacy to which she had devoted the following year, should be found at Clanpibroch Castle, where he assured her that the counsels of Sir Alfred and the convictions of his own mind, prepared him to occupy his future life in seeking that great object of Christian hope which had now attained its supreme value in the eyes of both.

Every reader of newspapers must have observed, in the *Morning Post* of Thursday last, the announcement of two marriages in high life, by the Rev. Dr. Murray of Gaelfield, Sir Thomas Grant, Bart. of Clanpibroch Castle, Inverness-shire, to Miss Eleanor Fitz-Patrick; and Sir Alfred Douglas, Bart. of Douglas Priory, in Mid-Lothian, and Bowmont Manor in Yorkshire, to Miss Howard, the lovely and accomplished heiress of Barnard Castle. Among the company present we observed Lady Susan Danvers, Lady and the Misses Montague, Hon. Mrs. Clifford, Miss C. and Miss A. Clifford, Miss Murray, Miss Porson, Hon. Col. Pendarvis, Major Foley, Sir C. Fletcher, Captain M'Tartan, and a numerous party of distinguished friends.

Among the *on-dits* in society it is currently reported that Lady Susan Danvers, once listened herself into the good graces of Sir Colin Fletcher with such persevering patience that, though a single yawn would have ruined her prospect forever, he actually, with much circumlocution, came at last to the point. The fair lady, having long had a ready-made attachment at the service of any very eligible match that offered, was found propitious on the present occasion, and lawyers and milliners are already in the full activity of preparation.

Captain M'Tartan was the only man at the Senior United Service Club who perceived much cause for astonishment when he one day found himself unexpectedly promoted to be an admiral and honored with a Guelphic ribbon, in consequence of his spirited conduct on board the "Champion, 74," of which particulars were given in his dispatches, dated the 15th September. Sir Donald M'Tartan, having been little on shore, is firmly persuaded that every young lady has much the same characteristics—that they are all good tempered, lively, fond of music, dress, and gayety—ready to marry the first man who asks them, and so smitten with epaulettes, that they will admire one on naval-blue shoulders when not to be seen upon scarlet. Since he became an ad miral, Miss Charlotte Clifford, who, to the certain knowledge of her numerous confidantes, had already refused or discouraged every other gentleman living, seemed in danger of finding it necessary to be in love with Sir Donald, when, to her great surprise, he announced an engagement to Miss Adelaide Montague.

Major Foley, having been quartered in Ireland lately with his regiment, was filled with dismay one morning to find that his little, well-turned compliments, and trifling civilities, were carefully registered in the heart and in the head of a fair Hibernian, possessing, among other *irresistible* recommendations, a squadron of brothers. Having been assured by them in strong terms of the pleasure with which they all anticipate a nearer connexion, he has found it impossible to disappoint them, and the marriage will take place at Tipperary without delay.

Colonel Pendarvis succeeded lately to Yorkton Abbey and the accumulated hoards of that avaricious old aunt, respecting whose penurious habits it had formerly been his amusement to relate so many anecdotes; but with the estate, he seems to have unexpectedly inherited all her saving propensities; and the very customs which he criticised in her have been, almost without exception, adopted by himself, while they are observed with ridicule and contempt by his younger brothers.

Nanny Muckleraith is at last restored to perfect composure and peace of mind. She can bear to see Martha the happy wife of William Grey. She has even learnt to rejoice in their contentment; while she devotes her own time to the charge of a school lately established in the village of Clanpibroch, where in useful and active employment she finds a degree of happiness never experienced before. The only fault her scholars find with their teacher is on account of her being extremely rigid about discouraging all excesses in dress, and invariably confiscating the necklaces of glass beads and the gilt ear-rings in which the girls delight to adorn themselves.

Dr. Murray, it is whispered, will probably be Moderator of the General Assembly next year; and as no event of equal importance ever occured before in the annals of his sister's life, he has found occasion to exercise the most indulgent forbearance in suffering a multitude of pleasing anticipations and active preparatory measures, with which she is already persecuting his few hours of leisure.

Mr. Armstrong is commissioned, by a friend who entertains the highest opinion of his taste and judgment, to choose some first-rate pictures abroad, for which first-rate prices will, of course, be exacted; and he has lately been exhibiting one or two "perfect gems" in London, which the Duke of Cairngorum and other connoisseurs pronounce to be *chefs-d'œuvres*, beyond all price.

Miss Marabout and Miss Porson are both at present looking out for situations as "finishing governesses," having each obtained the most satisfactory testimonials from a variety of distinguished families, to whom references can be given. Both profess to teach all the usual branches of education, music, drawing, and languages, besides every kind of useless or useful knowledge, and also, as Miss Marabout expressed herself—

"PRINCIPLES OF COURSE."